That Time I Accidentally Took Over The Mafia

Rebekah Sinclair

An Accidental Series
Stand-Alone

Triggers

Please read carefully before proceeding. This book is packed with intense, heart-racing moments, explicit content, and enough emotional turmoil to make you wonder if you've accidentally signed up for a reality TV show.

Side effects of reading this book may include:

- Heart palpitations (thanks to the sizzling chemistry and dramatic tension)
- Uncontrollable laughter (likely at the sarcasm and witty banter)
- A sudden desire to grab a gun, pull off insane stunts, and fall in love with the wrong guys for all the right reasons
- Intense cravings for risotto (sorry, it's part of the package)
- Potential confusion between fantasy and reality (especially if you find yourself daydreaming about mafia men with big... egos)

Trigger warnings include:

- Explicit violence and gore (we've got blood, explosions, and enough dramatic deaths to make you wonder if this is a Netflix crime doc)
- Graphic sexual content (steamy scenes that make the risotto look tame, Dom-daddies and mommies with a little triple-penetration on Santa's naughty list.)
- Abuse of power (psychological manipulation, power dynamics, and a heavy dose of alpha males)
- Murder, attempted murder, and bloodshed (because, you know, it's a mafia book)
- Emotional manipulation and betrayal (expect feelings to be messed with)
- Themes of family trauma and loss (you might want to grab a tissue, or five)
- Threats of rape and sexual violence (not just in the background, it's lurking, but we promise it's handled carefully and with intent)
- Drugs, alcohol, and general mob behavior (including, but not limited to, highly illegal activities, elaborate power plays, and getting away with it all)

If you're allergic to strong language, crude humor, or morally ambiguous characters, this may not be the book for you. But if you're all in for a wild ride with a seriously twisted romance, get your strap-on, grab your favorite drink, and get ready for a whole lot of accidental chaos.

*To the women who aren't afraid to get dirty
and make their men beg for it.*

One

I wonder if it's socially acceptable to let a guy, who's currently having sex with you, know that you've forgotten his name. For the past three minutes I've been staring at the ceiling, trying to remember, but—nothing. John? Jacob? Jingleheimer Schmidt? It's something basic, like him... like the date... like this sex.

A small part of me thought he'd be a freak in bed—classy in public, then BAM! Mr. "I'll Fuck Your Brains Out" would show up with some massive cock for me to worship all night.

But no. Not this Friday night. Not for Delaney Caputo.

Remind me to slap my bestie Stacie for setting me up with this guy. I'll never trust her judgment again. Ever.

This is a blind date, and even though I've got a birth control implant, there's no way I'm letting some random dude go bare in my "love canal." I offered him a condom, but he declined. He brought his own... smaller ones. Great. Just great.

I give up trying to remember his name and glance at the clock. Four minutes in, and it looks like he was ready to blow his load two minutes ago. What a champ, holding on this long.

I catch sight of my brunette hair in the lamp's reflection,

and... is that a gray hair? I swear, if it is, I'll riot. I'm only twenty-six! I'm too young for this. Too young for bad sex, too, and yet... here we are.

I should make an appointment at the salon. I'm due for a root touch-up anyway. I wonder if my regular stylist will be there. I need to update her on my next taboo stepbrother romance idea. (Hint: there are two stepbrothers. Twins. Eeek!)

His sweaty body shifts on top of me, and I remember I should be moaning at the right times, so I do. A little "uhh, yeah, right there" for motivation. I give his shoulders a small squeeze to seem like I'm into it. And of course, I'm squeezing my Kegels too. I have to get something out of this.

We all know pelvic floor strength is important for women's health.

Finally, he finishes, flopping over like a sweaty, huffing mess.

Thank God that's over.

Dude-man is barely able to move his arms, and his hands are floppy as he tries to form a coherent thought. He looks like a ridiculous T-rex. Just when I think he's about to ask, *"You came too, right?"*—he lets out a snore.

Cross my heart and hope to die, he fell asleep no more than ten seconds after coming. And—insert green "I'm gonna be sick" emoji—he's still wearing his tiny condom.

I sit up, the sheet draped around my chest, and cover my face with my hands. A literal face-palm.

Why me?

I sigh and check to see if Bob is available tonight. Of course, he is. My little pink battery boyfriend is always ready. "You're the only dependable thing in my life, Bob," I mutter, heading to the bathroom. Oh my god, I almost forgot my ear pods. That would have been tragic.

I scroll through my favorite faceless, thirst-trap creators for a good moaning audio. Thank you, Moanster23, for your service. We salute you.

I hit play with my ear buds giving me a surround-sound experience of a lubed hand sliding up, what has to be a massive cock. Bob buzzes to life, eager to serve and in 90 seconds, he does what Mr. Forgettable failed to do in five minutes. I wash my hands and face then pop in a probiotic suppository. Thinking about some titles for my next book, I go to my notes app to jot down ideas.

Just as I'm heading back to bed, I hear the little bell notification, letting me know that Moanster23 has posted a new audio. One more won't hurt, right?

I cut my eyes around my bathroom like someone is here to judge me and I decide another wonderful orgasm is definitely what I deserve after this night.

So, getting on my knees, I crank the volume and intensity up. Bob does it again, and I bounce up and down like I'm riding the cock I deserve. Moanster and Bob are my perfect partners. I watch the scrollbar on the video, timing it so I come when Moanster does and we all crescendo together to a second glorious orgasm.

Washing my hands again, I flip off the light and pad out to the darkened bedroom, remembering dude-face is still here. I debate waking him up, but then I notice the saggy condom still on his now-shriveled penis.

I actually do gag this time.

Grabbing a few tissues, I wrap them around his penis, and

remove the condom, cleaning up his–*mess*. I toss it into the wastebasket next to the bed. There is no way I'm letting his *goop* stay on my bed all night just because he couldn't be bothered to clean himself.

I'm too tired to deal with anything else, so I settle into bed. In the morning, I can kick out Mediocre-Marvin, hit the corner bakery for a flaky croissant breakfast sandwich and call the salon.

The sun shines bright, and the smell of bacon fills the air. I take a deep, appreciative breath before my eyes snap open. Wait a second—where's homeboy?

The bed is empty, and I growl in irritation. I had planned to tell him to hit the road this morning, but it looks like he wants to hang around for a post-bad-sex breakfast. Well that is *not* happening this morning.

I throw on a knee-length, silky robe and tie it at the waist. Hmm, I'll brush my teeth later—my morning dragon breath might help scare him off faster. I open the bedroom door, and at the same time, my bathroom door behind me opens. And there stands... Peter?

Ugh! Not even seeing him awake is helping me solve the mystery of his name. I should have looked at his ID last night. I'll remember that next time.

What? No. *Bad Delaney.* Next time, remember people's names—especially the ones you let fuck you.

"Morning!" he says, holding up his hand with a flat-lipped smile. "I was about to head out, but your—*nutritionists*—are here."

"Excuse me? My who?" I pinch my brows and tighten my robe's belt.

He points vaguely toward the stairs. "Your nutritionists. The ones cooking. They said breakfast will be ready in five."

I narrow my eyes, grab my phone, and head downstairs. If I have to call the cops at least I can use it to throat-punch whoever is downstairs first.

Do burglars usually cook for the houses they rob? Some sort of "pay it forward" thing? Or maybe Stacie sent me a sexy-gram to make up for... Adam? No, that's not it.

Well, if she did send me some Dick-Dash, she could have at least made sure dude-boy was gone.

I'm still thinking through possibilities when the sound of familiar voices from downstairs snaps me back to reality.

What. The. Fuck.

I freeze, my foot hovering on the stairs, hand clutching the railing as I stare with a gaping mouth into my kitchen.

I see Luca first, my long-lost stepbrother. His nearly-black hair is perfectly tousled—the most intentional mess I've ever seen. He doesn't glance at me, but I know he knows I'm here. He stiffens slightly, squaring his shoulders under the gray hoodie he's wearing.

The last time I saw him was six years ago my freshman year of college. He popped my cherry, then practically ran away with my blood still on his cock... his incredibly large cock... that I was most definitely *NOT* thinking about last night when I was bouncing on good-ole' Bob.

Now, here he is, just sitting at my table, clacking away on his laptop while Enzo, my old boss, paces outside on my balcony. Fucking Enzo.

Whoever he's chewing out should be thankful he's here on

my patio and not in front of them. I know firsthand what it's like to deal with him when he's pissed—it's downright terrifying.

Enzo's in a dark suit, with a burgundy shirt, sleeves rolled up and a tie, making his grey eyes look even more gorgeous. His dark hair is perfectly slicked, and at 6'4", you can't miss him. In fact, in a room filled with 6'4" suits, I still don't think I could miss him. Gravity seems to pull toward him, and it takes effort for me to look away from his ass when he turns around.

Because Enzo is double-caked here on this fine Saturday morning. *Dayum son.*

Enzo holds his phone to his ear with his shoulder and puts his suit jacket back on.

You know, I think my former boss must have come out of his mother's vagina wearing a three-piece suit. The only time I've seen him dressed differently was that weekend he spent filling my every hole with his giant dick, then he fired me on Monday. *Cocksucker.*

But it's Jax standing at the stove that shocks me the most. Not because he's wearing my pink apron that says, "Whip It Real Good," but because I had no idea he'd been released from prison.

It would seem getting arrested on your wedding day for a four-year prison stint doesn't come with a warning about your release to your abandoned bride.

I stand there gawking like a fucking idiot on the stairs. Evidently, I took too long making my presence known because Luca does it for me.

"Lenny's awake."

Psht. *"Lenny."* He's the only one that has ever called me

that. I roll my eyes, hoping he feels it with his hacker spidey-senses.

Jax looks up from stirring scrambled eggs and sets his gaze on me, flashing those knee-shaking dimples. Time seems to stop as he walks up with a steaming cup of coffee. "Hey there, Peach."

Two

"Don't you dare 'Peach' me," I snap, snatching the coffee from Jax. I might be furious that my exes are in my house, but I'm not stupid. I'll need plenty of caffeine to survive this morning—probably an amount that should come with a surgeon general's warning.

Jax grins, a trademark lollipop stick dangling from his mouth, and gives me a wink as he hands over the coffee. My coffee. Perfectly brewed, hot, and exactly how I like it. I take a sip. *Damn, it's good.* God help me, I needed this. Jax's grin widens as he watches me.

"You owe me twenty," Luca calls to Enzo, who's strolling in from the balcony. Apparently he's done traumatizing one of his poor employees for the time being and apparently they placed bets on how I'd react seeing them?

I guess I need a can of hairspray and a lighter to shake things up a bit. I would venture a guess they didn't plan on me coming in with a homemade flame thrower.

"What the hell are you three doing in my house? This is breaking and entering, you know." I tilt my head, locking eyes with Jax. "Wouldn't that violate your parole? It'd be a shame if you ended up back in prison so soon after getting out."

"Prison?" The voice comes from beside me, making me jump. I completely forgot about What's-His-Name. Poor guy. He's trembling like a lost lamb in a den of lions. "Are they prison nutritionalists?"

I offer him an apologetic smile, about to tell him, *Maybe you should go*, when Jax interrupts.

"He stays for breakfast," Jax says, pointing his half-eaten sucker at What's-His-Name while setting down a massive pan of scrambled eggs. Tossing the lollipop in the trash, he adds, "There's plenty, and it's ready."

Plenty? Oh, sure. There's plenty of awkward tension, plenty of weird silence, and plenty of... my ex-boyfriends in one space. There's also plenty of bacon, fresh biscuits, and cubed pineapple. Jax's grin stretches wider as he sets everything on the table, eye-fucking me the entire time.

Jax's nickname for me, "Peaches", is because of my love for fruit. Also, according to Jax, they make my pussy taste "damn delicious." Which, unfortunately, makes me glance at his mouth.

Fuck, that was a mistake. His smug smile tells me he knows exactly where my thoughts have wandered.

What I don't need right now is to think about his expert tongue on my vag. What I do need is to get all four of these bastards out of my house.

Luca piles a plate for Enzo, who gives him a wink as he takes it. "Thanks, babe."

Um, what?

Then Enzo casually rubs Jax's hip, nearly grabbing his dick.

Pardon me, sir?

Everyone sits at my table like some big, happy family of... lovers?

Questions flood my brain: *Why are they here? How do they know each other? How the fuck did they find me?* That last one answers itself: Luca, obviously. *When did they start screwing each other? Who's the top? Do they switch?*

My brain takes a nosedive. Do they all fuck at once? A vision of a three-way 69 pops into my head, and I can't stop myself.

"Is everyone here fucking each other?" I blurt, my brow furrowed in confusion.

"To be fair, we're not fucking your friend Matt," Luca says, finally looking at me. "And yes, that is his name," he adds with condescension.

"I know his name is Matt," I huff.

"Actually, it's Mark," pipes up Mr. Mediocre in a small voice.

Luca smirks, triumphant. I narrow my eyes and mouth, *I will kill you*.

Prick. He did that on purpose. He probably knows more about Mark's life than Mark does. He set me up to look like the jackass that forgot the guy's name. I mean I did forget his name, but my stepbrother doesn't have to point it out.

And how the hell did he know I forgot Mark's name?

As I sit, one interesting fact hits me: Every single one of these men has had their dick in me at some point. Hmm, small world, I think, sipping my coffee as I delay returning to the drama unfolding in front of me.

But Jax has other plans. "So, Mark," he starts, handing me a plate and turning to my petrified date. I'm pretty sure he's wondering if I spent any time in prison as he avoids looking at me.

"I saw those in the vase. You ole' charmer." He nods

behind him at the half-dead bundle of flowers Mark had when I opened the door last night. The plastic wrapper in the trash still has the 50% off sticker on it and I know Jax saw that too. I stab the fluffy eggs instead of Jax's brown eyes.

Mark hesitates. "Uh, yeah. I, uh, picked them up on the way over."

"Thoughtful," Jax replies, stuffing eggs into his mouth before he continues with my waterboarding. "And where'd you take our Delaney last night?"

Our Delaney? I glare at him, chewing my eggs. Damn it, they're delicious.

"Uh, Bristol's Grill & Bar on 9th. They have a really good two-for-$25 menu." Poor Mark shifts uncomfortably...again.

Jax's eyes widen like Mark just told him he personally invented fire. "Two-for-$25?! Classy. Do they have a Michelin star?"

I grip my fork, seriously debating stabbing him. Jax's smile only spreads.

"Uh, I'm not sure." Mark glances at me, desperate for help but looks away quickly. There's no saving him.

"Damn," Jax continues, glowing with fake enthusiasm. "You really know how to treat a lady."

Mark's face goes crimson. I swear, I hear his pride shatter. He looks like he might cry, and honestly, I don't blame him.

Enzo, meanwhile, ignores everything. I'm actually surprised he didn't stick Mark in the garbage disposal on sight and get to whatever they came here for. In fact, the seconds ticking by are driving my anxiety higher to know what the fuck is going on. Swirling his coffee like it's the only sane thing in this madhouse, he stands when his phone rings. "I'll be outside," he mutters, leaving without another glance.

The rest of us sit in tension, Jax clearly enjoying himself. He leans back, smirking. "So, Mark," he asks, entirely too casually, "tell me, how'd Delaney do in the bedroom last night?"

I sputter on my coffee, choking as I glare at him. This–mother fucker–did not seriously just ask that, did he? And now I'm supposed to sit here while he conducts a fucking interview about my—our—private business?

It doesn't matter that he has been balls deep in my private business... many times. But that was four years ago. You don't just drop into someone's kitchen with your pecks on display and talk to their fling about sexual performance ratings.

Mark looks like he is wishing he could just sprout a set of rocket boosters and fly right out of here, but Jax doesn't wait for him to answer. "Luca, play the clip."

My heart actually stops.

The room goes dead silent as Luca pulls out his phone with an expression that tells me I'm going to hate this. My stomach sinks as Luca swipes across the screen and then—oh no.

"Oh yes, just like that—" my own voice fills the room. Then a pause. The long, awkward silence where I forgot Mark's name and had to wing it with, "—yeah, just like that."

My face goes redder than a lobster in a pot. I can't look at any of them. Not at Luca's blank expression, not at Jax's smug smile, and especially not at Mark's face, which is so red it looks like it might catch fire.

Wait a god damn minute. My eyes, burning with rage now, fly to Luca. "Is my room bugged?"

He only smiles. This cocky son of a bitch.

Jax, as casual as ever, looks over at me, then back at Mark. "See, you can tell she's faking it." He's almost proud of himself for this. "When she's actually about to come–"

I swear I can feel my soul leaving my body.

This is the moment where I wish a tornado would pop down from the sky and swoop me off to another land. Perhaps Zeus could lightning bolt Jax in the asshole to stop him from whatever he's about to say next.

Just as I'm about to throw my coffee at him, Enzo bursts back into the room, his sharp eyes cutting through the tension like a hot knife through butter.

"Leave," he barks at Mark, his voice deep and commanding, not a trace of emotion or hesitation.

Mark looks like he's about to drop dead from embarrassment, but thankfully, he still retains enough control over his body to grab his boots and make a beeline for the door.

I can't even look at him. Not because I care—no, no, it's because I'm too busy mentally blocking out the fact that I just got exposed by my own damn voice.

Mark doesn't even look at me as he shuffles awkwardly by the door, trying to pull it open but it's locked. Then he pushes it. Sweet baby Jesus. Mark's face is a patchwork of red as he fiddles with locks.

When it's clear he'll be trapped here forever without help, I get up and unlock the door for him.

"I'll–call you?" he mutters, his voice cracking in embarrassment.

And I can't help but laugh because, what else can you do in a situation like this? "Please don't."

The second the door clicks shut behind Mark, I spin on my heel, arms crossed over my chest, a glare sharp enough to cut glass. I look at my three exes, all of them with smug smiles or impassive faces, and wonder if today is the day I commit my first and last triple homicide.

Three

"Okay, what the hell is going on here?" I demand, looking at all three of them.

Jax, as usual, tries to calm me down like I'm some kind of child throwing a tantrum. "Hey, hey. Take a seat, Dels," he says, his voice all too composed. But it's the solemn look on Enzo's face that catches my attention.

Luca is holding an envelope, and it doesn't look like it's going to end with me getting a fat stack of cash and a *"Sorry for your awkward morning"* note. Nope, this looks way too formal.

"Sit down, baby," Jax presses again, his tenor a little softer now, and I know this is serious.

But something in that tone, those gentle words, pulls at the pain in my heart that I've worked so hard to wall off. "Don't call me that," I say quietly, barely above a whisper and a flinch registers across his face.

I glance from Luca to Enzo, the two of them silent as they exchange some unspoken conversation that tells me everyone in the room knows what's in the envelope except me. Fine. I'll bite.

Taking the envelope from Enzo makes my stomach churn with anxiety.

Luca slouches in the chair, eyes locked on the paper, while Jax watches me like I'm an animal about to spook and run off.

I don't like this. I really don't like this.

Looking at the thick paper, the first thing I see is the large, audacious "C" for Caputo, and I know it's from my father. My estranged father.

I'm just about to crumple it and tell them I'm not interested in anything that man has to say when I catch the first line of the letter:

If you are reading this, I'm dead, and you are now a very wealthy woman.

What the fuck?

My heart thuds painfully in my chest, and for a split second, I want to throw this damn letter in the trash and pretend I never saw it.

But I can't.

Instead, my fingers curl around the edge of the envelope as I read the rest.

A very wealthy woman who is in very grave danger.

The letter continues, but all I can focus on is the fact that my father is dead—and that he wrote a pre-planned letter to cover the scenario. Who lives a life like that? I wonder as I look around the kitchen like the answer is here somewhere.

"Keep reading," Luca mutters. His voice is almost too calm, like he's already expecting me to freak out.

He can't know me *that* well. We spent a few months together in college before I gave him my virginity. The next night, my father introduced me to stepmom #5 and my new stepbrother: Luca. The man who spent the night before fucking me into oblivion. He looked horrified, like I'd just grown a second head made entirely out of dicks.

Until today, I hadn't seen him since. Not a picture, not a mention.

Not that I looked.

You are now the heir to the Caputo family. Your life will change dramatically, and there is no going back. This empire is yours.

I sit there, dumbfounded. The words blur as my brain tries to wrap itself around what I'm reading, and I realize my hands are trembling.

The next line hits me like a freight train:

I have kept you in the dark about this life for a reason. You will soon learn why. Be careful. There are people, very close to you, who would do anything to see this empire fall.

Trust no one.

"Trust no one?" I blink, feeling like the floor has just dropped out from under me. "This is some sick joke, right?" My mind spins as my eyes rush over the letter, skipping words and going back to reread the same sentence three times. It still doesn't make sense.

"What empire?" I demand, my voice pitched high as reality begins to sink in.

I look to each of my exes, desperate for an answer, but all I see is sympathy on their faces. Every one of them is staring at me like I'm some poor, lost kitten about to get eaten alive.

Except Luca. He's staring down at the table like he's made of stone.

"The Caputo Family Mafia," Enzo says, completely unfazed by my growing panic, as if he's explaining tomorrow's weather forecast.

I almost laugh, but it comes out more like a sob. "Oh, thanks for explaining that perfectly," I say, my voice dripping with sarcasm. "My father was a crime lord? And I'm... what? Expected to drop everything and go run it?"

I laugh again, but it's shaky and forced. The weight of what I'm hearing crushes me like lead on my chest. "Well, I have no plans to take the throne as some sort of mafia queen, so you three can fuck off." My tone is surprisingly even, but the words feel hollow, like I'm drowning under the weight of this new reality.

The worst part? I have no idea what to do with any of it.

My father was a business mogul who was never around. He shoved me off to be cared for by our staff, never coming to anything important in my life—birthdays, graduations—nothing. As soon as I could get away, I did.

He left me nothing but a legacy of silence and absence long before he died—and now he's left me this. A criminal empire. One I didn't even know existed. One I'm now supposed to lead.

"You're going to have to," Enzo says flatly, his serious tone snapping me out of my spiral. "You have six days to get to Chicago for the presentation of the will. It's imperative you attend, Delaney. This isn't just a formality—it's a matter of life or death."

I'm still in shock. "I don't want any part of this. I'm not going." I stand abruptly, ready to storm off. "This is insane, and you... you guys... why are you even here? You can't make me do this."

"Delaney," Jax says softly, his voice unusually gentle. "You don't have a choice."

I turn on him, ready to argue, but the words spill out before I can stop them. "What the hell do you want from me? You've all been out of my life for years, and now you're telling me I'm some damn mafia queen? And how are you all involved in this? Why are you the ones telling me?" I point between them. "Explain that. I deserve that much at least."

Jax hesitates, clearly weighing his words. Luca remains silent, stone-like, but Enzo speaks with calm authority.

"We're here because we're all connected to mafia families," he says simply. "You know my enterprise. It's a legitimate business, but it hides my family's other *work*." He stresses the word. "Luca's family has been mafia associates for years. Jax, too. We work together now."

I glare at the chair Jax pulls out for me, but I sit anyway, my legs too shaky to stand.

"Your father was the most powerful man in the country," Enzo continues. "The Capo dei Capi—boss of all bosses. Now that he's gone, a war has begun."

"The most powerful man in the country." The words feel

foreign as I repeat them, like I'm speaking someone else's language. "What do you mean... a war?"

Luca finally speaks, his voice low but intense. "Every family in the country is after the power your father left behind. But they can't take it unless you're out of the picture. And that's why you have to claim it—or someone else will. By force, if necessary."

I'm about to start laying into them—yell, demand answers, anything—when the sound of a floral delivery van pulling into my driveway derails me.

Seriously? Flowers? Now?

The white van creeps up the U-shaped drive, parking in the middle. A man in an all-brown uniform steps out, retrieving a large bouquet of flowers from the back. The sudden tension in the room feels like a punch to the chest. All three of them stiffen. Their eyes snap to the delivery guy like he's holding a ticking bomb instead of a bouquet.

"What the hell is wrong with you guys?" I roll my eyes, exhausted by the absurdity of the morning. "It's just flowers. People get them all the time. Not that any of you ever got me flowers," I add, giving Jax a pointed look. "Mike did, though."

"Mark," Luca corrects, as if it matters.

I glare at him. "Don't you have a Walmart to raid or something? I hear there's a sale in the keyboard aisle. You should go."

He shrugs, completely unbothered.

I scoff. "Ridiculous. No one has ever died from a floral delivery before."

"Delaney, stop," Enzo whisper-yells like a total psychopath as I open the door before the guy can even ring the bell.

It's just flowers. Right? How bad could it be?

I mean, they just said my father died so don't people get flowers during mourning. The fact that no one here knows my real name dawns on me and cold dread creeps down my neck.

I only use my pen name...always. No one from my past knows where I am so... who would know to send me flowers?

The delivery guy looks up from the bouquet, smiling politely as delivery people often do. Then, like some twisted magician, he pulls a gun from the middle of the arrangement.

For a split second, my brain freezes. Is he really holding a gun? In the flowers?

Before I can fully process the situation, Enzo barrels into me like a freight train. He shoves me out of the way so hard I stumble back into the wall, pain shooting through my shoulder.

"Enzo!" I start to snap, but he pins me to the wall with his body, shielding me.

Jax moves faster than I thought humanly possible. He pulls a gun—God knows where he was hiding it—and shoots the delivery guy square between the eyes just as I push Enzo off me.

I stand there, stunned, my mouth hanging open. The hole in the center of the man's forehead smokes slightly, and I can't take my eyes off it. Bright red blood trickles down his face as his body crumples to the ground like a rag doll. The bouquet scatters across the porch, mixing with the dark pool of blood spreading beneath him.

The world around me feels muffled, like I'm underwater. My ears are ringing, my heart is racing, and my legs feel like jelly.

Enzo, Jax, and Luca, on the other hand, are eerily calm.

Enzo closes the door with a deliberate click, as if there isn't a fresh corpse lying on my front stoop.

"What the fuck just happened?" I finally manage to whisper, my voice shaking.

Enzo grips my arm with more force than necessary, his expression grim. "We're leaving. Now." That commanding tone is what slaps me back.

"Like hell we are," I snap, jerking out of his grasp and storming toward the stairs.

I make it halfway up the stairs before Jax's voice cuts through. "Delaney."

I pause, turning to glare at him. "What?"

His smile is gone. For once, there's no humor in his tone. "You need to start taking this seriously. That wasn't just a warning. That was an attempt on your life."

"Oh, really? Thank you, Sherlock," I snap, my voice dripping with sarcasm. "Let me just pack a bag so I can move into your fortress of testosterone."

"We don't have time for this." Luca's voice cuts through like a blade, cold and sharp. "We're leaving now."

"Like hell we are," I retort, continuing up the stairs. "I'm not going anywhere in my bathrobe, thank you very much."

Four

Enzo knows how to do two things: fuck like the devil and piss me off. Right now, sadly, he's only doing one of those things.

We spent one whirlwind weekend together after months of resisting a workplace attraction. I gave him the best blowjob of his life, and on Monday morning, he gave me the boot.

Seriously, though, I can do this thing with my jaw—open my throat like a champ—and there is no length of cock too large for me. It turns Enzo into putty in my hands... especially when I slip a finger into his ass while he's coming.

But I'm getting off topic. Back to my heartache.

He threw me out onto the sidewalk in front of his high-rise and didn't even have the decency to do it himself. No, he sent the sixty-four-year-old HR lady to do the dirty work. Poor thing was crying hysterically, and somehow, I ended up comforting her—when I was the one getting fired.

That billionaire asshole didn't even give me severance pay.

Not that I needed it.

I've been publishing my stories since my second year of college and saving everything. I worked hard to make sure I'd never need to leverage my father's name. I wrote under a pen name, Dela Montgomery, and it was liberating. A fresh start.

When I got hired at Enzo's firm, Vincenzi Consulting Group, I stuck with Dela. No one knew who I really was.

The day Enzo had me thrown out, I packed up and moved to Seattle. Never looked back. I didn't need to. Instead, I poured everything into my books. Dela Montgomery became a bestselling author. My taboo series sold like wildfire.

Stepbrother romances? Check.

"My-ex-is-a-con" tropes? Love them.

"I-fell-for-my-billionaire-boss"? Always a crowd-pleaser.

No idea where I got the inspiration for those stories. Couldn't possibly be my fucked-up life and the three men who broke my heart. Nah.

As I move to storm upstairs, Enzo blocks my path.

"Move," I snap, glaring up at him. He's tall, imposing, with his perfectly tailored suit and that damn jawline I'd love to punch.

"Delaney," he says, voice low and sharp, "nothing about this is a joke."

I roll my eyes, pushing past him, but he grabs my arm—not hard, but firm enough to stop me.

"You need to understand what's happening," he says, his tone so calm it makes me want to scream. "Your life isn't your own anymore."

"When has it ever been?" I snap, yanking my arm free, "Oh, I know. When I got away from the controlling men that just fuck me... one way or another... and then set me out to be collected with the other garbage."

I ignore the flash of something in his eyes—regret? Guilt?

—and shove past him. The scent of his cologne hits me, all spicy cedarwood and expensive arrogance. My traitorous body responds with a shiver, but I don't let it show. *Bad vagina, bad.*

He doesn't follow, but I can feel his eyes boring into my back until I reach my room and slam the door with a satisfying bang.

The sound of tires squealing outside pulls me to the window.

Gunfire. Shouting.

It's like some low-budget action movie, but instead of extras, they're shooting up my actual house. Within five minutes of learning my father is dead, my front yard has become ground zero for a mob shootout. Perfect.

My exes are in the middle of it, returning fire with practiced ease. They duck, shoot, and shout orders at each other like it's just another day at work. They really need to work on some hand signals or something because they are loud AF. You can hear them across the entire neighborhood.

Speaking of which: down the street, a woman runs screaming, clutching her purse like it's a lifeline. A man ducks behind a car, phone raised over the hood as he records the chaos. Seriously? People are shooting at my house, and this guy's making a TikTok?

Shaking my head, I grab my black yoga pants and slip them on. Comfortable, practical. A sage green crop top follows, letting me breathe easier and conveniently pulling out the green in my hazel eyes.

Do I have time to brush my teeth? Yes. Yes, I do.

As I tie my hair into a messy bun, I glance out the window again. Jax moves with precision, firing, ducking, and firing again. He's still wearing my bright pink apron, the white stick of a sucker poking out of his mouth.

I watch as he takes down one attacker with a single shot, then pivots to the next with deadly focus. He's infuriatingly good at this, but the apron? The apron is ridiculous.

My gaze shifts as one of the attackers lets out a yelp. A neighbor's golden retriever has clamped its teeth onto the guy's ass, growling like a rabid wolf, shaking his muzzle back and forth.

"Oh my God," I whisper-laugh until I freeze in horror. "You better not, you fucking asshole."

The attacker shakes the dog off and raises his gun, but before he can aim, Luca takes him down with a shot to the chest. The dog runs off unscathed, tail wagging like it's just won a prize.

Okay, that is one bonus point for my stepbrother. But the others get nothing.

Shaking my head, I grab my bag and start packing essentials. Wallet, phone, laptop, charger. I pause, hand hovering over the drawer where my favorite book rests. *Do I really need this? Am I seriously thinking about taking a romance novel to a mob war?*

The sound of shattering glass snaps me out of it. A bullet whizzes past my head, embedding itself into the wall behind me.

I freeze, heart pounding, my breath catching in my throat. For a moment, all I can do is stare at the hole in the wall.

Are you fucking kidding me?

My fear morphs into anger, hot and sharp. I stomp to the window, yanking it open. "That could've hit me!" I yell out indiscriminately, not knowing which gun the bullet came from.

Jax looks up, completely unbothered. "Then get your ass down here. We need to go."

His tone makes me want to throw something, but I don't.

"You look fucking ridiculous," I yell back. He doesn't, he looks gorgeous.

The tattoos that run up his arms, somehow accentuate his muscles rippling as he moves. And his back, his wide shoulders and the way some of his tattoos creep behind him... oh my god, I think about him diving into me while I run my nails down that back.

I blink, shaking my head. There goes Her Royal Vagesty, taking the most inopportune time to remind me how long it's been since I've been well and properly fucked.

I stomp over to my closet and shove on my white sneakers. With my bag on my back and my phone in hand, I clomp downstairs, mimicking their voices. "Now, Dels. Meh."

Swiping car keys from the hook by the door, I take a quick look around for anything else I might need. This whole situation has moved past ridiculous and is circling back to comedic. There's a literal shootout happening outside, but whatever. Let the boys handle it.

With my bag on my back and my phone in hand, I head for the garage. My car purrs to life, silent as a whisper. Carefully, I pull around the side of the house, away from the shootout, and hit the gas as soon as I hit the street.

A glance in my rearview mirror shows Enzo sprinting after me like a lunatic, suit jacket flapping, his face a mask of fury.

"Seriously?" I mutter, laughing as I flip him off.

He doesn't stop, even pulling his gun and aiming at the car.

For a moment, I think he's going to shoot, but he doesn't. Instead, he yells, "Delaney, stop!"

Yeah, right, fucker!

I floor it, speeding down the street. One last glance in the mirror shows my own face—eyes narrowed, jaw set.

These assholes will learn I'm not some damsel in distress. I'm Delaney Caputo, and this is my life. I call the shots.

Five

I drive with my hands clenched around the wheel, the gears of my mind spinning just as fast as the wheels on my car. My thoughts are a chaotic jumble of bullets, mafia wars, and—God help me—my father's legacy.

Of course, I'm headed straight to Stacie's.

I've known her for four years now, ever since I moved to Seattle. We hit it off instantly, both escaping the pressures of the world by getting lost in coffee shops and the pages of a book. I was there, plugging away at my next manuscript, and she was there, reading one of my previous books—unaware that the woman she was reading was sitting right across from her.

I still haven't told her my real name. Four years of friendship, and I've let it go on like this. She only knows me as Dela Montgomery.

I've felt bad about it, honestly. I planned on telling her after I knew she was trustworthy, but the timing just never felt right. Then, after so long, it seemed weird. So, I just let it go. And now, here I am, driving to her place without a clue how to explain my real life. The one I left behind.

I call her as soon as I clear my street, my hands trembling as I pull up her contact.

"Stacie," I say, trying to keep the edge of panic out of my voice.

"Oh my God, what's happening over there? Where are you? The neighborhood app says there are gunshots near you," she practically shouts through the phone. "Are you okay?"

My heavy sigh fills the car. "It's... it's just so bizarre. You're never going to believe this."

I begin running through everything, starting with Mr. Mediocre Marty. (I know that is not right. We're moving on.)

I'm still in shock, but I know I need someone to process all this with, and Stacie is the only person I've trusted to be real with me—no matter how much I've kept from her.

By the time I pull into her driveway, I've just finished the part about the delivery guy getting a smoking hole in his head because my ex-fiancé shot him.

I can't shake the images of blood, gunfire, and chaos, no matter how hard I blink.

Stacie greets me at the door, eyes wide with concern. "What the hell, Delaney?" she asks before pulling me inside and yanking the curtains shut.

"So, this whole time, you had no idea your dad was a crime lord? That's so fucked up."

"You're telling me. And now I'm the head of his mafia empire." I barely register the words as I say them, but somehow, they sound so much worse coming out loud. "Like, go eat shit, dude."

Stacie looks at me, unblinking, before she pulls me into a hug. "This is insane. This is... unbelievable."

"I know," I mutter into her shoulder. "I'm still processing all of it."

She pulls back and looks me up and down, her eyes assessing. "And you're still here...in one piece?"

"For now," I say, trying to hold my own, though I'm secretly shaking inside.

"You're not doing this alone," she says fiercely, her voice sharp. "We're going to figure this out."

Stacie's kitchen feels strangely calm, like the world outside doesn't exist—even though everything inside my head is a fucking dumpster fire. She's standing at the counter, the kettle whistling as she prepares tea like we don't have an entire mafia conspiracy unfolding just blocks away.

I'm so lucky to have a friend like her. There's a literal gunfight going on because of me, and as soon as I get here, she just says, *"What the hell, De...laney?"*

Delaney.

The way my real name rolls off her tongue is like a pinball ricocheting around my brain. Not Dela. Delaney.

I freeze, setting my spoon down with a soft clink.

"So," Stacie says casually, pouring tea like it's nothing, "what's it like being the Caputo heiress?"

Another name she shouldn't know.

The walls of the kitchen suddenly feel too small, the air too thick. My mind starts to race—what else does she know? How long has she known? Why didn't she say anything?

A wave of heat runs down my body. A bead of sweat follows it down my back.

Oh my god, what if she is some kind of mafia spy, hired by my father to keep a secret eye on me. Or worse, what if she's here to kill me?

My father's words echo in my head, speaking to me as if he were here, a voice I've tried hard not to think about for a long time: *Trust no one.*

I glance at the tea she made. The creamy surface has settled now, but a thin, oily sheen floats on top.

Um, that looks suspicious. Especially when I see Stacie has no tea.

"Dela, are you okay?" she asks, using my pen name this time.

The curtains are drawn. I can't see out, and no one can see in. The music is playing too loud, muffling everything. Like the sounds of a struggle.

Suddenly, the walls of the kitchen feel too small, the air too thick.

Am I overreacting? Probably not. Something deep inside me screams, *Get out. Now.*

"I just need to use the bathroom," I say, forcing a laugh. "You know, splash some water on my face. Scream into a towel or something." My throat is suddenly dry but I'm pretty certain there is poison in the tea... at minimum, some kind of drug to knock me out.

"Yeah, of course." Her neck is flushed red, and I can see her pulse banging against her skin. She's nervous. Fucking perfect, Delaney. You pick the best friends.

The second I'm out of sight, I head upstairs instead of using the downstairs bathroom. I skip the fifth stair—it squeaks—and slip into the bathroom.

This is stupid. You should've known better. You've been played.

But how could I have known? I realize just how dark the hole I've been kept in has really been. A whole other world has been existing around me on the other side of a veil that I can't see through.

I need to think. And fast.

I slide quietly into the attached bedroom, glancing around quickly for something I can use as a weapon as I feel for my phone in my pocket. There is a faint squeak on the fifth stair. I freeze. Stacie freezes. Hell, the world freezes.

Shit.

Don't panic, maybe I'm overreacting. I'm just jumpy and obviously my nerves are fried from the guy's harassment and everything else. I'm sure she's just coming to make sure I'm okay. Or to see if I need some toilet paper, or something. That makes sense, right?

...Right?

Stacie's silhouette moves slowly up the stairs, but something about her posture—the shape of her shadow in the dim light—makes my stomach drop. It looks like she's holding something, something–

No, that can't be right. She can't possibly...

Yep, she sure is. She is screwing a silencer to the end of a fucking gun.

Fuck.

Well, apparently she is not worried about the toilet paper.

Okay. This is happening. My best friend—who's known me for four years—is about to kill me. No biggie. I got this.

I swallow hard, my pulse quickening. Panic surges through me as I back away from the door and ducking into the closet. The cool wood scraping against my arm as I quietly slide inside. I can't see anything in the dark, so I grab the nearest thing—a tennis racket? Really?

She has a silencer and I have...sports equipment. My heart

is pounding in my ears as I clutch it tightly, both hands shaking as I wait, listening to the sound of footsteps approaching.

The silence stretches, and it feels like the air itself is holding its breath. Then I hear the knob turning. Just a fraction of an inch. She's preparing herself. She knows I'm in here.

I imagine her on the other side of the door. Gun raised to the ceiling, hand on the knob getting ready to fling the door open.

I steady myself, every muscle in my body tensed and ready. The only sound I hear now is my own breath, shallow and fast, but I'm waiting. I'm ready for this bitch.

This is the moment. When she opens that door, it's either me or her.

The door is wrenched open, light floods the small dark space and I don't waste a second.

The racket connects with her throat in an uppercut. She stumbles back, choking, her gun flying out of her hand.

"Another point for me," I mutter under my breath, adrenaline surging as I jump over her and stomp on her hand.

"Oh, sorry!" I call out without thinking.

Shut the fuck up, you dumbass. She's trying to kill you, remember?

We're not polite to people trying to kill us.

I make a break for the stairs, taking them too fast. My foot slips on the last one, and I barely catch myself on the banister. My phone, naturally, decides this is the perfect moment to shoot across the floor like it's the main character at Disney On Ice.

I dive for it, but just as my hand wraps around the phone, I hear the unmistakable hiss of a bullet cutting through the air. It whizzes past my ear, so close that I can feel its heat.

At least she's a lousy shot.

Clutching my phone, I glance around like a woman who definitely does not have a plan. My choices are limited: kitchen utensils or my questionable survival instincts. I grab the first thing I see—a whisk—and hurl it at her.

It misses. Barely.

"Shit!" I hiss, grabbing a set of tongs next. They make a satisfying clang as they sail past her head, but Stacie dodges again, then barely has time to avoid the butcher knife I sent flying end over end. Her face twisting into something feral.

The sound of a bullet splintering the kitchen island snaps me back to reality. She's circling it, trying to corner me. I spot her reflection in the stainless-steel fridge. My options are dwindling fast.

Think, Delaney, think.

My eyes land on the pantry door, and I bolt for it. If I can make it through to the laundry room, I might have a chance to get to the garage.

"Please, please, please let me survive this," I mutter under my breath like a mantra as I throw myself into the pantry and slam the door behind me.

I hear her footsteps pounding down the hall. She's close—too close—and I can almost feel her hand reaching for me.

Just as I make it to the laundry room door, she grabs a fistful of my messy bun.

"Oh, fuck no," I snap, twisting around and swinging the spatula I don't remember grabbing.

The slap lands squarely on her cheek, leaving a red mark that's equal parts ridiculous and satisfying.

"You fucking bitch," she snarls, stumbling back.

"That's right," I sneer. "Don't forget it."

I make a run for the back door, praying I can escape this madness. My hand is stretching toward the doorknob when I'm yanked backward. Strong arms wrap around my waist, and a hand clamps over my mouth, silencing my scream.

Fucking Enzo.

"Let go of me," I hiss, thrashing in his grip, but he's got me pinned as he presses us both against the wall.

"Calm the fuck down," he growls in my ear.

Calm down? There's a fucking assassin in the room, and he wants me to calm down?

I'm about to shove my elbow into his ribs when Stacie stumbles into the kitchen, gun raised. Enzo sweeps his leg out, tripping her with the grace of a ballerina and the efficiency of a trained killer. She hits the floor hard, her gun clattering out of reach.

And then I notice Jax... on the fucking kitchen counter.

What in God's name?

He's standing on the counter like a man who has absolutely no business being there, hunched over as he pushes the fridge with all his weight.

I'm left frozen, watching the absurdity of it as Enzo keeps me in an iron hold.

The fridge tips, slow and deliberate, Jax rides it down until it crashes to the floor with a deafening bang.

There's a sickening splatter of blood as the heavy appliance lands on Stacie's head, cutting off her scream mid-shriek. The silence that follows is almost more horrifying than the chaos.

I stare at the scene, my mind blank. *This cannot be real.*

I may actually throw up.

Enzo's hold is loosening. He thinks I've given up. Not a chance mother fucker! I was only stopping to be momentarily traumatized by seeing someone's head get crushed and their brains ooze out.

Okay, that was too much. Let's stop while we're ahead.

I shove my head back into Enzo's nose, the satisfying crunch of cartilage sending a jolt of adrenaline through me.

"Fuck!" he roars, releasing me, taken by surprise.

I spin around, driving my knee into his groin with all the force I can muster.

"And that's for firing me," I snap, a mixture of rage and satisfaction bubbling to the surface.

I sprint for the door, flinging it open and making a beeline for my car. Luca is leaning against a black SUV, arms crossed, looking like he doesn't have a care in the world. He wiggles his fingers at me in a lazy wave.

"Arrogant prick," I mutter, flipping him the bird as I climb into my car. *Huh, would you look at that. I still have the spatula.*

I twist the key in the ignition. Nothing.

I try again. Nothing.

"Fucking Luca!" I slam my hands against the steering wheel, my frustration reaching its boiling point.

Enzo comes storming toward me, fuming. He might as well be a cartoon character—steam practically coming out of his ears.

"I don't fucking think so," I mutter, grabbing my bag and flinging the door open. I start to run, but I don't make it two steps before Jax is in front of me, pushing me back against the car with his body. "Damn," he drawls, his voice low and smooth. "I sure did miss you, Peaches."

I shove my knee into his crotch. Hard.

"Miss this," I snap, dropping my bag, I slap him across the face with the spatula. "Asshole!"

Slap.

"Ow!"

"Son of a bitch!" *Slap.*

"Mother—" *Slap.*

"Fucker!" *Slap, slap, slap.*

"Dammit, stop that!" he yells, throwing up his hands to shield himself. But I don't stop. Not until my arm feels like it's about to fall off.

Enzo grabs me around the waist, lifting me off the ground like I weigh nothing.

"Enough!" he barks, carrying me toward the SUV.

I kick, I scream, I thrash, but it's no use. He throws me into the backseat like a rag doll. I lunge for the opposite door, but of course—child lock.

"Ugh! Really?" I mutter, rushing forward, trying to climb into the front seats.

Jax climbs in beside me, wrapping his thick arm around my waist and hauling me back. His face red and splotchy from my spatula assault and I grin with accomplishment. He tosses my bag into the back and yanks the spatula out of my hand.

"Give that back," I snap, reaching for it.

"Not a chance in hell, Dels," he says with a smirk. "That thing fucking hurts."

"Good," I mutter. "It's the least you deserve."

Jax grins like a kid who just got away with something. Luca and Enzo climb into the front, the SUV roaring to life as we peel out of the driveway.

I glance at Jax, who's still smiling like an idiot.

"What are you so happy about?" I snap, my annoyance bubbling over.

His eyes meet mine, soft and teasing. "You're still angry with me," he says, his voice low.

"That means you still care."

I pinch him hard, pushing him away. "It just means I still hate you."

He chuckles softly, peeling the wrapper off a sucker, not believing a word I say.

Six

I cross my arms tightly, my patience hanging by a thread. "Take me back home," I demand, my voice sharp with frustration.

Luca, the ever-calm hacker who's probably the least worried about anything, gives me a sideways glance. "Not happening, Lenny."

I grind my teeth. "At least let me pack a better weekend bag, please. I'm not about to get stuck with only my old yoga pants and some ratty t-shirts for this... whatever the hell this is."

He doesn't even blink. "I blew your house up."

I pause, momentarily losing my ability to speak. "I'm sorry, what?"

He shrugs, as if discussing someone else's morning commute. "Dramatic, yes. But necessary. We needed them to think you could have been blown to bits. It'll take them a few days to sort through the pieces of flesh and chunks of skull to figure out you're still alive. The will reading will probably be over by then."

I blink twice, my head spinning. "Sure, because that's totally normal. Houses just blow up all the fucking time."

Luca doesn't even look fazed by my sarcasm. "Sometimes a

dramatic statement is needed," he says, sounding entirely too reasonable for my liking.

I want no part in all of this. None. I'm tired. I want to go home. I want to get back to my quiet life—writing steamy taboo novels under a pen name and avoiding confrontation. But Enzo, the ever-competent leader of this circus, pipes up, stealing any ray of sunshine I could hope to grasp in this shitstorm.

"Now do you understand how serious this is, Delaney?" Enzo says flatly, his tone brokering no argument. "This is no fucking game, and you have no choice but to trust us."

"The letter said not to trust anyone, though. Why are you three the exception to that?"

Enzo rolls his eyes.

"Dels, don't act like that." Jax almost sounds pleading, and I can hear real pain in there. Which I choose to ignore. Good. Serves him right.

"We contacted the executor of your father's estate the moment we heard about his death," Enzo says, cutting through the tension. "We knew where you were, and we also know we're the only ones that can get you to Chicago alive."

"How did you know where I was?" I cross my arms to stop my hands from trembling.

"I've always known where you were, Lenny." Luca turns his head back only slightly, not looking at me as he drops a giant bomb on my lap.

"Always?" I don't even recognize how small my voice sounds. Luca's jaw tightens, but he turns forward, not answering me. For six years, he's known where I was? And he still stayed away.

I'm not sure what to do with that information, so I put it

where I put everything else from my past—in an airtight box of trauma compartmentalization where I can pretend I won't think about it again.

A wave of resignation washes over me. The adrenaline from earlier is starting to wear off, and I slump back into the seat, staring out the window. The road blurs as I watch the scenery fly by, lost in my thoughts. This whole mess is spiraling faster than I can process.

I don't know how much time passes, and I must have fallen asleep because I'm jerked out of my stupor when the SUV slows down and turns. We pull into the parking lot of what looks like a rundown motel—one of those places that's one story, with a car parked directly in front of each room.

The whole vibe screams "Welcome, please come get murdered here." There's a drained swimming pool in the center, the water long gone, and it's nearing evening. I'm sure serial killers will start materializing out of the shadows after sundown.

This is not what I signed up for.

The guys stopped earlier for gas and food, but I said I wasn't hungry.

I'm starving, but my pride's keeping me from admitting it. I'm not hungry enough to ask any of them for anything. So instead, I just sit in the SUV, focusing on not pissing my pants.

Enzo stands out like a neon sign in a back alley, so Luca gets the rooms. He's the least likely to draw attention with his hoodie and casual cool. Jax is in the background with a fresh bag of suckers, probably from the gas station.

"Oh goody, a year's supply of annoyance," I grumble, folding my arms over my chest.

"Give me something else to do with my mouth and I

wouldn't need them." Jax retorts, grinning like a cat who knows he just ate the canary. "You're rooming with me tonight anyhow," Jax croons as he catches the key Luca tosses his way.

"No, I'm not," I snap.

"You are," Enzo interrupts as he walks toward the diner across the street, clearly unaffected by my protest.

Jax smirks and unlocks the door to the motel room, holding it open like he's doing me a favor. His hand's full of my bookbag and another I can only assume is not filled with my favorite snacks.

I walk into the tiny room and release a deep sigh. Insert predictable one-bed trope here. I just glare at Jax as he fills up half the doorway, smirking like an idiot.

Don't get me wrong, I've totally put the one-bed trope in like a dozen of my books. It's a modern romance classic. But that doesn't mean I want to live it in real life.

"Give me your phone," Luca demands.

"Get bent," I mutter, but he just grabs it out of my hand like it's no big deal. I huff, putting my hands up like what the hell?

"Use this one," he says, pulling out a burner phone. "I made you fake accounts on all social platforms, so you won't die of boredom. I've also changed all your passwords so you can't log into your existing accounts and blast your location like a lighthouse."

I open my mouth to argue, but he cuts me off. "It's six days, Lenny. You won't die."

Luca hands me the new phone and walks away. I throw it on the bed next to the weekend bag. It's packed with all my essentials. My brand of shampoo and conditioner. Clothes in my size. Everything I could need for a few days.

But also... lacey skimpy fucking underwear.

"Who packed this bag?" I ask, holding up a pair of red lace crotchless panties like I'm handling a grenade.

Jax's wicked grin fills my vision as he lounges on the bed, looking entirely too pleased with himself. He puts his hands behind his head, his biceps flexing...on purpose. "I did, of course." He winks, moving the sucker from left to right in his mouth with his tongue.

New goal in life: Don't think about Jax's tongue.

"You're not getting in my pants, you fugitive," I snap, tossing the panties in his face. "This pussy is a no-convict-zone, so you'll never see me in these."

"Never say never, Peach," he says, that smirk widening. "Besides, it's enough just knowing your little pussy will either be wearing the panties I picked out for you... or you'll be too stubborn and wear nothing. Either way, I win."

I hate him so much.

Too bad my "little pussy" hasn't gotten the message, apparently.

Thirty minutes later, I'm stepping out of the shower, feeling slightly more human—just enough to remind myself that I don't have to completely lose my mind just yet. I can always do that tomorrow.

As I reach for the towel, I catch a whiff of something... delicious? My stomach rumbles at the unexpected scent of food, and I find an empty motel room and a hot plate sitting on the bed when I open the bathroom door.

I dress quickly. Shockingly, not every pair of panties in the bag is crotchless, but I note the complete lack of pajamas, so I grab one of Jax's t-shirts. It swallows me whole and covers my ass. And I will not be admitting how wonderfully it smells like him. And I absolutely did not pull the collar up to my nose and inhale his scent like it was air.

Muffled voices sound on the other side of the door—probably the guys, talking shop or whatever it is they do when they aren't yelling at me. Not that I care. Cause I totally don't... care, that is.

I look at the food. It's cheesy pasta and a salad with an ice-cold Diet Coke. They even left me a glass with ice because I don't like drinking from the can. They still remember what I like, even the little things. I scowl at the plate, knowing exactly who this came from, and I refuse to be impressed by it.

Enzo—methodical, meticulous—he doesn't miss a detail. If something is needed, he'll make it happen, no questions asked.

He probably knew I'd be too stubborn to eat with them. Maybe he just didn't want me throwing a tantrum about it later. Either way, I'm not going to give them the satisfaction of knowing I'm eating. Even though they'll figure it out the second they see the plate empty, I'll still try to keep some illusion of control over this situation.

I shove the fork into the pasta, then my mouth, and it's so fucking good I moan.

Immediately, Luca quiets as if he heard me.

As I take another bite, he resumes talking on the other side of the door. His tone is low and purposeful, like he's discussing something critical.

"So, anyway, there's a trail of electronic info that's not adding up," he's saying. "I'm going to explore it more later. If I can connect the dots, we might have more answers."

I pause, my fork halfway to my mouth, narrowing my eyes. What the hell is Luca talking about? He's been deep in his little tech world for years, so he could be talking about anything. It's probably nothing related to my father's death.

Then Enzo speaks up, his voice sharp with suspicion. "Something's off with Caputo's death. It's not making sense."

Okay, well, there goes that theory.

He sighs, and I hear the frustration in his voice. "Old allies are turning on each other. It doesn't feel like just a power play. There's something deeper happening here. I lost another fucking land deal that had been all but rock solid before. Now they suddenly have another buyer? No. It smells fishy, so we need to find the barrel full of bullshit and take care of it."

I eat while they talk. I'm sitting on the floor behind the door so I can hear better. If any of them opens the door, I'll be squished like a bug.

When I'm done, I clean up my mess and put the tray on the dresser. The weight of the day presses down upon my chest as I lay on the motel bed, begging for sleep before Jax comes back.

It's times like this I wonder if a mother would come in handy. Someone to run to who can say, *"Oh, sweetheart, I know those guys are just cunt-wagons."*

Okay, maybe moms don't say that specifically, but some sympathy would be nice. Someone to run to with open arms for some advice and no judgment. But I don't even remember my mom.

I know her from photographs and old video recordings of family gatherings, but I have no memories of her on my own.

She went out on her sailboat—something she'd done a thousand times—when a squall rushed in on her. It took two weeks for them to find her capsized boat, but there was no sign of her.

What a terrible way to die. Drowning in an endless ocean. I close my eyes, feeling a little bit like that now myself.

I should suck it up and stop being a baby, but dammit, I want just a few minutes to feel pitiful for myself. I turn over, away from the door, hugging the pillow.

But I can't let this pull me under the waves. It will grab hold of me and never let me go until it yanks all the air from my lungs. At the end of the week, if this threat is over, I will move on and get back to something normal. Make a life for myself again. I've already done that once, so I can do it again.

I'll have to buy a new house since, apparently, mine is in splinters, but I can start over. I just need to make sure these men don't drive me to the brink of my sanity in the meantime. Which will be an accomplishment if we're being honest with each other.

As I drift off to sleep, I think of my mother again, her face soft and kind in the photos. And for the first time in a long time, I wish she were here to tell me how to keep my head above water.

Seven

The moonlight filters into my bedroom, and it's hotter than it should be for this time of year. I should open a window, but I can't bring myself to get up—not with the expert tongue currently lapping at my pussy. I'm naked, a light sheen of sweat covering my body.

"Please." The word escapes me in a breathy plea, though I'm not even sure to whom. My back arches, and my hand trails up my stomach, pausing to trace the curve of my breast.

The growl from the man between my legs is a sound of pure satisfaction. His approval only deepens when I pinch my nipple. His mouth clamps down hard on my clit, and my jaw drops as my breath catches. The pleasure coils deep in my core, a mounting pressure I can't ignore.

Sucking turns to licking, and two fingers thrust inside me with practiced precision.

God, I can feel how wet I am—even in this dream.

I roll my hips, matching the rhythm of my partner's skilled movements. I want to open my eyes, to watch him, but they're so heavy. If I open them, the dream will end before I come, and I can't have that.

Bang. Bang. Bang. A rhythmic thumping echoes from the

wall behind me, faint but unmistakable. Muffled groans and moans follow, distant and distorted, like they're coming from underwater.

My partner picks up the pace, and so do I, pressing my feet into the mattress to grind against him. A strong hand presses down on my thigh, keeping me open for him. That touch, that control, gives away his identity.

"Jax." His name is a breathy whisper on my lips. God, this man was put on Earth to eat pussy.

"Open your eyes, Peach." His breath cools the wet heat between my thighs. He pauses to kiss the inside of my leg, his tongue teasing my sensitive skin. His fingers never falter, their rhythm deliberate and relentless.

"Please, Jax," I beg, my grip on sleep slipping.

"Look at me, baby. Let me see those beautiful hazel eyes when you come."

His tongue circles my clit again, a wet, maddening rhythm. My eyes flutter open, and I'm met not with my familiar bedroom, but a ceiling that is a stranger to me. A brown water stain marks one corner, a reminder of a roof long overdue for repairs.

But all thoughts of the shoddy motel vanish when his tongue flicks hard and fast over my clit. His fingers thrust deeper, and I brace myself with one hand on the headboard. My other hand tangles in his hair—it's just as soft as I remembered.

"Fuck, Jax, don't stop," I whine, not caring how desperate I sound. This will be the best orgasm I've had since Enzo, and I swear I'll set this motel on fire if anyone takes it away from me.

Fully awake now, the muffled groans and banging from the

next room register clearly. I know that sound. Enzo is fucking Luca, and the walls of my pussy clench at the thought.

"You hear them, baby?" Jax pauses just long enough to torture me with his words.

Enzo's deep, possessive voice filters through the wall. Luca's groans follow, breathy and wanton. Then Enzo says, *"Good boy,"* in a tone that makes me fucking lose it.

Heat floods my body, radiating out from my core as my orgasm overtakes me. My entire body trembles, my cries filling the air. Jax knows I'm coming—of course he does—but I still have to say it, to declare that this award-winning tongue has me unraveling beneath him.

All while my two exes fuck each other into oblivion just a wall away.

It's real-life Moanster23, and I wish it were in hi-def surround sound. Hell, I wish they were here—with us—so I could watch, hear them clearly... join them.

"Yes, Jax. Keep going." My hips buck against him as I chase the aftershocks of my orgasm. "Please. Don't stop."

I have to be soaking his face. My god, I might actually die from this—and I'd happily march into hell if it meant living off the memory of Jax's mouth on me.

I've thought about this moment a thousand times, replayed it while I made myself come. But nothing compares to the real thing.

As my climax wanes, I reach for him, but he's already moving. He kisses his way up my body, leaving wet trails along my skin and breasts before his lips claim mine.

"Fuck me, Jax, or I won't be able to breathe."

His cock slips into me in one smooth thrust, and we pass

our shared moans back and forth as our mouths move in coordination like we never missed a day of this.

I clench around him, and a guttural growl escapes his throat. The rhythmic rock of his hips drives him deep, so deep that I know my next orgasm will hit me like a collapsing building.

"Tell me you missed me, Peach." His voice is husky, tinged with desperation.

"No."

I refuse to give him that. He left me standing at the altar like a jackass, clueless about what was happening. He doesn't get to know how that devastated me, how I cried for him, knowing he couldn't come back to me.

I rake my nails down his back, and he slams into me harder. "You can lie all you want, sweet Peach, but this pussy won't lie to me."

He shifts onto his knees, lifting my pelvis with him, keeping my legs spread for his viewing pleasure. His hands grip my hips tightly, holding me in place as he watches his cock slide in and out of me, slick with my arousal. The sight drives him mad, and I reap the benefits.

"Look how wet you are for me," he groans, his pace growing wild. "Look at you, split open on my cock, just the way you need it."

He spits on my clit, and my eyes roll back in my head. God, I missed that move. There's something about the way Jax spits on my cunt while he's destroying it that lights up every nerve in my body.

His thumb rubs circles over my clit as our bodies slam together. The headboard bangs against the wall, joining the cacophony of Enzo and Luca still going at it in the next room.

Together, we might actually bust through the wall, and I don't give a shit.

This man fucks like a god. He could tear the world apart with his dick in my pussy, and I'd be happy for it.

"Your cunt is choking me, baby. Are you sure you didn't miss me?" His words tease, his pace relentless.

My walls flutter around him, and he slows down just enough to threaten that he'll stop if I don't answer him.

"No! Jax, keep going," I plead.

He sucks on his thumb, his cock gliding into me with slow, deliberate strokes. He leans down, his breath hot against my ear. "Tell me what I want to hear, Peach, and I'll give you the world."

Oh, god.

He picks up the pace again, each thrust more intense than the last. The fire in my core reignites, burning hotter with every movement.

"Say it, baby." He kisses me, his lips demanding. He grabs my wrists in one hand, pinning them above my head. His thumb returns to my clit, drawing tight, torturous circles. "Fucking say it because this pussy is mine. You know it is. She's crying for me, Peach."

It's true. I haven't been this wet in years, and with just one touch, I'm Niagara Falls. But he slows down again, and I swear I might cry.

My eyes snap open, and I wrap my legs around his waist. "Fuck you. Yes." I glare at him, anger flaring in my eyes, but triumph dances in his. "I fucking missed you, and I hate you for it."

Jax releases my hands, his grip shifting to my throat as he pounds into me like his life depends on it. He hooks one of my legs over his arm, driving his cock deeper, and I swear I feel him swell inside me.

Is it possible for dicks to grow during sex? Because it feels like my cunt just became a cock extender. The thought vanishes as my orgasm crashes over me, consuming me entirely.

"That's it, Peach. Give it to me," he growls. His eyes, dark as the night, lock onto mine, swallowing me whole. My mouth drops open, and I mewl with every pulse of my cunt around his cock.

"Wake up this entire motel so they can hear how beautiful you sound when you come for me."

The strain in his face tells me he's close, his body trembling as he holds back his release. I dig my nails into his back, pulling him deeper into me. My sensitive clit rubs against the coarse hair of his pubic bone, and I know I'm seconds away from another orgasm.

"You're such a good girl for me," he rasps.

I bite his shoulder, muffling my cries as I curl into him. My breasts slide against his chest, and he grips the headboard, using it for leverage as he pounds into me with abandon.

"Are you ready for my cum, baby?" He sucks my nipple hard, and I yelp my answer.

"Play with your clit, Peach. Come with me. I fucking need it, baby. You don't know how badly I need you."

His voice is raw, desperate, and it pushes me over the edge. My hand finds my clit, and the combined sensation of his cock, his thrusts, and my touch sends me spiraling.

My walls clench around him, and he groans, his release filling me in hot, shuddering waves.

"Fill me up, Jax," I whisper, locking my ankles behind his back. "Give me every drop."

"Fuck," he groans, his face buried in my neck. Each grunt sends shivers across my skin as we ride the last ripples of pleasure together. "Delaney," he murmurs my name with reverence as we collapse onto the bed.

We lie there, tangled together, sharing quiet breaths. His hand strokes my cheek, his eyes searching mine. For a moment, the anger and pain between us fade, replaced by something raw and undeniable.

But I can't let go of the resentment, the betrayal. It's easier to hold onto the anger than face the truth of what I feel for him.

I turn my head away, breaking the fragile connection between us. Jax lets me slip off the bed, but he doesn't let me fall too far into the bitterness.

"You're still mad at me," he says, his voice low and heavy with regret. It's the kind of regret I never let myself show. "After everything... after all this time, you're still mad?"

I shoot him a glare, though it's not as sharp as it should be. "You lied to me. You kept things from me, Jax. You didn't tell me what you really did for a living. You didn't trust me."

"I was protecting you."

"From what?" My voice rises, the frustration spilling out as we stand naked in the dim motel room. His cum drips down my leg, and I hate it because I feel emptier with every drop that leaves me. "What were you protecting me from, Jax? From feeling abandoned? Because that didn't fucking work. You left me at the altar, and then you left me alone in the world when they took you away in handcuffs."

"You didn't wait for me." His voice is softer now, broken with pain. "Why didn't you wait for me?"

He takes a step toward me, and I instinctively step back.

"I looked for you, every day during the trial," he continues, his eyes pleading. Another step forward, another step back.

It's the same dance we've always done—pushing and pulling, never finding steady ground.

"You were charged with murder, Jax."

He winces like the word itself hurts. "You know it was a bullshit charge."

His fists clench at his sides. "That day… that was supposed to be the start of our lives together. I should have told you the truth about what I really did for a living, but I was trying to keep you safe."

Another step backward, and my legs hit the dresser. I have nowhere left to retreat.

"I hurt you, and you hurt me back. God, baby, I wrote you every damn day, but you never wrote back. You just… gave up on me."

His words hit me like a brick, and something inside me softens. He's right. I did walk away. I didn't wait for him. But at the time, I thought I had my reasons.

"I couldn't come to the trial," I confess, my voice trembling. I stare at my hands, unable to meet his eyes. "I couldn't be that close to you and not touch you. To have to walk away and leave you there… it would have ripped my heart apart."

My chin quivers, and I take a deep breath to steady myself. "I did write you—every single day."

Jax's sharp intake of breath cuts through the silence, his disbelief palpable.

I take a step toward him. "I read every letter you sent me. Over and over. Every day. But I never sent you anything. I couldn't."

My breasts brush against his chest as I take another step.

My hands find his taut muscles, and I feel him tense beneath my touch.

"I mostly told you how much I hated you," I admit with a dry laugh. It's not humor—it's the apology I never knew how to give.

He chuckles softly, his hands reaching for me. "I figured that part out on my own."

His gaze softens as he pulls me into his arms. I wrap mine around his neck, my fingers playing with the hair at the nape of his neck. "But I also wrote about my new job... my dickhead of a boss."

He grins knowingly. "Enzo."

"I wrote about my dreams too," I continue, a small smile tugging at my lips. "About wanting to publish more of my books. When my first book hit the best-sellers list... I imagined how proud you'd be."

"I am proud of you, Peach." His voice is warm, his thumb brushing against my cheek. "I always have been. I always will be."

Before I can respond, his lips find mine. The kiss is soft, unhurried, and it carries me somewhere far from the motel and all its ghosts.

He lays me back onto the bed, and when our bodies come together this time, it's different. There's no urgency, no frantic need to fill the silence. It's tender, deliberate, and filled with a warmth I've missed for far too long.

The climax isn't explosive—it's steady, like a wave cresting and retreating. When it's over, we lie tangled together, the quiet between us no longer suffocating but comforting.

His hand traces lazy patterns on my side as we stare at each other, lost in the moment.

"I'm sorry, Peach," he whispers, his voice thick with regret. "I'm so damn sorry I left you."

Just as the words settle, a sharp knock at the door shatters the quiet. I jump, reality rushing back in.

"It's time to go," Enzo calls from the other side, his voice brisk and insistent.

Jax pulls away reluctantly, but I tug him back for one more kiss, soft and lingering. "I'm sorry too."

He rests his forehead against mine, closing his eyes as if to hold onto this moment a little longer. His hands cup my face gently, as though he's afraid I'll disappear when he opens his eyes again.

But finally, he does, and his dimples greet me with a soft smile.

"Come on, Peach. Let's get dressed before your old dickhead boss beats the door down."

Eight

"I got you a hot chocolate."

It's a simple phrase, but when Jax handed me the disposable gas station cup this morning, I stared at him like he'd just sprouted wings and was about to start crowing. His brows knitted in confusion, and he moved his pink sucker to the other side of his mouth. The poor guy was probably wondering if I'd lost my damn mind. But that phrase, so casual, yanked me back to a memory—one I've been running from for years.

It was as if the words were carved into my brain, lying in wait for the right moment to resurface.

I hear my father's voice now, as if he's standing right beside me, saying the exact same thing.

"I got you a hot chocolate, il mio tesoro." *My treasure.*

I can see him so clearly in that moment, his hands steady as he placed the cup on the glass dining room table—the same table that once felt enormous to my child-sized perspective. Back then, everything seemed oversized and overwhelming. The table, him, his promises—they were all larger than life.

But now, as an adult, the table is just a table.

Everything that once felt so grand has shrunk in the cold light of reality. And that man, my larger-than-life hero, became small that day.

Something shifted in that moment. I don't know what it was, but that cup of hot chocolate—it changed things. Before he handed it to me, he was a giant in my eyes. Afterward, he became small. The pedestal I'd placed him on cracked and crumbled, leaving me with a man who wasn't all I thought he was.

And I—I wasn't his treasure anymore. At least not in the way he'd once made me feel.

He became the man who failed me, and now he's just a man who is dead. Another man from my past that I'll bury there, along with the ghosts of three others I thought I buried four years ago.

Jax stands there now, waiting for me to come back to the present. The hurt in his eyes is unmistakable. He thinks I'm offended or angry at him for some inexplicable reason. For something I don't even understand myself.

He pulls the cup back, his expression resigned. "Sorr—"

"No, Jax. It's fine." I force a smile, trying to brush it off. But the words don't feel like they fit anymore. The smile doesn't feel like mine. "I just... I remembered something."

We're back in the SUV now, the hum of the engine filling the silence. Trees blur past the window, their shapes distorted by the rain streaking the glass. The weight of the quiet between us feels suffocating, the air thick and heavy.

I catch my reflection in the window—haunted, distant. The ghost of a little girl stares back at me, small and alone, just like she was then. Just like I was then.

"Il mio tesoro," I whisper, the words barely audible even to myself. They carry more weight than they should. More pain. More distance between me and the woman I am now.

It's strange, isn't it? The way memories work. The more I think about it, the more I realize I can't remember what happened before that moment—before the shift. I don't remember life before he became that small man.

But I still remember that night with the hot chocolate.

The memory is like a lone photograph, faded and incomplete, yet vivid in its own way. I haven't thought about it in years. A lump forms in my throat, and I swallow it down.

There's nothing before that memory. No Delaney. No Mom and Dad. No Christmas mornings or chasing birds on the beach in summer.

Time didn't exist until that hot chocolate was set down in front of me.

It must have been around the time my mom disappeared. I was six when the lightning flashed in the dark sky and took her away from us. Just like the flashes in the sky now, dark clouds reflecting the somber mood this memory has left me with.

A burst of lightning outside jolts me, pulling me from my thoughts. My gaze stays fixed on the rushing landscape as rain pelts the window. The storm feels eerily familiar, a reflection of the one in my memory.

It's strange, the things you forget and the things you remember when you're a kid. The mind locks away details, only to release them years later, through the lens of adulthood.

While the memory of the hot chocolate is isolated, I remember the night my mother went missing with painful clarity.

I clutched my teddy bear tightly to my chest, watching the rain push against the tall living room windows. The room felt like a fishbowl, cold and dark. Lightning streaked across the sky in silver veins, each strike making me flinch.

My father opened the sliding door to the balcony, and I can still feel the breeze pricking my skin. I brush my arm now, trying to wipe away the phantom sensation.

He was on his phone, the other hand pressed to his hip. He wore a suit, as always, though his white shirt's sleeves were rolled up, the top button undone. It was the most informal I'd ever seen him, yet it made him feel like a stranger.

He didn't shut the door completely, and his words carried inside on the wind. "What do you mean there's no contact with the boat?" His tone was sharp, each clap of thunder fueling his anger. "Find her."

Then he saw me. He knocked on the window, snapping his fingers twice to get Rosia's attention. She usually left hours earlier, but she stayed late because of the storm.

Rosia nodded, ushering me away from the window and toward my room.

It was always like that after that night.

I didn't know what to think. I thought I'd done something wrong by overhearing his conversation. I thought his anger was directed at me. And when they found my mother's boat two weeks later, capsized, and empty, I thought his rage was grief.

But now I wonder...

What if he wasn't just sad? What if he was guilty?

What if it was his "work" that led to her death? The storm, the two weeks of waiting, the lie about the boat—it all seems clearer now, knowing what I know about him.

Was it the mafia that took her life because of him?

Maybe the same vendetta that took her life is the one that finally claimed his.

Even as I think this, there's a strange detachment, like the storm outside is mirrored inside me—chaotic, yet distant. A storm that isn't mine to own.

Nine

Enzo and Luca's conversation about the suspicions surrounding my father's death—about the strange activity and the war between families—keeps echoing in my mind. My eyes flick to them in the front seat.

Luca is driving, one hand on the wheel while the other grips Enzo's thigh in a possessive hold, drawing lazy circles on his leg. Enzo scrolls on his phone, unbothered.

Something about seeing them like this—it's comforting in a way I don't quite understand. Each of them hurt me, and I swore I would hate them for the rest of my life. But then I turned the dynamics of our relationships into dark romance books and became a best-selling author. My series all revolve around these three men:

My stepbrother.

My ex-fiancé.

My billionaire boss.

They may have tossed me out of their lives, but no matter how much I pretend I've moved on, the truth is they're burrowed so deep under my skin, it's impossible to remove them.

Pulling my gaze away, I open the burner phone Luca gave

me yesterday. I check the apps, and sure enough, several of the ones I use for mindless scrolling are already set up with fake accounts.

I search for news about yesterday's shootout—or, you know, my fucking house blowing up. But there's nothing. Not a single peep. If I hadn't been there, watching a swarm of shooters dart across my yard and pepper my house with bullets, you could argue I imagined it all.

But there were deaths. The florist, shot through the head. The attackers, their bodies scattered across my lawn like grotesque garden gnomes. And Stacie—she had a whole fridge dropped on her head like something out of a goddamn Acme cartoon.

And yet... nothing. No news. No chatter in the local neighborhood groups. Just silence.

Could they really have cleaned up that many bodies so quickly? Silenced the neighbors? How do you explain a house explosion?

The thought only fuels the nagging suspicion about my mother. Was she a victim of the mafia too, her death swept under the rug to protect secrets? Secrets that died with those who knew them.

Scrolling through social media, I let the short videos distract me, pushing away the heavy thoughts of hot chocolate, a ghostly little girl, and a murdered mother. I search for my favorite influencers and follow them.

Cutting my eyes at Luca, I bite back a sly grin as I refollow Moanster23. Luca keeps driving, still rubbing Enzo's leg, paying me no mind—but I feel like he'll be watching every-thing I do on this phone.

Moanster23 hasn't posted since the night of my date when

I relieved myself in the bathroom. I wonder if Luca will spy on the accounts I follow. Maybe he'll take a peek at a few of Moanster's posts. My favorites are the ones where his body is in the frame—never his face or hands, though. Those are usually... busy.

Just his ridiculously hot chest, with that birthmark on his left pec and a tease of his abs. A mic picks up the slick sounds of his lubed hand stroking his cock, his breathing, his moans. And the whimpers. God, the whimpers. They're award-winning.

I'm staring blankly at Luca and Enzo when the burner phone buzzes with a text.

I glance at the screen and roll my eyes. Of course, it's Jax.

He's programmed his name as:

Husband

I'll be fixing that immediately...

Douche Canoe

Much better.

Douche Canoe: see something you like up there?

Me: Has anyone told you how nosey you are?

Douche Canoe: yes

Douche Canoe: answer the question

Me: Suck a fat cock.

🪦 Douche Canoe 🪦: I have. both of theirs to be specific

I'm not commenting on that. Locking the screen, I drop the phone into my bag.

Buzz.

Ignored.

Buzz. Buzz.

Oh, a double text. The desperation builds. I slide the phone deeper into my bag, locking eyes with Jax the entire time. His glare of frustration is priceless.

Awww. Someone doesn't like this game.

Clearing my throat, I look to the front seat. "I heard you guys talking in front of the motel room door last night." I lean back, resting an elbow on the console between Jax and me.

"Has anyone ever told you that you're nosey?" Luca doesn't take his eyes off the road, but I hope the holes I'm boring into his head are burning.

Jax snorts a laugh, and I glance at Luca, wondering if he somehow knows what Jax just texted me. *That can't be though, right?* I give a weary side-eye glare at Jax as a possible co-conspirator.

"Has anyone ever told you to stop being a giant dildo?" I shoot back, but Jax chuckles.

Luca's navy eyes catch mine in the rearview mirror, stripping me bare. "I knew you were eavesdropping. No point pretending."

"Yeah? How would you know if you weren't eavesdropping yourself?"

His wry smile flashes before he looks back at the road. "Touché."

Jax flips the center console up and reaches into my bag, pulling out the burner phone and dropping it back into my lap. "I think we can all agree Delaney's got the right to know what's going on."

Buzz.

He wiggles his phone at me, like I don't know he's texting me.

With a groan, I reluctantly unlock the screen.

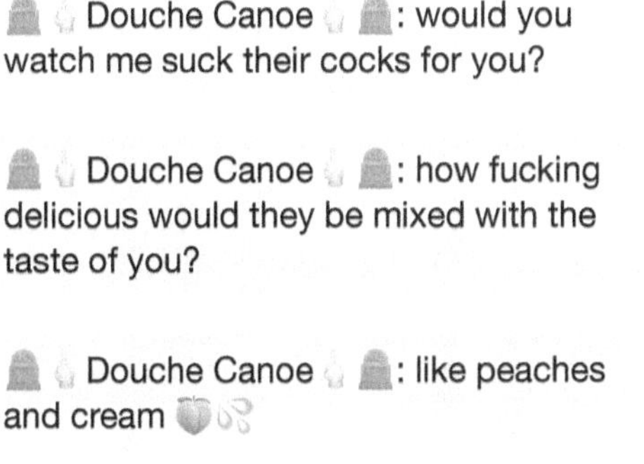

Now I'm wet. *Perfect.* My mouth hangs open for a moment before I snap it shut.

Enzo has been relatively quiet during the drive, but now he speaks, darkening his phone and resting his hand over Luca's. "Your father wasn't just the boss of the Italians. He was a strong ally with other families like the Russian Bratva. Since he's died, things have started to unravel quickly."

Douche Canoe: you use punctuation when you text

Douche Canoe: weirdo

Me: I happen to be a bestselling author. I can't help that my natural sense of excellence overflows into other areas of my life.

Enzo continues, his voice low but intense. "Old alliances have fractured. People who were supposed to stay loyal… aren't."

Douche Canoe: are your panties overflowing right now thinking about how much of their cocks I can fit down my throat?

I shift in my seat, and I can feel him grinning next to me.

Me: You just used punctuation. Super weird.

I cut Jax a warning glare, but he clearly doesn't take it that way, his thumbs flying across the screen again.

"And you found some fishy transactions, like money laundering? Does the mafia still do that, like the good-old-days?" I ask Luca. I catch the small twitch of his mouth, as if he wants to smile at my joke but doesn't want to give me the satisfaction.

Buzz.

It's Enzo who answers the question. "There's been a lot of odd electronic traffic we're tracking–payments that don't make sense. The kind of stuff that shouldn't have been moved, especially after your dad's death. It looks an awful lot like some-one's been cleaning up the tracks."

Douche Canoe : which pair of panties are you wearing? the red ones?

Me: You're about to get blocked.

"How can you tell?" I ask, genuinely curious, while also trying to ignore the growing heat from Jax's relentless flirting.

"Because it's the same type of stuff we would do when we move on a family's territory and take it over," Luca says, finally weighing in. "Except it's a lot sloppier. Intentionally so."

Douche Canoe : or are you not wearing any?

It's a natural reflex that makes me bite my lip, I swear. And it has absolutely nothing to do with the fact that I am not wearing panties and I would totally not mind if he checked.

Douche Canoe : I can just check for myself if you dont want to answer.

He's a mind reader. A telepath. He can hear my thoughts. That's the only explanation.

"So, someone is leaving messy electronic transactions on purpose?" The wheels in my mind are turning, secretly locking these details away to use in a future book. "Because that would distract you from the real stuff they're actually trying to cover up."

"She catches on quick." Luca means it like a sarcastic insult, but I know it's a genuine compliment. We may only have known each other for my first year in college, but I could read him like an open book then, and he's no different now.

"It's just a puzzle," he adds, glancing at me through the rearview mirror. "When I have enough pieces, I'll figure it out. I always do."

That seems to be the end of the conversation, so I look out the window again to see that we've driven beyond the storm. I wonder what their stake is in all of this.

Enzo said he was losing land deals. Maybe that's his schtick?

I'm wondering what could have roped Jax and Luca into this when Jax's warm hand slides across my thigh, pulling it slightly toward him. His touch travels north at an agonizingly slow pace, testing the waters. His other hand types rapidly on his phone.

Douche Canoe: shall we play a game?

I cut my eyes at him which I should not have done. He's brought out his heavy artillery. His sly crooked smile has brought out one of his dimples.

Me: What kind of game?

Luca and Enzo have fallen into a conversation about the safe-house we're heading to tonight and what time we should arrive.

Douche Canoe: the kind where I guess what panties ur wearing and then I get to check if I'm right

Me: What do you get if you win?

His slightly crooked grin morphs into a full-blown, shit-eating smile.

Douche Canoe: I get to slide my fingers into that wet cunt of yours

Jesus.

Douche Canoe: because I know you're soaking wet Peach

Me: Dry as the Sahara over here.

Me: And what do I get if I win?

Douche Canoe: peace and quiet for the rest of the ride

I raise my eyebrows and tilt my head in consideration, forgetting Jax is watching me like a fucking hawk.

Douche Canoe: choices, choices

Douche Canoe: whats it going to be Peach?

With some quick girl-math, this is a ten-out-of-ten win for me. He has a fifty percent chance of being right. But me? I either get his thick fingers in my pussy (and yes, it's totally bare and dripping wet) or hours of quiet time with my reading app and Moanster's posts.

Me: Place your bets, gentlemen.

His hand squeezes my thigh a little tighter as he works to rein in that soul-crushing smile.

> 🪦 Douche Canoe 🪦: I'm 💯 certain theres nothing between your cunt and these torturous fucking yoga pants

With his prediction sent, his devilish hand moves up my leg and slips under the waistband of my pants. His eyes close briefly, and he releases a quiet sigh as he bites his lip, meeting nothing but freshly shaven skin.

> 🪦 Douche Canoe 🪦: Oh Peach

He types out the message with one hand while his other runs along the lips of my pussy, confirming how wet I am.

> 🪦 Douche Canoe 🪦: Youre fucking killing me

One finger circles my clit while two others tease my entrance.

> 🪦 Douche Canoe 🪦: I'll make you come if you can stay quiet. Do you think you can?

He doesn't look at his phone for my answer; his eyes lock onto mine, daring me. I nod, parting my legs slightly.

The tension in the backseat skyrockets, but Luca and Enzo remain oblivious.

My god I forget how many skills this man has when it comes to my vagina. I'm not sure how it happens. The only thing I can think of is that he's a shape shifter. It's like his hand transforms and his fingers turn into tentacles but I'm coming in under two minutes. I'm surprised the door handle is not dented with the impression of my fingers as I squeeze it keeping quiet.

I nearly do it until Jax flicks my clit a few final times with his fingernail and it wrenches the quietest of whimpers from me.

Luca's eyes burn into mine in the rearview mirror, his grip tightening on the wheel.

"Jerk," I mouth at Jax as he withdraws his hand and licks his fingers clean, smug as ever.

Enzo, seated directly in front of me, turns his head slightly. Though he can't see me, the tick of his jaw tells me he knows what Jax was up to.

"This is not the time or place to finger-fuck our assignment," Enzo scolds, his voice clipped.

"What can I say? Our girl's tense." Jax leans back in his seat, shameless. "I'm just helping her relax a little."

I cross my arms, glaring. "I'm not a fucking assignment, you asshole. I'm a goddamn person."

Ten

There is no better nap than a road trip nap in the car. We stopped for gas earlier. I actually used the bathroom this time, with Enzo standing watch outside the door.

Jax bought nearly every snack and drink imaginable, holding up two bags of goodies that I was secretly excited to check out. I tossed him a big pink sucker with a roll of my eyes and then munched on peanut M&M's.

We passed some time playing a license plate game. Enzo even helped me cheat a few times, finding license plates and motioning to me discreetly so I could claim them before Jax did.

What a naughty boy the boss of the Vincenzi family has become.

The repetitive rock of the car was making my eyelids heavier by the second. Jax lifted the center console so I could scoot closer to him. His broad chest and the steady thump of his heart lulled me to sleep.

It's their soft voices that begin to pull me from my haze. "Is her seatbelt on?" Luca's deep voice is low.

"Yeah," Jax says right next to my ear. "Wake up for me, Peach," he whispers.

It's the sharp sound of a gun being cocked that has my eyes popping open. I sit up quickly, and instantly my heart is pounding in my chest. "What's going on?"

"Luca thinks we're being followed." Jax's tone is calm, and he's not faking his composure. It's genuine, honed, and practiced for probably years. All of them are cool as cucumbers on the surface.

Enzo pulls back on a gun, inspecting it just like they do in the movies, then releases it, apparently satisfied with whatever he saw. He looks back, his gray eyes running over me once. "It'll be okay." And for some reason, I believe it will be.

The car's blinker clicks as Luca moves us to the far-left lane, putting the wall to one side of us as the car keeps its pace down the highway.

Jax shifts, climbing over me into the passenger seat with the fluidity of someone who's been in this position too many times before. His gun is in his right hand, but his finger isn't on the trigger. He looks at me—dark, focused. His voice is softer now, but still serious. "Stay in the middle for me, baby."

I catch the way he looks at me. It's not just a question—it's a plea. A plea to be smart, to stay safe. His eyes are dark, as if the predator lurking within him is rising to the surface. I can see this isn't some game anymore. This is real.

"Can I hold my spatula?" I whisper, my voice coming out lighter than I intended, even though I mean it to sound firmer.

He smirks, shaking his head at my ridiculousness, but reaches behind us, pulling out the spatula. He holds it just out of my reach. "Just don't beat the shit out of me with it."

"No promises," I wink back at him.

"Keep an eye on the four cycles," Luca says, sounding like

something much more sinister than I have ever known him to be. It makes me wonder what the last six years have done to him because this is not the bright-eyed boy in my dorm that I fell in love with.

"I've got 'em," Enzo answers, his voice equally grim.

Luca has to change lanes again to pass a car that didn't move over. He does it with a curse and a glare at the driver.

I resonate with this so hard.

There should be an addition to the Ten Commandments: *Thou shalt not drive like a slow-ass bitch in the left lane; lest ye be yeeted from the road like the prick you are.*

Amen.

"Yeah, we're definitely being followed." Something shifts in Luca, and it's like he mutates into a professional race car driver. His foot is heavy on the gas pedal, and the SUV answers with a growl. "Head down, Lenny."

His eyes move constantly between the road ahead and the mirrors. I look behind and spot the motorcycles. They know he's onto them, and the chase ensues. Okay, here we go.

The four cycles surround us, two in the front, two in the back. They're closing in, trying to box us in, to slow us down. Luca doesn't flinch. He handles the wheel like he's done this a thousand times before. If this is a normal Monday for him, I'm in way deeper than I ever thought.

Without warning, Luca slams on the brakes, and I'm thrown forward. The seatbelt digs into my chest, pulling me back. My hands shoot out to catch myself on the front row seats, my breath catching as the world seems to lurch forward with me.

The motorcycles behind us didn't anticipate the move and

crash into the rear of the SUV. The collision makes every muscle in my body tense as metal strikes metal. One of the cyclists is thrown over the front of his bike, and his helmet crashes into the rear window.

It's an explosion of glass, and I scream, but no one hears.

Luca is already slamming his foot hard on the gas, reigniting the squealing tires and billowing smoke that drenches the cyclists behind us. Enzo's window is going down. His long legs push against the floorboards, and he extends the top half of his body out of the car.

With both hands on his revolver, he aims. One flash of his gun pops, and one of the cyclists in front of us goes down. His bike wobbles twice before it crashes to the highway, its momentum sending it skidding into the next lane.

The other cyclist in front does a quick maneuver and spins his bike around. It seems like a second passes, and he propels himself forward, riding between the wall and car.

Jax seems to know what's going to happen before I do, and he grabs the back of my neck, pushing my head between my knees. He covers me with his body as there is a bang, followed by another explosion of glass.

This time the fragments are in the seat next to me, and a breeze immediately rushes into the car from the blown-out window.

The SUV is a monster as it races forward, Luca calm and steady as he guides the car between the unsuspecting motorists commuting alongside a mafia car chase.

The cyclist that shot at us has turned their bike around again and is gaining speed on us. The other rider behind us picks his bike up, starts it, and races after his companion.

In the distance beyond them, more commotion on the highway catches my attention, and I squint.

"More are coming," I call out. "Looks like several Mustangs and some other model of car I don't know but fuck—"

I count the chaos that seems to be weaving between cars, just like we are.

"There's six."

"Good girl, Len." Luca's comment is quiet, almost like he spoke it to himself, but somehow it blasts around me like the wind billowing through the car. My stomach does that annoying flippy thing, and I swallow it down, getting back to the task at hand: not dying.

Jax and Enzo take action, somehow moving in sync without a word. Jax climbs over me again, his gun pointed at one cyclist while Enzo mirrors him from the other side. Jax hits his mark. Enzo misses, a curse ringing out as he ducks back into the car to avoid gunfire from the remaining rider.

The cars behind us are gaining, and Luca pushes the SUV harder. The car jerks in and out of traffic, forcing me to clutch the seats in front of me as if they were lifelines.

There's only one cyclist left, but the chaos is far from over. High-performance sports cars scream toward us, engines roaring like wolves on the hunt.

Luca is in his element, the car almost an extension of his body as he maneuvers through the madness. The remaining cyclist weaves through traffic, trying to keep up, but Luca is too good. It's as if he's analyzed the road ahead, mapping out the perfect path.

The motorcycle charges at us again, the rider determined. Luca abruptly veers two lanes over. The cyclist overcorrects, and Luca uses the opportunity to position the SUV on the rider's left, with the highway shoulder to his right.

Luca jerks the SUV toward him, forcing the rider onto the loose gravel of the shoulder. The bike spins violently, flipping end over end before crashing into the dirt. The rider is thrown clear, his body skidding across the highway. The wreckage of his bike arcs in an ugly slide.

"Fucking asshole," Luca mutters. Our eyes meet in the rearview mirror, and he gives me the faintest smile and a slight nod. It's both a question and a statement.

Are you okay?

It's going to be alright.

I nod back and adjust my grip on the seats. My legs ache from bracing against the floorboard during the car's wild movements.

The first round of the chase is over, but the next one is already bearing down on us. A fresh set of cars tears toward us like a pack of rabid animals.

"Roll all the windows down," Enzo says over the roar of the wind as he assesses the approaching storm of vehicles behind us.

My hand reaches for the knob, but Luca beats me to it, lowering every window that isn't already shattered. The roar of the highway and the wind engulf us, as if the chaos outside has broken into our fortress.

I grip the seat for dear life, my spatula firm in my grasp, as the SUV speeds forward, jerking through traffic. Luca's fingers dance over the wheel, his eyes flicking between the rearview and side mirrors.

Jax is quiet beside me, his jaw clenched as he surveys the

threat behind us. His hand rests on my knee, squeezing gently, then rubbing—a small tell of the nerves he's trying to mask.

I place my hand over his, giving it a firm squeeze, and it pulls his attention.

His rich brown eyes soften as they meet mine. He cups my jaw with his free hand, his lips crashing into mine in a hurried, desperate kiss. "Get ready for round two, baby."

"I'm ready."

Eleven

"They're catching up," Luca mutters, his voice calm but deadly. "Grab the larger firepower, Jax."

Jax shifts in his seat, twisting to open a long black crate in the back. His large frame moves lithely as he pulls out several semi-automatic guns, and my jaw nearly unhinges.

"What the fuck do you guys do for work?" My eyes widen as Jax hands a gun to Enzo and retrieves something that looks suspiciously like a small machine gun.

Are those grenades? Are these men Rambo? Why can't I stop asking myself questions? I clutch the handle of my spatula so tightly my knuckles ache, blinking rapidly to calm my racing mind. Enzo watches me take in the arsenal of weapons that they handle with practiced ease and his smirk is near deadly.

...For my panties that is because holy shit. If I were wearing any that look would make my undies combust on the spot.

"Welcome to the mafia, Delaney Caputo." He winks as he unbuttons his shirt, revealing a thin white undershirt that clings to every ripple of muscle. Then, as if it's the most normal thing in the world, both he and Jax lean out of the SUV's windows, guns in hand.

My. God.

My ovaries are planning baby registries. Her Vagesty has declared open season, rolling out the red carpet for fertilization.

Simultaneously, Jax and Enzo hurl small, heavy objects toward the first two cars pursuing us. I don't know what the hell they're throwing, but it's definitely not good news for the other guys. The objects land just ahead of both vehicles with deadly precision.

A heartbeat later, twin explosions erupt in fiery chaos. Flames billow into the air like a scene ripped straight from a Michael Bay movie, hurling the cars skyward. The shockwave rattles our SUV, and the heat washes over me, making my spatula slick in my grip.

"Holy shit," I whisper, my voice barely audible over the roar of destruction.

One car crashes nose-first into the pavement, flipping dramatically before landing on its roof. The second vehicle slams into one of its companions, crumpling like a soda can and sending the car behind it veering wildly off course.

Three down. The highway behind us is a graveyard of flaming wreckage and twisted metal.

Jax and Enzo don't miss a beat. The moment the debris clears, they line up their next shots, their weapons steady, their focus unnervingly calm.

"I need another clip," Enzo calls out, his voice casual, like he's ordering coffee. As Jax fires out the passenger window, I fumble in the back, rummaging through the arsenal.

Gunfire erupts in a deafening barrage, making me flinch as one car swerves violently, its tires screeching against the asphalt. The second car doesn't stand a chance—bullets rip into its side, and it careens into the guardrail with a satisfying crunch.

I blink at the sudden silence, my heart pounding against my ribs. My mind struggles to catch up with what I just witnessed.

"Well, that's one way to do it," I mutter under my breath, still dazed, as I hand fresh clips to Jax and Enzo.

Jax glances back at me with a smirk, his finger hovering near the trigger. "Thanks, baby."

I sink into my seat, my fingers gripping the seatbelt like a lifeline. This is real. I'm actually in the middle of a goddamn high-speed car chase. The absurdity of it all almost makes me laugh—or maybe cry. I can't tell anymore.

"We've got two left," Luca says, his tone steady yet urgent. His hands tighten around the wheel as he maneuvers through traffic with precision. "Enzo, check the sky."

The sky? What the actual fuck is in the sky?

My gaze darts to Jax and Enzo, who seem eerily at home in this chaos, like apex predators in their natural habitat. There's something about the adrenaline, the sheer thrill of it—it's intoxicating in a way I'm not sure I want to admit.

Luca slams the gas, the SUV growling as it lunges forward. I glance out the window, trying to spot what Luca meant, but Jax pulls me back into the center of the vehicle.

"Stay put, Peach," he says sharply, his frustration cutting through the chaos.

I clutch my trusty spatula, and I look behind us and see what Luca was pointing out. It's a fucking helicopter.

Sure, why not.

Perhaps a submarine will rise out of the fucking highway next. That would just be the cherry on top of this shit-show sundae.

"Get the rocket," Luca calls back, his voice a cold command.

Ex-squeeze me?

Jax moves quickly, opening a second case and retrieving pieces of a weapon that, when assembled, will undoubtedly launch us onto a government watchlist. He passes the parts to Enzo, who begins assembling them with unnerving precision.

The remaining cars surge closer, flanking us. Everything happens in a blur. Enzo pauses his assembly—the rocket launcher—as Jax fires at the car on the passenger side.

On the driver's side, a blue Mustang surges forward, its driver firing through his own windshield at Luca. Before I can scream, the Mustang's passenger door flies open, and a man leaps into our SUV through the busted window.

I shriek, swinging the spatula with all my might. The man recoils, clearly bewildered by my retaliation, but it gives Jax the second he needs.

Before I know what is happening the handle of a knife is sticking out of the man's eye socket and the other one rolls back into his head. "Cocksucker." Jax growls as he pushes the body out of the car. The SUV jolts as we roll over something heavy. I'll just pretend it's a pothole. *Definitely not a body.*

"You okay?" Jax asks, his eyes scanning me for injuries.

I intend to answer him, but Luca uses the SUV as a battering ram against the car on the passenger side and it steals my breath. I answer with an unflattering grunt while Jax holds me in place with his large arm across my body.

Luca catches the car on the front panel, and it spins wildly. The tires catch and the car is sideways. It lurches up, spinning again and again. Enzo throws another projectile and hits the car perfectly sending another fireball into the air.

If this whole mafia thing doesn't work out, I wonder if he

would join a pro baseball team because the man has an arm on him.

Luca somehow turns time into slow motion.

He wields the SUV like a fucking scalpel. Slamming the brakes and spinning the wheel, the SUV turns on a dime. As we begin our 360-degree rotation at top speeds, Luca's arm points out the window. His forearm muscles ripple as he grips the gun in his hand.

Pointed for the driver of the final car, Luca lined himself up perfectly and pulls the trigger. I don't see the bullet hit but the drivers head jerks back, and he's dead before I can blink. The last of the cars in pursuit of us barrels across the highway and slams into the wall at full speed.

Our SUV completes its rotation, having spun in a full circle and Luca smashes the gas pedal to the ground again. All of it took place in a matter of seconds.

My breaths are shallow and ragged. My knuckles are white from grabbing onto the seat beneath me with everything I have. Fast and furious, eat your fucking heart out.

Jax hands grab each side of my face, making me look at him.

I think I'm going into shock because the edges of my vision turn to static.

"Delaney," he says, his tone low and commanding. "You're okay. Look at me. You're okay."

I nod, the movement jerky as though I'm trying to convince myself as much as him. His thumbs stroke my cheeks in a soothing rhythm, though his body remains tense, coiled like a spring ready to snap. "Luca's not going to let anyone touch his girl."

His girl.

The words send a shiver down my spine, both thrilling and unsettling. At breakfast yesterday, it was "our Delaney." Now, it's "his girl." The possessiveness is maddening—and maybe just a little intoxicating.

I catch Luca's gaze in the rearview mirror. His piercing blue eyes are a storm of fury and focus, his jaw tight as his hands grip the wheel with no mercy. He glances at me briefly, a silent question in his eyes.

Are you okay?

The static fogging the edges of my vision begins to clear. I draw in a deep breath, finding my anchor in the controlled chaos that is Luca.

"The chopper," he says, his voice clipped. "That's all that's left."

His tone sends a chill through me. This isn't the Luca I knew back in college, the tech genius with a quick wit and a soft smile. This Luca is lethal, a weapon honed and ready to strike. And yet, he still glances at me with an unspoken promise of safety.

"Get the launcher," Luca orders, his voice calm but unyielding.

Jax moves with practiced ease, grabbing the remaining pieces of the rocket launcher and handing them to Enzo, who assembles the weapon with methodical precision.

Sure as shit, the helicopter looms behind us, its blades slicing through the air like a mechanical beast. Men dangle from its sides, their guns trained on us.

Jax leans out of the window, unleashing a barrage of bullets at the helicopter. The responding gunfire slams into the SUV, metal meeting metal in a deafening cacophony. I flinch as sparks fly, and Jax's broad frame shifts, shielding me instinctively.

The sunroof slides open with a hiss, and the wind howls into the cabin. My heart lodges itself in my throat as Enzo stands, the upper half of his body fully exposed. His white undershirt clings to him, already damp with sweat, and I swear the man has nerves of steel.

"Enzo!" I cry out, my voice cracking as he raises the rocket launcher. He braces himself, the weapon perched on his shoulder. The kickback from the launch jerks his body, and my heart stops, frozen in sheer terror.

A beat later, the missile finds its target.

The helicopter erupts in a spectacular explosion, fiery debris raining down like confetti. The wreckage plummets to the ground in a twisted heap, another explosion marking its final demise. Heat surges around us, and the SUV bucks slightly under the force of the shockwave, but Luca doesn't react. His focus remains razor-sharp as he steers us out of the danger zone.

There is nothing but destruction behind us for several miles. Plumes of smoke rise into the sky periodically marking the locations where the pursuers didn't survive my men.

My men.

I slump in my seat, my hands relaxing the death grip on my trusty spat. Enzo's gaze locks onto mine, his usual hardness absent, replaced by something raw and vulnerable. He leans forward, his forehead resting against mine. His hand cups my cheek, the warmth of his skin a stark contrast to the chill still coursing through me.

"We've got you, okay?" His voice is low, almost a whisper, and I don't know if he's saying it for me or for himself.

I nod, my own hand rising to cover his. "I know you do."

Twelve

It's dark when we roll up to an isolated home on a remote property just outside Butte, Montana. There isn't a damn thing out here for miles, and I can't help but think that's on purpose. It's too dark to take in anything beyond the immediate vicinity, and that alone is enough to tell me the isolation is intentional.

The house is large and one story, built primarily from stone. I can make out the dark outline of a building a short walk away, and dread washes over me at what it might be used for.

This place gives me the creeps—like something straight out of a horror movie, the kind with a haunted house and a dismembered body buried in the backyard.

Luca slams his door a little harder than necessary, stomping past me as I stretch, finally standing with my feet on solid ground. The back of the SUV pops open. Jax and Luca grab a few bags each, but Luca doesn't waste time with pleasantries and heads straight for the house.

I raise an eyebrow, watching him storm off. "What's got his bazooka bent out of shape?" I mutter, more to myself, though I'm sure the other two hear it.

"He just wants to figure out how we were located so quickly," Enzo responds, his voice low as he takes my book bag before I can protest. "Luca's planted dozens of false trails by now to throw them off. Someone got lucky, that's all."

"Three hits came after us today, Peach," Jax adds, his eyes narrowing, the usual playful spark gone. "We need answers, or you're not safe. Even here."

I glance around, the wind biting at my skin, the cold of the late night seeping through the remnants of the shot-up SUV. "And where exactly is 'here'?" I ask, gesturing to the mountains in the distance. It's a lot of wide-open space, with nothing but the house, a fancy-looking barn, and a fence stretching on for miles. There's no way this place is an innocent retreat. The mafia doesn't own places like this for fun.

"This is one of my properties," Enzo answers, but I can tell by his eyes he's withholding more.

My temper flares. "Okay, and?" I cross my arms over my chest, the chill in the air making my teeth chatter. "Do I need to play Twenty Questions every damn time? Stop fucking lying to me by hiding shit."

Enzo steps closer, his towering frame blocking the dim moonlight. "This is a house for Cleaners and Fixers," he says, his voice quieter now but edged with something I can't quite place. "Members of my family handle *associates* here who need to be bled dry for information or who've fucked up and get a visit from The Undertaker." He gestures toward Jax, then points to the barn. "That's where it happens. Bodies disappear here, Delaney. Does that answer it for you?"

I stand there, frozen, trying to process what he's saying. He just bluntly told me this is a mafia torture and disposal site. His family runs this operation. A dark, uncomfortable chill runs down my spine, but more than that, he just pisses me off.

Aren't I supposed to be leading a mafia dynasty by Friday? And they still want to pretend I can't handle the truth about everything. Well, fuck them.

I let out a short laugh. "Jesus Christ, you could've just said you kill people here and dump them in a mineshaft," I mutter, snatching my bag back from him and marching toward the house. "Dramatic-ass men."

Luca emerges from the house just then, locking eyes with me. His jaw tightens as he notices the bag in my hand. Without warning, he steps up to me, his face hard. "Give me that fucking bag."

"Bite my ass," I snarl, holding it out of his reach. But he doesn't care for my response. Without missing a beat, Luca rips the bag from my grasp and spills its contents onto the wooden porch like a kid's Halloween haul.

"What the hell?" I gasp, my stomach sinking as I watch my stuff scatter. Something heavy thuds as it hits the ground, and I stop breathing for a moment. *The laptop. The fucking laptop.*

Luca picks it up and glares at me like I've personally planted a homing beacon in his asshole. "This. They tracked us with this. Way to almost get us fucking killed, Delaney."

"Luc," Jax's tone is a warning, but Luca doesn't give a shit.

He's pissed, and I knew he'd find any reason to take it out on me. Hell, he's acted like he can't stand being in my presence most of the time since they abducted me.

My anger flares, and I turn on him, my voice rising in pitch. "I didn't ask to be kidnapped, Luca. If you recall, I was thrown into the car by a caveman after you blew up my fucking house. This is all I have left of my life, you dick."

Luca doesn't back down. "You ran, Delaney. In the middle of a goddamn shootout. You just left, like you were on your way to pick up fucking groceries while we risked our lives trying to get you out of there."

"Excuse me for not being the perfect captive and making your abduction easier," I snap, my voice shaking. "Perhaps call first next time."

Luca nearly snarls at me like an angry dog. "You have no fucking idea what we've done to keep you safe."

"Because you all treat me like I'm a porcelain doll about to fucking shatter. Well, I'm not." My voice echoes into the night as the shadows of the large mountains witness our meltdown. "News flash, big boy." I lower my tone and step up to him. It's not as intimidating as it should be since I'm about seven inches shorter and have to look up—but he gets the point. "I survived all three of you assholes making me look like a fool once, and I'm not aiming for a second time around."

He flinches at my words, but I keep going. I'm too wound up now to stop.

"I was just a cherry to pop, right? That's a pretty good notch for your bedpost, isn't it? Some top-tier bragging rights you got to deflower the Caputo heiress? Because you knew who I was, didn't you?"

"Enough," Enzo growls. His eyes, hard as steel, flick between Luca and me. The atmosphere thickens with tension, and I brace myself for more.

"I'm not on your payroll anymore, Mr. Vincenzi, but thank you for testing out how tight my pussy was and then throwing me to the curb. Is that why you went through so many assistants? Once they were dripping with your cum, you had no use for them anymore?"

Enzo's expression falters for a second, but something cracks behind his cold exterior. His eyes darken, his fists clenching at his sides. The silence between us is thick and suffocating.

"And you," I snap, turning to Jax, whose shock is plain on his face. We may have apologized for what happened after he got arrested, but we didn't even scratch the surface of everything before that. "Did you set your sights on making the mafia princess your old lady so you could have the empire when good ol' Pops kicked the bucket?"

Jax's voice is quiet but razor-sharp. "That's not true, Peach." His words hang in the air, but there's something in his gaze—something that tells me he's not innocent either. There's always been something, lurking in the shadows, that he's never admitted.

There is something else going on with each of them that I'm not privy to yet and I have a feeling it revolves around me. I can't decide if they are keeping it from me to protect me or if they are just cowards.

I snort a humorless laugh. "That's what I thought." I look between them, my anger simmering. "The three of you have lied to me since the day you met me, fucked me, and then tossed me. So, forgive me for not bending over and accepting your cocks like a good little cum dumpster when you show up out of the blue."

I spin away from them, heading for the house. My chest is tight, my hands shaking as I storm past Luca. "You showed up at my door, turned my life upside down, and I'm allowed to have feelings about it. You want the rest of this trip to go easier? Stop acting like I'm a fucking child who doesn't understand what the grown-ups are saying."

"Delaney," Enzo barks.

But I don't stop. I slam the door behind me, needing space. Needing a moment to breathe. I walk through the dark house with a scowl burning on my face and shut myself in the first bedroom I find.

I stand at the window, my arms crossed over my chest, staring at the full moon. Though we're in the middle of nowhere, it's not as dark outside as I expected. I catch movement in my peripheral vision.

Enzo is following Luca, trying to get him to acknowledge him. Luca opens the passenger door of the SUV, grabs something, and then slams the door, finally turning around to face Enzo.

I can't hear their argument, but it's clear they're bickering. Enzo throws his arms wide, gesturing angrily, while Luca dramatically rolls his eyes. I watch for a moment, noticing the heat between them slowly dissipating. Luca leans against the SUV, his head falling back against it as he gazes up at the moon —the same one I've been staring at.

Enzo steps forward and brackets Luca's hips with his strong hands. The tension drains from Luca's body, his posture softening as he gives in to whatever Enzo is saying.

With a hand on Luca's throat, Enzo pulls his gaze toward him. Their foreheads rest together for a moment before Enzo kisses him. It's slow, lingering—an intimate kiss where their lips remain still for a beat before they part, deepening their embrace.

Luca pulls Enzo closer by the waistband of his pants, pressing their bodies together, while Enzo holds Luca's face in his hands. They kiss again, but this time it's softer, more private. After a moment, they break apart, resting their foreheads together once more before slowly separating.

The sound of knuckles tapping on the door pulls me back, and I instinctively close the curtains, turning away from the two men I'm inexplicably drawn to.

"Yeah?" I call out, my voice thick with sorrow.

It's Jax, peeking his head in cautiously before opening the door wider. He stands in the doorway with the ivory weekend bag they brought for me.

"I thought you'd want your stuff for a shower and some clean clothes," he says.

The sadness in his eyes makes something in my chest tighten, cracking through the ice I've built around myself. I bite my lip, looking down at the floor for a moment before I take a deep breath and step toward him.

"Thanks." My fingers wrap around the brown leather handle, but he doesn't let go. I look at him, and I know what he wants. Damn it, I hate this part. I hate the vulnerability.

I want to pull away, to shut myself off completely, but I can't. I realize that, without them, I wouldn't have survived today. Death may not even be the worst thing that could have happened. What if the man who grabbed me had taken me? God knows what he would've done then.

A chill runs up my arm, and I shiver at the thought.

Jax gently runs a warm hand up my arm before cupping my face. I lean into his touch for a moment before he turns my face toward his.

"I'll tell you the truth if you want it, Peach," he says, his voice serious, almost sorrowful. "Just be ready to hate me once you hear it."

Thirteen

"You were a mark I was supposed to make disappear." Jax holds my gaze, unflinching, as I feel the weight of his words sink in.

He was supposed to kill me?

"The job didn't come with a picture, and it paid a shitload of money, so I took it. I knew the time and place. I knew the signal—a cupcake with a sparkler on the table," he says, his voice soft, almost pained.

A gasp escapes my mouth.

I remember that day. *My birthday.*

My father was supposed to meet me. He made yet another promise he never planned on keeping. That was the day I decided I was done with him—and the day I met Jax.

"You were alone, staring down at that cupcake like the loneliest woman in the world," he continues, shaking his head. A crease forms between his eyes, the memory haunting him. "I couldn't do anything but keep watching you, getting angrier by the second that someone would put a hit out on an angel."

He rubs his knuckle gently along my cheek—a tenderness I wasn't expecting.

"I fell in love with you from that single look. I knew I

couldn't let you get away. Someone else would just pick up the next hit and finish the job. So, I…" His voice trails off as he steps closer, one arm low on my back and the other cradling my jaw. "I went after you. Followed you into a few stores and then pretended to bump into you."

This was the part of our love story we always joked about. A bottle of red wine was in that bag, and it busted. It splashed up the front of my white sundress, and I looked like Carrie when the bucket of pig's blood was poured on her. We both just stood there in shock for a few seconds until I busted out laughing.

He took me to dinner to "make amends," and it ended up being the best birthday I ever had.

My mouth twitches at the memory, but the sadness creeps in again.

"I found out who you were after that, but I was already too gone for you. I tracked down anyone I could find associated with the hit and buried them. But I never found out which boss was behind it, and you never told me about your father."

Regret drips from his voice as he closes his eyes, like he's replaying every moment and thinking of what he would've done differently.

I run my hands up his arms, feeling his warmth, then around his shoulders to circle his neck. He breathes me in like I'm his lifeline.

"Now I know, you were never hiding anything. You just had no idea." He rubs his nose against mine for a moment, then pulls back to meet my eyes. "When they cuffed me and pulled me away from you, I never hated myself more for keeping this part of my life from you. I couldn't breathe thinking something could happen to you while I was locked up."

A darkness fills his gaze, a reminder of everything that could have gone wrong.

"So, what did you do?" I ask, my voice barely above a whisper.

A small smirk tugs at the corner of his mouth. "I called an old flame."

He chuckles when he sees my face fall in irritation at the mention of a former lover. "He wasn't part of a family, but he was an associate, like me. If something had a hint of a digital footprint, he could erase it, fabricate it, change it—anything. I called Luca."

My chin quivers, but I swallow my emotions.

"I begged him to watch the woman I love for me. To keep her safe. Oh, Peach..." He rests his forehead on mine and breathes deeply. "I just had no idea he loved you before I did."

"Jax."

He silences me with a kiss. "You have no idea how much our whole fucking world revolves around you, baby. Just talk to him. Please? For me?"

He cradles my face with one hand, the other clutching my tights, pulling me tightly into him. I whimper, wanting him to devour me, to make all of this go away.

"I can only tell you my side of the story, Peach. They have to tell you theirs."

I close my eyes, nodding. Jax exhales in relief and kisses my forehead. "Good girl."

His lips brush against mine, and I feel him smile, knowing he's about to lighten the mood with a teasing jab.

"What?" I grumble, bracing myself for whatever he's about to say.

"Just leave the attitude next time, little cum-dumpster."

I snort. It's loud, unflattering, but it escapes me anyway. And just like that, Jax does what he does best—he breaks the tension.

I take a step back, one eyebrow cocked. I grab the hem of my shirt, pulling it over my head, and drop it to the floor. "You know the best way to make me drop my attitude is to fuck it out of me."

My feet barely touch the ground as I walk through the dark, a chill creeping into my bones. The world around me is blurry, distorted, as if my mind is struggling to hold onto pieces of a memory I've locked away for so long.

I find myself looking into the reflection of the tall windows in the hallway, staring at that same little girl who waits at a table for a cup of hot chocolate—eyes wide and scared, breaths shallow, like the air has been sucked out of the room.

But the reflection isn't exactly right. The little girl isn't just looking at herself. She's walking, watching herself move toward something, her tiny legs unsteady, her body tense.

I know this is the same night. Something in me, deep down, knows it.

It's as if I'm aware of it in the dream. The little girl knows if she moves too quickly or makes noise, the dream will end, and we won't know what happens. It's as though she knows that I'll wake up, and she'll be left there alone—and that is the one thing she doesn't want.

I don't look away from the reflection as sound begins to fill the dream. Where there was silence before, yelling splits the stillness—sharp and guttural. A woman's voice. I don't recognize it at first, but I try to listen, try to lock onto it like a beacon in the darkness.

But the more I focus, the more muffled and distant it becomes, slipping away from me as if it doesn't want to be heard.

And then there is a second voice. One I know so well, one that has haunted me since childhood—it rings out. My father.

"You made me do this. You always make me do this," his voice thunders, harsh and cold, like a storm rolling in. He's not angry like he used to be, but his words are laced with venom. I flinch, feeling the sting of every word, every breath he takes.

Then a sharp crack against skin—too real, too close. I flinch again, the sound landing on my cheek as if the slap was for me. The little ghost in the reflection—me—stops walking. Stops breathing. Just keeps looking at herself.

It's like I'm not alone and scared. It almost feels as if someone is here with me, and it feels safer. But in truth, that little girl in the reflection was all alone that night—and she was terrified.

Another slap.

A cry out.

And I flinch again, my small hand rising to my cheek like it's my face being struck. With each blow, my heart races, my throat tightens. The world is spinning faster now. I can't look away from the little girl I once was—her wide, terrified eyes locked on a reflection that doesn't answer her.

Around me, the air seems to ripple, like the still surface of a lake disturbed. I'm waking up.

She breathes faster, tears welling in her large, round eyes. The fear is about to win, and she's about to cry out. She's scared to. She knows what happens when she does.

Just as she opens her mouth to scream, everything fades into the background, and the memory blurs into nothing. My hands reach for something to hold onto, but there's nothing left to catch. My eyes pop open, and I release a breath as if I've held it this entire time.

The room is dark. I blink, disoriented, my chest heaving with the remnants of the dream. My hands are shaking, and I'm sweating despite the cool air in the room.

I turn my head and see Jax beside me, his steady breathing the only thing that anchors me back to reality. His arm is draped around me, his warmth surrounding me like a shield.

I exhale slowly, trying to steady myself, forcing the remnants of the dream away. That must've been before the hot chocolate.

My father and mother... they were fighting.

And he was—beating her.

When it was over, when the damage was done, he gave me a cup of hot chocolate. His apology. His attempt to make me forget what I had heard, what I had witnessed. A fucking cup of hot chocolate, as if that could erase the violence that just unfolded in the presence of an innocent child.

But nothing could erase that. Not the way he'd sounded when he yelled. Not the feel of the slap echoing in my ears.

The truth of it makes me close my eyes in... I'm not sure what emotion I'm feeling. Shame? Shame for her—that she was abused by her husband and had to walk around like nothing was happening?

Or is it sorrow because I erased these memories from my

mind? Blocked them out, and now it's like that woman suffered alone. Her husband and her daughter were the only witnesses to her suffering. Her abuser is dead, and her daughter forgot. Now her pain is nothing more than a ghost that whispers in the broken crevices of my mind.

I press my hand to my mouth to stifle the sobs threatening to break free. Jax's body stirs against mine, his hand tightening around me like he's sensing my distress.

I turn into Jax and nuzzle against him. The arm around me hugs tighter, and he shifts his leg over mine. I soak in the warmth of him, his comforting smell, and the strength of his hold.

I let it chase away the memory of the night that sends a shiver down my spine.

I don't want to think about that man—that monster. I don't want to think about the father who once made me feel like his treasure, only to break me when I saw him for who he truly was.

As I lie in Jax's arms, a prisoner of my own memories, I push them back. I build my walls a little higher. The humor that I hide behind, the stubbornness that I pretend protects me from pain—I fortify myself with them so when I wake in the morning, no one will be able to see the truth that's hidden away within me.

Fourteen

This is the second morning this week I've woken up to an empty bed and the smell of bacon. After brushing my teeth and throwing my messy bun together, I pull on Jax's shirt and head downstairs.

Once again, he's at the stove, wearing nothing but pants. I run my hands along his corded muscles and hug him from behind, pressing my mouth between his shoulder blades.

He turns around, pulling me into a bruising kiss and grinding his hips into mine. "Fuck me, Peach. You can't put those lips on me while I'm cooking. I'll burn your breakfast."

I bite his lip, pulling it before letting it go. "You could always just feed me your cock for breakfast." I hop up onto the counter, and he hands me a steaming cup of coffee. "I wouldn't protest if I were woken up to your award-winning penis sliding into my mouth."

His smile would seduce the devil. "Noted."

Enzo rounds the corner, and I nearly pass out when I see him in gray sweats and a too-small T-shirt. I put my hand to my chest, acting like I'm having a heart attack. He rolls his eyes at my reaction, knowing exactly what I'm thinking.

"I half expected your pajamas to be a three-piece suit too."

"You know what I wear to bed."

It's nothing, everyone. He wears nothing to bed.

Enzo reaches around Jax, clearly copping a feel of Jax's semi, and murmurs, "Mmmm. Someone's having a good morning." He kisses Jax's shoulder. "It smells good in here."

I raise an eyebrow at their playful exchange, and Enzo shoots me a smirk and a wink before heading to the coffee pot.

"I could think of several things that would make this a much better morning." Jax leans against the counter, eyeing me while sipping his coffee.

Enzo looks over at him, still pouring a cup for himself, then looks at me. "Luca got rid of the computer and scrambled any trace of our route here last night, so we should be good until we leave tomorrow."

"Tomorrow?" I ask.

"We need a new ride, Peach. Our current one might draw a little too much attention."

Fucking obviously, Delaney. Stop being dense.

"I'm sorry for last night." Enzo's deep gray eyes hold me while he stirs his coffee. "We've—"

I hold up a hand, stopping him. "It's my fault. I shouldn't have snapped like that."

Jax erases the distance between us, standing between my legs and holding my face in his hands. "It's been a rough two days for you, baby. And you're right. You have every reason to be upset and react, okay?"

I nod, sipping my coffee, feeling a little more awake. The whispers of my parents' argument echo in my mind as Jax and Enzo fall into conversation. Perhaps the only way to bury this mystery along with my father is to figure out the answer to my theory.

"I've been thinking about my mother's death. What if it wasn't an accident?"

Jax and Enzo both perk up at this.

"I mean, now that I know my dad was a mafia warlord my whole life, I'm seeing my childhood in a whole new light. She was 'lost at sea,' never to be seen again. That sounds pretty mafia-ish if you ask me. What if she was killed by my dad—or because of my dad? And there have been hits out on me too... Maybe someone was trying to get to him through her, and now me?"

Jax stares at me, narrowing his eyes in thought, as if he's cataloging what he already knows and filtering it through a new lens.

"I mean, have you guys ever looked into her death?"

"No," Enzo answers immediately. "The focus has always been on Caputo. He is what leads to you."

"But what if it's not? What if it's my mother?" I take another sip of coffee, letting it give me courage. "The explanation of a boating accident was enough for you guys to dismiss it as unimportant and never even consider it. That would be the exact goal of someone staging a murder to look like an accident."

"That could lead us somewhere," Enzo says thoughtfully. "It's worth checking out because we don't have much else right now." His eyes flick over my bare legs, making my stomach flip.

I can feel the "but" coming. It's standing here between us.

"But—" *Called it.* "That was twenty years ago, Del. It may be hard to find anything, but we can try. Just don't get your hopes up."

I nod, understanding, but I'm glad they aren't fighting me on it.

I've always been indifferent toward my mother's memory because there isn't one. I know she existed, then she didn't. But I heard her voice last night, in my own mind. It didn't come from home videos; it came from me.

And now, there is something about finding out if she was murdered that feels important.

"You know," Jax begins, turning back to the stove. "Butte's full of Cleaners and Fixers."

"What are those? Mafia people?" My tone is a bit more excited than I probably should be, considering we're talking about reopening a twenty-year-old death.

The corner of Enzo's mouth lifts in amusement. "Yes, those are mafia people."

"Ooh, can we go talk to some?"

"They don't exactly sit down for afternoon tea, Peach." Jax rubs my thigh, cupping my ass, murmuring *"Damn,"* and then returning to the cooking.

"No. That would be too obvious." Enzo looks off thoughtfully. "But they do hang around a members club and reminisce about the old country every night." He raises an eyebrow at Jax.

"A members club? What, is that like code for a mafia old folks' home?" I take another sip of coffee.

Enzo laughs—a rare sound—but when he does, it makes his gray eyes gleam. "Kind of, actually. Butte's a nice spot for retirement, so it's full of goombahs."

My eyebrows shoot upward. "What kind of name is that? Does the mafia know those are little brown mushrooms in a video game?"

Enzo laughs again, and I feel a sense of accomplishment.

"The old country is Italy. The member's club is just that. A quiet life of retirement is more than most mafia families can hope for, but if they are able to hand off their duties to a successor, they can never really stop living the life." Enzo pours more coffee into my cup. "They sit around and talk about the same old stories as if they just happened. If anyone remembers anything about hits from two decades ago, this might be the best place to ask. We just have to be careful."

"Okay, so how do we do it?"

Enzo looks at Jax, who shrugs like he's agreeing with some unspoken question. Then Enzo turns his intense gaze on me. "Can I take you out to dinner tonight, Ms. Caputo?"

My stomach does a somersault. Inside, I want to scream, *"Fuck yes, let's go to dinner and talk to some old mafia goobers!"* Or whatever he called them. Instead, I hop down off the counter, pretending to be uninterested.

"We'll see. I have a very busy schedule." I huff on my nails and pretend to buff them on Jax's shirt that I've claimed. "I'll see if I can pencil something in."

Enzo licks his lips, accepting the challenge with a sharp gleam in his eye. "I'll call the shops and have someone deliver a dress."

"I'll think about wearing it." I walk away with my fresh cup of hot coffee, exaggerating the sway of my hips as I leave.

"Fuck, she's going to be the death of me," Jax says, returning to the breakfast that is nearly ready.

"Yeah, but what a way to fucking go, huh?" Enzo answers. "Now, come here and give me that mouth." His voice dips down just for Jax. I glance back, catching Enzo grabbing a handful of Jax's ass before claiming his mouth. And fuck, what I wouldn't do to be in the middle of that sandwich.

Fifteen

This whole thing should be weird—my three exes, who are now my boyfriends, showing up and whisking me across the country to become a crime lord. Me fucking one of them. Them fucking each other. One of us hating the other. All three of them have hurt me in the past. Badly.

Yes, I have daddy issues. Let's just admit it.

He was an emotionally unavailable, disengaged father who left my upbringing to boarding schools and our staff. Considering last night's dream, perhaps that was for the best.

But then I met Luca, then Jax, and finally Enzo. Each of them gave me something different. Each brought out something in me I had always wanted. And then they just—left. They fucking left.

But if Enzo and Luca have anything to say—similar to Jax —maybe there was more to what split us apart. Maybe something that can be healed.

But then what happens after that?

Do I want all of them? Yes, let's not even kid ourselves. If they would fill every hole I have at the same time and then cuddle with me afterward, that would be the perfect fucking life.

Am I okay with being the only taco in a three-way sausage sandwich?

One hundred percent, yes.

Do I get to have all three of them? Do all of them want me?

Jax, without question. Enzo, probably. But Luca?

He's avoided me all morning. I've heard him, but once he realizes I'm close by, he quietly moves in the other direction. Our history is the oldest. He had me first. He was my first.

The first man to look at me and actually see me. The first man who didn't tell me I was too loud or ask me to tone myself down. His tongue was the first to ever grace my pussy—and his dick, obviously.

He was the first one to ever come down my throat.

Luca is the reason I learned how to do the jaw thing. He carries a fucking monster between his legs.

Don't get it twisted—Jax and Enzo are big. Meaty. Girthy. Veiny.

And then Luca walks into the room. His dick arrives first, and he gets there a few minutes later.

I forgot where I was going with this.

But we spent months together at college. He never pressured me. We laid together in his dorm, and he spent nights just kissing me, letting me take my time giving myself to him. And when I let him claim me, I did it completely. I felt him in every inch of my being.

My pussy was still sore when my father had him and his mother over for dinner, announcing that they had gotten married the previous week.

Luca's mother was my dad's fifth marriage by that point, and these introductions were routine for me. But apparently not for Luca. He looked at me like I disgusted him and walked out.

And that broke something in me. I felt the fracture, and then I covered it with cement.

Then watching Jax fight the cops as they dragged him away from his almost-bride cracked it open again. But I slathered it up with a new layer, a thicker one this time.

And fucking Enzo spent months of heated looks, secret touches, and unspoken longings to soften me. He spent a weekend pounding through the cement—and my vagina. Then he tossed me out onto the crumbled pavement that was left when he was done with me.

And here I am, surrounded by them, wanting nothing more than for all three of them to break through that cement again.

I can't decide if that makes me weak—if I'm just begging to be hurt again.

But something in me can't stop when it comes to them. I'm fucking addicted to the fire in each of them. I want them to consume me with their flames until there is nothing left of me but ashes so I can rise out like a phoenix and do it all over again.

Maybe that means I'm fucked up. Or maybe that is the chaos that makes us perfect for each other.

Exploring the one-story house, it's fucking massive. The center features a large open space with a tall ceiling. Glass windows stretch to the top, offering an unobstructed view of the mountains on one side and open land on the other.

On each side of the home are two long hallways with other rooms—bedrooms and bathrooms—that lead to a central courtyard with a firepit and chairs surrounding it.

In one of those chairs, Luca is sitting, slouched low. He has no shirt on, and his lean build looks sculpted from marble. The geometric tattoos on his forearms stand out against his pale skin. His dark jeans are open, pulled low.

Enzo is on his knees. His mouth is consuming Luca's cock.

Up and down, he moves, his hand sliding along the length of Luca's dick, his tongue working the tip as he hollows his cheeks, sucking my stepbrother.

Luca watches him, his usually blue eyes nearly black, pupils blown wide. His mouth is parted, and he's breathing heavily with each descent Enzo makes down his length.

Luca thrusts his hips slightly, each movement making my pussy clench.

He raises one arm over his head, grabbing the chair behind him. His other hand fists Enzo's hair, and his thrusts increase. Fuck, he's getting closer to coming, and my cunt is dripping as I watch.

I slide my hand into my panties and swipe my arousal onto my finger, swirling it around my clit. My free hand grabs the window frame as I close my eyes, remembering how it feels to have Luca plunge into me.

When I open my eyes, my stomach drops—Luca is watching me. Enzo is still working him, still thrusting into him, still fisting his hair.

I remove my hand and back away, suddenly feeling like I'm intruding, like I don't belong here watching their moment. But the ache between my legs is killing me. The moisture that rubs between my thighs as I walk needs resolution, or I might not be able to breathe again.

"Jax?" I call out, my voice more panicked than it should be.

"Peach?" He's just ahead in the living room, and his face softens with relief when he sees me. "What is it?"

He starts to get up from the couch, but I push him back down and straddle him. I collide my mouth with his, fisting his shirt as my tongue invades him. His large hands grab my ass, squeezing hard and pulling me closer. He meets my fire with his own, but I need more.

"Fuck me, Jax." I break from our kiss, panting. "Eat my pussy and fuck me until I can't see anymore."

"Get up here." He lays down and pulls me until I'm sitting on his face. He rips my panties off with a tug, and one swipe of his tongue along my center has him growling, "Damn, baby, you're so fucking wet."

This sex god of a man does what he was put on this earth to do—he utterly consumes my pussy. He licks and thrusts his fingers into me until my legs are shaking. I'm humping his face, grinding against him as I shatter, my fingers tangling in his hair. My moans fill the house, but I can't stop.

The ache is still there. "Please, Jax."

"Shhh." He moves behind me. "I'm going to take care of you, Peach."

I'm still wearing his shirt, and he pulls it off me. I hear him unzip his pants. His free hand pinches my nipple, making me cry out in ecstasy. God, I need him now.

Jax pulls my hair back and thrusts into me with a single go. My cunt squeezes him, still pulsing from the orgasm he just gave me.

"Fu-u-uck, Peach, you're perfect."

He's ruthless. Exactly what I need.

The power of his thrusts slams into me, the sound of our bodies slapping against each other mixing with my mewling.

"Open your eyes, baby. We have an audience." He pulls back on my hair again, and I find Enzo and Luca standing in the open front door.

Enzo's hand is frozen on the handle. Luca is a stone pillar with his hands at his sides. His shirt is draped over one shoulder, and the top button of his jeans is undone. The grooves of his pelvis that run beneath his waistband make me whimper, knowing what waits beneath.

My cunt suffocates Jax to the point he grunts and throws his head back. "Fuck, Delaney. Do you like to see them watching you?"

He lowers himself closer to my ear, his voice a low growl. "Did Enzo fuck you on his desk? Bend you over just like this and make you come on his cock?"

God, he did—just like this. My breasts are slapping together from the pounding my pussy is taking, my cunt drenched for him.

"Does it make you wet knowing your stepbrother is watching me fuck you? Do you want his cock fucking you too?"

"God, Jax." I pant, another orgasm rising within me. "Don't fucking stop."

"What else does my little slut want, hm?"

He somehow fucks me harder, and I feel like I'm ascending to heaven when Enzo unzips his pants and steps toward us.

"Do you want a cock to fill that needy mouth?"

Yes.

"Say it, Peach." He pulls back on my hair, and I yelp at the pain that shoots directly to my throbbing clit. "Did you watch Enzo swallow Luca's cock and get soaking wet? Did you think about them stretching you and come find me to fuck you?"

I can't breathe when Enzo pulls his cock out. Fuck, I forgot how pretty it is.

"Fucking answer me." Jax growls, adding a finger to my clit and a smack to my ass. "You want to be our fuck toy, don't you? You want us to fill you with our cum?"

Enzo is right in front of me now. His hand circles his dick, stroking it as he tenderly holds my chin. "Tell me, Delaney."

It's the way he says my name, the deep timbre of his voice rattling through me, that has my eyes rolling back as an orgasm slams into me.

"Yes!" I finally manage to yell.

As my pussy clenches around Jax, Enzo fills my mouth. They claim me from both ends, and the only other sound I hear besides the pleasure passing between us is the slamming of a door as Luca walks away.

Sixteen

The vision of Enzo leaning against his luxury car is straight out of a dark romance novel—just before the guy whips out a massive dick and forces the woman to her knees. Then they drive off to their event while she has his cum dripping from her mouth.

Jesus, Delaney. Get it together.

Jax and Enzo ate me for lunch in the living room, so you'd think I'd be satisfied. They made use of every inch of that couch, and I'm pretty sure it would light up like the Fourth of July if you put a blacklight to it.

I'm giving myself the excuse that I haven't had good dick in four years. I'm just making up for lost time while there's an abundance of very large, very erect penises in my immediate vicinity.

Except one, that is.

Luca disappeared after he and Enzo walked in on Jax and me.

I don't know what he has to be so pissed about. I didn't bring the laptop to purposefully sabotage our trip. Hell, I didn't even plan on going with them. When I packed my bag, I was intending to hide out somewhere on my own. Kidnapping victim here, remember?

It can't be me fucking Jax or that Enzo joined in. Hell, I fucked them all first... I think, at least. And then somehow they all started fucking each other. The hypocrisy of that would rival the size of his dick. And that's saying something.

My heels crunch against the gravel as I make my way to him. The shoes are a perfect height—so they're not too terribly uncomfortable or making me walk like a newborn foal. The fitted black dress he had delivered hugs my body like it was made for me.

There can never be any doubt when Enzo says he'll make something happen—he does it to perfection.

An array of hairstyling tools and products was delivered, along with an assortment of makeup and nail polish in perfect shades. There was a single bottle of perfume with a note:

In a perfect world, this would be the only thing you wore tonight.
But if you must wear a dress, I hope you like this one.
E

After he devours me with his eyes, he wraps his arm low around my waist and leans close, smelling the perfume he picked out on my skin.

"You look amazing, Delaney." It's so quiet next to my ear, almost like he didn't want me to hear it, and it pulls a bashful smile to my face. My cheeks heat with the compliment as he opens my door.

After I'm seated, he rounds the car, sliding effortlessly into his luxury silver vehicle.

Enzo is sporting a black-and-charcoal-gray ensemble. It's

one of his favorite color combinations, and he wears it often. He takes my hand and looks at my nails. I painted them a deep crimson. It's not a flashy red; it's subtle, sexy.

With a kiss placed on my knuckles, he puts my hand back in my lap, then reaches across me to open his glove box. There's an array of silk pocket squares folded neatly in a case, and he picks one that's a close match to my nails.

Internally, I'm kicking my feet like a giddy fucking schoolgirl.

He knows I like it too because he smirks and winks as he fixes it in the pocket of his jacket.

"Details will matter tonight, Delaney." He drives with one hand, the other shifting gears and taking the corners like he owns them. He probably fucking does. I wouldn't be surprised if Enzo Vincenzi owned every inch of Butte, Montana. "You're going into the lion's den of old-school mafia tonight."

"So should I talk with my hands a lot and say things like, 'Eh, fuhgeddaboudit'?"

His eyes sparkle a little when he genuinely smiles, and I force myself to look back at the road. "I don't think that will be necessary." He looks me over a bit longer than he should, letting his eyes run down the length of my legs.

"Eyes on the road, pervert."

Now he releases his smile unbidden and takes my hand, shifting gears without letting go.

Yeah, that's hot. The kitty is definitely purring.

"You shouldn't use your real name tonight or mention your father."

I assumed that, and I figured I'd go by my middle name, Marie. I'm sure there will be two dozen Marie's there, for how common a name it is with the Italians. Nearly my entire dorm at boarding school was full of Marie's.

How does one go about asking details on a possible murder-for-hire that's two decades old? A nervousness coils in my stomach now that we're on our way. I've never knowingly been around mafia members before.

Plus, I'll be asking about a ghost from my past that does a great job of staying there.

Enzo didn't use the valet, opting to park himself for a quicker exit if we need it. The first thing I notice about the members club is the gilded façade of the brick building. It looks like it was designed for someone to drop dead from the sheer amount of gold leaf in the damn place.

The second thing is the crest in the center of the building and the ornate-looking R initial. A remembrance of the past, and I'm curious about the building's history.

It looks like it could have been an old theater for how lavish it is.

"What's the R for? Ridiculously overdecorated?"

He snickers and shakes his head. "Romano. My family acquired the building about thirty years ago from the Sicilians."

I *knew* he owned this place. I wonder what else.

A river runs close to the rear of the building, parallel with the street, and a cool breeze dances off its surface. But the shiver that runs down my back has nothing to do with the chill—it's the ominous feeling I get looking at this imposing building.

Enzo opens the door for me, and his steady hand finds my lower back as we head inside. My heels click against the marble as we walk into the lobby, and it's like stepping into another world. Velvet-lined walls in deep burgundy, gold accents gleaming in every corner, and chandeliers hanging down in heavy, glimmering clusters make it feel like something out of a Gatsby party.

The air smells of cigars and aged whiskey, with an undercurrent of expensive cologne. The whole place screams excess, and I can't help but roll my eyes.

"Not exactly the local steakhouse with a deep-fried onion, you know?" I mutter half under my breath, but Enzo's the only one who hears me. He cuts his eyes at me and walks with the confidence of a man who owns the entire room.

The lighting is dim and inviting, and the host greets us like Enzo's name is a password that opens every door. He's treated like royalty—and probably is mafia royalty, the rich bastard. I half expect a red carpet to unfurl beneath us, but instead, the man behind the desk is already shepherding us through with a reverence that seems far too real to be forced.

"Mr. Vincenzi, always glad to have you visit the club," he says, his gaze lingering on me a little too long before flicking back to Enzo. I offer him a tight smile and nod, making a mental note to never come back here unless I absolutely fucking have to.

I'm used to crowds and gatherings. When I have a new book releasing, there's usually a tour: stopping at bookstores, meeting fans, and autographing their books. Aside from writing, that's my favorite part about being an author—the comments they share with me in those few minutes at my table.

I'll just pretend like this is a signing.

And all these people are readers… old, male readers… who look at you like you should be sitting on their plate instead of the rare steak they ordered.

"Isn't it, like, a general rule of thumb that mafia men gouge out the eyes of anyone who dares look at their lady?" I tease, though the staring is making me a little shifty.

Enzo suddenly turns his six-foot-four frame toward me, towering over me. I stop abruptly and crane my neck to meet his gaze as he pulls me against him. My hands go to his chest on instinct as he lowers his mouth near mine.

"Are you?" he asks, his eyes flicking between mine.

"Am I what?" I whisper back, the room suddenly stifling.

"My lady?" His mouth is a millimeter away from mine. So close, but not actually touching.

I open my mouth to answer, but nothing comes out. I don't know.

"Hmm." He looks disappointed. Then he leans to the side and kisses my cheek. He lingers a moment, and I realize, from this angle, it looks like we're locked in a passionate kiss—a public claiming. He pulls away, and the cold of the room wraps around me tightly. "They're just curious."

Enzo puts my hand in the crook of his arm and escorts me the rest of the way into the dining room. Looking out the windows that surround us, I spot the river behind the building and the beautiful sunset casting the sky in golden hues.

"Curious why?"

"Because I've never brought a woman out with me in public." Then he looks me dead in the eye. "Ever."

Well. Isn't that something.

With a deep breath, I stand taller and let their gazes slide over me. They're trying to figure out how I fit into this godforsaken mess. But I need other things out of tonight, and I've got to find a way into the conversations to get what I want.

The host leads us to our table and removes a marble table marker etched with the name Vincenzi. It's secluded from the rest of the room, but not by much—we have the lay of the land from here and can see every table.

Looks flick our way, linger a second, then dart off as if they were never here. I can already tell this is going to be one of those dinners where the air is thick with cigars, secrets, and lies.

Enzo pulls out my chair for me and slides it back gracefully. For someone who's never graced the public with a woman on his arm before, he's pulling it off perfectly.

He sits across from me, the setting sun's last light flickering over his dark hair and the deep wood paneling that surrounds us. There's something about him in this place—the way he belongs here. He's surrounded by people who respect him. Hell, they've practically kissed his feet as he walked by, but I can see the lines of tension in his jaw. The tightness in his shoulders. The darkness in his eyes as he casts them around the room.

"You own this place, don't you?" I ask quietly, noting the grin he quickly wipes away. "Like, actually own this town—not just the members club. It's yours?"

"You've always been perceptive. I own this club. I own this town and everything around it."

He nods once at the waiter, who scurries over. Enzo speaks low into his ear, and I narrow my eyes at him.

"I knew it." I rest my chin in my hand, elbow on the table. "You took those turns too comfortably for someone who doesn't own everything in this valley."

He takes my hand on the table, rubbing his thumb over my knuckles. "Not everything, apparently."

I take my hand from his and smooth my dress over my thighs, suddenly nervous with my back to the room. It seems

Enzo can sense my unease because he leans closer and lowers his voice. "Give me your hand again."

"Enzo."

"I just want to show you something."

I hold my hand out, and he guides me beneath the table. "What? Are you showing me your gum collection you've been sticking under here since you were a little mafia baby?"

He actually chuckles, and I think I might pass out.

My fingers run along something metal and cold fixed to the underside of the table. I gasp when I realize what it is. It's a gun in the perfect spot for him to grab quickly should he need to.

"Now," he says, releasing my hand and straightening himself. "Feel under your side of the table. Jax made a visit earlier to make sure the place was ready for our visit. Just in case."

"I don't want to touch a gun. What if I shoot my vagina off?" I whisper, one hundred percent serious.

This time, he straight-up throws his head back and laughs. The poor waiter looks like he's going to have a stroke, witnessing the rarest event on Earth right here alongside me.

"You'll be fine. Trust me." He gives the waiter his attention, examining the label of a wine bottle and approving it.

I carefully let my hand feel the underside of the table, confused for a moment as I make out what it is. Enzo watches me, his sharp gaze catching every movement while the waiter pours our wine. When I finally realize what I'm touching, my mood shifts instantly.

"My spa—"

Enzo shushes me and looks around, cutting off my outburst.

"Sorry. My spatula," I whisper. "I feel better now."

He shakes his head in disbelief, picking up his glass and holding it out toward me. "You have a six-foot-four, two-hundred-and-fifty-pound killing machine at your beck and call. I've crushed men's skulls with my bare hands, and you prefer a spatula to keep you safe?"

I clink my glass against his and take a drink. Of course, it's my favorite wine. "First of all, don't disrespect The Spat, okay?"

"Oh my god, you've given it a nickname." He pinches the bridge of his nose and closes his eyes before lifting his glass to his lips.

"Second of all, you better have washed those skull-crushing hands before you stuck them in my pussy this morning."

I sit back, satisfied, sipping my victory wine as he sputters and chokes on his. He stands abruptly, straightening his suit jacket before he buttons it. He holds out his hand for me to take. When I stand, he leans down, his lips brushing against my ear.

"You're getting spanked for that later."

Mmm. Activate kitty purring in three... two... one.

"Now, let's get that perfect ass of yours to the dance floor so the vultures can start circling you."

Seventeen

Enzo leads me onto the dance floor, and the moment we step into the center of the room, the music seems to fade into the background. The soft, intoxicating melody of a saxophone drifts through the air, but I'm far more aware of the man holding me flush against his hard body, as well as the eyes following us as we glide across the polished marble.

His hand on my back is warm, steady, and—as usual—commanding. I can tell by the way his grip tightens ever so slightly when we reach the crowd that he's not just leading me through this dance—he's nervous.

Leaning in, he keeps his voice low enough that only I can hear. "Just remember, we need to find a way to ask about your mother's death, but we can't be obvious. They'll sense something's off. This group is too fucking bored and nosy to miss a single detail."

I nod, my hand running up his chest, just under the lapel of his jacket. I can feel the tension in his body. The pressure in the room is thick, suffocating, and it seems all eyes are on us. "Got it. Don't worry. Just casual conversation like: 'Hey, let's tell our favorite death-by-drowning stories. You go first.'" I tease, a sarcastic edge creeping into my voice.

Enzo's lips twitch into a hint of a smile, but it's gone before I can properly appreciate it. "That sounds perfect." He pauses, his eyes scanning the room as the music swells around us. "Just keep it subtle—and keep that smile of yours intact. Let them think they're getting exactly what they want, and you'll have them eating out of your hand... just like the rest of us." He adds a wink for good measure.

Before I can reply, an older man steps into our path, holding his hand out to his wife, who catches up. His suit is crisp, impeccably tailored, and he has the look of someone who has seen it all—along with the liver spots on his hands. The slight tilt of his head, the calculating glint in his eyes—they scream experience with manipulation.

"Mr. Vincenzi," the man says, his voice thick with age and authority, "may I cut in for a dance with this beautiful young lady?"

Enzo raises an eyebrow, but his politeness is flawless. "Mr. Moretti, I thought you'd never ask," he replies smoothly, his voice warm with deference as he takes a step back. "I've had my eye on this young vixen all night." Enzo takes the hand of the old man's wife, charming her into oblivion in an instant.

"Of course, Enzo," the man—Mr. Moretti—says with a chuckle, his eyes lingering on me.

Enzo offers me a half-smile and, with a brief but meaningful glance, places my hand in Mr. Moretti's. "Enjoy your conversation, Marie," he says, his voice hushed, a trace of something in his eyes that's hard to pinpoint. He tenderly leads the older woman into the steps of the dance, leaving me with the older man.

Mr. Moretti takes my hand, his other on my back at a respectful level, but his gaze never quite leaves my face, and I don't like that too much. "Marie," he says thoughtfully, "a beautiful name. My lovely wifes, as a matter of fact." He takes the first steps into the dance, and I move with him. "I must admit, I'm intrigued. It's not every day we see someone on the arm of Enzo Vincenzi. He's an elusive one, I'm sure you know."

I offer a polite smile, feeling the weight of his curiosity, but I don't reveal anything beyond the veil. "I'm sure Enzo is a very private man," I reply, my voice sweet but neutral.

Mr. Moretti raises an eyebrow, clearly intrigued. "Indeed. And a man of power. You must be someone special to catch his attention like this."

I suppress the urge to roll my eyes. "Perhaps I am a mere escort, Mr. Moretti, no more, no less." I offer him a sweet, measured smile. "Here tonight, gone in the morning."

His gaze sharpens. "Oh, you're much more than that. Tell me, how did you come to be in such... esteemed company?"

I meet his eyes directly. "Perhaps it is I who am the esteemed company, Mr. Moretti."

Mr. Moretti's smile stretches into something more calculating. "Ah, I see." He pauses, as if weighing his next words carefully. "May I ask, have we met somewhere else? You look rather familiar."

My stomach feels like it's tumbling boulders. I was afraid this might happen—someone recognizing any familial similarities to my father. "I just have one of those faces."

This seems to satisfy him, and he goes back to his line of questions as I try to figure out how to work mine into the conversation. "You know, my son is a man of equal stature, just as successful as Enzo. Perhaps you've heard of him?" He leans in slightly, his tone lowering with a touch of pride. "I'd be happy to introduce you to him, if you're interested."

Well, that's laughable. If his son was truly on Enzo's level, he wouldn't need to be making introductions for him.

I smile, but it's all teeth. "I'm flattered, Mr. Moretti, but I think I'm perfectly content with the company I have."

He laughs softly, and I cast a glance at Enzo that says I'm done with this one. "Of course, Marie. Of course." He leans back, his gaze lingering on me a little too long, but thankfully Enzo comes back for me.

It only takes a moment before another older man cuts in, and then another.

The contact transfers of so many colognes on my dress are going to give me a headache.

None of them lingers on my curiosity about how long they've been in "the business" or any other excuse I make to try to steer the conversation toward events two decades ago.

All of them want to talk about Enzo. His business dealings and property acquisitions dominate the discussion. It's clear this is a man's world.

To them, I'm merely "the little woman," an accessory to Enzo for the night. Their interest in me is superficial, clearly hoping I'm a floozy who overhears too much and might let something slip. They're vultures, circling for scraps.

But I give them nothing, primarily because I honestly know nothing. Despite the whispers and insinuations, Enzo and I have been strangers to each other since he fired me. The current pig sweating through his suit and droning about land deals is grating on my nerves.

I realize now that Enzo likely anticipated this. That pisses me off even more.

This mafia empire isn't built for women—it's an enterprise made by men, for men.

My eyes wander, ignoring the old man in front of me.

He rambles about Enzo's property acquisitions, describing how he swallows up deals like a shark. He even mentions silent purchases—territories acquired without names on the deeds, cloaked in mystery.

Frankly, I'm zoning out. My gaze shifts to the dark booths keeping secrets under shrouds of shadow. A ringed hand emerges from one booth, holding a wineglass marked with red lipstick. I watch the matching red nails—bloody talons—tapping the rim as the server refills the glass. The woman's fingers are stacked with gold rings, each one an ornate statement.

Hmm. She probably didn't even have to speak a word.

This society is engineered to keep women invisible, relegated to the shadows while men claim the spotlight.

Though I can't see her face, I feel the weight of her stare, nonetheless. I wonder if that will be me in twenty years—sitting silently in some booth, appeased with wine while the men take credit, start wars, and hold all the power.

This can't be all there is to this mighty and powerful regime. There has to be more.

Enzo must sense my patience wearing thin because, when he catches my eye, he excuses himself from his latest dance partner and strides toward me.

When he takes my hand from the sweaty man who's been pawing at me, I exhale sharply.

"I need some air," I mutter, my voice tight with frustration. Turning on my heel, I leave him there.

Eighteen

"Delaney," he whispers, reaching for my hand. "It's not safe."

Ignoring him, I leave the dining room, cutting down a hall and pushing through the door of the ladies' room.

Of course, it's as equally opulent as the rest of the place—lush, tufted benches and marble on top of marble. I lean over the sink, scrubbing the soap into my arms harder than necessary, wishing I could wash away their lingering stares, the brush of their hot breath, and the desperation in the air.

Mirrors surround the bathroom, reflecting every angle of me—distorted, exaggerated—not letting me escape even myself.

The door swings open behind me, and I don't have to look to know who it is.

"Delaney," Enzo's voice is low, almost cautionary, but that tone only makes my temper flare higher.

He closes the bathroom door behind him with a firm click, locking it. His sharp eyes scan the empty stalls before landing on me. His jaw is tight, his expression unreadable. The tension between us could be cut with a knife.

"Oh, so sorry I didn't obey my orders," I snap, my anger

rising, bubbling to the surface like the heat surrounding us. "I just needed a second, Enzo." I return to scrubbing my hands.

"You needed air. Not to disappear." His voice is just behind me, almost a warning, but I refuse to let it sway me.

I turn to face him. His large frame fills the space, and his expression remains unreadable. His eyes lock onto mine, a mix of frustration and concern.

"No, I needed some fucking space, Enzo," I say, my words clipped. "Since you knew not a single one of those men would have anything useful for me. I was just a pawn for them to see how close they could get to you and suck your cock."

He steps forward, closing the space between us. His eyes narrow with that familiar intensity I can't escape. The heat radiating from him makes the air between us crackle. But I refuse to back down.

"You needed to see this for what it is, Delaney." His gaze hardens, the lines around his mouth tightening. "This is your reality now. The power, the position—it all comes with a price. You think you're going to waltz in, and these men are going to bend a knee to you for a sweet smile and your pretty face?" He lets out a harsh breath. "You've got to be stronger than that. They won't respect you until they see you're willing to bleed for it."

I stare at him, my breaths ragged, my chest aching. My head pounds with the adrenaline coursing through me. I want to scream at him, tell him how much he's hurt me, how much he's fucked up my life.

But it's not just him. It's me, too. I'm caught between this world, between the man I once trusted—the man who made me feel something I thought I'd never feel again—and the cold, harsh reality that he just used me like a pawn in a game.

"You put on such a big production, making me feel good about myself, pretending like we had some agreed-upon plan, while you really just sat back and watched me get passed around to all these men with eligible sons like I'm a fucking hooker." My voice shakes, the heat of the room closing in around us. "I'm not going to let you treat me like that again, Enzo. I'm not your plaything. You can't just use me and throw me away whenever it's convenient for you. I know how you love doing that."

His jaw tightens, and for a brief moment, his eyes soften with regret, but it's quickly masked by his usual hardness. "This isn't a game, Delaney. I'm here to make sure you're ready for what's coming."

"Why is that your fucking job? And why do you have to treat me like I don't matter in the process?" I snap, my voice cracking with emotion I didn't expect.

Enzo reaches for me, his grip tight around my wrist as he pulls me toward him. I push back against him, my heart pounding, confusion, and rage swirling together. He's so close, his breath mingling with mine, his eyes locked onto me like he's trying to find a way to get through to me.

"I never said you didn't matter," he says, his voice low and controlled, but with an undercurrent of pain. "You matter more than you'll ever know."

"You don't need to say it. You show me I don't fucking matter when you make love to me for days, tell me I'm yours, and hold me like I'm something important." Tears threaten to surface, and I barely hold them back. "Then you show me I'm nothing more than trash when you throw me away. Is that what will happen at the end of the week after you parade the Caputo heiress around your town?"

Pain flashes across his face like I've slapped him. I push away from him, and he takes a step back.

"You should've tossed a roll of bills at me when you threw me out of your building too. You never paid your whore for services rendered."

Something snaps in him. He surges forward, leaving no space between us. The marble counter bites into my back as his hand grips my throat, holding me still.

"Every word I said was true. Every touch, every fucking kiss." His gaze falls to my mouth like he'll die if he doesn't claim it soon. "You don't know what happened that day. Why I—"

"Then fucking tell me, Enzo." I grip his wrist with one hand and the counter with the other. "Stop acting like I'm supposed to just erase all the pain because you're here trying to do some noble thing for your mafia empire."

"I'm not doing this for me, Delaney." His voice rises, filled with frustration. "I would burn all of this to the fucking ground if it could die, but it won't. This beast is rooted too deep to ever be destroyed, and it will never stop coming for you."

"I've been fine all this time until you three showed up."

"You haven't been fine. It's been coming for you for years. You just never knew it because we were always there. In the background, in the shadows, making sure none of it touched you. We thought—fuck!" He releases me and turns away, pacing.

He paces twice more, running his hands through his perfectly styled hair. "We thought we could protect you better if we stayed away." He stops, placing his hands on his hips and shaking his head like he's replaying his regret.

"I didn't want that weekend to end," he says, his voice softening, his chest heaving with the effort to control his emotions. "I wanted to spend more time with you. I had Sandra clear my calendar for the week. I—" He swallows hard, his gaze flicking to the floor before returning to me. "I got one of the interns to cover your duties."

He looks at his reflection in the mirror, guilt shadowing his features.

"I had them come in early so, when you got to the office, I could surprise you. Take you away and keep you all to myself." His voice drops lower, as if confessing this secret makes it real all over again.

My breath catches as he looks back at me, his eyes soft but heavy with pain.

"You used your fake name when you came to work for me. I didn't know you were Caputo's daughter until after."

"After what?" My voice is barely above a whisper.

"After the intern was shot in the head by a long-range sniper who mistook her for you."

The gasp that escapes my lips feels like it echoes through the room. My hands fly to my mouth as the weight of his words hits me like a freight train.

"She just happened to have hair a lot like yours," he continues, his voice steady but lined with grief. "Similar build. She was sitting at your desk because I asked her to." He shakes his head, his hands falling to his sides as if the memory still haunts him. "Luca ran into the building like a lunatic only a minute later."

"Why would Luca be there?" I ask, my voice shaky as my brain struggles to process this revelation.

"Of course, Luca was there. Haven't you figured it out

yet?" Enzo's gaze hardens, though his voice remains steady. "Luca has kept you hidden all these years. Delaney Caputo's digital footprint is so confusing, no one even knows what you look like or where you've gone. Hell, some people even think you're dead."

My brow furrows as I try to piece this together. "I don't understand."

"He walked away from you first," Enzo says, stepping closer. "But he never left."

The pieces start clicking together, Jax's earlier story interweaving with this new revelation. Jax had asked Luca to keep an eye on me, but...

"He's done so much to keep you safe, Delaney. Because he loves you. Jax loves you. I fucking love you."

The words hang heavy in the air between us as Enzo reaches for me, cupping my face with his hands. His lips claim mine in a kiss so full of passion and desperation it steals the breath from my lungs.

"We've poured everything we have into keeping you alive," he says against my lips, his forehead pressed to mine. "Luca tracks every job that's been put out on you. We make sure they never fucking touch you."

He points toward somewhere beyond the club. "These mines—those fucking mines are a mass grave for the assassins who signed their death warrants the moment they took a job on your life."

"What the fuck..." I whisper, my voice trembling.

"How come there was nothing on the news?"

"You don't know how good our boy is, do you?" Enzo's pride for Luca is evident, his smirk tinged with admiration. "Luca put out news reports of a local gas leak and evacuated the entire block. I had the window repaired, and we took care of the body. Then we used a cadaver to make her a fatality of the gas leak." He shakes his head, regret flickering in his expression. "She got thirty seconds of airtime on the news, and then she was forgotten forever."

The enormity of it all feels suffocating. "Why would you all do this?"

The question seems to break something in him. Enzo wraps his arms around me, lifting me to sit on the counter and pulling me into his chest. The warmth of his embrace feels like a lifeline as I bury myself against him, inhaling his scent.

"If you think we wouldn't rip this world apart for you, Delaney, you're fucking crazy."

A startled laugh bursts from me, breaking the tension. Maybe I am crazy. Maybe we all are.

I grab the lapels of his jacket and pull him toward me, the confusing emotions coursing through me demanding release. My lips crash into his, and his approving growl vibrates through me as his hands tighten around my waist.

Enzo pulls back just enough to rest his forehead against mine. "Luca and I agreed we need to work together to keep you safe. Jax too, even from inside prison. We knew we would die to protect you. But we didn't want to leave you with the guilt of our deaths."

He pauses, his voice thick with emotion. "It was better to make you hate us. To hope you'd one day forget about us." His hand cups my cheek, his thumb brushing against my skin. "But I can't do it anymore, Delaney. I can't take another breath if I have to stay away from you again."

He claims me with a bruising kiss.

I'm drowning in the weight of his words, the confessions

that tore apart the foundation of my anger and replaced it with something far more terrifying—understanding. Everything he's done, everything they've done, wasn't out of cruelty but out of desperation to protect me. And yet, the scars remain, jagged and raw, etched into the parts of me that still ache for them.

They've carried my burdens in shadows, buried bodies in my name, and orchestrated a lie so elaborate that it kept me hidden even from myself. I should feel suffocated by the enormity of it all, but as Enzo's embrace holds me, I feel something else—a flicker of hope, a fragile thread that maybe, just maybe, we will survive the chaos they've unleashed—us, together.

The thought terrifies me as much as it comforts me, but in this moment, with his hands framing my face and his lips married with mine, I can taste the regret on his tongue, and I choose to let myself believe it.

Nineteen

A tear runs down my cheek as I kiss him back. My fingers thread through his hair, and I circle his hips with my legs, grinding against him. "I don't want to make a mess on your pants," I say in a low tone, my mouth so close to his that my lips brush against him as I speak.

"I don't fucking care, Delaney. Soak me." He thrusts against me, and I smile, biting my lip. He knows instantly what this look means, and he stops. It's the look that says: I have a secret.

"I swear to God, Delaney." He takes half a step back, placing his hands on either side of me. Eye level with me, the tempest raging in the gray storm clouds of his eyes makes my smile widen.

He glances between my legs, then back at my eyes. He runs his finger down my lips, slowly tracing down my chin and chest. "If I reach between your legs and find out you let those cocksuckers dance with you—put their fucking hands on you —when you had no panties on..." He clenches his jaw, biting down as I push my chest out for him.

He lowers the top of my dress, freeing a breast and taking my nipple hard, making me cry out. The path his finger takes feels like the longest trip of my life. He pulls his mouth away from my breast to look into my eyes when his hand finally slides between my legs.

His thick finger runs up the lips of my bare pussy, and my eyes roll back at his touch.

He fists my hair, pulling me out of the pleasure. "You fucking brat." His lips dominate mine, his tongue commanding me to open for him. He digs his fingers into the fleshy part of my hip, then pulls away. Sliding me off the counter, he spins me around, pushing me over and lifting my dress.

Oh, fuck yes.

He unzips his pants and takes his cock out, sliding it between my legs while his hand rubs my ass. Slowly, he pistons his hips, covering his dick with my arousal. He kicks my feet wider, positioning my hips where he wants them, keeping one hand on my back to force my chest flat against the counter. The biting cold of the marble makes my nipples pebble.

"You like to fucking make me a madman for you, don't you, Delaney?" he asks, rubbing my ass cheek, keeping me in anticipation.

"Yes," I pant.

He leans down, placing kisses where he's about to strike, and I whimper for it. Sitting back up, the head of his cock slides against my clit, and my leg starts shaking.

"Did you get wet when I said you were getting a spanking earlier?"

"Yes," I whisper.

I feel the wind from his hand a split second before the smack lands on my cheek, making me yelp as my pussy tightens.

"Let me hear you, baby." He rubs my ass where it's warming from the impact, and it tingles so good. I need more. "Did I make you wet?"

"Yes," I manage, my voice nice and loud.

"Good girl." He kneads my cheek, then reaches around to circle my clit. My mouth drops open, and I release an exhale of pleasure. "And you danced with that old motherfucker while your cunt was weeping for me?"

SMACK!

"Yes."

SMACK!

"With your bare pussy, soaked under this short fucking dress I picked out for you?"

"Oh, fuck," I moan, unable to answer over the throbbing of my clit.

"Words, baby. Use your words." His hand massages my cheek, then slides between my legs, finding how wet I am. He plunges two fingers into me as his other hand collides with my left cheek. "Tell me."

"Yes, yes," I breathe as he pumps his fingers into me. "I was soaking fucking wet for you with no panties on. And you know what?" I try to sit up and look at him, but he pushes me back down again, the hand in my pussy leaving me empty, and I want to cry over it.

"Be fucking careful with your words, angel."

SMACK!

He leans down, pulling my hair to raise my head. His cock slides back between my legs as he moves his pelvis against me. "Now, tell me."

"He moved his hand down just enough to know I had no

panties on." I bite my lip, knowing what I've unleashed upon myself—and I fucking need it.

He straightens, keeping my hair in his grip and his cock moving between my legs.

SMACK!

SMACK!

"You're fucking mine."

SMACK!

"Do you hear me, baby? You fucking belong to me."

The thrusting of his cock against me is torture. He hits my clit, but I need to feel him deep inside me, claiming my body like he's claiming me with his words.

"Enzo, please."

SMACK!

"Tell me you're mine, Delaney."

SMACK!

My ass is burning, my clit is throbbing, and my thighs are soaked. "Put me out of my goddamn misery and fucking admit it, Delaney."

"I'm yours, Enzo," I confess because it's fucking true. He belonged to me the first moment he looked at me in his office. I knew he wanted to make me drop to my knees right there.

"I've always been yours."

I'm up and sitting on the counter before I can process what happened. The cold clashes with my red-hot ass cheeks as he slams into me, pinching my clit and demanding my pleasure obey him. Within two strokes of his dick, my walls are clenching around him, and I'm throwing my head back as my orgasm crashes over me.

He circles my throat, pistoning hard into me. "This pussy

is mine, baby. We've ruined you forever, haven't we?" He squeezes my throat and slides me closer to the edge of the counter so he can access my clit more easily. "Wrap your legs around me—I want to feel you come again."

I do, and he fingers my clit, rubbing circles and ripping more moans from me. "Yes, fucking sing for me, Delaney. Let the whole fucking club know who you belong to. Whose cock is ruining you."

I come again, grinding my hips with his thrusts and he sticks his fingers in my mouth, "Suck," He commands, chasing my orgasm with his own. When the waves of ecstasy slow, he rolls his hips softer. His grip on my throat turns tender, and he rubs my skin with the pad of his thumb.

Keeping himself inside me, he wraps me in his arms, and I circle his neck with mine. He kisses me, and I feel the sorrow for every second we've spent apart flow into me with his embrace. I feel it in how he tightens his hold, as if the thoughts of how he could lose me consume his mind.

He kisses me faster, and when my hips move again on their own, he reaches between us and gives me more of what I want. His fingers coax another wave of pleasure, a softer one this time, while he keeps claiming me with his tongue.

As we pull away, panting, he leans his forehead against mine and looks into my eyes. "I love you, Delaney. I think I was born loving you because I knew it the second I first saw you."

I hold his cheek with my hand and kiss him again. "I love you."

"I know this doesn't fix everything, angel. And I'll spend the rest of my life making it up to you if you let me. But right now, I need you to understand—every step we've taken, every decision we've made, has been to protect you. Even when it hurt. Especially when it hurt."

His words are a mix of desperation and conviction, his eyes pleading with me to believe him. And damn it, I want to. I want to let go of the anger and the pain and let myself believe, but the pain is what has held me together all this time.

But trust doesn't come easy—not after everything.

I swallow hard, forcing the lump in my throat down as I look into his eyes. "We need time, Enzo. It doesn't make everything okay. But... I hear you."

His grip on me tightens, his forehead pressing against mine again as he breathes a relieved sigh. "That's all I'm asking for. Just give us a chance to show you."

I nod, the weight of his words settling over me like a heavy blanket.

With our breathing returning to normal, he helps me off the counter, and I pull my dress back down, fixing the top in place to cover my breasts again. "You gave me a hickey on my titty," I mutter, smacking at him.

He's not even sorry. "Good. Now everyone will fucking know these are mine too."

"You're a Neanderthal."

"I'm so much worse when it comes to you, Delaney baby." He circles my throat and kisses me again quickly, as he tucks his beautiful cock back into his pants.

I reach for a towel, and he yanks it from me, backing me into the counter again.

"*My* girl is going to walk through *my* club with *my* cum dripping down her legs. Don't you dare fucking clean your pussy up. Do you understand me?"

I clasp my hands behind my back and smile. I watch closely so I can see the exact second when he turns feral as I say two words I've never said before.

"Yes, Daddy."

Twenty

"On your fucking knees."

How he's instantly hard again, I have no idea. But any chance to have this gorgeous cock in my mouth, I'm going to take it. This isn't a punishment; it's a reward. I guess he likes being called "daddy" by his little brat.

It doesn't take long before he's fisting my hair, and I'm swallowing his cum as he grunts out my praises. Helping me stand, he just looks at me for a moment before licking a bead of cum running from the side of my mouth. He sucks on my bottom lip and gives me a quick swipe of his tongue before I pull away with a giggle.

He's acting like a teenage boy who came in his pants after copping his first feel.

"Now, get out so I can freshen up. I totally look like I just got my brains fucked out in the bathroom."

Enzo's smile could brighten any of my darkest days, and I can't help but stare at him when he does it. "You totally did just get your brains fucked out in the bathroom."

"Yeah, I did." I grab his hip and lean up to kiss him. "And it was some good dick too." I lick his bottom lip, and he groans, rolling his head back and closing his eyes.

"Please, can we just go home? We have so much more fucking each other's brains out to do."

It makes me chuckle, and my stomach does somersaults.

"No, I'm hungry. So, feed me." I pause, realizing my mistake. "Something other than your dick. And your fingers," I quickly add, making him resign. "Food, then fucking."

"Fine." He kisses the tip of my nose and steps toward the locked door.

I'm sure there's a line a mile long of poor old ladies nearly wetting their panty liners, waiting to use the bathroom.

Sure enough, Enzo leaves, and within a minute, an older woman comes in as well. I catch her eye in the mirror and give her a courteous smile and a nod. It must smell like sex in here. There's no mistaking what just went down, but she's a lady, and we both act like everything is normal.

I'm fixing my makeup when she exits the bathroom stall to wash her hands, and I remember who she is: the wife of the first asshat who danced with me, Mr. Moretti.

"Hi, Marie, my name is Marie too." I break the silence with something polite.

"Oh, my name is not Marie." She answers, her old age making her voice shake. "I'm Eloise. Pleased to meet you."

"I apologize. I could have sworn Mr. Moretti said his 'lovely wife's name is Marie.'" I mock his tone, and she smiles, but it doesn't reach her eyes.

"Ah, his first wife. He always preferred her over me."

Great, now I'm the asshole.

"Oh, I'm sorry." I instantly feel bad for her. That must feel horrible, knowing your husband still loves his first wife. "May I ask what happened to her?"

"It's rather tragic. But he had a debt he couldn't pay."

Oh my God.

"She paid it for him, with her life."

"Holy shit."

"Yeah, holy shit is right. My father was a hard boss, but in some territories, you have to be." She takes out a cigarette from a silver case and closes it. She clicks a button, and a small flame from one of the case's corners lights it for her. She releases a plume toward the ceiling. "Then I was his second punishment. He had to marry me to show his loyalty and all. Provide an heir, all that jazz. Except the bastard is impotent."

I gasp. This old lady is a riot, and it gives me an idea. "He tried to hook me up with his son, though."

"His wife stepped out on him. There was a rumor the child belonged to Caputo."

My heart skips a beat at the mention of my father, then rushes forward again.

"But it wasn't. Us ladies talk. We know who's fucking who, so we don't cross each other... most of the time." She winks. "She was having an affair with one of the lower-level members of her father's crew. Moretti just can't admit that because then everyone will know he has a limp dick."

It makes me snort.

"So, did this Caputo guy ever get in trouble with his wife over the rumor?" I ask, fishing for information.

"Oh, he was a widower by that point." She looks off thoughtfully. "Or maybe he was on his second wife? I can't keep them all straight."

"How did his wife die? Was she also killed, you know..." I run my thumb across my neck as if slicing it. "...to pay a debt?"

"No, that was a tragic time for the families. Stella Caputo was very loved. Died in a freak boating accident. Terrible."

She looks off as if remembering her, and I find myself wanting to ask more. I never knew she was so loved by the other families. My father was beyond heartbroken over it, but hearing this, she must have truly been amazing. It makes me want to find out more about her now.

Perhaps if I can get Luca talking to me again, he can help me uncover some things.

"There was never any suspicion around the boating accident, though?" I try to keep my voice even as I pretend to clean up nonexistent lip gloss.

"No one would dare step against the Capo." She shakes her head with conviction.

"What does that mean?" I play dumb to keep her talking.

"The boss. The boss of bosses. He is the family leader of all the Italian families. It would be suicide."

"Well, I did hear some gossip about the Caputo's." I lower my tone, even though it's just us in here. "I heard Caputo had a daughter that someone put a hit on. Maybe they already got her mom, and she was next?"

"That poor girl." Eloise looks truly ashen now. "So many of us regret we couldn't step in and help her."

"What do you mean?"

I may pass out depending on her answer—or have a fucking heart attack, because I swear my heart has never beat faster in my entire life.

"If we could have taken her, raised her, so many of us would have. But Caputo wouldn't hear of it. He was the one putting hits out on his own daughter."

I try to mask my horror, but I'm not pulling it off well because Eloise puts her hand over mine on the counter.

"Why on earth would he do that to his own daughter?"

She smiles with sympathy, hopefully feeling sorry for my ignorance and not because she somehow recognizes me.

"Her mother's inheritance, my dear. He couldn't collect it for himself if he killed her." Eloise taps her cigarette ash into the sink and wets it to put it out. "He needed it to look like an accident."

Just like... a boating accident.

Twenty-One

My heels announce my arrival as they click sharply against the polished marble floors, echoing through the room like a warning. The low hum of conversation falters momentarily as eyes flick to me—some lingering too long, while others glance away quickly, pretending they're not staring. But there's no hiding from the sharp attention of the mafia world.

Enzo, meanwhile, remains an impenetrable figure, looking deadly as ever. Leaning slightly back in his chair, his leg crossed over his knee in the perfect balance of control and arrogance, he exudes effortless power.

The dim club lighting casts most of him in shadow, but a strip of soft, golden light breaks across his sharp features—illuminating his eyes, filled with intent, and watching me closely. In his hand, he swirls a lowball crystal glass filled with rich amber liquid, the ice inside clinking as he tracks my every step.

When I approach, his eyes devour the lines of my body, the muscles in his jaw tightening ever so slightly. He stands smoothly, his towering form somehow imposing despite the slow grace of his movements. Pulling out my chair, he guides me into place at the table with a quiet, commanding hand. I hesitate for a split second before speaking.

"Um, breaking news," I begin, but pause when his hand cuts through the air, signaling for me to wait.

The staff moves in swiftly, placing silver chargers before us in perfect synchronicity, their movements rehearsed and polished. I don't miss the subtle exchange between Enzo and the server—the unspoken understanding that flows with years of familiarity. The scent of the rich Italian feast fills the air, and my mouth waters instantly, distracted by the lavish display before me.

It smells amazing. A full spread of decadent Italian dishes, precisely prepared and beautifully plated—antipasti skewers glistening with vibrant colors, the richest pastas cooked to perfection, seafood dishes adorned with fresh herbs and lemon zest. My senses overload as I take in the familiar dishes, a reminder of the world I've come from and the things I've left behind from my former life with my father.

"Okay, so," I start again as Enzo pulls my chair closer to his side of the table, wanting me nearer to him.

"That's better. Go on," he murmurs, his voice rough but calm.

"That was cute." My hand snakes onto his thigh as he grins with masculine pride, putting several helpings of the array of antipasti on a plate for me.

The intimacy of his proximity shifts something inside me —his presence a steady anchor, even as my mind races with the revelation I've just uncovered. This new, relaxed demeanor of his could be addicting if I let myself slip into it.

I grab a spear of burrata con pomodorini e basilico—the delicate cheese paired with fresh basil and sweet cherry tomatoes. Using my teeth, I slide the tomato from its skewer, savoring its burst of flavor, ripe and tangy against the rich olive oil and aromatic herbs. A nostalgia creeps in—a fleeting warmth in my chest as I remember similar meals at my family home.

The feeling turns cold as memories of myself eating alone at long, empty tables flash through my mind. The comfort of this food—simple yet exquisite—stirs a sadness hidden deep within me.

"So, that first old fogey that fondled me..." I begin, casting a teasing glance toward Enzo. The smile that pulls at my lips is sharper now as I pull a piece of burrata from the skewer and take a bite, savoring it.

Enzo's eyes darken immediately. His hand, which had been lightly brushing the edge of his glass, clenches the crystal a little tighter as his lips press into a thin line.

"Is your ass already missing the palm of my hand, Ms. Caputo?" he murmurs, his voice low, sending a shiver of heat through me. The lethal edge in his tone almost makes me forget my playful teasing.

"Don't send me on a murder spree before we've had the main course. I ordered you lobster risotto, and I know for a fact you'll regret it for the rest of your life if you miss out on the club's risotto," he adds, his eyes softening just enough to show that underlying affection.

My heart skips a beat as his words linger in my mind. Lobster risotto? It's practically part of my DNA. I close my eyes, imagining the dish—the creamy risotto with tender lobster, the subtle flavor of saffron, and a hint of lemon. A dream in a bowl.

"Enzo, if you could slather me in risotto and eat it off my

body, I'd die happy," I say, letting the words roll off my tongue with an ease I don't usually allow.

"Fuck, Delaney," he growls, draining his whiskey in one go. His gaze shifts toward the ceiling as he quickly signals for another drink. "Just get back to your news."

I grin—the playful energy between us undeniable—but I push the teasing aside, remembering what I'd learned.

"Right. Mr. Moretti," I start, but then pause as I take a bite of honeyed melon wrapped in melt-in-my-fucking-mouth prosciutto, moaning my appreciation.

The small grin pulling at the corner of Enzo's lips makes me pause.

"You like watching me here? In your club, wearing your dress, eating your food." I take another bite.

"I do." He refills my wine glass, setting it back on the table. "I enjoy bringing you the best things the world has to offer and laying them at your feet. I won't deny that."

Dammit. *Cue my purring kitty once again.*

Despite the heaviness of the reasons that forced us to reunite and brought us out tonight, I'm having a good time. The opulence and dancing, definitely the bathroom fucking— that is at the top of the list of highlights for the night.

Now, this amazing food and an incredibly romantic Enzo looking at me like I'm a goddess he was born to worship...

It pulls a chord within me that makes me feel weightless and heavy all at once.

I take his face in my hand, and he closes his eyes at my gentle touch. Leaning forward, I kiss him with a tender swipe of my tongue against his lips.

"Thank you for taking me out tonight." I rub the tip of my nose against his. "I'm having a good time."

He kisses me back, quickly but reciprocating my affection with a display of his own.

"You don't have to thank me, angel. I'll bring you the world if you wish it."

I clear my thoughts with a drink of wine, then continue.

"Moretti is a piece of shit. I had a nice bathroom chat with his second wife." I pause, my eyes twinkling with mischief. "Apparently, his first wife was a whack job because he fucked something up."

Enzo's laugh is quiet, but his smile deepens with amusement. He leans back, shaking his head slightly, as if accepting the truth in my words.

"Moretti would fuck up a one-man job at a deli," Enzo says with a small smirk, his voice casual but tinged with disdain.

I can't help but laugh at that. "Did you just make a joke?"

Enzo's smile is brief, but it lingers in his eyes as he looks at me, unabashedly satisfied with himself. "Don't get used to it."

I lean closer, my body naturally gravitating toward him. I pull him closer by his necktie, my lips inches from his ear. We lock eyes for a second, a silent understanding passing between us.

"But I want to get used to it," I whisper, my voice thick with desire, and I can practically see him melting under the weight of my words. The storm in his eye's flares to life, igniting something darker.

"Okay," he mutters after a moment. But just as the tension builds, we're interrupted by the arrival of the servers.

One clears his throat, and if looks could kill, the glare Enzo gives him would reduce him to ash on the spot. The man doesn't flinch, merely acknowledging the second server who arrives with a new glass of liquor for Enzo.

"Your whiskey, sir."

"Thank you."

But before I can dive back into the conversation, the server passes a shallow white bowl in front of me. I almost feel a wave of bliss crash over me, ready for the delicious fragrance of the lobster risotto to engulf me.

My shoulders slump in disappointment as I stare at the bowl making its way to the place setting in front of me.

Mushrooms. The one fucking thing I have an allergy to.

I try not to let my disappointment show, but it's impossible. Enzo notices it immediately and looks down at the dish, sensing my unease instantly.

The server speaks as he sets the bowl in front of me. His voice barely above a whisper, and a chill runs down my spine.

"Your father sends his regards, from the grave."

I freeze. The world seems to slow, everything around me blurs. Some innate instinct within me takes over, like some mafia sleeper cell resting dormant in my blood until this very moment. My hand moves swiftly beneath the table, finding the trusty spatula hidden there, and with a swift motion, I fling the bowl of hot risotto into the server's face.

Enzo's hand reaches beneath the table, where I know his gun is stashed. As the server reacts, taking a step back with scalding risotto coating his face and covering his eyes, I slap the ever-loving horse shit out of him with "The Spat." His head jerks to the side, and he reaches into his vest.

Enzo fires, and the bullet hits his temple with a sickening finality.

I feel the hot spray of blood and other fragments splatter across me, and I grimace. The sound of his body hitting the floor, a gun sliding across the marble, is drowned out by the chaos that erupts around us.

"Ugh," I mutter under my breath. "I think his brains went into my mouth."

But Enzo doesn't let me dwell on it. His hand pulls me behind him, his gun aimed at the chaos now unfolding in the dining room.

The walls themselves seem to pulse with danger, as if the very foundation of the club is alive with the promise of violence. The air grows thick, and before I can process what's happening, the lights flicker, throwing the room into brief darkness before the storm of gunfire explodes. The ceiling splinters with an eerie crack as men dressed in black, like shadows, begin rappelling through the jagged openings.

Their guns drawn, they land silently, their boots making barely a sound as they prepare to strike. Armed guards emerge from hidden panels in the wall, and in the blink of an eye, we're surrounded by Enzo's men in suits, all armed with guns.

It's all-out pandemonium.

My eyes snap to the far side of the room, where a massive cannon of a gun is set up at the only exit, aimed directly at us. We're on the third floor, cut off from escape as an invasion roars to life around us.

The sudden realization hits like a wave—the inevitable is crashing toward us, and it's going to be a bloodbath.

For a fleeting moment, as time seems to slow, two thoughts cross my mind with sharp clarity: I wish I could have spoken to Luca… and I wish I could have had a bite of that damn lobster risotto.

Twenty-Two

The chaos around me is a symphony of violence—sharp and brutal, but somehow controlled. Enzo's men move like a well-oiled machine, springing into action with deadly precision. They're calm in the storm, each one moving with purpose, doing exactly what I would expect from someone raised in this world. They take cover behind columns, upturned tables, and anything else they can find. They fire with unshakable accuracy, cutting down attackers as they appear. It's like a dance—if you can call it that—violent, precise, and practiced.

Enzo doesn't miss a beat. He's everywhere at once, gun raised, eyes sharp. His movements are fluid and efficient—like he's done this a thousand times, which I guess he has. I watch as he fires shot after shot, each one hitting its mark, the men around him following his lead without hesitation.

I find myself holding my breath, caught in the moment. There's something about watching them fight, watching them protect, that makes my chest tighten. It's not just about survival—it's about dominance. About being in control of the situation when everything around you is falling apart.

I'm so caught up in the scene, in the rhythm of the fight,

that I don't realize how close the attackers are getting until one of them rushes forward, gun drawn. I grab what's near, taking a plate that has fallen on the floor, and hurl it like a frisbee, catching the man in the face.

"Fuck yes! Take that, asshole!" My victory is short-lived when there's a pop next to me. The man goes down, and Enzo's hand is on my arm, pulling me back behind cover.

"Fucking stay down," he growls, his voice low and harsh, eyes scanning the room. "It's not safe."

It's a command. And damn him, he knows I'm not going to listen. My gut twists as I watch him and his men push back the invaders, calm and deadly as they take control of the room. But I can't just sit here, hiding behind a pillar, doing nothing. I have no weapons. I don't even fucking know how to use a gun. But damn it, I can fight. I need to.

There are innocent people here in harm's way because of me. I see several motionless bodies on the ground, their clothing telling me they were patrons of the club who lost their lives in this.

I'm about to argue, to break free from his grip, when something catches my eye. Across the room, just past a cluster of gunfire, I see Eloise. She's huddled in the corner, fear written across her face, with nothing but her hands to protect her. She's shaking, her eyes darting around in panic, clearly overwhelmed by the chaos unfolding around her.

I swallow hard. I can't just leave her there, unprotected, while we're all fighting for our lives.

"Delaney," he snaps, his voice hard, commanding. "Stay the fuck behind cover until one of my guys can get you out of here."

Not a fucking chance.

I'm already mapping a route to Eloise, my pulse racing in my ears. The sound of gunfire, the shouting, the chaos—it all fades into the background as I focus on how to get to her.

Crouched on the ground in my heels and dress, I'm about to lunge forward, my path set.

I feel a sharp tug on my arm before I can leap forward. Enzo's hand is around my wrist, pulling me back. "What the fuck are you doing?" he growls, his voice cold and dangerous.

"I'm not sitting here like a pussy while she's over there in danger, Enzo." I yank my arm free, meeting his gaze with fire in my own. "You told me they wouldn't respect me until they saw I was willing to bleed for it," I say, my voice low, matching his intensity. "I'm just doing what you said."

Enzo's jaw tightens, his eyes flicking to Eloise, then back to me. He takes a step toward me, his voice hard as he grits out, "I didn't mean right now."

I cross my arms, defiance radiating off me. "Beggars can't be choosers. I'm the Capo dei Capi, right? So, we do what the fuck I say—which is, we go save her."

The tension between us crackles, and for a moment, I think he might snap. But then, with a deep breath, he steps back. "Fine," he mutters, his voice clipped. "But don't think for a second you're doing this without me."

Enzo gives his team a few hand signals to communicate the plan. He looks like a baseball coach, talking to a runner on base with something that looks eerily similar to interpretive dance.

In a second, there's a wall of his soldiers in front of us, and several push out, engaging in hand-to-hand combat. Enzo thrusts the black handle of a blade into my hand. "If it's you or them...always make it them."

I nod, then we move.

Staying close to the back wall, I run in a crouch to the other side of the ballroom.

"Eloise," I say, my voice steady despite the chaos. "We need to get you out of here. You're coming with me."

She looks up at me, her eyes wide, her mouth trembling. "I —I can't," she stammers. "I'm too scared. I—"

"I've got you," I snap, grabbing her arm and pulling her to her feet. "Trust me. We'll get you out of here."

I give Enzo a tight nod, not even a second of hesitation before I reach for Eloise again. She's frozen, her fear still visible in her trembling form, but with one last look at Enzo, I push forward. "Let's go," I say, my voice firm.

She lets me hoist her up. Her age makes it difficult, and I see two others—a couple hiding under a nearby booth.

"We need to get them out," I hiss at Enzo.

"The panels." He nods as two men approach him. He raises his handgun like it's another part of him. Pulling the trigger, a bullet lodges in the head of one. Enzo pulls another knife from somewhere, and it flips through the air, end over end. The serrated blade cuts through its victim with ease until the point exposes itself out the other side of the man's head.

It's fucking gross.

"Grab who we can and let's go, but they get out first," I call over the noise, and Enzo nods in agreement.

He whistles once, his sharp signal cutting through the mayhem. His team recognizes their boss's call. "Get them out," he commands, picking up a discarded gun from the ground and continuing his oppressive fire at the men attacking his club. His girl.

The wall of protection is back, and we get several of the

club's patrons out. Eloise goes first with one of Enzo's soldiers shielding her.

"Even if we do get out, they'll just follow us into the walls." I finally realize there's nowhere for us to go. We'll just be chased into secret passages, running like rats in a maze until they gun us down.

My eyes land on the bodies around us. The ninjas—or whatever they are—that fell through the ceiling were some of the first to die. Around their belts, I see what I think are grenades.

"Enzo," I call out. He half turns to me, but he keeps his eye on his enemies. "Let's blow up the dining room."

"What the fuck?" he calls back.

"We're trapped! We have nowhere to go."

"Dammit." He growls, pausing to reload his confiscated gun.

"Here." I hand him a clip as I look to the window with the river below. "Enzo, blow this place into the sky and take me for a swim." My gaze is heavy with what we need to do. "It's not just about protecting me but those who can't protect themselves."

Enzo is looking at me and doesn't see the attacker coming at him from behind. I panic as I call out his name and throw my blade like I just saw him do. I miss my target but get close. The blade slices the assailant's face badly enough for Enzo to turn and pull his gun.

Two pops later, the man is on the ground, his wide, dead eyes staring at me as his life fades.

"All right. Let's go for a swim."

Twenty-Three

Enzo's counterattack appears frenzied, but it has purpose. I can see the strategy in it. What appears to be random spurts of hand-to-hand fighting, followed by a pushback with gunfire, allows Enzo's soldiers to move about the large room, helping patrons make their way to the back walls.

Gunfire echoes through the club, mingling with the screech of chairs, shattering glass, and the desperate cries of bystanders.

Enzo and his men move with calculated precision, coordinating with military-like efficiency to clear the room. I watch as they drag terrified civilians into secret passages hidden behind walls, ushering them to safety while the rest of the men hold their ground, gunning down the invaders one by one.

But Enzo doesn't stop—not for a second. His eyes are focused, sharp, scanning the room for every possible threat. His team takes care of business while he ensures the safety of the people here—of me. I can see it in the way his muscles tense, his every movement purposeful.

I remain behind the blockades, helping move those who need assistance to the tunnels within the walls. Some are injured, and I avoid looking at the ones lying motionless on the ground.

"Ninety seconds, Delaney." His tone is low and menacing, leaving no room for argument. In less than two minutes, all hell is going to break loose.

The large artillery gun is nearly set up, and when they start using it, none of us will make it out. I can see the large-caliber rounds from here. If one were to rip through a human body, there would be nothing left.

Two of Enzo's men are preparing the explosives we've taken from the bodies of those who broke in. Several guards are armed with grenades to throw, and Enzo is handling the large bundle.

We will be the last two out, causing a distraction so the patrons can escape through the walls. It's me they're after anyway, and by extension, Enzo.

An older woman stumbles, nearly out in the open and exposed to the gunfire. She's slipping on broken glass, spilled food, and blood. I dart out for her just as Enzo yells for us to get down. I cover her with my body and feel Enzo's heat as he covers me.

The explosion rattles the ground and vibrates the chandeliers above. I expected a spray of debris, but it never comes. Peeking behind me as the blast dissipates, I see Enzo has flipped a table on its side and is holding it to shield us.

"Thank you." I cup his face, then help the woman to her feet. One of Enzo's guards takes her, and they disappear into the darkness of the passages behind the walls.

Enzo takes the bundle of explosives, his finger holding the tab. When he pulls it, the countdown will start, and we'll run for our lives.

"Can you run in those, baby?" he asks. His eyes are wild, and I know he doesn't like this plan, but we have no other options. No one is coming to help because all the mafia families are either sending someone to kill us or are busy killing each other. I have no idea where Jax and Luca are, and frankly, I'm trying to ignore the possibility of what that could mean.

If these men attacked Enzo's house first and caught them off guard... If they are already—

I can't finish the thought and swallow it down, focusing on Enzo and what we're about to do. "Yeah, I'll be okay."

He releases a huff of resignation and pulls me into a kiss. "You better not fucking die," he growls, taking one last look at the anarchy.

"We'll see you on the other side, boss." One of his men pats his shoulder. I see them take their positions, and emotion washes over me. The loyalty Enzo's men have to him, their training, their devotion—it gives me hope. He's a good leader for his family, and that's enough to know we're going to make it out.

An assault of explosions will blast around us as we run for the window. Enzo will throw the bundle at the heavy cannon blocking the doorway. As long as we don't get shot, it should be fine.

"We've got thirty seconds to make it out of the building once I pull this pin, okay?"

"Got it." I nod, steeling myself internally to make the push toward the other end of the building. Then comes the hard part.

We have to run straight through a large glass window and jump three stories down into the freezing river below. No big deal at all. Super glad this was my idea.

Enzo looks down at the bundle, his finger pausing on the tab. Then he releases a deep breath and pulls it. We're up and running. The first few steps are tricky amid the shrapnel littering the floor.

Enzo lobs the explosives, the mesh bag of bombs arcing through the air. His gun fills his empty hand, and he reaches for me with the other.

It's a hard push toward the windows, and I focus on them as we race forward.

Enzo's soldiers hurl their own grenades, and they explode around us, forcing the attackers to take cover and giving us the best chance of making it out. I only hope they survive and can help the bystanders escape.

Enzo raises his gun, shooting the window until his clip empties. He throws the gun through the window, shattering it just before we leap into the air.

Enzo turns his shoulder into it and yanks me to him as we jump from the building. He takes the impact of the window at the same time the bombs detonate, sending us free-falling three stories to the water below.

The explosion is huge.

It races out of every window, shattering the glass. The blast feels like a punch to the gut, but Enzo took the brunt of it, shielding me from everything he could.

I feel his arms go slack, and I panic.

No. Fuck you, don't you dare.

He slips away from me, and I reach for him. It's too dark to see, but I know he's unconscious. I just pray he's still breathing.

The water is like needles on my skin as we crash hard into

the river. It is not graceful. Unable to control our descent, the water feels like cement.

Immediately, I push everything down and start reaching for Enzo, but I can't find him. I can't breathe. I can't see.

The current carries us downstream in an instant. I kick myself to the surface, sputtering and opening my eyes to look for Enzo. Thank God, he's close, but he's facedown, and my heart crumbles.

He can't be dead. He fucking can't be.

I kick toward him and wrap my arms around his wide chest. It takes everything I have to hurl him around so he's facing the sky.

"Enzo!" I call out, grabbing his face and trying to wake him, trying to see if he's still alive. "Enzo! Wake up."

It's a struggle to keep both of us above water, and the river churns around us. I hear the zip of bullets racing by, followed by the sharp bursts of automatic gunfire aimed at us.

"If you can hear me, take a deep breath!" I inhale a big gulp of air and pull us beneath the surface, kicking hard with the current to carry us downstream quickly. I push aside the horrifying observation that he didn't react at all.

I can't hear any more bullets, and I'm not even sure if I would feel them pass us in the water, so I stay submerged as long as I can. This feels like an action movie playing out in a real-life nightmare.

It's nearly impossible trying to hold onto Enzo. He's a fucking giant, and it's exhausting me. My lungs burn, and the frigid water stabs at my limbs, stealing what little strength I have left.

The light above the water's surface darkens briefly, then

brightens again. I think that means we've passed under a bridge. If so, the shooters can't possibly reach us now.

I push myself to the surface, gasping for air as I haul my lifeless Enzo with me.

My Enzo.

He's dragging me down with every kick. Every muscle screams against the biting cold, and I'm having a harder time keeping my grip on him.

He's going to fucking drown, and it's going to be my fault.

The thought crushes me, acting like an anchor pulling me under. But I fight against it. I kick, push, and swim, trying to reach the opposite shore, but the current is carrying us too fast.

I try to get on my back and hold Enzo so we can float, but it's no use.

I'm coughing and sputtering on the water I'm ingesting as my vision darkens. I can't take a full breath, and it feels like gravity is increasing tenfold.

Blinking furiously, refusing to stop, I fight against unconsciousness and keep swimming. Maybe the river will slow soon, and I can make it to shore. I cling to that hope, forcing myself to hang on just a second longer.

A bright light shines in my eyes, forcing me to shut them tight against its intensity. It's gone in an instant, and I frantically look for the source. Terror competes with the chill of the river as I think our attackers have found us again.

But thank fucking God, I see the most beautiful sight I've ever beheld: Luca and Jax at the next bridge, standing by a massive black SUV. Luca removes his jacket, something slung over his shoulder, and climbs over the bridge's railing. Holding on, he times himself to dive in just ahead of us.

"Luca." It comes out like a garbled plea, but he hears me.

Pain flashes across his face, and I see fear in his eyes. But I'm so fucking happy to see him and Jax. No matter what, I know they'll get us out of this river.

"We're going to make it," I tell Enzo, hoping he knows he's going to be fine and that we'll all be together.

Tears blend with the water assaulting me, but I focus on Luca. His hard gaze locks onto mine, acting like a tether.

With his arms outstretched, Luca dives into the river. I feel his grip on me before he surfaces, and my heart splits in two with relief.

"I've got you." Luca's dark hair clings to his face, and he shakes his head to clear it so he can see. The weight of Enzo is dramatically lighter with Luca's help. In seconds, he secures a harness around Enzo, letting go of me only briefly. Then he's holding Enzo's collar with one hand and wrapping his other arm tightly around my waist.

"Luca." His name is all I can manage, my thoughts too scattered for more. It becomes my prayer.

"Jax will pull him up, okay?" he yells over the current.

"Don't leave him!" Panic surges through me at the thought of losing Enzo. "We can't leave him, Luca. He's not waking up." Tears stream down my face as the reality of our situation sinks in.

"I won't leave either of you, Lenny." His grip on me tightens, as if to prove his point.

Suddenly, the thick rope fixed to Enzo's harness pulls taut, but we're carried under the bridge before it catches, halting our movement in the current.

"There's only one crank, so we're going to have to climb," he calls out as I watch Enzo being lifted from the water. His head lolls, his limbs are slack, and my heart shatters. "He'll be okay. Just hold onto me, Lenny."

He kicks hard, grabbing another rope secured to his own harness. Hand over fist, he pulls against the water. "Get on my back and hold on tight. No matter what, don't let go, or I'm coming in after you."

"Okay," I manage, though I know he's not looking for an answer.

Luca grabs the rope over and over, pulling us upward. "We're almost there," he huffs, his voice strained but determined.

I adjust my grip and look up just in time to see Jax hauling Enzo over the railing. Seeing him so vulnerable, so still, feels like a violation of the natural order of the universe.

Enzo is sturdy. An immovable pillar of resolve. Not this lifeless body being dragged from the river.

With a few more pulls, the top of the bridge is within reach. "Don't let go yet, Len."

"Okay." My answer is weak, barely audible. The thought of Enzo dying is crushing me, like the river's current still has a hold on my soul.

Luca braces his feet against a knot in the rope and reaches for the railing. His muscles strain, cords tightening as he lifts us higher. "Grab on now, baby. You can do it."

I stretch my arms toward the railing, but my muscles feel like jelly, useless and weak. Gritting my teeth, I dig deep, grunting with effort as I pull myself upward. "Good girl, Lenny. Keep going. You're almost there."

Luca continues to support me, his hand steadying my back. Finally, I manage to hook my knee over the edge, and with one last push from Luca, I'm on the bridge.

I immediately turn back, reaching for Luca's harness. My fingers fumble, but I don't stop pulling, determined to help him climb. He moves quickly now, hand over hand, until he's finally over the railing.

As soon as he's on solid ground, Luca's arm snakes around me, holding me tightly. We collapse against the railing, both of us trembling with exhaustion and adrenaline as Luca holds me upright.

But the moment of relief shatters when I see Enzo's body lying still. Jax is over him, performing mouth-to-mouth.

My knees buckle, and I crumble to the ground. Luca catches me, his arms wrapping around me like a protective cocoon as we sink together. He holds me tightly against his chest, his long legs bracketing me like a shield.

"It'll be okay, baby. It'll be okay," he murmurs, his voice low and soothing. But I can't look away from Enzo. Not for a second.

Jax leans over Enzo, his face tight with concentration as he forces air into his lungs. Over and over. Desperation rolls off him in waves. My pulse pounds in my ears, each beat dragging on like an eternity.

Then, a miracle: Enzo's chest jerks once, then again, more violently this time. I gasp, hope surging through me.

He's breathing. It's shallow and ragged, but it's breathing.

"Enzo?" My voice cracks, barely a whisper. I'm afraid saying his name might shatter this fragile moment.

Jax quickly turns Enzo onto his side, and he begins coughing violently, expelling water from his lungs. Relief crashes over me like a tidal wave. He's alive. He's really alive.

I reach for him instinctively, my fingers trembling as they

touch his damp face. "Enzo, please..." My voice is thick with emotion.

His eyelids flutter open, his gaze unfocused but alive. When his eyes finally lock on mine, they fill with recognition.

"Delaney..." His voice is a raspy whisper, barely audible over the sound of the rushing river and my pounding heart. But hearing him speak breaks the weight crushing my chest.

"I'm here. I'm right here," I say, pressing my forehead against his, feeling his warmth even through the cold dampness.

He winces slightly, the pain hitting him, but his lips twitch into a weak, familiar smirk. "You're... crazy," he mutters, his voice rough but teasing.

I let out a shaky laugh, brushing his wet hair away from his face before kissing his cheek, then his mouth. "Yeah, well... you're lucky I'm crazy enough to keep you alive."

Jax exhales a long, relieved breath, sitting back as he wipes his face with the back of his hand. "Holy shit, both of you are going to fucking kill me one day," he mutters, a mix of relief and irritation in his tone.

Luca's arm tightens around me, and I feel the strength of his hold, a comforting anchor in the storm. His other hand grips my hip like he's afraid to let me go. He's trembling, and I don't know if it's from exhaustion or the emotional weight of the moment.

I turn in his embrace and cradle his face in my hands. His hold feels like a shield, and I bury myself against him, pressing my face into his neck. "You fucking scared me, Len," he murmurs, his voice raw with emotion.

"You came for us," I whisper, my breath caressing his skin.

"Always, Lenny." His forehead rests against mine as he

takes a deep breath, closing his eyes. "A day won't pass that I won't be here for you, baby." He cups my cheek, pinning me with his piercing gaze.

"Luca—" I choke on his name, unable to form another word.

"Shhh." He kisses the top of my head. "Later, okay? We've got to go."

I pull back slightly, needing to see him. He winces, and my heart twists at the sight of his pain. "I really fucking want to kiss you right now, Lenny." His thumb brushes my bottom lip, his gaze lingering on my mouth.

"Then kiss me."

Twenty-Four

The zing of a bullet snaps through the air, and my body tenses instinctively. Everyone flinches and ducks—of course, this is how it's going to go down, right when I was about to get kissed senseless for the first time in years. Seriously, the universe is a cock-blocking asshole.

"Give me a gun," I demand, eyes narrowed as I scan the landscape around us, ready to take out my anger on the assholes who ruined my moment. But before I can even complete my sentence, Jax is already up, gun in hand, firing off shots. The body of a sniper falls from the rooftop of a building across the bridge with a sickening thud. At least we're good at this whole shoot-first, ask-questions-later thing.

"Calm down, Rambo," Luca mutters, rolling his eyes as he stands up and effortlessly lifts me in one smooth motion, tossing me over his shoulder like a sack of potatoes.

"Hey! I can walk!" I thump my fists against his back, but I know it's a lost cause. He's already moving with purpose, his grip strong and unyielding.

"I know you can." His hand slides up my leg, giving my ass a swift smack. Well, that's one way to remind me I'm not wearing panties. I don't think I realized it until that exact moment and—oh, look—Jax turns around just in time to catch the entire show. *Awesome.*

"Goddamn, that is the prettiest thing I've ever seen," Jax drawls, his voice thick with amusement as he stares unabashedly. "Never seen a more gorgeous pussy in all my life."

"Christ almighty, Delaney," Luca growls under his breath, his gaze darkening as he lowers me to the ground near the SUV. "This is fucking painful." It's more to himself, but I hear the undercurrent of frustration—and something deeper.

I place my hand on his arm, feeling the heat of his muscles under his jacket. His jaw clenches. "It doesn't have to be," I murmur, my voice quiet, just for him.

Luca looks at me, and for a second, the weight of everything seems to press down on him. His lips tighten, and his gaze hardens. "Later." His voice is clipped, but the unspoken promise lingers in the air. He opens the door for me. "We need to talk," he adds, his eyes flicking to my mouth before he looks away.

I get in with a small nod, silently agreeing because I know we need to hash things out. But honestly? A part of me wouldn't mind a ride on his giant disco stick first.

I need to look for some cream or something, or I'll be chafing soon from the monstrous amounts of cock I'm getting these days. Her Vagesty has been rusty and dusty for four long years now, never satisfied by the few dates I've gone on. I'm surprised she hasn't gone into shock, getting orgasms from someone other than Bob.

As I slide into the back seat, Enzo is next to me. He looks like shit. Paler than I've ever seen him, his eyes are half-lidded but still watching me. His exhaustion is evident, but I don't want to bring it up. I don't need to add more fuel to the fire.

I don't even get my own door fully shut when he shifts toward me, his hand circling my waist and tugging me into his lap. "You're cold," he mutters, his voice rough and low.

"Are you making up excuses, so I'll sit in your lap?" I raise an eyebrow, the sass practically dripping from my words.

"Abso-fucking-lutely." He doesn't even hesitate, tipping my chin up and pulling me in for a kiss. His lips are urgent, his hand at my back, fingers digging into my skin. It's like he's trying to anchor himself to something—to me. I can feel the tension in his body, the remnants of everything we've been through tonight.

I let him pull me in deeper, a soft groan escaping him as I shift, settling into his lap more comfortably. His other hand is at my hip, squeezing and rubbing like he's trying to dissipate some of the chaos clearly taking over him.

The car pulls off, taking us out of town and back toward Enzo's property. A fleet of black SUVs passes us, heading into town. I let the weight of the evening—the gunfight, the dead bodies we couldn't save, and nearly losing the man holding me —float away with the retreating vehicles. I bury it for now, soaking in the warmth of Enzo's body.

"The cavalry's heading to the club to clean up," Enzo murmurs into my ear, his breath warm against my skin. His hand continues to rub circles on my back. "Get some rest, angel."

I hum softly, feeling my eyes grow heavy as I relax into his embrace. The tension from earlier slips away, replaced by the sense of safety I feel when he's near.

Before I know it, I'm drifting, lulled by the rhythmic motion of the car, my head nestled against Enzo's chest. His hand brushes through my hair, and I let out a soft sigh, unable to keep my eyes open for much longer.

"Wake up, baby," Enzo whispers, the words pulling me from the edge of sleep. It feels like only a second ago he was telling me to relax, and now we're already at his home. He kisses the top of my head, and I blink my eyes open, stretching my arms and arching my back as I shift in his lap. My ass presses against him, and, of course, he reacts immediately.

I feel the telltale hardness of him beneath me. Damn, these men. My back feels like it's made of steel, but my body—oh, it's not complaining. Not one bit.

A soft, guttural moan escapes his throat, and I swear I could melt right here. That sound? That moan? *Moanster23*'s got some serious competition. It's enough to make me want to climb him again, right here in the backseat. Enzo leans in, burying his nose in my hair, his lips brushing against my ear.

"Stay with me tonight."

It's a request, not a command, and I need zero convincing. If it means blowing up a dozen more buildings to get into this man's bed again, I'd do it in a heartbeat.

I look back at him, pulling his lips to mine. The kiss is desperate, hungry, the fire between us reigniting as my heart races and my body answers the call. It feels so good to be wanted by him—by them. No one has ever looked at me the way they do, back then and now.

The car finally pulls to a stop in the driveway of Enzo's estate. Jax opens our door and offers me his hand to help me out, but he doesn't let my feet touch the ground. Instead, he lifts me effortlessly into his arms, and I instinctively wrap my legs around his waist, clinging to him as he carries me toward the house.

"You scared the shit out of us, Peach," Jax growls, his tone softening when my lips find his. He kisses me as he walks, with the kind of confidence that says he knows every step and trusts himself not to trip or drop me. The slow burn of his kiss doesn't falter, not even when we reach the smooth stone of the front patio.

Setting me down, he gives my ass one last squeeze before opening the door. "Go shower and change. We're going to unload the car and get updates from the team."

I nod, my head spinning from everything that's happened, but there's still an ache in my chest that needs to be dealt with. One problem at a time. "Do me a favor? Make sure he gets off his feet sooner rather than later?" I cut my eyes at Enzo, who doesn't seem to think he needs to take it easy after his near-death experience.

"Anything for you, Peach." He winks at me before jogging off to Enzo. Instead of relaying my message, he grabs the front of Enzo's shirt and demands a kiss, his mouth crashing into Enzo's with ferocity.

Before I reach the door, I catch a glimpse of Luca standing at the back of the SUV. His eyes meet mine, and for a moment, so much is unspoken between us. He's not angry—not really— but there's a tension between us that only a conversation can fix.

I blow him a kiss, my fingers grazing my lips, and he gives me a slow, sexy grin in return. That's all I need. It's a promise that we'll talk, that we'll fix it. Eventually.

But not tonight.

I turn away, stepping inside the house, and as I close the door behind me, Luca steps forward, closing the gap between Jax and Enzo. They break apart, and Luca claims his own heated kiss from our grumpy billionaire. The embrace is raw, full of unspoken things—maybe even a little relief that we're all still standing.

The image hits me like a punch to the gut, a reminder of how close we came to losing him today. My throat tightens, sorrow wrapping its claws around my heart and squeezing the air out of me. It's suffocating. Tears sting my eyes, but I force them back, blinking hard to push the heaviness away.

No. He didn't die. He's alive. He's here. He's with us.

That thought steadies me. We're going to figure this shit out, all of it. We'll find a way to break through this chaos and get to Chicago, where I can finally put all the pieces together. Once they've finished cleaning up the destruction we left behind, once they've buried the bodies of the people who dared to come after us... we'll be together.

And then?

Then I'll take my place. A mafia queen, no longer just a pawn in someone else's game. I'll accept my role because that is where I belong—with them right by my side. Nothing —*nothing*—will ever separate me from these men again. Not the blood spilled, not the lies, not even the war itself.

They're mine. And I'm theirs. And nothing will ever change that.

Twenty-Five

Enzo's large bathroom is all dark-gray slate with matte-gold accents. It's minimal, polished, refined, and sexy. The massive walk-in shower has no fewer than a thousand shower-heads. Obviously, that's an exaggeration, but water comes at me from everywhere.

I play with the settings, putting the water just below the temperature of magma. Adjusting the sprayers and jets, I fiddle with the keypad on the shower wall. Ambient lighting and music create the perfect symphony, and I am finally ready for my shower.

I was going to just use Enzo's shampoo and soap, but I should have known better. Everything I love is here—my brands of shampoo, my favorite scents of soaps and scrubs.

It makes me want to cry. It's like they've all been holding their breath, waiting for me to come back into their lives.

But I giggle instead when I see enough lube to stock a sex store. I look through the flavored ones, guessing which ones Jax picked out, before picking up the peach flavor and then putting it back.

With the world's best water pressure, I wash my hair twice, then put in conditioner. I scoop out a big dollop of sugar scrub and use a mitt to exfoliate my legs and feet. Rinsing my body off and tipping my hair back into the spray, chills run down my spine. I feel the warmth of Enzo's eyes on me and turn my head, finding him leaning against the doorframe.

His button-down shirt is untucked and open, giving me a fantastic view of the muscles sculpting his chest and abs. He's ditched his tie, socks, and shoes, looking the most relaxed and casual I've seen him in a long time.

Arms crossed over his chest, one ankle crossed over the other, he just watches.

Jax's arm appears, sliding around Enzo's chest. He's wearing only his dark jeans, unbuttoned, the zipper slightly down, giving me a glimpse of the thin line of dark hair disappearing under his waistband.

I grin at them and wring the excess water from my hair. Walking to the end of the floor-to-ceiling glass wall that keeps the water in the giant shower, I lean my head against it.

"You know, I bet if I scoot over, we could all squeeze in here together."

Accepting my invitation, they stride toward me, removing their clothes. They meet me at the shower, taking me in, devouring my wet, naked body with their gazes. My skin tingles everywhere they look, my nipples pebbling from their proximity.

I greedily take in their sculpted bodies—the unrestricted view of Enzo's beautiful dick. It really is the prettiest cock I've ever seen. I'm not sure what it is about it that makes it so gorgeous, but my mouth waters as I look down his shaft. I outright groan when Jax fists his own.

Enzo's large hands take my hips, guiding me back to the sprayers, and Jax follows, his hands sliding along my body. I kiss

Enzo's chest, rolling my tongue around one of his nipples. Enzo slides his hand along Jax's wet skin and cups his ass. Jax pulls our brooding boss into a kiss, groaning appreciatively at the taste of Enzo.

"Let us take care of you?" I kiss Enzo's chest again, softly, with reverence. He almost died today. In fact, I think for a minute there, he did. Jax brought him back to life, and I know neither of us wants to consider how differently tonight could have ended.

Enzo palms my jaw, angling my face to him for a kiss. It's deep and rich, filling me with reassurance that he's here, that he's not leaving—not this time. Jax reaches between us, his hand wrapping around Enzo's cock, stroking him while placing kisses on his shoulder.

"Will you let us make you feel good?" Jax squeezes Enzo's dick, and Enzo's mouth drops open. He releases a moan that I catch when I seal my lips around his again.

"Say yes, Enzo." I run my tongue along his full bottom lip.

"Fuck, yes." He closes his eyes and tips his head back as I add my hand to Jax's, and we work his hard length together.

I select a flavored lube and pour a generous amount into my palm. Setting the bottle aside, I rub my hands together and drop to my knees on the warm, tiled floor. With one hand on each of them, I stroke their cocks, the lube allowing my hands to glide easily.

Jax is first. Swirling my tongue around the head of his cock, I suck it into my mouth. "Fuck, Peach," Jax groans, his muscles tightening. I stroke Enzo's length as I work up and down Jax's shaft, taking him fully into my throat. Relaxing my jaw, I swallow him entirely, sucking and building pressure until his groans echo around us.

Pulling back slowly, I circle Jax with my hand and turn to Enzo. "Jax is going to fuck you. I'm going to drink your cum." I squeeze him, running my tongue the full length of his erection.

"Christ," Enzo breathes, his voice shaky.

"I'll let you pick out the lube he uses to fuck your ass." Without waiting for an answer, I grip his hips and take him into my mouth, sucking him the way I know he likes it—hard. He loves it rough, with teeth grazing his shaft and nails biting into his thighs.

"Oh, Delaney," he moans, fisting my wet hair as he thrusts shallowly into my mouth. The sharp sting of his cock pushing deep into my throat draws a muffled grunt from me.

"I *said* you could pick out the lube, Enzo," I tease, pulling back just enough to speak. "I *did not* tell you to fuck my mouth like a brute." I stroke him, placing light kisses along his length as Jax's hand slides between Enzo's cheeks, teasing his hole.

"Be a good boy, Enzo, and I'll fuck you like the slut you are." Jax's voice is rough as he bites Enzo's ear, his hand squeezing Enzo's firm ass. "Is that what you want? To be our whore?"

"Yes," Enzo whispers, his voice trembling. Reaching out, he grabs a bottle from the shelf.

This powerful mogul, the head of an empire, wants to surrender control. It's his release, his trust. Tonight, he's giving that to us.

I keep my eyes on Enzo as I lavish his cock, my lips sliding over his heated skin. Jax drips lube onto his fingers, letting it run down, and Enzo's eyes track the movement like he's hypnotized.

"Are you ready to come for us, baby?" Jax licks the column of Enzo's neck as he works a lubed finger inside him.

"Please." Enzo's head falls back, his hand tightening in my hair. I watch Jax's arm flex as he pumps into him.

I pull back with a pop, releasing Enzo's cock. "I think our good boy deserves another finger." I run my tongue along his shaft. "Do you want another, Enzo?"

"Yes," he gasps.

Jax withdraws his finger, teasing him. "Say please."

"Yes, please. I want another," Enzo pleads, his voice hoarse.

"So good for us." I take him back into my mouth, my teeth gently grazing his skin as Jax rewards him with a second finger.

We work him slowly, building his pleasure in waves without letting him crest. Jax sucks on Enzo's nipple while his cock brushes the back of my throat, drawing soft, desperate noises from him.

"Do you like our queen on her knees for you?" Jax adjusts his fingers, hitting a spot that makes Enzo moan.

"Yes. She feels so good on my cock," Enzo murmurs, his hands curling into fists. He's holding back, letting us keep control of his pleasure.

"Are you starving for my dick, Enzo?" Jax's teeth graze Enzo's neck as I nip at the head of his cock.

"Fuck, please," Enzo pants, his voice trembling with need.

Jax slicks his cock with lube, positioning himself behind Enzo. "Hands on the wall," he commands, teasing Enzo with the head of his dick. Slowly, he pushes inside, drawing a guttural groan from Enzo.

"I love fucking your ass, Enzo." Jax moves with long, deliberate strokes, his pace matching my mouth's rhythm. "You're so tight." His hand smacks Enzo's cheek, and we both pick up our pace.

I squeeze Enzo's cock as I suck him harder, my teeth grazing him lightly. His moans grow louder, his pleasure building.

"I'm going to fill you with my cum because I know you're a slut for it, aren't you?" Jax's thrusts grow sharper, his voice rough.

"Yes. I love it," Enzo cries, his voice breaking.

I take him deeper, his cock hitting the back of my throat as I work my tongue and jaw in tandem. My fingers find my clit, circling it as my arousal pools low in my belly.

"She's fucking herself while she sucks you," Jax growls, his hips snapping into Enzo. "Do you want to come now, Enzo?"

Enzo nods, unable to form words.

"Don't come until Delaney does," Jax commands, his tone firm. Enzo groans, his body trembling as he holds back his release.

"You're doing so good for us, Enzo. Such a good boy. I think I'll fuck you again," Jax teases, his voice dripping with promise.

"Yes," Enzo gasps, his hands flattening against the wall. He's on the edge, waiting for permission.

I thrust my hips harder against my hand, the pressure on my clit building to a breaking point. My orgasm crashes over me, my cries muffled as I suck Enzo's cock. The sound of my pleasure pushes him over the edge.

Jax pounds into him, his own climax shattering as Enzo's release floods my mouth. I drink it down, savoring every pulse of his orgasm. As the tension leaves my body, I grip his hips, pressing my face to his pelvis, showing him how deeply he's buried in my throat.

"Christ, Delaney," Enzo huffs, his body sagging against the wall. He turns, leaning his forehead against Jax's.

"You're so perfect," Jax murmurs, kissing Enzo tenderly before pulling out of him.

I rise slowly, placing a soft kiss on the tip of Enzo's cock before standing.

"But we're not finished with you yet," Jax says, his gaze flicking to me with hunger. He turns off the water, pulling me to him. My back presses to his chest as Enzo's lips find my neck. Their hands roam my body, reigniting the fire in my veins.

"I want to watch you come on his face, Peach," Jax murmurs, his lips brushing against my ear as his hands slide down my waist as he looks to Enzo. "And I'm going to fuck you again while I watch you suffocate on her cunt."

Enzo nods with a breathy exhale, his cock still hard against my hip. He lifts me effortlessly, cradling me in his strong arms. Our mouths meet immediately, hungry and desperate, as he carries me out of the bathroom. His hands grip my ass firmly, teasing me as the head of his cock brushes against my wet folds.

I pull back slightly, meeting his gaze with a sly smile. "You know Jax didn't tell you to fuck me, right?" My tone is teasing, but my grip on his hair tightens, a silent warning.

Enzo smirks, clearly tempted to disobey, but he doesn't. He knows who's in charge tonight. When we reach the bedroom, he sets me down on the edge of the bed, his hands lingering on my hips. I lean in, nipping at his bottom lip. "Good boy," I whisper, my voice low and full of promise.

"Fuck, Delaney," he growls, his hands roaming my back as I

arch into him, pressing my breasts against his chest. "I want to fuck your ass, angel." His voice is rough, filled with longing as he grips my ass and squeezes.

I laugh softly, shaking my head. "Likewise."

Enzo groans, his head rolling back as he looks at me, a mix of frustration and need in his eyes. "You'd love that, wouldn't you? Me with a strap-on?" My smile is wicked, and his answering curse is delicious.

He falls back onto the bed, pulling me to straddle him. I grin, his hands run up my thighs as I lean over him. His erection teases my asscrack as I work my hips, torturing him. "Behave," I whisper, pressing a soft kiss to his lips and he groans in frustration.

Jax whistles from behind us, his gaze locked on my ass. "God, why couldn't I have been born with two dicks? Then I could fuck you both at once."

Laughter bubbles out of me, lightening the intensity of the moment. "I love this pretty pussy," Jax growls, his finger running up my slit, making me shiver. "Now, go smother him with it, baby."

Turning back to face Jax, I straddle Enzo's face. He doesn't wait—his tongue laps at me eagerly, and I cry out, my fingers threading into his hair. Jax positions between Enzo's legs, lifting his hips and sliding inside him again with a low groan. The movement sends a ripple through Enzo's body, his moans vibrating against my core.

"Kiss me," Jax demands, his hand gripping my jaw. His lips claim mine in a firm but tender kiss, his tongue sweeping into my mouth as Enzo's tongue flicks over my clit. The dual sensations are almost too much, and I press harder against Enzo's mouth, grinding against him.

"That's it, baby," Jax whispers against my lips. "Come for us. Let me see how beautiful you are when you drown him."

The tension in my body snaps, my orgasm crashing over me in waves. I scream their names as the pleasure consumes me, my thighs tightening around Enzo's head as he drinks me in.

As the aftershocks ripple through me, Jax adjusts Enzo's hips, making room for me to slide down. "Now, ride his cock, Peach," he commands, his voice low and rough. "Bounce that pretty pussy on him and let him fill you with his cum."

I obey, straddling Enzo and sinking onto his waiting cock. He lets out a guttural moan, his hands gripping my hips tightly as I begin to move. "Holy shit, angel," he breathes, his voice raw.

Jax watches intently, his hand sliding to my clit to circle it as I ride Enzo. My movements are frantic, the pleasure building again as I watch Jax's dark eyes burn into mine.

"You're so fucking beautiful," Jax whispers, his fingers working me expertly. "Fuck him harder. Make him lose control."

I pick up the pace, my nails digging into Enzo's chest as I take him deeper. His moans grow louder, his hands guiding my movements as his climax builds. "I'm so close," he pants, his voice shaking.

Jax leans down, his mouth brushing my ear. "Come with him, Peach. Let him feel you fall apart."

The intensity of his words pushes me over the edge, my orgasm shattering through me as Enzo finds his release. He spills inside me with a roar, his body trembling beneath mine as I collapse toward Jax.

The room is filled with the sounds of our heavy breathing, the scent of sex lingering in the air. As the last waves of pleasure fade, Jax pulls out of Enzo carefully, his hands gentle as he helps me slide off Enzo's spent body.

Enzo wraps his arms around me, pulling me close as Jax joins us on the bed. The three of us lay tangled together, their hands soothing and grounding me as exhaustion takes over.

But even in this moment of calm, my thoughts drift to Luca. I need him. I want him here with us, not outside this room, alone. Jax notices the shift in my expression, his hand brushing my cheek as he leans in.

"He'll come around, Peach," Jax says softly, his voice filled with quiet confidence.

Enzo presses a kiss to my shoulder, his arms tightening around me. "Trust us, angel. He just needs time."

I nod, swallowing down the ache in my chest. For now, I focus on the warmth of the men holding me, letting their touch chase away the lingering shadows.

Twenty-Six

I should have let Enzo rest more, but my vagina was especially ravenous. I woke him up with my mouth on his cock in the middle of the night, only to be thrown onto my back and pillaged by him. Then, this morning, I gave him gentle kisses and stroked his cock until he woke up with a sly smile.

He pulled me on top of him and whispered to me as I rode him—how much he missed me, how sorry he was that he left me, and how he wants me here, with them, every day. It healed something, mending a deep crack in my heart that he had inflicted before.

I leave Enzo asleep, lying on his stomach with one leg bent. He's hugging the pillow I slept on, his face buried in it. Jax didn't sleep with us. I think he wanted to give us some time alone—or maybe he didn't want to leave Luca. Perhaps a bit of both.

In nothing but my birthday suit, I walk through the hall to my room for a pair of underwear, then head to Jax's room and steal a new shirt.

The sounds of life float through the house as I head to the kitchen, where I find Jax and Luca sitting around the table with a pile of papers and folders. Jax is standing, leaning with one hand on the table and the other pointing to something in the pile in front of them. Luca is sitting, his laptop pushed to one side as he drinks a cup of coffee.

They both hear me coming, and Jax straightens, meeting me as I walk over.

"Nice shirt." He grins, pinching the fabric between two fingers and pulling me to him by it. He gives me a morning kiss, a swipe of his tongue teasing me for more, but he pulls away. "Go sit. I'll make you a plate." He pats my ass as he walks to the counter. "That shirt is going to be my favorite shirt now."

"I'm stealing another one tomorrow," I call back, padding over to the table.

"Then that one will be my favorite tomorrow." He's so damn cute when he winks at me, those mouthwatering dimples on display.

"Good morning." I rub Luca's chest as I walk around him, then invite myself to sit on his leg. I'm careful not to put my ass in his lap. I know he wants to talk about... us, and while I love teasing him, I want to respect that impending conversation.

"Lenny," he protests halfheartedly as his hand moves to my thigh.

I turn and cup his jaw with my hand, placing a soft kiss on his cheek. "You jumped into a raging river for me." My eyes scan his, and I see them soften. "Don't push me away now." Emotion rises within me, and my voice cracks on the last few words. "Can I just sit next to you?"

I move to stand, but he tightens his hold on my hip, his other hand grabbing my inner thigh. "Don't—get up."

The rush of warmth that surges through me makes me

grin, and he leans his head on my shoulder. "You're trouble, Len. You know that? Trouble with a capital fucking T."

"Well, I work hard at it, so thank you for the compliment." I wriggle back and forth with a sing-song tune, and he growls.

"You're going to have to be still, though."

"Hm, we'll see."

Jax sets down a plate of pancakes, and I may burst into a multi-orgasmic state just from looking at it.

"Oh my god, Jax." I literally drool as he sets the plate in front of me. "Marry me."

"I tried to once. I'll gladly try again." He smirks when I smack his arm. "Just let me know when you're ready for Wedding 2.0, and I'll be there."

If I've died and gone to heaven, then I'm so damn glad the sky daddy let me through the pearly gates. Three fluffy pancakes steam on the plate, topped with roasted peaches, nuts, and warm maple syrup. Jax delivers a small bowl of cream, and I remember our texts.

"Peaches and cream." I chuckle. "You slut." My jab at his earlier text earns me another wink as he puts a fresh sucker in his mouth.

I cut a decent-sized bite, making sure to get a little bit of everything, and the food makes love to my taste buds. If I wasn't dead before, I am now. The pancakes are buttery soft, the tender peaches oven-roasted in a cinnamon bourbon glaze, and the toasted nuts add a perfect crunch. It's so good I close my eyes, lean my head back, and release a satisfied moan as the flavors burst in my mouth.

"Jax, goddamn," I mutter, shaking my head as I cut another bite. I turn around, giving this one to Luca. He squints at me but lets me feed it to him. "You couldn't cook like this before the slammer."

"Yeah, I worked in the kitchens and picked up a few skills. I had to do something to pass the time other than jack off thinking about you two and working the prison network for information on the Caputo heiress murder-for-hire."

"Oh my god. I nearly forgot," I say between bites, taking a drink of orange juice. "Fuck, he even freshly squeezed the oranges, didn't he?"

"No, but he made me do it. Every single one." Luca grumbles, taking a piece of the pepper-and-brown-sugar bacon. "I'm getting him a goddamn juicer for Christmas."

"Well, it's delicious."

Luca is grumpy on purpose, but his fingers tenderly rub my thigh with such softness that I know he's faking it.

"So, I chatted up this old lady in the bathroom. She said my dad was the one that put the hits out on me. Is that true?"

"No, he was the first person I looked at once I found out your name was at the top of the mafia kill list." Luca holds my leg firmly, as if making sure I know I'm safe now.

"Dang, the top?" My eyebrows rise as more pancakes disappear down the hatch. Luca taps my leg and nods toward the plate, so I spear another bite for him. "Open."

He raises an eyebrow at me, as if to say I'm pushing it, and I return it with a sly grin.

"It's an underboss within one of the families trying to make a power grab, or it's a rival clan like the Irish," Jax says, stealing a piece of bacon and dodging when I try to stab his hand with my fork. "Everybody wants to be top dog."

"Yeah, well, there's only room for one bitch at the top."

"Oh, I love it when you're feisty." Jax goes for another piece of bacon, but I successfully fend him off this time.

I set my fork down, looking at the two of them, and lean in. "So, who's trying to make me the next 'Caputo casualty,' and why?" I ask, my voice steady, though my brain is still trying to process the fact that I'm now a pawn in some twisted mafia chess game.

Jax doesn't answer right away. Instead, he slides a thick stack of photos across the table—blown-up, high-quality color images that scream professional surveillance work. This isn't the grainy black-and-white stuff from TV crime shows. This is the work of someone who knows exactly what they're doing.

"These," Jax says, tapping the stack, "are from our surveillance on the Serrano family." He meets my gaze, his eyes serious. "I know you don't know who they are yet, but trust me, you'll want to."

I look down at the photos, scanning them quickly. There are people coming and going from various buildings, cars parked in random spots. It's clear someone's been tailing these people for a while now.

"Who are they?" I ask, trying to make sense of it all.

Luca leans forward, pointing to one specific photo—a man in a tailored suit walking through a back alley with a briefcase. "This is Marco Serrano. Mid-level guy in the Serrano family. We've been tracking him for months. He's trying to make some serious power moves." He pauses, letting the weight of his words sink in. "And not in a good way."

Jax picks up where Luca left off. "He's been making connections with some unsavory types—arms dealers, money launderers, you name it. Whoever's trying to destabilize the

Caputo family, Marco's definitely got his fingerprints all over it."

I swallow hard, the pieces starting to fall into place. "You think Marco's behind the hits on me?"

"He's too much of an idiot to be the mastermind, but he's definitely acting like a fixer," Luca responds, his hand tightening on my thigh. "If he's involved, we can use him to get to the boss behind it all. This isn't just about taking you down. It's about getting control of the Caputo family—and the power that comes with it."

I lean against Luca, trying to let the information sink in. The weight of it presses down on me. This isn't just about surviving anymore. It's about winning, taking control, becoming who I was meant to be.

"Well, I'm not planning on sitting around and waiting to get taken down." I stare at the two of them, my resolve hardening. "Let's lure him out. I'll be the bait. If he's an idiot—"

"No." Luca doesn't even let me finish.

"Yes," I snap, partially turning so I can face him. "If you wanted to lock me in an ivory tower, then you should've done that when you kidnapped me."

"Do you even know what you're asking for?" Luca's face flushes with frustration. "It takes a lot to keep you safe, and you want to just piss on that and throw yourself into the line of fire? No fucking way."

I get off his lap now, carrying my plate to the sink, needing some distance. "Well, by all means, keep being a brooding asshole and keeping me in the dark. That's working so wonderfully for you." I set the plate down with a little more force than I intend.

Luca stands, pushing the chair back like it offends him. "You'll do this our way."

"Then you don't fucking know me at all. Perhaps you should've stayed around an extra few minutes to at least wipe my blood off your cock before you ran away." I regret the words the instant they leave my mouth.

"Dels," Jax's tone is a low warning.

"No, fuck this." Luca grabs his phone from the table and stomps toward the hall. "Let her go off and get herself killed so the last six fucking years can be a goddamn waste."

I give Jax my back, leaning against the counter with my arms folded over my chest, staring at the kitchen floor. I ignore the scrape of Jax's chair and the sound of his footsteps approaching. He tosses his half-eaten sucker in the trash and stands in front of me.

He rubs his hands up my arms and then tilts my chin so I'm forced to meet his gaze.

"I can't help you two fix each other," he says softly, his eyes searching mine.

"He doesn't want to fix anything. He just wants to lock me in a bubble," I mutter, my voice low and raw. I circle Jax's waist with my arms, holding him, never wanting to let him go as he cups my face gently with his hands.

"Luca is just frustrated he hasn't figured it out yet. The world's best hacker, and he's missing one key," Jax murmurs, leaning down to kiss me tenderly. "It's the one thing he needs to make sure the girl of his dreams can live a safe life."

I snort, trying to push back the emotions welling up in me.

"No, ma'am. Don't you scoff at that." His eyes lighten with amusement, and one of those irresistible dimples makes an appearance. "You are the girl of our dreams, Delaney."

"Oh, I have no question about that," I reply with a small smile, my anger melting under his touch. Jax matches my smile with his own, shaking his head slightly. "The 'safe life' part. I'm supposed to be the queenpin of the Italian mob. Are you going to convince me that will be a safe life?"

"Point taken." He grins and kisses me again, his tongue brushing mine in a teasing swipe before pulling back.

"I need to protect myself," I say, my tone firm.

Jax raises an eyebrow, a sly grin forming on his face. "Oh, don't worry, Peach. We'll make sure you're ready for whatever comes. Starting with teaching you how to use something better than a spatula."

I lean back in mock offense, trapped between the counter behind me and the solid wall of muscle in front of me. "Don't disrespect The Spat. It kept me alive at the club last night. You're telling me I'm going to have to rely on something else now?"

"The Spat?" Jax repeats, his grin widening. Clearly, he doesn't appreciate the weapon's nickname. "It's great for close-range, but I'd prefer your enemies not get close enough to use a fucking spatula."

I roll my eyes, trying not to smile. "Fine, I'll upgrade The Spat to something that actually kills people from a distance. Happy now?"

Jax nips at my neck, sending a shiver down my spine. "You'd be surprised how fun it is to shoot a gun. And how satisfying it is to know that when shit goes down, you'll be able to handle it."

"We'll see about that when I throw up after killing someone," I mutter, reluctantly giving in. "But I'm in. Teach me everything."

"I'll teach you, Peach. But just remember—guns aren't just tools. They're a commitment. If you're going to carry one, you need to be ready to use it when the time comes. No hesitation."

I meet his gaze with a steady nod. "Oh, I won't hesitate. I'll bust a cap, on the spot."

"Okay, Al Capone, take it easy." Jax chuckles, stepping back and stretching. I make it very clear I'm enjoying the view of his low-riding sweatpants and the deep-V that disappears into his waistband. "First, let's get you dressed. While I'd prefer to keep you in nothing but my shirts twenty-four-seven, you need pants on, at minimum."

"Fine, party pooper." I jump into his arms, wrapping my legs around his waist. He holds me effortlessly. "Where are we going to practice shooting?"

"The barn." Jax points toward the building on the property—a place I know they use for torture, interrogation, and disposal.

Perfect.

Twenty-Seven

The property stretches wide and quiet around us as we walk toward the barn. The house is a distant silhouette behind us, and up ahead, the barn—more like a large, nondescript metal building—blends into the landscape. It looks about as inviting as a low-budget horror movie set, and I can't stop imagining body parts being severed by machetes inside.

Jax, however, looks completely at ease, walking beside me like we're just taking a stroll. His hand brushes mine occasionally, and I try not to focus too much on how calm he is while I'm fighting off images of past massacres that have likely taken place here.

"This place is beautiful," I comment, scanning the vast expanse. "If you don't think about the number of people who might have been murdered here at some point."

Jax laughs, his grin lighting up the otherwise dark atmosphere. "Trust me, Peach, no one's died here recently. Just a lot of very interesting conversations."

Recently. I narrow my eyes, skeptical. "Oh, I'm sure. 'Interesting conversations' while the body bags are getting zipped up and the lawn's getting hosed down." I nudge him with my shoulder, poking at his side where I know he's ticklish. "If I find a dismembered body in there, I'm punching you."

"Baby, you know you can be rougher with me than that," he winks.

I roll my eyes, but the tension breaks with a playful laugh. "What's that?" I nod toward the black case in his hand. "Some kind of secret weapon?"

"You'll see," he teases, clearly enjoying my curiosity.

I glance up at him, trying to keep my tone casual despite my nerves. "So, what exactly is your role in this whole mafia thing? I know you're Enzo's right-hand man, but what does that actually mean?"

Jax swings our hands as we walk, acting like we're heading to a picnic instead of a barn that could be hiding God knows what. "I'm the fixer, the cleaner. Whatever needs to be done, I plan it, set it up, and if it goes wrong, I clean it up. No trace, no evidence. I make sure no one gets caught." He says it so casually, like it's just a job—not a life-or-death thing.

"Wait." I pause, curiosity taking over. "So, if you're the world's best cleaner, and you've been fixing all these jobs... how'd you end up charged with murder?"

Jax's smile fades, a flash of seriousness crossing his face as he pulls us to a stop. "We all have something tied up in this, Peach. We protect you, and someone comes after us. I've killed people, but I didn't do what they said. I was framed."

I gasp. "So, how did you get released?"

Jax smiles. "You really need to stop underestimating Luca." He brushes a lock of hair behind my ear. "Luca owed me a favor. I called it in to protect you."

I press my lips into a thin line.

"Come on." We resume our trek to the murder-barn, and

he continues. "Later, Luca figured out it was a setup. He hacked the prison records, put in a transfer for me, and altered my charges to accessory to burglary. When I got to the new place, my release was six months later."

He looks at me seriously, his voice low. "I sure as hell wouldn't have done anything to risk being taken away from you. So, someone did it for me. That's what I'm after—finding the asshole who tried to bury me in a cell for the rest of our life together."

I feel the sincerity in his words, a warmth spreading through me. I reach up, brushing a stray strand of hair from his forehead. "I believe you. You do what you do because you're good at it. And it keeps you, Luca, and Enzo safe."

He leans down, pressing a soft kiss to my lips, his voice teasing again. "What we do is in the name of our goddess, Delaney Caputo."

I smile against his lips. "You shameless flirt." We're nearly at the barn, but my questions keep coming. "What about Enzo and Luca? You said all of you have something in this."

"Someone is going after Enzo's business, his properties— snagging land purchases out from under him. He's lost millions. It's a territory grab but without the bloodshed." Jesus. "Luca needs to find that last piece of the puzzle that has eluded him. He's chased a shadow for six years. He needs this. He needs it to come to an end."

So, that's it. Jax was framed. Enzo's territory is being invaded, and Luca is taunted by a mystery. The investment they have in this goes deeper than just me.

Jax pulls me back from my thoughts with a kiss to the back of my hand and gestures toward the barn. "Ready to see the magic?"

I take a deep breath, feeling a mix of nerves and anticipation. "Ready as I'll ever be."

Jax opens the door smoothly, and the cold air from inside hits us. The unknown is waiting just beyond the threshold, but I'm not backing down now.

"After you, princess."

I look at him, a small smile tugging at my lips. "If there's even a hint of blood in there, I'm blaming you for my mental trauma."

Jax just grins back, and I feel the spark between us flicker again. "I wouldn't have it any other way."

We step into the barn, and I take in my surroundings, half-expecting a blood-splattered scene straight out of a horror movie. Instead, it's more like a storage space where you'd park an RV for the winter—nothing ominous about it at all. The shelves are stacked with random tools, cans of motor oil, and a pile of old blankets. If I don't think about it, it could just be a regular garage.

Jax, on the other hand, doesn't seem fazed at all. He strolls in, his hand brushing mine casually, while I'm stuck picturing a crime scene.

I raise an eyebrow. "So, where's the blood and the bodies hanging from meat hooks?" I look around like I'll find them tucked behind a stack of boxes.

Jax grins, stepping up behind me and getting close enough to drop his voice in a creepy way. "Oh, those are far below ground," he whispers, leaning in like he's sharing a dark secret. "Where no one can hear their screams." He even shudders exaggeratedly, and I feel a chill run down my spine.

For a second, I can't tell if he's joking. I mean, it's Jax—he can't possibly be serious, right? But the idea of a subterranean torture chamber flashes through my mind, and I can't help but shudder. Maybe he's not entirely joking.

I eye him suspiciously. "I'm not sure if you're joking or if you're really about to drag me into a creepy hole in the ground." I cross my arms over my chest, half-expecting him to break into laughter.

Jax, ever the smooth talker, just keeps grinning. "I'd never let you go down there alone. It's more of a two-person gig." He winks at me, and I roll my eyes.

"You're a sick bastard, Jax. I bet you love seeing me squirm."

"Only when it's fun," he says with a wink, completely unapologetic.

I look around again, processing what he's said. It's a lot less creepy than I imagined, but I still picture some poor soul tied up in here, getting tortured while Jax casually munches on a sandwich.

"Alright, no more creepy basement torture talk, Jax. You might actually convince me you're a psychopath. You'd ruin that cute smile of yours."

Jax flashes a grin. "I'm your psychopath, Peach."

I roll my eyes but can't help smirking back at him. This guy never takes anything seriously.

Then, with a flick of his wrist, Jax opens a cabinet door and reveals a hidden button. The shelf behind it rises with a smooth whirring sound, exposing a compartment beneath.

I freeze. "Holy shit. There really is a torture chamber down there, isn't there?"

Jax laughs, unaffected. "Relax, Delaney. Nothing sinister. But you don't leave evidence from a 'conversation' out in the open, do you?"

"Yeah, sure," I mutter. "Just a little spot for 'conversations.'"

I'm starting to think therapy might be on the horizon after all this.

Jax completely ignores me, a grin still on his face as he walks past the opening, inspecting the shelves of guns. He selects a few handguns, his movements smooth and practiced, like he's done this a thousand times.

"Here," he hands me a couple boxes of ammo as though we're just grabbing some snacks for a movie night. "We're going to need a lot of these."

"Hey, I resent that," I say, taking the boxes, trying to shake the unease in my hands. I follow him through a door, and as it closes behind us, I feel a quiet, unspoken tension.

My eyes widen in surprise as I take in the space: it's like a legit training facility, with booths for individual shooters, targets on pulleys, and a smooth floor.

Jax steps up to one of the booths, grinning. "Yeah, not exactly what you'd find in a regular garage, huh?" He positions himself like he's done this a million times. "Alright, time to teach you how to protect yourself."

I walk over to a booth next to his, the weight of the ammo in my hands feeling a lot more real now. The air smells like gunpowder, and the hum of the pulleys fills the space.

"Okay, let's do this," I say, trying to hide my nerves with a touch of sarcasm. "How hard can it be? Point, shoot, end someone's life. Easy peasy."

Jax turns to me with a wicked smile. "Don't worry, baby. By the time I'm done with you, you'll be using that gun like it's a part of you. You won't even remember The Spat."

I gasp in mock offense, clutching my chest. "How dare you

speak of my Spat so soon after she sacrificed herself for me." I look upward, pretending to address the heavens. "May you rest in peace, baby girl."

Jax rolls his eyes but can't help the grin that follows. "Let's get going. I need to make sure you leave here ready to fight for your life." He pats the space next to him, his eyes twinkling.

"Alright, first things first." He picks up a sleek black handgun and holds it out for me. "This is your new best friend. Semi-automatic. If you're going to be in this world, you need to know how to handle one."

Jax takes his time explaining everything, showing me the parts of the gun, making sure I can point them out before moving on. He steps closer, guiding my hands through the motions of loading and unloading the gun, his attention unwavering.

I focus, trying to ignore how his gaze feels like it's pressing against me. It's hard not to notice how close we are, how much his warmth radiates into me.

Jax's grin never fades as I nail the parts of the gun, one after the other. "You're a quick study," he says, clearly impressed.

I don't let myself think about how good he looks when he handles the guns with such mastery.

"Good girl," he says quietly, his deep voice vibrating the air around me.

Concentrate, Delaney. You're learning how to be a killer. You're definitely not hoping Jax will get you off using the barrel of one of his guns. Not at all.

Jax hands me a pair of safety goggles and earbuds. As I put them on, he steps behind me, his body close enough that I can feel the heat radiating from him. I try to concentrate, but his presence is hard to ignore. The faint scent of his cologne mixed with the essence of gunpowder is intoxicating.

My pulse quickens when he leans in closer to adjust my stance; I swear I can feel the heat of his breath on the back of my neck.

His hands move to mine, guiding my grip on the gun. I can feel his fingers press into mine, and my body reacts before my brain can process it. I shift slightly, but Jax's hand follows, sliding slowly over my hip. His touch sends a jolt of heat straight through me, and my skin tingles as his hand drifts toward my inner thigh.

It's okay. We're totally focused… on something. I forgot what. Oh, the guns. Not Jax's hand, which is very close to my vagina.

He leans in closer, brushing my ear with his mouth as he speaks in a low, husky voice. "Good. Just like that."

Holy fucking shit.

"Feel the gun, Delaney. Let it become an extension of you." His wandering hand squeezes my inner thigh, his nails gently raking my skin.

My breath catches, and I bite my lip to suppress a moan. "Jax… you're being distracting," I whisper, though I know I'm not really complaining. Judging by his grin, he knows it too.

"I know," he murmurs, his fingers trailing down my side, my body still humming with heat. "Do you want to play a game?" he asks, placing a kiss behind my ear. His hand moves to rest on a small black box nearby.

Jax's games typically result in me being unable to walk from the sheer number of orgasms he gives me. But the guns make me nervous, and not knowing what's in the box is killing me. I know he won't tell me unless I agree.

"You know," I say, putting the gun down and turning to

face him, "there's a splatter horror movie where the killer says that. They're in a creepy slaughter barn too."

His eyes gleam with a dark shine, and he raises one eyebrow, silently waiting for my answer.

"Yes, I'll play."

He turns me back around, his massive frame pressed against mine as he opens the black box. A grin spreads across my face when I see what's inside.

There's a small pink butt plug and a matching toy curved like a hook. Next to them is a little remote control. "Well, pink is your favorite color."

"If you're in a gunfight for your life"—he moves my hair aside and kisses my neck—"you won't be in a quiet, still shooting range." His right hand slips into my pants, under my soaked panties. His middle finger moves in slow circles around my clit while he continues to kiss my neck. With his left hand, he grabs a gun, quickly flicks the safety off, aims, and fires three times.

I gasp, my breath catching as his finger never loses tempo, his mouth never stops, and I can see from here that the bastard hit the center with each shot.

"Oh my god," I pant, unsure if it's from seeing how well he shoots or the fact that I could come in about thirty seconds.

"So, you're going to wear these," he says, running his finger down the edge of the black box, "and I'm going to stand over there with the remote." He pulls a packet of lube from his pocket and places it on the counter. His hand slides under my shirt and bra, pinching and rolling my nipple with deft fingers. I moan, leaning against him and clutching the counter.

"I'm going to edge the shit out of you until you hit the center. And then I'll let you come."

Just as my climax begins to swell, Jax pulls his hand away. I release a shocked huff, which only makes him chuckle as he sucks his finger clean.

"Pants down, Peach. Get on all fours on the couch." Jax rips the corner off the lube packet with his teeth, spitting it on the ground.

"Aye, aye, Capt'n," I salute before reaching for my pants.

"We'll see how bratty you still are when we're done here." He smacks my butt as I lower my pants and head for the sofa.

Oh, baby. I could keep this up all day. And he fucking knows it.

Jax places the black box on the arm of the couch in front of me and sanitizes his hands. He grabs the small plug first, hesitates briefly as he lubes it, then slides it along my center and presses it against my clit. I hear the click of a button, and the plug vibrates. I yelp, clutching the leather couch.

"Holy shit."

He leans down to my ear as he slides the plug toward my ass. "We're going to have a lot of fun, baby." Jax kisses behind my ear, then focuses on easing the plug into me.

"Good girl," he praises when it slips all the way in.

"Now, pants up and turn around."

I comply, and Jax grabs the second toy, rubbing lube around the shaft and bulb. He holds my gaze as he reaches into my pants, sliding the shaft along my pussy before easing it in. My mouth drops open as he works it in, stealing a kiss and sucking on my bottom lip.

"I'll make sure it's in the right spot, okay?" he whispers, his breath tickling my lips.

I nod, and he presses one of the remote's buttons. The pink toy comes to life, instantly putting Bob to shame.

"Oh, Jax," I moan, clutching his broad shoulders as he moves it around, watching me for reactions. The bulb fixes on my clit, and the sucking motion nearly sends me into orbit. My loud moan echoes through the empty range.

"There she is." Satisfied, he adjusts the intensity, making me rise onto my tiptoes as an orgasm rushes forward, then dials it down to nearly nothing.

"Asshole," I pant, trying to catch my breath.

"Let's see what you've got."

One hour and three boxes of bullets later, we leave the warehouse. Jax slings his arm around my shoulders, and I release a satisfied sigh after earning my six glorious orgasms.

Twenty-Eight

The little girl is back in my mind, stuck, frozen in that reflection in the window. Her wide, scared eyes stare back at me, and I want to tell her it's okay—that we can move past this—but she's trapped. I'm trapped.

She's stuck in that moment, but I need her to move. I need me to move.

I've spent so long locked in this memory, trying to forget the weight of it, trying to bury it in some dark corner where I wouldn't have to face the truth of it. But she's still there, preparing to wait for her cup of hot chocolate and a man who's supposed to love her but never did.

Chills run up my spine, and I hug myself, rubbing my arms to chase away the gooseflesh as I look out the window at the expansive valley. It's when my eyes focus on my reflection that the little girl comes back to me.

I close my eyes and blink hard, trying to shake the memory free, to bring it into focus. When I open them again, the reflection has shifted. I take a few steps back, and the little girl is gone. I'm looking at myself. But the sadness in her eyes still haunts mine, and it feels like something inside me hasn't changed. I'm still carrying that fear, still trying to make sense of what happened.

I turn my head toward a hallway where light spills from an open door, waiting for the sounds of my parents' argument that I know will soon reach me.

The voice of my father booms like thunder, finding me first. My mother's voice—desperate and pleading—follows. Her words are lost in the noise. No matter how hard I try to hear them, they keep dancing away from me. I can't tell if it's the absence of understanding what she is saying, or merely the sound of her voice, that makes me shiver. But I can't stop it.

I force my foot to move, taking one step forward, then another toward the hallway. It's dim around me—dark outside with low lights on around the quiet house.

I pass a table against the wall. A vase of flowers is still fragrant, but I can't see any color in the soft petals that have wilted, dried, with some crumbled pieces resting on the table's surface. I stop, trying to look at the framed picture. I see me and one of my parents. I see smiles. It feels happy, but I can't tell who it is.

The edges of my vision blur, darkening as the details try to hide themselves from me.

The first slap rings out, and I twist my head toward the source. My body tenses as I instinctively wince, feeling the sting of the sound echo through me.

My cheek warms, and I press my fingers to it again. Had he hit me too? Or am I just feeling the pain of this moment with my mother in the memory?

I rub my eyes again. "Focus," I tell myself as I step through the doorway and see blurred stairs before me. They are wide, lavish, with deep red carpet—the color of blood. The same color I painted my nails.

I fan my hand out before me, looking at them when another slap echoes, and I look up.

"You'll thank me for this one day," he barks at her.

I see her now. In vivid detail, my mother. She has medium-length dark hair, lighter than mine and shorter, falling just below her shoulders. Her face is red where she was struck, and I look at my feet, touching my own cheek again.

"You can't take this from me," her voice is shaky, but she puts bravado behind it.

Her scream reaches me first, then the thudding of her body falling down the stairs. She jerks and tumbles, powerless, crashing against the hard steps.

I freeze. I can't look away. I'm rooted to the spot, watching, helpless.

Her arm begins to bleed, and I'm stuck, staring at the white bone protruding from her arm. She's twitching, her body lying in a curled position, facing me. Her face is already bruising, her lip busted as blood covers her teeth.

She tries to smile at me. Tries to soften what I'm seeing. But that is impossible. "Happy birthday," she whispers before her eyes close and her head thumps to the floor.

My eyes are wide, and my brow is pinched as I look up at my father. He's standing at the top of the stairs, breathing heavily, his chest rising and falling in sharp, erratic bursts. His eyes are wild, his face contorted in a way that sends a chill down my spine.

He's looking straight at me.

The mask he wore, the hero I thought he was—it's gone.

All that's left is the monster behind it, standing there, looking back at me.

It's the moment the illusion cracked.

The moment I stopped being his treasure.

Twenty-Nine

My mind is like a flower petal caught in the wind, floating somewhere between what I've learned and what I can't bear to fully accept. The images keep spinning around the revelation, like a hamster on a wheel I can't seem to stop. The pieces are all there, but the truth is still too heavy for me to wrap my hands around.

My father killed my mother.

There's no romanticized version of her drowning on a sailboat and leaving behind a daughter and a grieving husband. No storm or two-week search for her that I've clung to for years. No—he knew where she was the entire time. He covered up her death like it was just another inconvenience in his world.

Maybe it was an accident. A mistake in the heat of the moment. But the cold truth is still there—he killed her. And I —I was there. I saw it, but I couldn't understand it. Not then. Not at that age.

I wipe away the sudden sting in my eyes, the feeling of helplessness creeping in, and I find myself closing off that memory again. It's too much. But I know I can't let it go. Not now. Not when it could have been the beginning of everything.

And that's where the second part of the puzzle clicks into place.

Maybe Eloise's rumor wasn't so far-fetched after all. Maybe my father didn't just want me out of the way because of any inheritance. Maybe he saw me as a witness to his crime—his biggest regret—and he tried to silence me before I could remember. He knew. He always knew. He was afraid I'd remember and bring his empire down.

Maybe that's why I was the one he kept closeted all these years—his little insurance policy. The daughter who would never speak out. Because if I had... If I had just understood what was happening... maybe I could have stopped him. But I couldn't, and I didn't.

Maybe that's why the hits started. Maybe he wasn't just protecting his empire. Maybe he was protecting himself from me.

I shake my head, trying to clear the fog that clouds my mind, but it doesn't work. All I can see is his face, the man I used to idolize. The man who destroyed my childhood with something so heinous my child's mind locked it away.

Locked it away in the same manner Luca locks himself away from me.

His presence feels like a weight on my chest, a constant reminder of the distance he's putting between us, the way he keeps stepping away whenever I try to get closer. His anger, his frustration—they come out in his silence, in the way he shuts down every time I push him.

Maybe that's his way of protecting himself. Maybe he's afraid that I'll break, or I won't choose to forgive him.

But that's not the part that stings the most.

No, what stings is the part I'm too scared to admit: Luca

was my first. My first boyfriend, my first love, my first lover. And when it came time for him to choose—he chose to walk away.

He was the first one who chose to leave me behind. And that cuts deeper than anything else.

I don't know how to fix this. I don't know how to bridge the distance between us when every time I try, he pulls away. He keeps choosing the distance over me.

"Lenny?"

I blink and look over at Luca, surprised to see him standing right in front of me, his eyes guarded. I didn't even realize he'd come into the living room; I was so lost in thought. My mind is a jumble of unfinished memories and half-formed conclusions, none of which make any more sense than they did when they first hit me.

"I'm sorry," I say, barely recognizing the crack in my voice. "I was just... thinking."

Luca nods, taking a step closer. "I can see that."

I swallow, trying to push past the walls I've built around myself. "Yeah. Just... stuff."

He looks at me for a long moment, his brow furrowed as if he's trying to read me. "Anything you want to share?"

I open my mouth, but the words don't come out. How do I tell him what I'm feeling when I can barely sort through it? That I miss him even though he's right here. That it hurts each time he pushes me farther away and then sleeps just down the hall.

How do I tell him he's still breaking my heart after all these years?

So, I don't. I change the subject.

"Have you found out anything about my mother's disappearance?"

Luca exhales, stepping farther into the room, arms crossed. "I've gone through all the files, all the reports. The boat was signed out of the marina the night she went missing, the storm hit, and the Coast Guard didn't deploy until the morning because of it. The boat was found capsized, no sign of her. Case closed. She was declared dead a month later."

The sharpness of his words lingers, and I press my lips together, not letting the anger inside rise.

"Well, keep looking. Look for any evidence of a cover-up. There has to be something more. Other boats signed out that night. Maybe from other marinas? Or maybe someone else checked the boat out—someone who wasn't my mother."

He shakes his head, as if this is all a waste of time. "We're talking about a case that's been closed for two decades, Len. Your mother's death isn't some grand conspiracy. She didn't make it through the storm."

His words cut deeper than I expect, and my breath hitches. But I'm not going to back down.

"It wasn't the fucking storm." My voice is low, but it carries. "My father pushed her down the stairs."

Luca freezes. He blinks at me like he didn't hear me correctly. "What?"

"He killed her."

There's a flicker of disbelief in his eyes, followed by a mixture of confusion and... anger. He stands there for a moment, jaw working, trying to process what I just said. "You've always said how devastated he was."

"Yeah, well, he was acting. You men seem to be good at that."

He narrows his eyes but recovers quickly at my jab. "Why didn't you tell us that earlier?" His voice is sharp now, frustrated. "What the hell do you expect me to do with that information, after I wasted half a fucking day chasing my tail?"

"Well, I apologize for being a waste of your time. Maybe because I didn't remember until now," I snap back, my temper flaring. "If you saw your mother killed, you wouldn't exactly be excited to remember it either."

I see his jaw tighten, his cheeks flush red, and the muscles in his neck visibly straining. "You need to fucking watch what you say," he growls. "I'm done here."

Before I can respond, he turns, walking toward the hallway. My heart races with a mix of anger and frustration. Every time he gets like this, it's as if he builds a wall between us. And once again, I can't break through it. I'm fucking tired of it.

"Don't walk away from me," I snap, stomping after him. "I'm sick of this."

He doesn't look back or slow his pace. But I'm done being the one to always back off.

I catch up to him in the hallway and grab his arm.

He spins around too quickly, and before I know it, I'm slammed against the wall. His chest is pressed against mine, his breath coming in sharp bursts, his eyes stormy with emotion. The tension between us crackles, a mix of frustration, longing, and something I can't quite name.

"What do you want from me?" he yells, his voice breaking.

"You! All I want is you." The words burst out of my throat, heavy and suffocating.

His body stills for a moment, as if he's holding back. And then something changes. Something inside him snaps, and without warning, his lips crash against mine. It's a kiss that feels like the world is collapsing around us, an overwhelming rush of heat and need. It's raw, desperate—like he's finally letting go of everything he's been holding inside.

I melt against him, my hands instinctively moving to his chest, feeling the heat of his body under my fingertips. His lips are insistent, pushing against mine with a fierce urgency, as if he's trying to say everything he can't put into words. His hands slip around my waist, pulling me closer, and the kiss deepens, consuming me. I match the intensity of his kiss, my own body reacting, responding to his every movement.

The taste of him is intoxicating—rich, urgent, and so hauntingly familiar it makes my heart ache. His tongue brushes against mine, and I can feel the weight of everything between us—the years of distance, the unresolved pain, the unspoken words. It all builds, a simmering storm that's finally breaking free.

My chest heaves, my pulse racing as I press myself even closer to him. I can feel the tension in his body, the way he's fighting to keep control, but I don't want him to. I want to feel everything. I want to feel him. I want to break down every barrier he's built and finally reach the man beneath the anger and the distance.

His hand grabs my throat, and his desperation moves from my mouth to my neck and collarbone. "This is what you want, Len?" His voice is deep, raspy, and full of need.

"Yes." My answer is just as desperate. More. I need more.

He sucks and nips at me, pinned to the wall by his body, and presses his knee between my legs, confining me more. "You want me to take you right here in the fucking hallway?"

My hands are all over him, pulling at his hair and holding onto him, afraid he'll pull away.

He strikes out quickly, snatching both my wrists and pinning them above me. "Bury my cock in you?"

"Yes, Luca."

His pupils are blown wide, the black nearly consuming the rich blue. He unbuttons my pants and shoves his hand into my panties, finding me soaked. "Of course, you're fucking wet." He licks up the column of my neck, and I gasp when he shoves two fingers into me, thrusting hard and palming my clit. "Because all you want is to complete your collection. Is that it?"

Confusion and pleasure collide within me, and I can't speak as he consumes me.

"You fucked the two of them, and now you only need me to get you off too." He kisses me hard, our teeth colliding. The taste of blood mingles with the fire coming off him, but it's not passion. It's just anger. It's not what I want.

"Luca." I gasp, pulling back from him.

"You wanted this; I'll fucking give it to you." He works my pussy with his fingers, and I can't stop the reaction of my body to his touch. I've starved for it, but I feel out of control. He feels out of control.

"No, Luca." I try to pull my hands down, but he tightens his iron grip. "Stop!" I push against him with my body, but his mouth is on mine again, silencing me with another bruising kiss. Tears well in my eyes as I fight against the orgasm that is betraying me. I don't want him like this. This is not Luca.

It's not my Luca.

He's shaking, his muscles so tense like he's still fighting against something. So, I stop fighting. I force myself to relax. I steel my face to a neutral expression as tears streak my cheeks.

"No, Luca." My quiet command breaks whatever possession took him over. "Not like this. Please." My chin quivers on the last word, and he blinks, like a fog clears from him. He yanks himself back from me as if touching me burns him, putting his back to the other side of the hall.

Horror drenches him, and he looks at his hand as if it doesn't belong to him, then looks back at me.

"Luca." I put my hands out in front of me, but they are shaking. I take a half step toward him, and he stumbles back, farther away from me. "Tell me how to reach you." I whisper my plea.

"J–Just," he chokes on his emotions as they pour out of him. Tears glisten in his eyes, and I can finally see past the façade his anger gives him.

It's loathing. For himself.

He—he hates himself.

"Just don't."

"No, please don't—" ...Go.

But he's already gone.

A choked sob wrenches out of me as I slide down the wall, my tears falling with me.

Thirty

That's where Jax finds me—a crumpled mess on the floor of the hallway, sobbing, holding myself, trembling like a fucking leaf. He looked like he was going to have a brain aneurysm before I could muster the words to tell him what happened.

Even then, all I could say was one thing: "Luca."

I didn't see Enzo standing behind him, but Jax's head snapped toward him. Something silent passed between them. I've never seen Enzo so angry. He just turned and walked to the door at the end of the hall. He slammed it so hard the glass inset shattered, and I flinched.

Jax's face filled my vision. His rich brown eyes held me and brought me back from the void I was falling into. He carried me into my bathroom and filled the tub. He undressed us both and picked me up like a bride, settling me on his lap and using a shallow dish to gently pour the hot water over my back.

Enzo arrived at some point, kneeling down beside the tub. His thumb so tenderly stroked my cheek as he looked at me, trying hard to calm the raging storm in his thundercloud eyes. He kissed my cheek, then rubbed Jax's throat, kissed the top of his head, and left us alone in the bathroom.

Jax took care of me—drying me off, giving me one of his shirts, and lying in my bed with me. He never stopped rubbing me, holding me, and talking in a low voice. At some point, I stopped crying, and my body relaxed into him. He told me stories, trying to get my mind off the heavy thoughts crushing me.

My heart feels like it's in a thousand shattered pieces after Luca. The weight of it sits heavy in my chest, suffocating me with every breath I take. I can still see his angry face in my mind, hear his words cutting through me. He was so closed off, so distant. I don't know how to fix this, how to reach him when he keeps pushing me away.

Eventually, the smell of something amazing wafts into the room, and my stomach grumbles in response.

"You hungry, Peach?" Jax whispers, placing a gentle kiss on my temple.

I nod. He helps me up, wrapping a blanket around me and rubbing my arms.

"You okay?" Jax's voice is soft, but there's concern in his eyes as he watches me. He's not asking for anything more, just wanting to know if I'm still breathing, if I'm still here with him.

I don't answer right away. What is there to say? I'm not okay. Not when one of the men I care about shattered me two hours ago. Not when I'm caught between a war, an empire, and the three of them, struggling to make sense of everything. But somehow, Jax knows how to make me feel like I don't need to explain it all.

"Come on." He leads me into the living room with his arm around me.

The kitchen is filled with the sounds of clattering pans and sizzling food. Two chefs are working feverishly in the massive kitchen. The fragrances filling the space instantly make me feel warm, and my mouth waters.

"Enzo brought in the chefs from the club tonight," Jax explains, his voice laced with hope that this might cheer me up. "Special request for you. Life-changing lobster risotto, I think he called it."

I raise my eyebrows, surprised. My heart stirs a little—it's one of my favorite meals, and for some reason, it feels like a lifetime since I've had it.

"Lobster risotto?" I ask, trying to keep the sadness out of my voice. "Really?"

"Yep. Just for you," Jax smiles, nudging me forward as I watch the chefs work.

Enzo is in the living room. Like Jax, he's shirtless, wearing a relaxed pair of lounge pants. A warm glass of wine is in one hand, and a remote is in the other. Flames rise in the fireplace with the push of a button. Lights provide a low, warm glow, and the framed picture over the mantle lifts up, receding into the wall to reveal a television behind it.

He notices us and immediately walks over to where I'm standing. His hands frame my face, gently cupping it. His gaze softens as he looks down at me, his thumb brushing over my cheek.

"I'm so sorry, angel," he murmurs, his voice low and sincere. "I hate seeing you hurting."

"I don't want to cause problems between you," I whisper, my voice cracking. The words tumble out before I can stop them. "I know I'm messing things up. I can't seem to figure Luca out, and I'm just—"

"No," Enzo interrupts softly, shaking his head as he strokes my cheek with his thumb. "This isn't on you. You haven't done anything wrong. You're not messing anything up. You're not causing problems. You're just... being you. It's okay to feel what you're feeling, Delaney."

I can feel the heat of his hands, and I lean into him. He's right, but it doesn't feel like it.

"I wish I could fix this for you, baby," he whispers, leaning his cheek against the top of my head and wrapping his arms around me.

"You can't," I say, my voice thick with emotion. "You can't fight this for me."

Enzo's hands cup my face again, his voice firm but gentle. "I know. But we'll work through it. Together."

Pain forms a lump in my throat because we aren't. We aren't together, and right now, I know I can't be around Luca. It's too raw, too painful. But it also tears at me knowing he's hurting too, alone. Jax and Enzo are both here with me. Who does *he* have?

"Where is he?" I ask suddenly, needing to know.

Enzo sighs deeply, his eyes flickering with something unreadable. "There's a guest house on the property. He'll stay there tonight. In the morning, we leave for the next safe house. We don't want you worrying about anything."

My chest tightens with the weight of his words. I don't want Luca to be angry, but I can't just ignore the hurt in my heart either. We need to work this out—before we lose each other for good.

Tears threaten to well in my eyes again, but I fight them back. "I don't know what to do, Enzo."

"You don't have to fix anything right now," he says, his

voice low but steady. "Just take it one step at a time. Let us help you, let us be here for you."

I look up at him, feeling the sincerity in his eyes, and something shifts. Maybe it's not about fixing everything at once. Maybe it's about taking it slow, letting things happen as they're meant to.

Jax slides into view behind Enzo, his grin easy as he puts a hand on my shoulder. "Dinner's ready, Peach. Enzo's going to let us torture him with our favorite movie." He grins and winks, lighting up my dark heart.

"*Legally Blonde!*" I exclaim, and they both chuckle. Enzo adds an eye roll, just to make sure I know he still doesn't agree it's one of the greatest gifts to the world.

The weight on my chest doesn't lift completely, but maybe the night will offer me a small reprieve. I follow them to the couch, trying not to think about the distance between Luca and me, about the unresolved hurt. For now, I just want to enjoy the men who are here, doing everything they can to bring me some comfort, if only for a little while.

It's going to be okay. I have to keep telling myself that.

Jax and Enzo carry in several arranged platters of snacks and appetizers. Enzo commands me to take the middle of the couch while he pours a glass of my favorite wine.

"Sit," he orders, his tone playful but firm.

"Bossy."

He winks at me. "My specialty."

Jax brings three steaming bowls of the most amazing combination of ingredients.

The one. The only. Lobster risotto.

Enzo takes two of the bowls, giving one to me before

sitting next to me. Jax starts the movie and retrieves his wine-glass from the mantle, lip-syncing to "Perfect Day" and dancing his way over to the couch with a very drawn-out shoulder shimmy. Even Enzo has to laugh.

I nearly pass out from my first delicious mouthful. Enzo was right. It's life-changing. I'll never see the world the same way again.

Jax takes our empty bowls, and Enzo refills my glass. "Babe, you have some competition in the kitchen," I tease Jax when he returns. "Seems you're not the only chef who can give me a full-on mouth-gasm with their food."

He chuckles as he resettles on the couch, his ever-present cockiness evident in his voice. "Peach, if anyone but me gives you a mouth-gasm, I'll shoot the poor bastard in the head and fuck you right on top of his dead body."

I burst into laughter, shaking my head at how morbid he can be. "God, you're twisted."

"You should know—I have no competition." He circles my throat and pulls me into a quick kiss. "It's me giving you that mouth-gasm, baby. That's my lobster risotto they made, so they'll live to see another day."

Jax stretches out at one end of the couch, his legs draped across Enzo's lap. I'm perfectly squished in the cozy space between them, my legs hanging over Jax's as Enzo covers us all with my blanket.

The movie plays, and Jax and I continue torturing Enzo by reciting every iconic Jennifer Coolidge line. He massages my hand, then Jax's feet, before crumpling his forehead at the "bend-and-snap" scene.

"How can you like this so much?" he groans.

"First of all," Jax begins, taking a fresh bubblegum-flavored sucker from his mouth, "Elle Woods is a Gemini with a double Capricorn moon. And her signature color is pink. We're practically twins."

Enzo is secretly into it. By the time the big courtroom reveal happens, he gasps when (*spoiler alert*) a perm takes down the criminal.

"Damn, I never would have guessed," he scoffs, then rolls his eyes when he catches Jax and me watching him instead of the movie. "Oh, get over it."

Jax convinces Enzo that the only way I might ever smile again is for him to practice the "bend and snap" with us. Enzo nails it perfectly on the third try, and when my face hurts from laughing, he picks me up with his hands under my ass.

I circle his waist with my legs and wrap my arms around his neck. "I hope this proves I'll do anything for you, Delaney Caputo." He kisses me with a swipe of his tongue that sends my stomach into cartwheels. "If that means I have to suffer through a pink cinematic trainwreck with the mob's new queen and its most lethal Fixer, I'll do it."

I can't help but smile. "I accept this level of devotion and nothing less." I return his kiss, deepening it, running my fingers through his hair.

"You deserve nothing less." The sudden seriousness in his eyes softens the lightheartedness, if only for a moment. Then he kisses my nose.

Jax runs his warm hand over my exposed ass cheek, squeezing with an appreciative grunt. His hand slides down, and based on Enzo's reaction, I'd bet he helped himself to a nice handful of Enzo's cock as well.

"I think we've all earned some dessert." Jax kisses Enzo's cheek, then raises his eyebrows in some lame secret signal.

"Oh, dessert time," Enzo catches on, grinning.

"What's for dessert?" I ask, looking between them with suspicion.

They both grin wickedly.

"You'll see."

Thirty-One

Enzo carries me to my room, then carefully sets my feet on the floor. He smiles when I cross my arms and furrow my brow. "You're so fucking cute when you're trying to be pissed."

"I am pissed." I put as much fire as I can into my answer, but he knows it's bullshit.

He stands behind me, pulling me to him and I feel how hard he is. His hand covers my throat and his thumb presses against my pulse. "Excited. Intrigued. Aroused. But not pissed, angel." He kisses my cheek and disappears to the closet. "Stay put."

I hear a drawer or two open, then close before he returns with a thin, silk nightgown. It looks so small in his large hands and it's a beautiful shade of magenta. One of my favorite colors. It's just above knee length with a revealing slit up one side. Trimmed in matching lace with thin straps. It's so pretty.

"Arms up, beautiful." Enzo's voice is low and husky and floods through me.

He removes Jax's shirt and it drops to the floor. His thumbs gently run over my pebbled nipples, and I suck in a breath. He helps me into the nightgown, his hands slowly mapping my curves with appreciation.

"You won't need these." He whispers against the shell of my ear. With his hands splayed on my hips, he slowly drags my panties down, kneeling as he goes. I step out of them, and he firmly rubs each of my ass cheeks, massaging them and moving his strong hands in a circle. "Fuck, Delaney." He kisses one side, his grip firmer as he keeps rubbing my ass. He peppers kisses on the other side before he stands and spins me to face him. "I'm going to need to be in this ass soon."

"Holy shit."

His body pushes me against the counter. His hand holds the back of my neck as one holds my thigh, lifting my leg so he can grind his hard cock against my bare pussy. Enzo's tongue pushes into my mouth and I whimper into his. "Thank fuck, Jax needs a few minutes to get ready."

I chuckle and he moves to my jaw, then my neck. His dick sliding against me. He lowers one of the straps of my nighty and sucks on my nipple. I bow my back and drop my head. Scratching my nails against his scalp as he lights my body on fire.

He drops my leg and lowers the other strap, exposing both breasts and lavishing them with his hands and skillful mouth. "Enzo," I pant, wanting him to touch me but my plea makes him pull away. Fixing the straps and helping me stand up straight again.

"Just one more final touch." He raises my hand, kissing my knuckles and opens a drawer next to us.

I smile and shake my head at the contents. "Do you guys have lube stashed in every corner of this house?"

"Pretty much." He smirks, looking through the drawer for

something specific. He pockets a small bottle then retrieves a peach color tube that looks like lip gloss. "Turn around."

I watch in the mirror as he squeezes a small amount of product onto his thick middle finger, and I can only hope he's about to put me out of my misery and slide that into my wanting pussy.

"Lift your gown so I can see that pretty cunt," Enzo commands, his voice steady and firm. He exudes control, and I feel myself surrendering to it, letting go of every thought as his will becomes my own.

I do as I'm told, the soft fabric brushing against my skin as I raise the gown. A low, approving moan rumbles in his throat, and I shiver under his gaze. Reaching around me with one hand, he uses two fingers to part my folds gently. His middle finger brushes against my clit, spreading a clear gel that immediately warms and tingles as it touches me.

"Oh, fuck yes," I whisper, my voice trembling as I lean back against him, my head resting on his shoulder. My eyes flutter shut, and a wave of pleasure courses through me.

It feels surreal—like dreams really do come true.

Enzo continues to circle my clit with slow, deliberate movements, the gel amplifying every sensation. His touch is firm but teasing, dipping just inside me before retreating, leaving me desperate for more.

"Let's go," he murmurs, pulling his finger away. I gasp at the loss of contact, but before I can protest, he presses his finger to my bottom lip, coating it with my arousal. His slate-gray eyes meet mine in the mirror, dark with desire. "Don't lick your lips," he warns, his tone carrying a promise of punishment if I disobey. The temptation to test him flits through my mind, but the anticipation of what's to come outweighs it.

Taking my hand, he leads me to the table where Jax is arranging a platter of sliced peaches and a small bowl of caramel. There's a single chair with a suctioned bar and a soft pillow at one end. The setup feels both elaborate and intimate.

"Jax says there's only one way you like to drink bourbon," Enzo says, his lips quirking into a smirk as he hands me over to Jax.

Jax holds a bottle of dark-amber bourbon in one hand, his gaze traveling the length of my body. He takes a slow swig, then steps closer, gripping my hair and tilting my head back. His mouth crashes against mine, the taste of bourbon and heat igniting something deep within me.

We both moan—his low and guttural, appreciating the gift Enzo left for him on my lips. As the bourbon trickles from the corner of my mouth, Jax doesn't let a single drop go to waste. His tongue follows the trail, licking me clean before he pulls back, his dark-brown eyes smoldering.

"On the table, baby," he commands, his voice rough but full of promise.

The liquor warms me from the inside out, and the gel Enzo used between my legs has my clit pulsing with need. I already know that as soon as Jax's mouth touches me, I'll come undone.

Jax places the bourbon on the table, revealing the carefully arranged platter of peaches and caramel. Enzo adds a bottle of lube to the mix, and together they move to either side of me. Enzo lifts the hem of my nightgown, ensuring it doesn't bunch beneath me as Jax gently helps me onto the table.

"Lay down, arms above your head, angel," Enzo instructs, his tone soft but commanding.

I rest my head on the pillow, my arms reaching for the bar

suctioned to the table. Before I can process what's happening, a pair of soft wrist cuffs are secured around my wrists, fastening me to the bar. My heart pounds, both from the vulnerability and the undeniable thrill of what's about to happen.

Jax picks up a slice of peach from the platter, popping it into his mouth with a smirk at Enzo who grabs Jax's neck and pulls him into a kiss. They share a glance—something unspoken but charged passing between them. Jax licks his thumb clean, his cocky grin firmly in place.

Enzo's warm hands trail up my thighs, spreading them gently. "Let your knees fall to the side, angel," he murmurs.

I comply, my breath hitching as their gazes roam over my exposed body. The hem of my nightgown rests high on my hips, leaving me completely bare beneath their scrutiny.

Enzo takes a seat in the chair positioned at the end of the table, his large hands caressing the soft skin of my inner thighs. "You have all the control here, Delaney," he says, his voice low and soothing. "If you want us to stop, just say it. Okay?"

He leans forward to kiss my leg, his lips warm and gentle against my skin. The intimacy of the gesture contrasts sharply with the raw heat in the room.

Jax's hands move to my breasts, kneading them through the silk of my nightgown before pinching one nipple, sending a jolt of pleasure straight to my core. My back arches instinctively, a soft moan escaping me.

"Words, Peach," Jax urges gently. "If you want us to stop, we need to hear you say it."

I smirk despite the haze of desire clouding my mind. "Should I use a safe word? Like spatula?"

Enzo chuckles, his grin matching mine, while Jax rolls his

eyes. Their banter is grounding, a reminder of the trust woven into this moment.

"Just relax, okay?" Enzo says, his gaze holding mine. His gray eyes are intense, filled with desire and reassurance.

Jax steps to Enzo's side, watching as his hands slide up the back of Jax's legs. Enzo leans forward, pressing soft kisses to Jax's abdomen, inching lower with each one. Jax's hands thread into Enzo's dark hair, his fingers tightening as he tilts his head back, his breath hitching.

The waistband of Jax's pants dips lower on one side, revealing the deep V of his pelvis. Enzo's lips trace the lines of his hips, his tongue darting out to taste his skin.

"Fuck, that feels good," Jax groans, his voice rough with need.

Enzo doesn't respond, his focus unbroken as he moves to the other side, the tension thickening as the fabric lowers further. The dark trail of hair leading downward grows more visible, teasing what's to come.

When Jax's pants finally drop, Enzo takes him fully into his mouth in one swift motion. A deep, guttural moan escapes Jax as Enzo works him skillfully, his hand gripping the base as his tongue swirls along the shaft. Jax's stomach muscles clench, and his hands tighten in Enzo's hair.

"Christ, Enz," Jax breathes, his body trembling under the assault of pleasure.

Enzo licks a long, deliberate line up Jax's length before pausing to drizzle a spoonful of warm caramel syrup over him. The rich amber liquid glides down Jax's skin, and Enzo follows its path with his tongue, licking him clean as Jax groans above him.

When Enzo stands, his lips find mine in a slow, intoxicating kiss. The taste of caramel lingers on his tongue, mingling with the heat of his breath. My body reacts instinctively, my back arching off the table as I press closer to him.

Jax moves to my side, his breath warm against my skin as he blows gently over my center. I let out a soft moan, and Enzo swallows the sound, deepening our kiss. The tension between us crackles, and when Enzo finally pulls back, I'm left panting, my chest heaving.

He sits up, his hands braced on either side of me. My gaze drops to where Jax is behind him, his hand sliding into Enzo's pants to stroke him. Enzo's head falls forward, a groan rumbling in his throat.

"Let me see," I whisper, my voice thick with desire.

Enzo's gaze locks with mine, his thumb brushing over my bottom lip. "You want to see my pretty dick, angel?"

I nod, my tongue darting out to wet my lips. His finger slips into my mouth, and I suck on it, my eyes never leaving his.

Jax lowers Enzo's pants, and his heavy cock falls free, brushing against my exposed core. The sensation sends a jolt of electricity through me, and I gasp, my body trembling.

Jax's hand wraps around Enzo, stroking him slowly as his lips trail over Enzo's shoulders. With a wicked grin, Jax slaps Enzo's cock against my clit, the rhythm teasing and torturous. Each tap sends shockwaves of pleasure through me, and my legs twitch involuntarily.

Enzo's grip on my jaw tightens, his pupils blown wide as he groans. "We're going to taste so fucking good together."

Turning to face Jax, Enzo commands, "Sit." Jax immediately obeys, sinking into the chair and pulling Enzo's cock into his mouth. His movements are eager, his head bobbing as he takes Enzo in deeply, eliciting another moan.

"Can you taste her pussy on me, baby?" Enzo asks, his voice hoarse with pleasure.

Jax pauses long enough to hum an answer, but Enzo doesn't let him linger. He pulls back, stepping aside and gesturing for Jax to move closer to me.

"Taste her for yourself," Enzo says, his voice low and deliberate.

Jax's eyes darken as he reaches for the spoon of warm caramel. Holding my gaze, he lets the syrup drip onto my center, the warmth spreading over my sensitive skin. The first touch of his tongue is slow, deliberate, and utterly maddening. He keeps his eyes on mine, the heat in his stare making my breath hitch.

Stars dance behind my closed eyelids as Jax's tongue swirls around my clit, his movements purposeful and reverent. My pulse thrums in time with his strokes, the pleasure building with each passing second.

"She's sweet, isn't she?" Enzo murmurs, lowering the strap of my nightgown to expose one breast. He picks up a partially frozen peach slice from the platter and presses it against my nipple. The cold shock makes me gasp, and he immediately soothes the sensitive skin with his warm mouth.

Jax's worshipful attention on my pussy combined with Enzo's skilled ministrations to my breast sends me spiraling. My moans fill the room, unrestrained and desperate. I feel like I'm on the edge of falling into the best pleasure of my life.

Enzo shifts his attention from my breast to my other nipple, his mouth warm and wet as he licks and sucks. The frozen peach slice drips slightly against my skin, the cold trailing down to where Jax's tongue is working magic. The sensations collide, a heady mix of heat and chill that leaves me trembling.

Jax pauses just long enough to whisper against my skin, "So fucking sweet, Peach." His voice is rough, reverent, and it sends another wave of arousal crashing over me.

Enzo straightens, watching Jax as he devours me. His gray eyes darken, the intensity of his gaze making my breath catch. He reaches into his pocket, retrieving a bottle of lube and squeezing a small amount onto his palm. With deliberate movements, he strokes himself, his head falling back as he exhales sharply.

"Fuck, you're beautiful like this," Enzo says, his voice thick with desire. "Spread out for us, taking every touch we give you."

Jax lifts his head, his lips glistening as he grins up at Enzo. "She's fucking perfect," he says, his fingers sliding inside me with ease. My back arches off the table as he curls them just right, hitting that spot that makes me see stars.

"Don't stop," I gasp, the words spilling from me without thought. My hands tug against the cuffs securing me to the bar, desperate for something to hold onto.

Enzo chuckles low in his throat. "She's so eager, isn't she?" His tone is teasing, but the hunger in his eyes is undeniable.

"Fuck." Enzo opens his mouth and exhales his pleasure. Fisting Jax's hair again, Enzo pulls him off me, and I complain.

"You want his mouth back, angel?" Enzo asks but doesn't wait for my answer. He licks Jax's lips and then kisses him deeply, still sliding his hand along his cock. "Let's cool your little Peach down first. Then I'll let you have your dessert back." Enzo nods to the plate, and Jax takes a frozen slice of fruit.

I anticipate it on my pussy, but the intensity of it touching me wrenches a pleasured yelp. He rubs it around me, and I move my hips, only to have Jax stop and hold me still with one hand. "Don't move, Peach."

He keeps his grip on me and watches me while he rubs the frozen peach around my clit. He's going to fucking make me come with it, and one side of his mouth lifts when he sees I realize it. "Yeah, you're going to come for us, Dels. So fucking much." Within seconds, the orgasm washes over me in warm waves. I arch my back at the intensity, heightened by the cream Enzo prepared me with.

"Goddamn, that's the prettiest thing I've ever watched." Jax makes sure to run the cold peach slowly up my slit, making my legs twitch when he flicks it on my throbbing clit. He feeds the peach, covered in my juices, to Enzo, who makes sure to suck Jax's fingers as he takes it.

"Fuck, she tastes sweeter than I thought she ever could," Enzo says, chewing the peach and swallowing it, then leaning down to kiss Jax. "Are you ready to have some cream with your peach?" Enzo bites Jax's lip, tugging on it.

Jax whimpers his answer and I nearly lose it at the sound.

"Give me your fingers." Enzo grabs the lube and drips it onto three of Jax's fingers. "Now get your mouth on her cunt and show me how badly you want to taste us." Enzo fists Jax's hair and pushes his face to my pussy.

Jax eats like he's been starving for a month. I call out... for anyone. Jax. Enzo. God.

Enzo pumps his hand along his cock, watching Jax and my face. "Don't come, Delaney. Not until I tell you that you can come," he commands, panting as his arousal builds. It's now that I realize what's happening.

It's a scene from one of my books—the billionaire boss and ex-fiancé crossover story. They're recreating it, adding their own twist with the peaches and caramel sauce. The realization sends a shiver through me, the line between fantasy and reality blurring in the most delicious way.

I moan and close my eyes, pulling on the cuffs as pleasure coils tight in my belly.

"I'll spank that pretty cunt for being a brat, so don't fucking push me, Delaney," Enzo warns, his grip firm on Jax's hair as he devours me. The threat—a tantalizing promise—makes me tremble. "Jax, oh God." Enzo's head falls back, his mouth open as he groans. His hips pulse forward, his cock sliding through his hand.

"Ah, fuck, Jax. Give me another one." His voice is hoarse, and I know he's teetering on the edge, just as I am.

Jax's fingers press against Enzo's ass, sliding in smoothly. The deep groan from Enzo matches the mounting pleasure building inside me.

"Please," I cry out as Jax nips at my clit, the swelling orgasm impossible to hold back. His expert mouth and fingers combined with Enzo's commanding presence have me unraveling.

"You want his fingers too?" Enzo asks, his voice heavy with approval.

I nod, my wrists straining against the cuffs. "Yes. Please."

"Go ahead, baby," Enzo grants permission. "You're giving me three—let's give our queen three as well."

It's heaven and hell wrapped into one. Jax can make me come in thirty seconds flat, and we've timed it before. Yet, the ache between my legs is insatiable, and I want nothing more than to let go.

Jax curls his fingers inside me, his tongue maintaining its relentless rhythm. The tempo builds as my legs tremble uncontrollably. "Oh my God," I whisper, squeezing my eyes shut as I teeter on the brink. "I'm going to—"

"I'm warning you, angel." Enzo's voice cuts through, tight and commanding. "Not yet, baby." He fists Jax's hair, guiding his movements. "Fuck." His breathing grows ragged as he works his cock faster, his knuckles white with the effort.

"Enzo..." My voice is a desperate plea.

"I know, angel. Just—ah." Enzo's words dissolve into a guttural groan as he pulls Jax's head back by his fisted hair, spilling his warm release against my pussy. The sensation is overwhelming, the wet heat pushing me closer to the edge.

"Oh, fuck, Jax. Harder," Enzo gasps, shuddering as the last waves of his orgasm crash over him. Jax works his ass and keeps his pulsing fingers in my pussy. This man can do anything.

I'm writhing, pulling against the cuffs, the ache for release unbearable. "Enzo, please. Let me come. Please," I beg, my voice cracking with need.

Enzo smirks, his hand still tangled in Jax's hair. "Now eat that pussy drenched in my cum, Jax. Drink your peaches and cream until she drowns you."

Jax doesn't hesitate, diving back in with renewed fervor. If I thought he was devouring me before, I was sorely mistaken. His tongue is relentless, his fingers pistoning into me deeper, harder. My legs tremble violently, the pleasure teetering on the edge of pain.

"Enzo, please," I cry out, my walls tightening around Jax's fingers. "Let me come. Please."

"You're so pretty when you beg," Enzo murmurs, leaning over me. He runs a lubed finger up the curve of my ass, pressing gently against my hole. His other hand cups my breast, squeezing as his finger slides into me.

"You can come, angel," he finally allows, his voice a low growl. "Come while I finger your pretty ass and get it ready for my big cock."

I nearly go into orbit.

"The next time I fuck you, I'm going to bury my dick in your ass, angel," Enzo promises, his voice dripping with raw need. His words are a spark, igniting the orgasm that crashes over me like a tidal wave. My body tightens around Jax's fingers, trembling with every stroke as wave after wave of pleasure consumes me.

They play my body like an instrument, coaxing every last ounce of pleasure from me with perfect precision. I lose all sense of time, my cries filling the room as my hips move instinctively, seeking more.

"Give us another one, angel," Enzo commands, his tone leaving no room for argument.

"Holy shit," I gasp as his mouth closes over my breast, his teeth grazing my nipple while Jax's tongue keeps its relentless pace. My body obeys their demand, another orgasm barreling through me, leaving me breathless and boneless on the table.

"That's it," Enzo praises, his voice thick with satisfaction as he pulls his finger from me. Jax replaces it seamlessly, keeping me full as his mouth continues to worship me. The sensations are overwhelming—too much, yet not enough all at once.

"Jax," I whimper, my hands straining against the cuffs as his teeth graze my clit, sending a sharp jolt of pleasure through me. "I can't."

"You can," Jax replies, his rich brown eyes locking with mine. "One more, baby. Fall over the edge with me, Dels."

Enzo drops to his knees. His mouth devouring Jax who takes a second to relish in the pleasure. His mouth drops open as a gasp leaves him. He closes his eyes before opening them and returning his attention to me.

The edge feels razor-thin, my body trembling violently as Jax's fingers curl inside me, hitting that perfect spot. His tongue flicks over my clit with maddening precision, coaxing the orgasm he wants from me.

"Come with me, Peach," Jax murmurs, his voice muffled against my skin as he grunts against Enzo's mouth and tongue working his cock. His words are my undoing.

My body shatters, the orgasm ripping through me with an intensity that leaves me sobbing with relief. Stars burst behind my eyelids, and I arch off the table, every nerve ending alight. Jax doesn't stop, his mouth and fingers milking every last tremor from me until I'm trembling, spent, and utterly broken.

"Fuck me," Jax breathes, sitting back in the chair, his chest rising and falling rapidly.

I blink, struggling to focus as my vision clears. Enzo stands, his cock still hard as he drags it along my swollen core, drawing a soft moan from me.

My vagina is a whore. I've been wrecked by orgasms, yet my pussy clenches, hungry for another.

Enzo leans over me, his hand sliding under my neck as he kisses me deeply. Jax's cum is still in his mouth, and the salty tang mixes with the taste of my arousal. I moan into the kiss, my body reacting instinctively, craving their touch despite being utterly spent.

Cum drips from the corner of my mouth, just like the bourbon earlier. Jax leans over, his thumb swiping the droplet before pressing it to my lips. I suck it clean without hesitation, and his dark-brown eyes smolder with heat.

"Good girl," Jax murmurs, his voice full of approval. His lips find mine, his kiss hungry as he devours me, tasting both of us on my tongue.

Enzo shifts lower, positioning himself at my entrance. His hands grip my hips, his strength undeniable as he pulls me to the edge of the table. With one powerful thrust, he buries himself inside me, filling me completely.

The stretch burns in the best possible way, and I cry out, my hands gripping the bar above me. "Oh, God. Enzo."

"You take me so well, angel," he growls, his grip tightening on my hips as he sets a punishing rhythm. Each thrust drives me higher, the pleasure overwhelming after everything they've already given me.

Jax watches from above, his hand stroking my cheek. "Look at you, Peach. So fucking perfect for us."

Their touches linger like a brand on my skin, I realize something undeniable: with them, I don't just feel alive—I feel claimed, seen, and utterly unstoppable. But as I take Enzo's pounding cock, wholly spent but craving–needing more, a small, nagging thought whispers in the back of my mind: we're not complete yet. And I feel that vacancy on the other side of me, knowing only one person can make us whole.

Thirty-Two

The house is quieter than usual this morning. Maybe it's the looming weight of the will reading tomorrow, or maybe it's the silence after last night's chaos, but either way, the tension is thick—and so are my sore muscles. My mind is running in circles, trying to piece together the puzzle of my mother's death. I still don't have the answers I need, and it's driving me insane.

But there's a flicker of warmth I can't push away. Last night—Jax and Enzo—they took care of me. And I mean really took care of me. Lobster risotto. My favorite movie. Laughter. And then, the kind of love that makes me feel seen, heard, and cherished. For the first time in a long while, I felt cared for, like I mattered in a world that's constantly shifting under my feet.

I can't help but smile at the memory, even as the anxiety bubbles under the surface about moving on to our next safe house. But I can push that away for now. For a moment, I let myself hold on to the feeling of being surrounded by the men I love, their hands on me, their attention focused on me like nothing else mattered.

Jax's lighthearted presence helps more than he probably

realizes. As I sit on the kitchen counter, my legs dangling and my head spinning with a thousand worries, he's in his element. Breakfast sandwiches.

The smell of eggs and bacon fills the kitchen, and I can't help but relax a little. Jax moves around with an easy grace, making it all look so effortless, like the chaos in my head doesn't even touch him. He doesn't hesitate, doesn't overthink things—he just does.

"You're good at this," I say, my voice soft as I watch him work. "I think you missed your calling. You should've been a chef instead of a professional troublemaker."

He flashes me that grin of his—the one that always gets under my skin in the best way. "Nah, I think I like being your favorite troublemaker better. Food's just a bonus."

I chuckle, leaning back on my hands, allowing myself a moment of peace. It's easy with Jax. It's like I can breathe without all the weight of everything pressing on me. He makes everything feel simpler, even when the world is anything but.

I let myself relax for a second, but as the last of the sandwiches are packed, the knot in my stomach returns, knowing we'll all be heading out soon. That means I'll have to face Luca after yesterday.

"Ugh, I hate this," I huff, partly whining. I lay back on the cold marble counter with my arms spread wide.

Jax stands between my legs and slides me closer to him, then leans down and places kisses on my stomach. "I'll be right here with you the whole time, okay, baby?"

He holds out his hands, and I reluctantly take them. Pulling me up, he wraps a strong arm around my waist. His other hand threads through my long hair, gripping the back of my neck. His kiss is reassuring and confident before he breaks away, resting his forehead against mine.

"You're the strongest woman I know, Peach," he says, his eyes softening as he watches me. "Don't let this mess with your head."

I take a deep breath, nodding against his chest. "I just want to get it right this time."

Jax pulls back slightly to look me in the eyes, his gaze soft but steady. "We're in this together, okay? Just... take it one step at a time."

The SUV is packed, and we're standing by it, waiting. Jax's arm is around me, grounding me. His warmth settles me, and for a brief moment, I can breathe easy, even though everything feels like it's about to come apart.

The front door opens, and the sound of footsteps on gravel breaks the silence. I don't have to look up to know it's Luca and Enzo coming out. My stomach tightens just thinking about it—the tension, the things we haven't said, and the things we did say.

Jax's arm around my waist gives me a sense of security, but when Enzo and Luca come into view, I feel like I'm standing on the edge of a cliff.

Enzo takes Luca's suitcase and gives me a wink as he walks to the back of the SUV. Luca shoves his hands in his pockets and doesn't look at me. His eyes are bloodshot, and he looks terrible. The wall between us is too high to climb over. My heart aches at the sight of him, but it also hurts because I know he's the one who put it there.

Luca opens his mouth, then pauses, like he's weighing what he's about to say. Finally, he speaks in a voice that's too soft, too full of regret. "I'm sorry," he says, his eyes still on the gravel. "There's no excuse for what I did. I fucked up. I said things"—he flinches—"did things... that are unforgivable." He finally looks up at me, and another crack forms in my heart. "It'll never happen again."

His words hang between us, heavy with meaning. My mouth opens, but no words come out. There's so much I want to say, but the lump in my throat won't let me. Before I can find my voice, he turns, walking to the SUV and getting in without another word. It feels like a door slamming shut between us.

Jax's arm tightens around me, and I let myself lean into him.

Enzo shuts the back of the SUV and gives me a kiss on my head. "Are you okay?" he asks, his eyes searching mine.

I nod, keeping my voice steady even though everything feels broken inside me. "Yeah," I whisper. "I'm fine."

Jax opens the back door for me, and I slide into the seat. He follows in beside me, his presence a silent comfort. The SUV starts up, and we begin to drive, the tires humming against the road as the scenery changes.

I close my eyes for a second, just trying to breathe. The faint scent of Luca's cologne lingers just in front of me, but it feels like he's a million miles away. It's like I'm standing between two worlds—one with him, one without.

The plan from here is simple: drive for an hour, then board Enzo's private jet. We lost a day letting him rest after nearly being blown up and then drinking half the river. Honestly, I'm thankful we don't have to spend a whole day driving. The plane ride to Wisconsin will only be a few hours, so I'll have plenty of time to lose my mind thinking about the reading of my father's will tomorrow.

As the miles pass, the tension between Luca and me remains thick. We haven't said a word to each other since we left the house, and I'm not sure what to say. My mind keeps flashing back to everything that's been left unsaid between us.

Luca, ever vigilant, is the first to break the silence.

"Someone's tailing us," he mutters, his voice low but sharp as he points to his side-view mirror.

Instinctively, I glance back, like I have any idea what it looks like when a car is tailing you. To me, it just looks like other cars on the road, driving like we are.

Jax, who's been clearing a row of colorful blocks on his phone, tilts his head to get a better look, then bursts out laughing. "It's Marco Serrano. That fucking idiot."

They mentioned him yesterday when we were looking at the photographs. Marco Serrano is the underboss they've been keeping an eye on, hoping he would lead them to the person trying to wipe me off the planet.

"We can't let him follow us to the airfield," Enzo says, his tone clipped and focused as he drives. "He can't know where we're going."

I turn toward Jax, my mind already clicking through options. "You know, we could always do my idea." I suggest, a smirk forming. "Use me as bait."

Luca's jaw tightens at the suggestion. He doesn't respond, but I catch the sharp tick in his muscles.

Jax looks at me, his grin widening as he picks up on the plan. "I love how your mind works, Peach. Yeah, let's do it. He's dumb enough to follow you on a spur-of-the-moment decision."

Enzo looks between the two of us in the rearview mirror

but says nothing, trusting our judgment. He exits the highway and turns toward a small gas station just up ahead.

Sure enough, Marco Serrano follows. He pulls into the other side of the gas station, like that makes him invisible.

"We wait here," Jax says, nodding toward the station. "You go to the bathroom, and when Marco follows you like the idiot he is, we'll take care of it."

"Okay." I give Jax a wink as I grab my phone and stick it in my back pocket. "I'll be right back," I say, pushing open the door and stepping out of the SUV.

I walk toward the station with deliberate steps, making sure to glance back over my shoulder as my guys pretend to pump gas at the SUV. I can feel Marco's eyes on me, his presence like an itch I can't scratch.

I head inside, pretending to ask for the bathroom key. With it in hand, I step back out, making a show of looking casual, even tossing my hair over my shoulder as I head toward the bathrooms at the back of the building. Marco doesn't even try to hide—he's leaning against the wall, trying to look nonchalant but failing miserably.

When I round the corner where the bathrooms are, I stop, leaning casually against the wall with my arms crossed. A devilish grin spreads across my face.

This is kind of fun.

Marco rounds the corner, and I swear he yelps like a startled puppy. What kind of kidnapper yelps?

"Hey there," I purr, my fist striking out for his nose before he can respond. Marco stumbles back with a grunt, and before he can recover, Jax and Luca are there, flanking him like two imposing vices.

They grab Marco with practiced ease, pinning his arms as

Jax shoves something in his mouth to keep him from yelling out. Enzo pulls up in the SUV, the back already open. In one smooth motion, they shove Marco inside and Luca jumps in too, slamming the door before anyone can notice.

I can't help but feel a little thrill at the efficiency of the plan. I toss a glance at Jax, who's already wiping his hands clean with a smile.

"Nice work, Peach. If you were my bait, I'd happily let myself be captured by you." He winks.

"Okay, but I do actually have to use the bathroom, so I'll be right back."

When I return a moment later, feeling a little grungy from the less-than-hygienic gas station bathroom, the guys are about to shut the back of the SUV again. Curious to see how they subdued Marco, I peek in and immediately burst out laughing.

"Don't worry, it's clean," Jax says, grinning like a cat that got the cream.

"A peach choke ball? Are you serious? That's all you guys have to kidnap him with?" I fold my arms over my chest, pretending to be offended. "How come I didn't get a choke ball?"

Jax shrugs, the mischief twinkling in his brown eyes as we climb back into the vehicle. "We can definitely recreate your kidnapping if you'd like to make some modifications to the abduction."

Enzo chuckles from the driver's seat, glancing at me in the rearview mirror. "I'm sure we can arrange something."

"I'm absolutely into primal play, Peach," Jax says, his hand resting on my knee. "If you ever give me the 'if you catch me, you can fuck me' line, I might die on the spot from happiness."

"Hmm, noted." I raise an eyebrow. "You just had that choke ball in your bag? For emergencies?"

Jax's grin turns deadly. "It's Enzo's. Ask him."

Enzo chokes on his coffee, coughing as he turns red. "It was a birthday present. Last year."

"Hmm, also noted." I glance back at our unconscious passenger, bound, and gagged, before settling back into my seat next to Jax. Today is going to be an interesting day.

Thirty-Three

If I don't think about it too much, I could pretend I'm walking up the steps to a private jet that is going to drop me off in Fiji instead of Kenosha, Wisconsin. Not that there is anything wrong with Kenosha, but it's only an hour from Chicago, where tomorrow my fate will be sealed, and I'll inherit the mafia.

I would much rather be in Fiji.

The jet is charcoal gray and lavish. It's very Enzo—polished and sophisticated, luxurious but not flashy. Enzo and Luca carried our unconscious companion in first. There's a bedroom in the back of the plane... yes, mile-high club, here I come. Except we have a short, balding underboss in there with a peach choke ball in his mouth. Not exactly setting the sexy mood.

I ascend the stairs with Jax behind me, carrying my bookbag. The pilots stow our luggage while a cabin attendant greets us inside, and I immediately roll my eyes.

You've got to be kidding me. The sexy stewardess cliché? Really?

She's about my height and age, with blonde hair styled back in a low, neat bun. Her uniform is a gray pencil skirt and vest over a white button-down shirt with short sleeves. The top few buttons are open, revealing a healthy amount of cleavage. They must not have had her size when she ordered her uniform because it's so tight she looks like she was poured into it. She stands perfectly on a pair of black heels and is sporting an obnoxiously bright shade of red lipstick.

My guess is she's hoping to smear it all over at least one of their dicks before the flight is over.

She looks at me with a close-lipped smile, a short nod followed by a "hm," and it instantly sets me on fire. I'd bet my ass she isn't going to greet Jax that way.

Sure enough, as soon as she sees him, she all but lays down and opens her legs.

"Mr. Donovan," she says, practically sucking Jax's cock with her eyes as he steps in behind me. "A pleasure to have you flying with Mr. Vincenzi today." She rubs her hand down his forearm and places her hand over his on my bookbag handle. "I'd *love* to take this from you."

Interpretation: I'd love to put your cock in every hole I have, Mr. Donovan.

She even goes as far as to bat her fucking eyelashes.

Bonus points for Jax when he moves out of her reach like she's infected with the plague.

"Where is my spatula?" I mutter calmly, looking around me. Jax lifts the corner of his mouth in a smirk, but it vanishes quickly when he looks back at the stewardess. Before he opens his mouth to address her, I do.

"Look, honey," I begin, stepping between her and Jax. She raises a perfectly plucked eyebrow at me, clearly not a fan of my presence on the plane. "There won't be any titty-fucking on today's flight, so you can put the girls away. And if you touch one of them again, I'll break each one of your little manicured nails right off your fingers and then shove them up your bleached little asshole. Got it?"

She scoffs, but I walk past her into the cabin, sitting down in one of the seats a little too hard. I cross my arms and look out the window, pissed at what they probably did with that woman on previous flights. And then they have the audacity to have her on this flight with me here as well.

I know we haven't really settled everything between us. We haven't talked about what anything means for us beyond not dying until tomorrow. They said they love me—still, they love me—and then bring me on a plane with one of their flings.

"Peach," Jax says, sitting down and immediately turning to me with a pleading voice. At the same time, Enzo emerges from the back, with Luca behind him.

When Enzo sees the stewardess, his face turns red, and that familiar look of impending doom settles in his eyes. It's like a switch flips, and his handsome features somehow turn harsher, deadlier, and even more fucking beautiful.

"Why. In the fuck. Are you. On my plane?" he growls, his voice low and dangerous. The poor girl is speechless. She opens her mouth, then closes it again like a fish gulping water.

"I—I didn't think..." That sex-kitten voice is gone, and now she's just scared.

"I warned you. The next time you show up for one of my jobs, I'm breaking your fucking hands." He stalks through the plane.

"Oh," I murmur, more under my breath than anything else, but Jax hears me. "Jinx," I tease. That's basically what I just said. Jax snorts a quick laugh and grabs my knee. Luca stays in the hall, not entering the cabin, leaning casually against the wall. He's so effortlessly handsome it actually hurts to look at him and not get to touch him.

"I t-thought you only meant your Colorado resort," she stammers. "Mr. Vincenzi, I apologize." She's crying now, tears falling down her face as she stumbles back.

"Let me make this crystal fucking clear for you." Every inch of Enzo's six-foot-four frame looms over her like the grim reaper. The pilot and copilot come out of the cockpit, hearing the commotion. "If I ever set eyes on you again, anywhere on this planet, I'm putting a fucking bullet right through your skull." The pilot and copilot retreat into the cockpit hearing death threats. Smart move. "Now get the fuck," Enzo cocks his gun. "off my plane."

Dayum.

She all but sprouts wings and flies down the stairs. I see her stumble a bit in her haste—clearly not accustomed to running for her life in heels. She should practice if she's going to work for mobsters.

Jax leans to me, quietly whispering, "If I had a pussy, it would be soaking wet right now. You know what I mean?"

Despite the irritation that boiled inside me, which is now cooling, I can't help the smirk, "I do actually."

"I'll be right back," Enzo says, casting a dark glance at Luca before looking at me.

"I was going to say, Peach," Jax rubs his thumb along my cheek, his voice soft and teasing, "you don't have to worry about her." He pulls my chin to him for a kiss. "But Enzo's made that crystal clear." With a quick wink, Jax leaves me, heading to the wet bar at the front of the cabin.

The question of what happened lingers on my lips when Enzo returns from the cockpit, looking a little less like death incarnate. He walks the aisle back toward Luca. Without hesitation, Enzo wraps one arm around Luca's waist and cups his face with the other.

"I don't know why they booked her," Enzo says, his voice almost pleading.

"I know, babe," Luca replies, his tone resigned. He grabs Enzo's wrist, pulling his hand gently away. "It's fine." He leans up and kisses Enzo, their movements tender and familiar.

"I'll make sure it doesn't happen again," Enzo reassures him. Luca nods in acknowledgment, his expression softening.

Enzo shifts his attention to me next. "Come here." His tone matches the gentleness he used with Luca.

"I'm fine," I say, half-rolling my eyes.

Enzo huffs and pulls me from my seat, sitting down himself and tugging me into his lap. "Don't lie to me. I know you were angry seeing her. I know how that looked, Delaney."

"What did she do to Luca?" My fingers thread through the hair at the nape of his neck, and my other hand rests on his chest.

"I brought my staff to Colorado for a weekend ski retreat. She was one of the servers hired to tend to the guests. She spent the weekend trying to fuck Luca," Enzo explains, his voice tight. "She ignored his rejections and touched him..." He pauses, his jaw clenching.

Rage builds in my chest. I know where this is going.

"She touched him inappropriately while he slept."

"Oh, I will fucking kill her." My gaze darts out the window, searching for any sign of her. "Give me your gun. Jax taught me how to shoot."

Enzo's smile—a mix of affection and menace—could solve all my problems. "I should have thrown her off the fucking mountain that day like I wanted." He rubs my leg, his anger simmering just under the surface. "I told the agency she's never to work one of my events again."

"You don't need to explain things to me. It's clear she wasn't wanted here."

"But I do, Delaney." His stormy gray eyes meet mine with sincerity. "She didn't greet us when we boarded, or else I would've tossed her ass down the stairs then. She's the kind of woman who works jobs like this so she can sell herself to the rich clients. Fuck a few billionaires, get a couple thousand in tips, and hopefully become a full-time mistress for one of them."

"Hey, I respect the hustle."

"But it's disrespectful to you." He tucks a loose strand of hair behind my ear, his touch lingering. "We wouldn't do that to you, angel." His gaze is almost pleading, and I feel the weight of his words.

I nod and kiss him softly. "Thank you for explaining it." My nose brushes against his as I lean closer. The squeeze of his hand on my thigh and the glimmer in his stormy eyes make my heart flutter. The ever-terrifying Enzo Vincenzi is a closet teddy bear.

The engines roar to life as Jax presses a button, retracting the stairs and sealing us inside the plane. With a message from the pilots, we all take our seats.

I return to mine as Enzo sits across the aisle with Luca. Jax plops down beside me, the two of them acting as a buffer between Luca and me. Fastening his seatbelt, Jax stretches his arms and pulls me close. Propping his feet on the seats across from us, he crosses one ankle over the other, his body a wall of warmth and ease.

"Next time we're on this plane," he whispers against my ear, his breath sending a shiver down my spine, "I'm taking you in the bathroom and eating your sweet pussy."

I smile and turn to him for a quick peck on his full lips. He winks, unwrapping a pink sucker and popping it into his mouth. His masterful tongue rolls the candy around as he fidgets with the wrapper, finally crumpling it in his fist.

One hour into the flight, with three more before we reach Kenosha, Jax and I are engrossed in a fast-moving card game. He accuses me of cheating, as usual. Enzo places a fresh glass of diet soda in front of me with a kiss to the top of my head, then sits next to Luca, his hand possessively resting on Luca's thigh.

Luca is focused on his laptop at the small table in front of him, breaking into our captive's cell phone. Enzo's hand slowly slides upward, his forearm flexing as he teases Luca. I catch the subtle movement and the way Luca's blue eyes flicker with warning before darting to mine. Embarrassed I was caught spying, I look away quickly.

Jax and I start another round. The first cards we lay down are two queens. I slap my hand down before he can, claiming them with a victorious grin.

"How are you so fucking fast?" Jax exclaims, mock-offended.

"I'm just where I'm supposed to be, unlike you." I smirk as we continue laying cards one at a time.

"Not fair. I was locked in the tank... unlawfully, I'll remind you." He grins, laying down double aces and claiming them with a triumphant flourish.

"I'm not talking about prison. You conveniently left Enzo and me to handle a shootout all by ourselves." My tone is teasing, but I know the truth—He and Luca were securing a new vehicle that wasn't riddled with bullets.

Jax sets his cards down, his playful expression hardening into something serious.

"Jax, I was only teasing," I say quickly, reaching for his hand.

"I don't tease when it comes to the people I love being safe." His voice is steady, but there's an edge of intensity. He squeezes my hand gently. "We didn't get a call, and the club's silent alarm didn't alert us, or else we would have fought through hell to get to you. We paused on the bridge, seeing the smoke from the club, and tried to call you both."

Enzo shifts in his seat, his jaw tightening as he exchanges a glance with Jax and me. "But I pushed the silent alarm myself. Are you telling me someone disabled it before the attack? How would they have had the time?"

Luca's fingers freeze on his keyboard. He looks up from his laptop, his face hardening as if processing something monumental. Then he returns to his screen, his fingers flying faster across the keys. After a few moments, he mutters a curse under his breath and slams the laptop shut.

We all stare, waiting for him to explain.

"There was a blackout net cast over the whole fucking town," Luca finally says, his voice low and steady. He pushes the table away and leans forward, resting his elbows on his knees.

"What is a blackout net?" I ask, throwing out the first olive branch since his apology this morning.

Luca's eyes meet mine, and for a moment, the entire world feels like it pauses. He clears his throat, his gaze unwavering. "It's a digital net. A hacker's tool that blocks all signals from coming in and going out. Calls, texts, everything. It's invisible. Completely undetectable."

"So how did you figure that out if it's invisible?"

Luca's jaw tightens, the weight of his next words evident in his posture. "Because... I invented it." He leans back slightly, letting the revelation hang in the air. "And I only showed one other hacker how to do it."

Thirty-Four

The jet touches down, and it's barely lunchtime. A new black SUV waits for us just a few feet away. Jax and Enzo load our captive into the back. He's awake now, drooling, and won't stop trying to talk to us. Apparently, he doesn't understand the purpose of a choke ball.

Luca adds our luggage, and Enzo insists I sit in the front. He doesn't want me close to the underboss in case something happens, so Jax and Luca take the backseat. It's not a far drive to the next safe-house, and the route is beautiful, winding through a serene countryside.

We turn off the main road and pass two decorative gates on either side, each proudly displaying the letter **B** for Bellini—Luca's last name. You can tell this was once a fully functioning farm. The land is still well-maintained, and most of the buildings, including a stable, remain intact. I wonder if there are horses inside. I've never ridden one before.

This is Luca's childhood home—the Bellini farm. It's been in his family for generations. I remember him talking fondly about it. He promised to bring me here one day, though I would have preferred if we were on better terms when he did.

As we pull up to the main farmhouse, its charm is undeniable. The footprint of the original home is surrounded by an expansive two-story upgrade. To the side, a detached four-car garage matches the aesthetic. The buildings are painted white with black accents, creating the quintessential farmhouse look.

Stepping out of the car, I take in the surroundings and inhale the scent of fresh grass. It's lovely here.

Luca wastes no time opening the back of the SUV and dragging Marco onto the ground by his collar. Leaving him on the gravel drive to struggle, Luca retrieves several bags, then strides toward the covered porch. "I'll be inside," he calls back.

Jax grabs the remaining bags, hoists Marco off the ground, and tosses him back into the SUV before slamming the door. Enzo looks at me with a mix of caution and apology, though his expression leaves no room for debate.

I brace myself for whatever he's about to say.

"Don't look at me like that," he begins.

"No, *you* don't look at *me* like that," I snap back, folding my arms over my chest.

"We have to go have a..."

"A *'conversation'* with Mr. Serrano," I finish, grinning as I wrap my arms around his waist. He pulls me into a firm hug. "Just be careful, okay?"

Enzo visibly relaxes, clearly expecting more resistance from me. But I knew this was part of the plan when we decided to nab Marco. They're going to press him for any information they can get.

"Don't worry about us, angel. You'll be okay while we're gone. Luca won't—"

"I'll be fine." Rising on my toes, I kiss him. "Maybe... he and I can talk."

Enzo nods, his gaze softening as it flickers between my eyes.

He seems to decide it's out of his hands because he hugs me tighter, his heartbeat steady against my ear. "We're going to be... a while," he says, stepping back.

Jax gives me a quick, chaste kiss on the cheek before climbing into the passenger seat.

"Where are you going?" I call as Enzo rounds the car to the driver's side.

Jax rolls down the window, hanging his arm out. "Luca has his very own murder barn!" he announces gleefully, like they're heading to an amusement park. Marco's muffled cries from the backseat punctuate his declaration.

"You're incorrigible!" I yell back as the SUV drives off, following the gravel path past the house and deeper into the property.

Turning back to the farmhouse, I take a deep breath and step inside.

The interior exudes warmth. The soft scent of aged wood and leather is instantly inviting. It's almost too cozy, like a home that's been lived in for generations. The kind of place where the floors creak in all the right spots and every corner tells a story.

The walls are lined with framed photos—Luca at various stages of his life. Baby pictures, school portraits, and those awkward teenage years when he looked like he was still learning to walk upright. It's oddly comforting to see him like this, smiling in that way only Luca can. I kind of want to reach through the frame and ruffle his hair, imagining how soft it must have been.

One thing strikes me as odd: there are plenty of photos of Luca with people I can tell are clearly his family, but not a single one of his mother. My finger hovers over one of the frames as I frown. I only met her once—when my father introduced us. Luca had bolted out of the room faster than I've ever seen anyone move and her absence here feels deliberate.

Maybe she wasn't part of the picture for a reason.

That awkward night is burned into my memory—my father trying to present us as a "perfect family." A week later, he casually mentioned their marriage had been annulled. That was the day I packed up and left, determined to avoid Stepmom #6. My first love ruined over a week-long marriage.

I got my own townhouse and learned how to survive on my own. That's when I met Jax. He was... exactly the distraction I needed. And he was very good at it.

Walking past a room with double glass doors, I pause, catching sight of Luca inside. The office is simple—bare walls, a few shelves, and several computers stacked on a desk. He's hunched over a keyboard, fingers flying with the precision of someone who knows exactly what he's doing.

It reminds me of just how skilled those hands are... if you're picking up what I'm putting down.

Ever since he discovered the blackout net, it's like he knows where to find that shadow he's been chasing. He's determined to uncover that final, elusive piece of the puzzle. The intensity in his expression makes me wonder how much of the Luca I used to know is still there—the one who made me laugh until I cried.

I linger for a moment, watching him work. But I can't bring myself to say anything. Not yet. Instead, I head toward the kitchen, my stomach growling like I haven't eaten in days.

The kitchen feels serene, a stark contrast to the rest of the house. It's functional yet personal, with an organized lived-in charm. The fridge is stocked with fresh produce, the bright colors inviting. Someone must have recently arranged every-thing—it looks pristine.

My eyes land on a bundle of fresh basil, vibrant and green, alongside plump cherry tomatoes, and soft mozzarella balls. I grin, knowing exactly what I'll make: penne pasta with toma-toes, mozzarella, and basil.

It's simple but comforting, the first thing I ever learned to cook—taught to me by Luca.

I toss the ingredients together with olive oil, balsamic vine-gar, and a dash of red pepper flakes for flavor. As I take a bite, I'm transported back to that tiny dorm kitchen, where Luca and I used to whip this up between study sessions. It's a bitter-sweet memory of a time when I was utterly, hopelessly in love with him.

And then he broke my heart.

No time like the present to find out why.

Thirty-Five

I walk into Luca's office, balancing two bowls of pasta. I set one down in front of him, and he doesn't move for a second, still staring at the computer screen. His fingers hover over the keys, frozen.

He closes his eyes, and I know exactly what's happening. Every memory of us cooking this very thing together floods back to him, and I can practically feel the weight of it in the room. It's painful.

"It's just pasta," I lie, trying to make light of it.

"No," he whispers, eyes still shut tight, as if letting the moment wash over him. "it's not."

"I know it's not," I reply quietly, my voice soft.

I sit down in the chair across from him and stretch my legs, resting my feet on the adjacent chair. I spear a few pieces of penne and eat, the comforting familiarity of the dish grounding me.

Luca leans back in his chair, grabs his bowl, and turns toward me. We eat in silence, neither of us in a hurry to break it.

The encounter in the hallway yesterday afternoon still lingers, like a bruise I don't know how to treat. It was explosive, but not in the way I had hoped. The rush of emotions—anger, pain, longing—still stings in the back of my throat. I can see it now, that young man who once gave me everything, tucked in the way Luca holds himself now. Deep down, I know he's still in there. That 23-year-old college kid who took all my firsts—the first love, the first heartbreak. He's still sitting here, just like he was that day he ran away from me.

The last six years feel like a void between us. But today, right now, it's like none of it happened. I'm here, and I'm ready to finally understand why he left.

Taking his empty bowl I place it in mine, sitting our dishes in the seat I just occupied.

Closing the laptop behind me, I slide it back and sit on his desk. I set a pack of playing cards from my back pocket down next to me and tap them twice.

"It's your shuffle."

Luca's forearms are resting on the chair's arms, fingers clasped in front of him. He cracks his knuckles slowly, his gaze fixed on the deck of cards. His expression is neutral, but I can see the storm brewing in his eyes, swirling with conflict.

"So, this is how we're going to do it?" His voice holds the weight of unspoken words, but he doesn't say them.

I nod once, a simple gesture, but it carries everything. "Yes."

His eyes flick to me, then back to the cards. Without another word, he sighs and picks up the deck, shuffling with the practiced precision I remember so well. He was always good with cards—spending hours shuffling, perfecting tricks until they flowed seamlessly.

I was always fascinated with his hands. The deft movements of his fingers across his keyboards. The elegant mastery over the way he handles these flimsy cards. How they felt holding me, drawing out the first stirrings of pleasure from my body.

And here he is now, still flawless, handling the deck with the ease of someone who's been doing it his entire life.

I raise an eyebrow at him, watching as he flicks the cards between his hands. A tiny, fleeting smile tugs at one corner of his mouth. It's not much, but it's enough to make my heart flutter with hope.

The smile doesn't last. The walls go up again, and I can feel the tension in the air like static before a storm. But it's a start, I think. A crack in the armor that I want to shatter.

This is a game we used to play when we were getting to know each other. If I pulled an even card, I got to ask a question. An odd card meant Luca had his turn. And the face cards... well, those meant we got to get even more personal. Black for me. Red for Luca. We can ask for anything we want. A kiss, a touch... something more.

A simple game, but one that somehow always managed to make us dig a little deeper into each other's souls.

Luca sets the deck down, sliding it closer to me. "Go ahead." he says, his voice almost tight.

I touch the first card, feeling the cool against my fingers as I flip it over.

Two of hearts.

I stare at the card, my question already clear in my mind. "Why did you run away from me?"

It's simple, but the question hangs between us, laden with the years of hurt, longing, and confusion. The moment stretches, Luca's silence suffocating the air around us as he looks at me, his jaw tightening.

Luca's breath hitches slightly, his gaze shifting downward as if the weight of what he's about to say is too much to bear. He's been carrying this for six years, and the words seem to strain his chest as he speaks, each one slow and painful.

"I hacked into the mob's network. It was–a prank really— just fucking around, you know?" He shakes his head, swallowing hard. "I found a hit on someone, and the payout was ridiculously high. Way more than the usual. I knew something was wrong about it. No one in their right mind would turn down a job like that for that kind of money."

I close my eyes, knowing it was about me.

He pauses, his fingers thrumming on the desk, but he doesn't look at me, still looking down. "I traced it to a meeting location and dug around on who lived there. The cyber-protection was a fucking fortress, and I couldn't get inside with my computers. I needed to know who the hell was getting hit."

His voice cracks just slightly as he says the next part. "The second you walked into that room, Lenny... I knew. I knew you were the target. You were the one they were going to kill."

His jaw tightens, and I can feel the regret rolling off him like a palpable force. "I couldn't let that happen. I had to do something. I had to stop it. I didn't care what it meant—I just couldn't let you die."

I'm quiet for a long time, my breath catching in my throat. It feels like a thousand different emotions are crashing into me at once. Fear, pain, confusion. But the one that cuts the deepest is the silence.

"But you stayed away. Even after that night, even after all of it, you never came back." My chest aches as I stare at him. "You just... disappeared. You didn't–you didn't come back for me."

Luca's eyes close, and he rubs his hand over his face, frustration evident in his movements. "One question, one answer, Lenny," he says quietly, his voice tinged with something darker than regret. "Those are the rules."

My mouth opens, but I stay quiet for a beat, trying to steady my thoughts.

He pulls a card from the deck, his fingers shaking just slightly as he reveals it. Two of clubs.

He looks at me, eyes dark and full of something unspoken. Something heavy. "Your question, Len," he says softly.

I want to understand him so badly, but the more I try, the more impossible it feels. He's been an enigma this entire week —a phantom I can't quite grasp, each time I try slipping through my fingers.

I look at him for a long moment, my heart pounding, the words coming to me before I can even stop them. "Why do you hate yourself?"

Luca's hands tremble ever so slightly as he places the card back on the table, his eyes never meeting mine. The room feels unbearably still, as if the air itself is waiting for him to speak.

"I had to protect you," he finally says, his voice raw, barely a whisper. But his words don't seem to hold the weight I expected. There's something underneath them, something heavier.

I press him further, unable to contain the need to know. "Luca, why do you hate yourself?"

He looks at me then, eyes wide and tortured, and for the first time, I see the flicker of something truly broken in him. His shoulders slump, as if the weight of whatever he's been carrying is finally getting to him.

And then he answers, his voice thick with pain. "Because I killed her."

The words hang in the air between us, and for a moment, I can't breathe. "Who?" The word barely escapes my lips, a breathless whisper.

He swallows, his gaze locking onto mine. "I killed my mother, Lenny."

Thirty-Six

uca's confession hangs in the air between us, thick with regret, guilt, and unspoken pain. The truth of it—the weight of it—almost suffocates him. Luca killed his mother. That must be why there are no pictures of her. But there's more. I can see it in his pleading eyes as he watches me.

I have to be careful. He already thinks he's a monster. If I'm going to reach him, I can't let him stay trapped in this belief. I can't let him believe he's beyond saving.

I need to show him—show him that he's still the man I love, the man who used to hold me like he was afraid to let go, even for a second.

Without another word, I slide off the desk and into his lap. With my heart pounding in my chest, I straddle him, settling onto him. His body tenses beneath me. He exhales a shaky breath, his fingers tightening briefly on my waist before he shakes his head, his voice low and strained. "Delaney... you shouldn't. I don't deserve this."

I shake my head, cupping his jaw gently and bringing his face closer to mine. "You deserve this. You deserve more than you think."

His eyes are a mixture of confusion, disbelief, and something else that makes my heart ache. I wrap my arms around his neck, pulling myself closer, feeling the heat of his body against mine. "Luca," I whisper softly, brushing my lips near his ear. "Draw my next card for me."

His eyes search mine, and for a moment, I think he's going to push me away. But instead, he seems to crumble, his heart pounding like a drum against my chest. Slowly, he moves his forehead to rest against mine, and I close my eyes, savoring the moment.

It feels like I've waited forever for this—to hold him like this again.

His entire body trembles as he takes the next card. I don't need to look at it to know it's my question. I set it up this way to get what I want from him—what he needs from me.

Two of diamonds.

I keep my eyes fixed on his, my voice steady despite the storm brewing inside me. "Do you love me, Luca?"

His grip on me tightens, his hands moving to my hips as if he's afraid I'll disappear if he lets go. His breath is ragged, and his voice cracks when he speaks. "I never stopped loving you, Lenny. Not for a second."

A tear slips down my cheek, and we're both breathing heavily now. "It's your card next," I whisper, my lips brushing against his. He shudders at my gentle touch.

I bring him with me to grab his next card. He runs his nose up the column of my neck as I lean back. He takes me in like it's the first breath he's taken since the night we parted.

With a victorious smirk, I show him the card, knowing exactly what it is. *Ace of spades.* A black face card. I get to ask him to touch me any way I want, and he has to do it. It's the rules of the game.

His sapphire eyes flick to the card, then back at me. "You stacked the deck." His arms snake around me, pulling our bodies flush, our mouths only a heartbeat away.

"You taught me well." I cup his jaw, leaning even closer. My quiet words caress his lips as I claim my reward. "Kiss me."

"Len..."

"You can't break the rules." I move my hips against him, feeling how hard he is. "Kiss me, Luca."

He cups my face, his thumb tenderly grazing my bottom lip. His eyes flick to my mouth for a moment, then back to my pleading gaze. He tilts his head, his lips moving slowly across mine—not quite kissing me yet, but savoring every second, every inch of contact.

Finally, he closes his eyes, and his lips meet mine.

It's slow at first, tentative, as if he's afraid that if he moves too fast, this moment will disappear into thin air. But it doesn't feel like hesitation—it feels like the first time all over again. His hand moves to my back, the weight of it grounding me, as his other arm snakes around my waist, pulling me closer. I can feel his body, tense and warm, and the steady beat of his heart under his shirt. It makes my pulse quicken in response.

I melt into him, letting my hands slide to his neck, holding him closer as though I want to absorb every ounce of him. His kiss deepens just slightly, his tongue tracing the line of my lips with a quiet insistence that makes everything inside me coil and burn. With every soft press of his lips, I feel the layers of distance, of years apart, begin to peel away.

It's a kind of kiss that makes everything else fade into the background—the world dissolving into nothing but the feel of him: his warmth, his touch, the way his lips move with mine.

There's something desperate in the way he touches me, but

it's not frantic—it's deliberate, as if he's making up for lost time, trying to show me how much he cares, how much he regrets, how much he's never stopped loving me. Each kiss is a question, a plea for forgiveness, and as I respond, I feel a sense of release in both of us. We don't need words right now; his touch speaks louder than anything else could.

For the first time in years, I feel the weight of him—really feel it. Not the anger, not the distance, but the quiet intensity he's always had. The boy who used to kiss me like he had all the time in the world, like I was the only thing that mattered.

And I know, deep down, this is the Luca I've missed. The one who used to make me feel like I was the most important thing in the room.

I lean into him, my body responding to the way he holds me, the way he kisses me like he's trying to communicate everything he's been holding back. His fingers trail down my spine, light and deliberate, sending a shiver through me. It's a subtle touch, but I can feel the history between us in it—the comfort of being held by him, the unspoken apologies, the regret, and the love. He's not saying it, but he's showing it in the way he touches me.

His lips pull away just for a moment, and I'm left wanting more. His eyes lock onto mine, dark with emotion, and for the first time, I see the raw vulnerability in them. He's still holding me close, but there's something softer about the way he looks at me now—like he's finally letting down the walls he's built around himself.

"Lenny," he whispers, his voice hoarse and thick with emotions he doesn't know how to name.

I trace his jawline, my thumb brushing over the rough

stubble, trying to tell him everything with just a touch. "I'm here," I murmur. "I'm right here."

And for a moment, it's just us—no past, no hurt, only the present.

But as he kisses me again, I realize this isn't just about physical desire. It's about connection. It's the ache of six years, the pain of what we've both lost, but also what we still have. And Luca's touch tells me that he's ready for that. He's ready to let go of the past, to let me back in, and maybe, just maybe, to forgive himself.

"Please tell me I draw another face card next," he murmurs against my lips, his voice low and full of longing. His hands tighten their grip on me, anchoring us together.

"There's nothing but face cards now," I reply with a mischievous smile.

"Thank fuck for that." He captures my lips again, his kiss more urgent this time. He holds me tightly as he stands, kicking the chair back in the process. He places me on the desk, setting me down gently. My legs wrap around his waist, drawing him closer, as I rock my hips against him. The heat between us is electric, building with each touch, each kiss.

He trails his lips down my neck, across my collarbone, and back up again. His voice is a husky whisper in my ear. "Can I take you to my room?"

"Yes." The word barely escapes my lips before he's carrying me out of the office, our mouths colliding as he takes the stairs two at a time.

He bumps into the doorframe, jolting our kiss to an abrupt end. "Fuck, sorry," he pants, then captures my lips again, swallowing my giggle. He kicks the door open and steps inside. The desperation in our kisses grows as we strip away the layers between us. Shoes hit the floor, shirts are yanked over our heads, and we collide again.

It's pure fire. Every touch ignites something deep within me, something only Luca can reach.

I fumble with the button on my jeans, partially unzipping them when he picks me up again. I cling to him, my hands cupping his jaw as I kiss him hard, pulling a deep, guttural moan from him. The sound reverberates through me, sending a delicious shiver down my spine.

He crawls onto the bed, laying me down at its center, his lips chasing mine the entire way. His weight presses into me, grounding me, as we grind against each other. His hands find the clasp of my bra, and with one fluid motion, he frees me. He doesn't even look as he tosses the garment aside, his mouth descending to my exposed skin.

His lips latch onto my nipple, teasing it with his tongue before gently nipping at it. The sensation sends a jolt of pleasure straight to my core. He gives the same attention to the other side, his hands roaming my body as if trying to memorize every inch of me.

He kisses down my body and when his hands get to the waistband of my pants he works them down. I lift my ass, helping but as soon as my pussy is exposed his mouth is consuming me.

"Oh, thank god," I whisper as he runs his tongue up the slit of my cunt, groaning in pleasure at the taste of me. I run my nails through his hair, pushing him into me as I move my hips. I need more, more friction, more of his fingers. I need to be spread bare for him, so he knows just how much of me he owns. "More." Is all I can muster as his mouth caresses my pussy with just as tender a kiss as the one we shared in his office below.

He keeps eating me while he resumes pulling my pants off me. When one leg is free, he hikes my knee over his wide shoulder and deepens the fervor of his licks, the swirls of his tongue around my clit. "Fuck, Luca."

He doesn't miss a beat, pulling off the rest of my pants so both my legs are wrapped around him, my thighs locking his mouth around me as I try to move my hips with each swipe of his tongue. Luca's grip on me is firm.

His arms are wrapped around my legs, his hands pull the lips of my pussy back, exposing my clit to him. Keeping me at his mercy. He flicks my clit with his tongue, and I feel my orgasm burning within me, begging to be released for him.

He moans again when my legs twitch around him, loving the pleasure he knows he's giving me. I add my own noises, unable to stop telling him how good he feels, how much I missed him. Each phrase burrows inside of him, wrapping around the blocks of the wall he built, and I make each one of them crumble until I'm shaking around him. Calling out his name and grinding hard onto his mouth as my climax plows into me.

He keeps licking, slowing his movements as my orgasm ebbs away. Each time his tongue brushes across my sensitive clit, my legs jolt. Luca kisses my pussy several time as I keep rubbing his soft hair, scratching my nails on his head.

Luca climbs up my body, his mouth leaving a trail of kisses as he moves. His face hovers over mine, and the evidence of my pleasure lingers on his lips. He kisses me deeply, and I taste myself on him, a mix of desire and intimacy that makes my heart race. His hands frame my face, his thumbs brushing over my cheeks as if I'm the most fragile, precious thing in the world.

"You taste so fucking good, baby," he whispers against my lips, his voice thick with emotion and want. His hands trail down to the waistband of his jeans, and I help him work the button loose. My fingers brush against his as we tug the zipper down together, and I can't wait another second to feel him. "I've missed you so fucking much."

We both moan when I run my nails up his shaft. The soft skin pulled tight with the bulge of his erection. Our eyes are locked onto each other. I grasp him, getting as much of him as I can when I wrap my fingers around him. He's so fucking big.

My other hand cups his jaw and I rub his cheek. "You're no monster Luca." I lean up and kiss away the sting he feels with my comment. "But this," I squeeze his cock harder, stroking him while I lick his lips. "This is a monster and I want you to destroy me with it, baby."

"Tell me first," He thrusts his hips into my hand a few times before getting to his knees, his firm body on display for me. "Are you still my girl?"

My legs are spread wide, and his massive hands rub my inner thighs, but I can't answer him. My expression drops and my eyes go wide when I look at his chest, a wave of heat running down my body at what I see.

"You asshole!"

Thirty-Seven

Luca remains kneeling on the bed, shirtless, his gaze locked on me with an almost arrogant smirk playing on his lips. His pants are open, and half of his massive cock has joined the party—the other half waiting to be released. My eyes travel over his chest—smooth, defined, and sculpted just the way I remember—and then pause, landing on something that hadn't been there in college but is staring me in the face now.

Even though this is the first time I'm seeing it in person, it's no stranger to me. It's the same mark I've seen—probably hundreds of times—on my phone screen.

I blink a couple of times, trying to make sense of it, before I slowly lift my eyes from his chest to meet his. My jaw drops. He knows exactly what I've figured out, and his grin widens, smug as ever.

"You asshole," I growl, still processing it, my brain struggling to catch up to what I'm seeing. Luca's smirk deepens, and I swear he's holding back laughter.

My heart pounds in my chest, and I feel a mix of disbelief, pure attraction, and feral jealousy.

"You're Moanster23?!" I exclaim, the realization rushing out like a floodgate bursting open. I sit up, pushing against him, but he quickly captures my wrists and lays us down, pinning my arms over my head.

"The hot, mysterious guy who's been making me moan like crazy is you? Moanster23, really?" I shake my head in disbelief at the heat of the situation.

"Took you long enough to figure it out." He nips at my mouth, but I turn my head away.

"No, I'm mad at you," I quip, though my legs, holding him captive, and my grinding hips are not playing along.

"You don't remember the first time you sucked my dick?" He moves to my neck, biting me there and kissing the spot. "I couldn't stop myself. The noises... fuck, you felt so good."

Oh my god. I remember. "I called you my little moanster." My body goes slack as I resign myself to the memory of the username I apparently gave him.

"Honestly, I thought you would've figured it out sooner." Luca leans in, whispering in my ear, his breath warm against my skin. "Did you really think I'd let you have all your fun with some random fuck face online?" His fingers trail over the curve of my hip, sending a shiver through me.

For a moment, I'm speechless. All I can do is stare at him, caught between the shock of discovering his secret and the undeniable pull between us.

"Eight hundred forty-seven times you called out my name when you were coming to those videos." He licks up the column of my neck, and I exhale deeply.

"How do you know that?"

"You know exactly how I know, Lenny." He rubs his bare shaft through my wet slit, teasing my clit with the thick head of his heavy cock. I roll my eyes closed. "The same way I recorded you faking yet another orgasm with some pencil dick you gave a sympathy fuck to." He grinds harder, like he's punishing me for every cock that's entered my pussy these last six years.

That's a punishment I'd happily take.

"The same way I heard you gasp in your motel room when Jax licked your pussy." He moves faster, straight-up fucking my clit with his cock, and I'm going to come again soon. "The same way I know you wanted Jax to guess your panties so you could have his thick fingers fuck your wet cunt in the car." He slides two fingers into me, and I swear I see a choir of angels behind him.

"I'm always fucking there, Lenny. Listening to you. Watching everything you do."

"Holy shit." I hold onto his wrist as he adds a third finger. I have a stalker. My stepbrother is my stalker.

"I woke Enzo up to fuck me while I listened to you, Len."

"Luca," I pant. I have to remember that.

Book title. *Oh my fucking god, this feels so good.* Don't forget.

My stepbrother is my stalker.

"I choked on his cock so I could pretend I was suffocating in your cunt." My walls clench around his fingers as he talks directly into my ear. "He slammed his dick into my ass and asked me if I was thinking about your wet pussy while he jacked me off."

"I'm going to come, Luca."

"You know what he said to me when I told him yes?" He sucks on my neck and pulses his hips against me, thrusting his fingers faster. "'Good boy,'" he whispers, and I lose it. The choir of angels sings hallelujah as I come undone on his fingers to him telling me how Enzo fucked him.

"Holy shit," I gasp, catching my breath as the waves

subside. He slides his fingers out of me, licking each one, smirking like the devil. "Oh, fuck me." I drape my arm over my eyes, just trying to come back to earth.

"Trust me, I'm going to." Luca laughs, and I feel the bed shift. He strips off his pants, officially releasing the kraken. Ladies and gentlemen, clutch your pearls, pucker your butts, and have plenty of lube because this will be the best ride of your life.

But I can't make it that easy on him. "You dick!" I push at him, pinching him and moving to a new spot to pinch again.

"Ow! What the fuck?"

"You stalked me! And Moanster has over two hundred thousand followers, you asshat." I pinch and pinch again. "All those women, all those men listening to you jack off for me."

Pinch.

Pinch.

"If I had The Spat here, I'd slap the shit out of you like I did Jax." I try to find a new spot, but he pulls my hands behind my back. He crushes me with his weight, and I thrash around to no avail.

"Those are bots, Lenny." He's enjoying this, smiling and nearly laughing while I'm pissed as hell. "They're just fake accounts, Len." I give up my fight and let his words sink in. "Every account is fake, babe. Every engagement is just a program." He takes my lip between his teeth and pulls. "I only have one follower, and every post is for her." He lets me go, and I circle his neck with my arms.

"Really?"

"Just for you." Luca nods, wrapping his arms around me. I lock my feet behind his back. "When you were letting... pop quiz, Lenny. What was his name?" He looks at me incredulously. "Your poor date."

"Oh shit... what was his name?" I look off in thought. "Maverick? Marshall!" I call out, knowing that's not it. "Jerry... McGuire?"

Luca laughs and shakes his head. "Mark. When you gave poor Mark the best vagina he could ever hope to experience, I posted for you because I knew you'd be going into the bathroom with your little pink fucking buzzer."

I gasp. "Are you jelly?" My shit-eating grin widens because this motherfucker is jealous of a sex toy.

"Fuck yes, I'm jealous." He kisses me hard. "If you didn't call out my name so much when that thing made you come, I might've stolen it and blown it to pieces."

"You are fucking crazy!" I laugh.

"I'm fucking crazy for you, Lenny." He kisses the tip of my nose. "Did you think it was perfect timing that another post uploaded just before you left the bathroom?"

Oh my god.

"I jacked off watching you fuck yourself with your little toy. I uploaded it for you. Then I jacked off again watching you do it again." He fists his thick cock and rubs it against my clit. "But if I don't sink my dick into you in the next minute, I may die, Lenny."

"Well, we can't have that, now can we?"

Thirty-Eight

"On your fucking knees, Lenny. I've missed the way you lube me up."

I don't know how I became the luckiest woman on planet Earth, but I'll do anything I can to not jinx myself.

I get on my knees and bend back with my arms behind me, pushing my chest out.

Luca gets some lube from the bedside table drawer and squirts it on my chest. I gasp at the chill, but Luca has the gaze of a predator, and it heats me to the core.

"God, I've missed having my hands on these tits." He palms both my breasts, pinching my nipples while he pushes my breasts together, spreading the lube around generously.

I smirk. "You didn't do this with Jax or Enzo?"

He rolls his eyes at me. "My boyfriends don't have the rack my girlfriend does." He gives me an extra pinch for good measure.

His girlfriend.

"And... no other girls?" I find I'm holding my breath, and I'm not sure I have the right to. I fucked other people, which he apparently knows very well.

"There haven't been any other girls, Len." The deep-blue oceans within his eyes darken. "Only you, baby."

Oh, I like that very much.

My face heats, and I know my cheeks are turning pink. Luca winks at me, then slides his dick between my tits, and I feel it in my pussy, releasing a moan.

I lean my head forward and open my mouth.

"Oh, fuck. That's my good girl, Len." He slides slowly, watching the head of his cock enter my mouth while my breasts lube his dick. He pulses with short thrusts into my mouth, letting me enjoy sucking him. "Okay, Len." He helps me sit up with an arm around my waist. "You ready to bounce your wet pussy on my cock?"

"God, I was born ready."

Luca lays down, and I straddle him. With one foot flat on the bed, I grab him with both hands, sliding up the length of him easily with the lube.

"Fuck, Lenny."

I position him at my entrance and take him slowly. He stretches me with his head, and I go up and down a few short times before taking a few more inches. God, this is exactly what I've needed. I've never felt more full, more secure than when Luca is balls-deep inside me. He's so fucking big, there isn't room for anything else.

Unless...

I pause, and Luca gets worried. His hands squeeze my hips. "Are you okay?"

"Yes." I take another inch or two, making him moan when I tighten my pussy around him. "I was just thinking, though." I put my knee down and start my ride, even though he's not fully inside me yet.

Yes, girls, we've got another three inches or so before I'm wholly and completely impaled on this megalodon of cock.

"I was thinking... would another dick fit in here... if you were already fucking me?" Down another inch or two, I go. "Or another two dicks?" I lean down and lick his lips.

Luca closes his eyes and squeezes my hips. "Lenny, you'll fucking kill me if I think about feeling their cocks fuck you while I'm fucking you." When he opens his eyes again, there is something feral looking back at me, and somehow, I grow even wetter.

I'll put a bit of triple penetration on the good ol' wish list for Santa Claus this year.

"You would like that?" I grab my tits, squeezing them and pushing them together while I let myself down the rest of the way.

"Oh, yes, Lenny. You feel so fucking perfect." He tilts his hips as I ride him. Up and down, grinding my clit on him, leaning forward so he can kiss the ever-loving soul out of my body... and he never falls out.

Again, luckiest woman on the planet.

"You would make me come so hard, Luca. Your fat cock stuffed inside me with Enzo's and Jax's."

"Mmmh, Lenny, God, keep going."

It's been so long since he's been inside me, but I never forgot what he felt like. It's almost too much but in the most perfect way. He's so careful but, at the same time, unleashing himself on me.

"All of you thrusting inside me, filling me with your cum together."

I play with my clit while I ride him. He watches every second of me, absorbing my tits bouncing, my face when

I change my rhythm and feel him in a different part of me.

"You're so beautiful, Lenny, riding my dick. I love seeing your greedy fucking pussy take every inch of me." His grip on me helps as my orgasm approaches. "Are you going to come for me again, baby? Will you let me feel your cunt strangle my cock?"

"Oh my God, Luca." I let my head fall back as I tighten around him and keep swirling my finger on my clit. "Luca, I'm coming again."

He fucks me from the bottom, grunting and moaning, but he doesn't come. When my climax is over, he quickly flips me to my hands and knees, setting himself behind me.

With another squeeze of lube on his hand, he strokes his cock and then rubs my pussy, getting me ready for him again.

He thrusts into me, sliding slowly but not stopping until he's fully inside. "Goddamn it, Lenny." Luca pumps into me. I lay my chest on the bed, arching my back and using my hold on the covers to push myself into him, meeting his thrusts with my own. "You're so tight."

"Fuck, yes. Just like that."

"I want to hear you say my name, Lenny." He fucks me like I'm dying, and it will save my life. And at this point, I think it just might. "Eight hundred forty-seven times you called out my name when you were coming to those videos. On your fucking vibrator." He pounds into me. "It's me fucking you now, and I want to hear my name when you come. Because this pussy is mine, isn't it?"

I'm too busy groaning into the mattress to answer, so he smacks my ass.

"Tell me, Lenny. Tell me you belong to me." His thrusts turn feral, and the feeling of him shoots up my spine. He grabs a fistful of my hair, pulling my face out of the sheets. "I know I'm the only one who fucks you this deep, Len. Fucking tell me."

"Yes."

"Say it. Tell me this is just for me. No one else touched you where I am now." He smacks my ass again. "Only my cock can reach this far into you, baby. I own this. It's fucking mine."

"Yes, Luca." I cry out. "Only you." He reaches around and fingers my clit. I place my hand over his, and we work my pussy together. "It's always been you, baby."

He pulls me up, my back to his front, and turns my chin to him. His tongue invades my mouth with renewed hunger. I reach behind me and hold onto his neck, pulling his hair, and I get my very own whimper. God, it does something to me.

Our bodies are moving together, both of us working to a climax that we ride out together. I start to come first, and he pinches my nipple as his other hand rubs circles on my clit. His mouth swallows my moans as the waves of my climax make me squeeze his thick cock.

He pushes me down, putting my chest back to the bed and grabbing my hips in a bruising grip. "My name, Lenny. We don't stop until you lose your voice screaming my fucking name."

I feel the chill of his lube on my ass, then he gently eases his thumb into me.

"Oh my God, Luca."

"That's it, baby. You'll be so fucking full of me, you'll feel me for a week." He fucks me hard while he holds his thumb still in my ass. It's the added pressure, the added fullness of it that pulls me into an orgasm. He reaches around and pinches my clit, working me in every way possible and wrenching screams from me.

His name flows off my tongue in worship, and waves of pleasure roll over me again and again. "Good fucking girl, Len." He removes his thumb from my ass and grabs my hips again for his own release. "Your pussy is going to swallow every drop of my cum, baby. You feel so fucking good."

With my chest flat on the bed, I reach back between my legs. Running my hand up his thigh, I cup his balls.

"Oh, fuck, baby." He calls out when I squeeze him.

"Come for me, Luca." He grunts as I work him with my hand and meet his thrusts while I clench my pussy around him. "I'm a fucking whore for your cum. I need it." I squeeze and massage his balls, and he moans each time. "Please let me have it. My pussy has been starving for you, Luca."

He pumps his release into me with a roar until he's spent. Still sheathed in me, he pulls me up so my back meets his chest, and he holds me, peppering kisses on my shoulder and cheek, then on my mouth again.

His cock slides out of me and his hand is there. His cum leaking from me, into his palm. Luca keeps his mouth on mine, devouring me. After a moment, he runs his hand up my abdomen and my breasts until he's gripping my throat possessively. His cum dripping along my body and down his wrist.

"Say it again, baby." With his other hand, he rubs his cum into my skin, pinching and rolling my nipple. Marking me, like a claim. "Say you're mine." His kiss turns gentle now. His hand slides back down my body, cupping my pussy.

I thread my fingers into his hair, panting as my heart

pounds in my chest. "I've always been yours, Luca. Forever." I add with gentle smile at the warmth that spreads throughout my body.

"I love you, Lenny." He kisses me again. "I'll love you until the day I die."

Thirty-Nine

I rest my chin on Luca's chest, my hand rubbing lazy circles around the soft tuft of dark hair, my fingers tracing the mark on his chest. I see now it's a tattoo, but I can't tell what it is. My lazy circles match the ones he is drawing on my back. My hair, still damp from our shower, is splayed on the pillow behind me.

The silence is easy; just filling the space with each other is enough amid the heaviness of what Luca has unloaded. He told me how he killed his mother: he strangled her with his bare hands.

The same hands that fascinate me so much. The hands that hold me so fiercely and love me so tenderly.

When he hacked into the mob's dark web, he was determined to learn about the hit because it was his mother who accepted the job. The payout was huge, and he wanted to know whose life was worth that much. When he couldn't find a way into my father's home with his computers, he met her there at the door.

She had worked for three months to seduce my father, knowing his penchant for taking on wives. She never really

"

intended to marry him; in fact, the marriage wasn't even legal. She only wanted to get close enough to come back and kill me.

It was going to happen the night my father introduced us. She was going to plant a device that would disable my father's security system at a certain time. Luca says it was like a bomb but an electronic, silent one.

She would only need long enough to slip inside the house. From there, her virus would overwrite the cameras' feed with one she pre-recorded. She would be free to take her time with the kill and stage it as if my father had murdered me. I would be gone, and so would he.

But she didn't get to do any of that because Luca met her at my father's front door just before he opened it. She had no choice but to play along as if she'd brought her son to meet her fiancé. What luck—my father had also called me to dinner for the same thing.

Luca didn't know who would walk into the room. Horror washed over him because he knew his mother was planning to kill me—the woman he loved.

He knew immediately what he would have to do, so he left to prepare himself.

Luca came back that night and intercepted his mother before she could trigger her bomb. He pleaded with her not to go through with it, but she refused. She owed a crime boss, and this was the only way to clear her debt.

He told his mother that I was the woman he had fallen in love with at college. He had spent months telling her all about me, about Lenny. She never connected his nickname for me with Delaney Caputo—the mark she was going to kill.

Even after learning that, she was still going to do it.

So, Luca did the only thing that would keep me safe. He

tackled her to the ground and straddled her chest, pinning her arms to her side. He strangled her. He watched the life leave her eyes. He sat there, in a dark corner of my father's property where the cameras didn't reach, and he called a Cleaner, telling him he would owe him a favor that could be called in anytime.

He called Jax.

While he waited for Jax to arrive, he watched me sit on my balcony and cry over him. He watched me dial his number, trying to call him, and then cried himself when he silenced my calls and sent them to voicemail.

He decided then that he couldn't be with me and protect me. So, he promised himself he would stay away. He would watch me live my life from a distance and protect me.

He thought it would only take a few weeks... months, at most. Luca was going to find who put the hit out and he was going to end them himself. Then he was going to come back to me and beg my forgiveness.

In the nearly two years following that night, he and Jax had a few casual flings, but Jax went off the grid for a while—because he was hunting me. When Jax watched me cry over a cupcake through the scope of a gun, Luca watched Jax through a scope of his own. He watched Jax pause, and something inside him made him pause as well. Luca followed Jax as he followed me and saw the second Jax fell in love with me.

He knew the moment I burst into laughter at the spilled wine that I would fall in love with Jax too. So, he kept hunting my hunters. He stopped watching, not wanting to see me fall for someone else.

Then, before he knew it, it was my wedding day—the day I was going to give myself over to someone forever, and it wasn't going to be him. Luca got wasted, and then he got a call from an inmate, one looking to cash in a favor. Jax, arrested at the altar, asked Luca to watch over me.

He laughed maniacally and told Jax everything. That yes, he would watch over the woman Jax loved, but Jax needed to know he loved me first.

Luca and Jax worked together then. Jax from prison and Luca tending to everything on the outside. He became a killer, a fighter, a getaway driver, a sharpshooter. He became whatever the job needed him to be. And he kept me safe.

He told me the same story Enzo did about the girl who was shot sitting at my desk—how they cleaned it up and took care of her respectfully for becoming an innocent victim in this war against me.

Luca and Jax became close. Through countless jailhouse phone calls, visitation days that left them both wanting more, and letters where they could say what they really wanted to say.

Enzo could give Luca something Jax couldn't: a physical connection. Someone to come back to after a rough job and someone to wake up with. Someone to hunt with and someone to miss me with.

I brought the three of them together, and they fell in love trying to save me. They comforted each other when they couldn't comfort me, and in sharing me, they formed a love that could last through anything.

But it wasn't complete without their muse, and they were going to live without me as long as they could keep me safe. But not Jax. He dreamt of a life after the hunt, when they could come back to me, tell me everything, and beg for my forgiveness. It makes me smile, knowing Jax has gotten most of his wish—hopefully the most important part.

The hunt is still on, but we're together now.

Luca was ready for it to end in death—mine or theirs—and he didn't want to hope. That washes away my smile, and a tear runs out of the corner of my eye. He lived each day knowing it might be the one where he finally watched someone kill me because they failed.

I close my eyes and inhale deeply, his scent wrapping around me, grounding me. I wish I could take it all away, make it better, but I know it's not that simple. Still, it feels like I've peeled back a layer of him that's been buried so deep. I can't help but think it's my fault that we're all tangled in this mess together.

But I won't run from him. Not now. Not after knowing everything he's done for me; for us.

I can feel how tense he is beneath me. His body is a wall of muscle, taut and stiff, as he tries to push the conversation out of his mind. I don't let go of him, my arms wrapping tighter around his chest. He doesn't say anything, but I feel the way his chest rises and falls under my touch—slow and steady, trying to calm the storm inside him.

"What is this tattoo of?" I trace over the shape with my index finger. It's not defined, more like a smudge of paint.

I sense him smile. He turns over, facing me, pulling me close so we can tangle our legs together. His large hand rubs my hip and slides down my thigh.

"You never told me you were a virgin." He leans forward slightly, rubbing the tip of his nose against mine. I close my eyes and hide my face against his chest.

"It was embarrassing!" My pitiful excuse is muffled. The moment he realized it flashes in my mind, and I pop my head back up. "No, you didn't?" I accuse, looking at the tattoo and placing my hand over it.

The marks fit my first and second fingers perfectly. He smiles again, just like he did when I figured out he was Moanster23.

"I didn't want to hurt you, and I tried to pull out, but you made me stop. Then you put your hand right here on my chest." He covers my hand with his, holding it against his heart. "As soon as I left your dorm the next morning, I went to the tattoo shop and had them ink your bloody fingerprints on me."

I wrap my arms around his neck, a wide grin spreading across my face that matches his. "Luca Bellini, that is simultaneously the most sadistic and romantic thing I've ever heard. Why does that turn me on so much?"

His hands run up and down my back. "Because we're the same brand of twisted, baby. It's why we're meant to be together." He kisses me, and my tongue begs his mouth for entry. He gives it to me. "But I have a confession."

"Oh God." I tease, rolling my eyes and collapsing onto my back.

He pulls me back with a chuckle and leans close to my ear. "You were my first too." He kisses the shell of my ear before looking at me.

"You mean to tell me," I roll over, pulling him on top of me so he can settle between my legs, "that this—behemoth of a cock"—I grind against him, making him growl as his dick hardens—"had never before graced a pussy before mine?"

He chuckles, and the sound of it seals up some of the cracks in my heart. "You're very poetic."

"I try. I'm a pretty good writer. You should read some of my stories."

He grinds against me now. "If you think I haven't already

read every single one of your books, then I'm hurt." God, every word he says makes me want to kick my feet like a giddy little girl. Instead, I bite my lip and watch his gaze move down to my mouth. "You took all my firsts too, Lenny. The first hand—other than my own—to make me come. The first tongue"—he licks my lips—"to ever taste my cock."

Fuck me.

Please actually. Like please... fuck me... disrespectfully, of course.

I kiss him softly, gently, and he responds in kind. Slowly, but with an intensity I can feel down to my bones. I feel him relax, just a little, as his lips move against mine.

I pull away just enough to see his face, to look at him with all the tenderness I've been feeling—all the emotion bubbling up from somewhere deep. His eyes are still dark with the weight of everything he's been carrying, but there's something softer there now, a flicker of hope.

"I love you, Luca," I whisper, my hand gently cupping his cheek.

"I just don't want to lose you again," he says, his voice thick with emotion. The words are raw, desperate in a way that almost breaks me.

"You won't. I'm right here, Luca," I reply, running my thumb across his lips. "Right here. And I'm not going anywhere."

He breathes deeply, his fingers digging into my hip as he pulls me closer, burying his face in the crook of my neck. It's like he's trying to hold on to me, to keep me tethered to him, like I'm the anchor he's been searching for. I can feel the weight lifting off him, just a little, with every breath he takes, and it gives me hope that we can rebuild what was broken.

I focus on the steady rhythm of his breath, the warmth of his body grounding me. For the first time in what feels like forever, we're just two people in this moment, unburdened by the chaos swirling around us. I feel safe here, in his arms, like I've finally found a place where I belong.

But the moment doesn't last. A sharp, shrill sound rips through the calm, slicing the air with a jarring urgency. My heart skips a beat as the alarm blares, sending a cold wave of fear over me.

Luca's eyes snap open, his body stiffening immediately. He pulls away from me, eyes wide with shock, panic flashing across his face for a brief second before his usual calm takes over. But there's no hiding the raw emotion in his gaze—the worry, the fear, the anger.

"What the hell is that?" I whisper, my voice tight, fear creeping into my chest as the blaring alarm echoes in my ears.

Luca doesn't answer immediately. His jaw clenches as he stands up, his body tense, like he's ready to spring into action. He glances back at me, his eyes dark with something I can't place.

"Stay here."

Forty

"No." I shake my head, my heart pounding, the alarm still blaring through the house. Each shrill wail adds to the tension. "I'm not sitting here waiting. We face this together. We've already survived too much to be apart now."

Luca's eyes narrow, and for a moment, I see that familiar flicker of exasperation—the same look I've seen a dozen times this week when he tries to push me away. But it's not working now, not after everything we've shared, everything we've talked through. I won't let him push me out of the equation.

With a growl of frustration, Luca steps toward me, his hands gripping my face with unexpected tenderness as he leans down. His kiss is brief, chaste even, but it's full of heat and annoyance. When he pulls back, his forehead presses against mine.

"I fucking love how stubborn you are when it's not directed at me," he mutters.

I can't help the soft smile tugging at my lips, but the moment is fleeting. Luca's eyes harden again as he pulls away, grabbing his phone from the bedside table. With swift motions, he taps at the screen, his fingers moving faster as he brings up a security feed on the TV in his bedroom.

The grid flickers to life, and I freeze, my stomach dropping when I see the cameras. Dozens of men, all dressed in black, swarm across Luca's property. I can barely make out their movements, but the way they move in coordinated chaos—armed, tactical, precise—makes my blood run cold. It's like watching a military operation unfold on my doorstep.

"Oh my God, Luca." I glance at him, feeling the weight of the situation settle in. "You know that scene in *Kill Bill* when she fights the Crazy 88s?" My voice comes out barely above a whisper, the question hanging heavy between us.

"Yeah, I was just thinking that." Luca's expression doesn't waver until he snaps out of the initial shock. "We need to get dressed," he says, his voice steady despite the rising tension, "quickly. And I need to get you to the safe room. Now."

Right. We are both very naked. And very much under attack.

He's already moving before I can respond, his eyes locked on the screen like he's memorizing everything before he turns away. He pulls a gun from the bedside table next, inspecting it. There's something about the sight of his giant cock, the shifting muscles of his abdomen as he pulls back the weapon, or maybe it's the cloak of death he seems to drape over himself, preparing to kill everyone setting foot on his land... but... it's definitely doing something for me.

"That is the sexiest thing I've ever watched in my life."

Luca places the gun on his dresser with a boyish smirk, and I follow him into his closet, pulling on a pair of panties and a sports bra from my bag.

"You have a thing for some gunplay, baby?" he asks, looking me up and down before turning back to his rack of all-black clothing. I'm pulling up my yoga pants, trying not to hyperventilate over the idea of him fucking me with his gun.

"I'd be glad to watch you come all over the barrel of my Glock, Lenny," he says with a smirk, the timbre of his deep voice extra rich.

"We should maybe pin that for later." I pull a shirt over my head as Luca, sadly, puts away his megalo-dong. I wrap my hair in a messy bun, and he quickly dresses in black tactical pants, a black shirt, and boots. "Just how did we get here from five days ago? Hmm, what a journey."

He looks every inch the lethal predator, and that only intensifies when he opens a drawer full of weapons that could rival those in any spy movie.

Luca checks guns, sliding them into holsters I hadn't even realized he had. Clips of extra ammo go into the pockets of his pants, along with several concealed knives. He takes a vest from his closet and puts it on. A rush of relief washes over me until I look back at the screen, and it seems like the attackers just keep coming.

"How far away are they?" I ask, still looking behind me at the screen.

"We've got about five minutes," he answers, taking a quick look. "Okay, you're going to strap up." He comes to me with another harness and vest in hand.

"I would prefer to strap-on... but fine." I tease as he clips a belt around my waist and straps around my thighs. He shakes his head at my choice of humor in the midst of certain death.

He offers me a gun resting in his palm, and it looks so small in his hands. "Check the weapon and the safety." Luca is watching me, testing me with the gun.

With a deep breath, I run through everything Jax taught

me. Apparently, I pass my test. I earn a kiss on my head and a "good girl."

I'll take both of those any day of the week, thank you!

Luca fixes the gun in one thigh holster and lets me check another weapon. I holster this one myself, then secure the knife he gives me close to one of the guns. My heart is beating a million miles a minute, and having weapons strapped to my body is not helping.

Satisfied we are fully armed, he closes up the rest of the weapons, and they disappear into the closet like they were never here. "Come on."

He heads for the stairs and goes down them quickly, his pace brisk as the minutes tick by.

We head to the kitchen, and he grabs a spatula from the jar of utensils, giving it to me with a roll of his eyes. "For luck." He winks at me when I grin at him like an idiot.

I do feel better having this silly thing in my hands, and I'm not sure what it is about this trauma-fest of a week that has gotten me so attached to a fucking spatula, but there is no time to ponder it.

Luca presses a combination of keys and buttons on the double oven, and it swings open like a door—a thick-ass door made of metal.

"No way!" I gasp, following him in. "This is just like in the movies."

"Yeah, except we very well may die, Lenny."

"Oh, yeah. I mean, that part sucks."

He walks me back to another door, and we step into a hidden room at the center of the house. The rest of the home seems built around this, its sole purpose to conceal it. I suppose when your family has a long history of associating with the mob, things like this are pretty standard.

The room's lights turn on automatically when we enter, and screens flicker to life.

I avert my eyes quickly, accidentally glancing at the goddamn murder-barn scene of bloodshed. I think I see a finger falling to the ground, and Marco now looks more like a *Marc-oh-fuck-no*. "Oh, my fucking God."

There was a large dark hole where his ear should be. Blood caking his shirt on both sides so I can only assume his other ear has been removed too, van Gogh style.

He's definitely lost some skin on his hands and forearms. The thought of what else is something I try to push out of my mind.

"Sorry, Lenny." Luca's fingers fly feverishly across the keyboard, and the screens change in an instant. A red light in the top corner of the room starts blinking silently.

"What is that?" I ask, my voice tight.

"My silent alarm. I need to call Jax and Enzo up here." He's still typing furiously, his frustration mounting. He suddenly slams his hands on the desk. "Motherfucker! I've got you now."

"What?" My stomach knots, the fear growing more tangible by the second.

I mean, I was scared before, but you know... if Luca wasn't worried, I wasn't worried. But now? We've got a SWAT team of assassins descending on us, I've got guns strapped to my legs, and my other boyfriends are torturing someone in the murder-barn completely oblivious to the situation.

So, we can agree I was at least pretending not to be worried.

"Where are you?" Luca's blue eyes scan each of the screens

quickly, searching. "I know you're here, you bastard." His gaze fixes on one screen, and it seems the figure in the frame knows it. A masked man, rifle in hand, is staring directly at us.

"Luca, who is that?" My voice is barely a whisper.

"Nico Santoro," he growls, curling his lip as anger burns in his eyes.

I gasp, my hand flying to my mouth. "Nic."

Luca's old roommate in college. They were always neck and neck in everything—top of their class, best friends, constantly in competition with each other.

"He's the one I taught how to do a blackout net."

"And you're not friends anymore?"

"I outgrew his childish need to compete." Luca sits up and opens a drawer beside the desk.

Surprise—it's full of guns. We're all shocked.

He takes a silencer from the top and screws it onto his gun. Then he grabs a pair of brass knuckles, slipping one into each pocket.

"Luca." I can't hide the tremor in my voice now as I see how close the horde is getting to the house.

"I have a strong suspicion he helped fabricate the evidence that convicted Jax. He's the reason Jax was put away on a murder charge—for life." Luca's jaw tightens as he looks at the screen, urgency building in his eyes. "He's the secret to the strange transactions, the last-minute land purchases in Enzo's territory—all of it. He's the one helping whatever boss is trying to kill you."

"So, what does that mean?"

Luca tilts his head, tucking a few stray hairs from my bun behind my ear. "It means I'm going to beat him to a pulp until he stops breathing." He cups my face and kisses me.

"Okay," is all I can answer, the impending doom weighing heavily on me.

"This is a safe room. Once I close those doors, no one will know you're here. You can get out anytime, but no one can come in. Got it?"

I nod, trying to swallow the knot in my throat while twisting my hands around the spatula.

"It's nearly dark. They're going to swarm the house. It will be quiet. Nic knows better than to come in here with guns blazing." I nod again, pretending to understand the strategy. "You can watch me on the screens, but no matter what happens, you can't leave this room, Lenny."

He bends down so his eyes are level with mine. "I mean it. No matter how many bullets you see enter my body—"

"Stop it!" I cry out, tears welling in my eyes.

"No. This is serious." He kisses me quickly. "No matter what, promise me."

I can't. I can't promise that. But I can lie so I nod.

Luca relaxes slightly and glances at the blinking red light. "When it turns green, Enzo and Jax are on their way. Okay? They'll get here." He kisses me again. "Fucking Christ, Lenny. Please stay in here." He leans his head against mine, and I can't lie to him again. He already knows the truth.

"Don't die." I take his face in my hands, holding him just like he's holding me.

He pulls me into a kiss that feels too much like goodbye.

"Go," I choke out. "Go kill everyone and get your ass back here. They're here to hurt your incredibly sexy girlfriend who has no gag reflex."

He gives me a crooked grin. "Say that again."

"That I have no gag reflex?"

"No, silly girl. Say you're my girlfriend again."

I smile, and for a moment, amid the chaos surrounding his family's old home, there's peace. I stand on my tiptoes to reach him better. "I'll say it again when you come back to me. So don't fucking die, or I'll come out there and kick your ass myself."

His smirk widens as he cups my ass with one big hand and kisses me, his tongue sweeping into my mouth. "Yes, ma'am."

Forty-One

I watch Luca, my chest tight with nerves, as he slips out of the safe room. The door clicks shut behind him, and I hear an ominous lock further away. It's the false door being closed, sealing me in here, hiding me from the mayhem that is about to take place. The seconds stretch into what feels like hours. My heart beats too loudly in my ears as I stay frozen in place, waiting. I need him to be okay—I need him to survive this so we can all be together.

If he thinks I won't come out of this room when he needs help, he's sadly mistaken.

The silence in the room feels suffocating, the weight of everything about to unfold pressing down on me, making my heart thump in my chest and sweat roll down my back.

The screen of small grids shows me the feeds from all the security cameras. I watch the shadows moving toward the house, the assassins closing in like a swarm. They're calm, controlled—trained to kill without a sound. It's impossible to tell how many there are.

They move as one, flowing toward us with deadly precision. A few are already inside, creeping through the hallways like ghosts. They're professionals, probably just like the men

Luca has faced before. But he's alone, and that makes my stomach coil with dread.

I glance at the lightbulb in the corner behind me: still red.

A wave of heat crawls up my spine when I catch sight of Luca standing in the shadows just outside the room, his back against the wall, knife in hand, so still I nearly miss him. The gleam of the blade catches the low light from the hallway. His posture is tense, but his movements are controlled and ready. He's a predator, waiting for the first of his prey to get close enough.

This is the quiet stillness of a man who knows he's untouchable, who's ready to tear through anything that stands in his way.

I watch as he shifts, silently putting the long knife away and retrieving something else—too small for me to identify. Four attackers come into the room from four different locations, all of them just as silent as Luca. One opens the front door; another climbs in through a window they've quietly opened. Two come from opposite hallways.

None of them are aware Luca is watching. Waiting.

In a flash, he moves his arms, then goes still again, melting back into the darkness.

It's a motion so practiced it could be a dance—fluid but deadly. Every step is calculated, every movement precise. It's as if the whole house holds its breath, frozen in time, the tension thickening the air.

The silence in the house is broken only by the softest thuds as their bodies fall to the floor. No struggle, no noise. They just drop without a sound, their blood pooling beneath them.

I can't breathe, my throat tightening at the sudden violence. I want to look away, but I can't. I have to watch.

Something dark moves on another screen. It's Luca. He's already left that room and is moving through the house he knows so well. His eyes stay fixed on the next target, a deadly calm taking over him. Another attacker comes into view. Another quick slash of his blade. Another body.

I sit frozen in the safe room, my heart racing, my hands shaking as I watch him. There's no hesitation in him. No mercy.

He rounds a doorway into a room. An arm shoots out with a blade aimed for his throat. He grabs the wrist, bending it with a sickening crunch. Luca's blade disappears into the attacker's chest twice, as fast as a cobra striking.

Luca pulls his gun, the silencer making the bullets whisper across the room as he shoots two attackers climbing in through the room's windows.

Someone from the hallway lands a punch to Luca's lower back. He bends with the pain for only a second before turning and slicing the throat of his victim. The body falls, and the now-familiar dark pool of blood seeps across the floor. Luca is careful not to step in it as he moves on.

They aren't trying to kill him. They're trying to capture him.

That awareness is more terrifying than the swarm of attackers. Because catching him will end in torture—likely long and painful before he's graced with death. And likely with me at his side.

My stomach coils, bile rising in my throat. I nearly puke and grab the small trash can under the desk, but it subsides.

My breath catches in my throat as I glance at the red lightbulb again, still glowing steadily in crimson blood—just like the blood being spilled all over the house.

Enzo and Jax are still at the murder barn, unaware of the hell breaking loose here. They don't know Luca needs help. They don't know the entire house is crawling with enemies.

Desperation claws at my chest, but I fight it. I can't panic. I have to focus. I have to stay calm. But how can I? Luca is out there, alone, and I'm here—watching him fight, unable to do anything but clutch my fucking spatula.

I glance back at the security monitor, my gaze locking on Nico, still staring at the same camera, his eyes fixed on the screen, completely detached. If I didn't know better, I'd think he was watching the whole thing like it was some kind of sick game. His face is masked, giving nothing away.

I don't trust this. Why is he just standing there?

Looking away, I turn my attention back to the feed, my eyes searching for Luca.

He's crouched in the corner of his office—the very one where we ate pasta only hours ago.

Four attackers are closing in on him, and he has no way out except through them.

Two of them come in first, and Luca hurls our lunch bowls at them like frisbees. Each shallow bowl strikes them in the throat. They double over, clutching their necks and gasping.

With two fluid pulls of his trigger, Luca drops the two attackers behind them. Then the two choking join the pile of bodies collecting on the floor.

Luca steps over them casually, checking his gun and loading a new clip.

He looks into one of the cameras, and my heart stops as my fingers reach for the screen. He winks, giving me a small smirk before continuing his hunt.

Bodies drop in his wake as he moves with quiet precision

through the farmhouse, which now looks more like a slaughter-house. There must be no fewer than two dozen bodies strewn across the house.

He's making his way across the living room when he stops —just freezes, his gaze focused as if listening intently. And I see why as I look at the other cameras. Six more are headed for him, and he's out in the open.

They come in firing, and Luca is forced to jump behind a sofa. He rises just enough to kill three with efficient shots to the center of their foreheads.

One falls with Luca's knife sticking out of his chest, its last beat taking place around his blade before it stops forever.

The last two attackers come at him from both sides, forcing a two-on-one fight. Luca holds his own, taking some hits but dodging most and landing even more on both of them.

I can see Luca's face—focused and determined—as he fights back with raw power. His fists fly, his body moving with deadly precision. He's a force of nature, too dangerous to stop.

"He's Jason Bourne," I whisper at the screen as he snaps the neck of one attacker before capturing the other in a chokehold.

Luca's legs wrap around the man while his arms squeeze the life out of his body. The man claws at Luca's arm, trying to break free.

Luca moves so quickly it takes me a second to process what happened. He reaches into the man's eye socket, yanks out his eyeball, and shoves it down his throat as the man tries to scream.

"Spat, did you see that shit?" I mutter. It's disgusting—but also, a flex.

I take another look at the red light... still fucking red and

I'm scared to turn on those screens. Afraid I'll see a different reason why Enzo and Jax aren't coming. A vision of them lying dead on the cement floor with Marco tied to his chair flashes in my mind and I brace my hands on the desk to steady myself.

They'll be fine. I'm sure there is a reason they aren't coming. They are just having too much fun taking fingers from Marco. Maybe Jax is putting on a little puppet show with them. Or Enzo is making Marco eat them...

Jesus Delaney.

I'm going insane here and it's only been a few minutes but that doesn't seem like it would be a stretch given what Luca just did.

As I'm thinking through a plan to get out of here and make a run for the murder-barn, I panic when I see the screen Nico had been filling is now empty. He's finally joining the fight and I rake my eyes over the screens until I see him.

I wish I had just kept thinking about finger puppet shows.

Pure terror runs down my body when I see Nico standing at the double ovens. His fingers running over the seams and cracks. He knows the panic room is here. He knows Luca is in the house fighting, so that means he knows I'm in here. *Alone.*

I stick my spatula through one of my holster's belts loops and pull one of the two guns strapped to my legs. I check it again, just like Jax showed me.

I find Luca again on the screens. He's surrounded by several men and is holding a gun in each hand. "Come on baby." I whisper, then I look back at Nico.

He's found the hidden seam of the door and draws a knife. My heart rate skyrockets as I prepare myself for some company.

Nico jams his knife between the thin line, and a shriek pierces the air. The sound is deafening, making my heart lurch in my chest. I immediately cover my ears, wincing, the noise too much to handle.

But then, in an instant, the entire house goes into an automatic lockdown. Thick metal doors, hidden and almost invisible when not activated, slam down with a force that vibrates through the walls. The windows, too, are sealed shut in an instant. They drop down like heavy, impenetrable walls of iron, blocking all access to the outside.

One intruder making his way through one of the windows was sliced cleanly in half. One leg, one arm, his torso and head lay in a bloody heap on the floor. That means his other leg, arm and ass are in a pile on the porch.

I freeze for a moment, breath caught in my throat. The house is sealed tight, trapping us inside. No one can get in. That's the relief, the only bright side. But it also means no one can get out. We're locked in here with Nico and the rest of the men who came to kill us.

It takes Luca all of two seconds to drop every attacker in the room but not before one of them gets a shot off and I pray it didn't hit him. Luca is a storm rushing out of the room, heading for Nico.

I look for buttons, desperate to stop the blaring alarm and finally find a flashing one. Pressing it, the deafening shrieking ends, leaving my ears ringing.

Luca's former dorm-mate, now enemy seems to know Luca is coming for him. He abandons the hidden entrance to the safe room and points a gun at the stairwell he knows Luca will be coming down.

Except he doesn't.

I hold my breath, waiting, unable to find Luca on the monitors.

Just as worry chokes me, dreading the worse has happened, a body comes crashing from the ceiling above Nico who turns his gun up, firing a shot into the body that crashes on top of him. But it was just a member of his own crew, no longer alive thanks to the man dropping from the ceiling next like death coming to claim his next soul.

Luca doesn't waste a second, aiming his gun and shooting Nico. He lands a shot in the shoulder because Nico rolled out of the way, avoiding a bullet to the brain.

Luca brings his gun down, striking Nico in the face but Nico kicks Luca's hand, sending the gun flying across the room and Luca stumbling to the side.

It's enough time for Nico to get up and for Luca to arm himself with another gun. Nico is on the retreat as Luca opens fire until the clip is empty. A new gun is in his hand, and he keeps firing, pushing Nico further into the house and away from the safe room.

My hands are shaking and another glance at the red light ends all resolve. I punch the other screen and bring it to life, seeing what is taking place in the murder barn.

"Fuck me in the ass," I groan when I see Enzo and Jax holding their own against their own horde of attackers.

"It's about time you came out from behind your screens, Nic," Luca calls out, tossing his empty gun to the ground. His hands move casually into his pockets, but I know he's putting on the brass knuckles.

"You may as well have blasted a homing beacon, Luca. After six years of chasing, it took no effort at all to track you down today." Nico snorts a laugh, removing his mask. A long scar runs the length of his face, from the center of his forehead down his left cheek to his jaw.

Movement on two of the monitors pulls my attention. A masked attacker is sneaking up behind Luca. I need to do something. But Nico is facing the safe room door. If I open it, he'll see me in an instant.

"Odd, it's almost like I meant to draw a rat out of a sewer," Luca spits on the floor. "And here you are."

His gaze darkens as he takes his hands out of his pockets. Nico spots the brass knuckles.

"Can't fight me like a man?" Nico taunts.

"I'm not the one who overcompensated by bringing every armed guard I could throw a coin at," Luca replies, circling him.

I can't tell if he's drawing Nico somewhere specific or if they're about to turn the house into a UFC octagon. Either way, Luca and Nico have always been near equals in everything they do. I steel myself, knowing Luca is about to take a few hits.

"You come to *my* home for *my* girl. You should have stayed behind your screens, because you're not leaving here alive," Luca speaks calmly, as if they're comparing hacking techniques. "You'll swallow every one of your teeth and drown in your own blood right here."

Luca widens his stance, raising his fists. With one hand, he motions twice, telling Nico to bring it on. "So, let's go."

Nico moves as fast as Luca, flicking a blade across the room. I gasp, my hands flying to my mouth as the two lions collide.

I look at each of the screens. Enzo and Jax are still knee-deep in attackers, but they're holding their ground. Movement on another screen catches my eye. There are still assailants inside the house.

I take note of their positions—six in total—and with a deep breath, I open the drawer next to me.

Screwing a silencer onto the tip of my handgun, I check it once more, adding two extra clips to my pockets. My hands are shaking, and I struggle to steady them.

If these guys go after Luca, it'll be Nico and all of them against him. I have to help. I can't leave him out there alone, sitting in here and watching him get killed when I can do something about it.

All right, Delaney. You can do this. You're a stone-cold killer.

I take a deep breath and release it. *You're a bad bitch with a spatula.*

I grip the door handle, inhaling deeply one last time before opening it.

Forty-Two

I may have a heart attack as I move quietly through the safe
room's door, my heart pounding in my chest. The spatula
tucked into my belt feels more like an old friend than a
weapon, but right now, it's the only thing keeping me sane. I've
got my silenced gun in hand, and I'm determined to do this.
The sound of fists landing on flesh, followed by the crash of
Luca and Nico slamming into walls, barely registers as I creep
into the kitchen, trying not to draw attention.

I contemplate just shooting Nico, but I can't risk hitting
Luca. I'm not a good enough shot, and they're all over each
other. Trying hard to push their brawl out of my mind, I ready
myself for the next few minutes. I can do this.

"If it's you or them… always make it them."

All right, get ready, motherfuckers. Time to kill some bad
guys.

My focus sharpens as I hear movement from the hallway
beyond. The six gunmen are making their way to the center of
the home where the fight is happening. One of them is
creeping toward the large room behind Luca, who is too busy
with Nico.

I crouch low behind the kitchen counter, silently moving

into position. The adrenaline thrums in my veins, but I force myself to focus. My hands are steady, though my legs are shaking. I adjust my grip on the gun and brace my stance, keeping my eyes locked on the empty space beyond the living room.

The seconds drag by as I wait, heart hammering. My breath is shallow, but I know better than to let it shake my aim.

Then I see the shadow—just a flicker, but enough. My target moves, and I track him as he crosses the space. He's almost in place.

I hold my breath, steadying my gun. The world around me feels like it's slowing down, every second stretched as I wait for the perfect shot. His shadow inches closer, my finger hovering over the trigger.

Then—I pull the trigger.

The shot is silent. The only sound is the crack of glass as I shatter the window behind him, sending shards flying into the air. The first gunman drops, his body falling back as I hit my mark.

I exhale, feeling the rush of success flood through me. It's not the loud, triumphant feeling I imagined. Instead, it's the steady calm that comes from knowing I did what I had to do.

Luca's attention snaps to me, and it costs him a punch to the jaw. He knows I'm out of the safe room, and I can tell by the scowl in his eyes that he hates it. But he can't do anything else but focus on Nico.

And I've got five more guys to look out for.

I reposition myself quickly, keeping the counter between me and the hall. The next two are coming from the left—I can feel it in my gut. They're smart, working in tandem, trying to corner me. I steady my breath, the gun firm in my hands, my heart pumping adrenaline into my veins.

As they step into my line of sight, I aim. The shot rings out, but it's too high, the bullet grazing the wall just beside one of their heads. They duck back into the hall, and I curse under my breath.

I move swiftly, just like I saw Luca do—striking, then shifting my position across the kitchen. I can hear their footsteps—quick, sharp. They're close. The tension builds in my chest as I ready myself for the next move.

Good thing I moved when I did.

One of the men bursts out from the hallway, gun raised, firing where I had just been. My pulse spikes, but I'm already moving, sliding behind the fridge for cover. I wait, breath shallow, and then aim again. This time, I don't miss.

The bullet hits his shoulder first, sending him stumbling back. I don't hesitate. Jax's voice replays in my mind, reminding me to make small adjustments, not big movements.

I fire again, hitting his neck. The man crumples, and my stomach churns at the sight of the blood on the wall. The shot feels wrong, the finality of it weighing heavily on me. But I push it aside, focusing on the next targets.

I take a deep breath, trying to silence the rush of guilt. I think back to the targets in the shooting range and the promise of a reward for each one hit. It's just like that, Delaney. The targets are just... a little different.

Four more to go.

I hear them before I see them and position my gun at what I think should be the right height to land a body shot—the next two rounding the corner together, unaware of me. They've just stepped into my sight when I pull the trigger, taking one down with a shot to the head.

My heart skips a beat as his head explodes on the wall

behind him. There's so much blood—I didn't think that could be real. That kind of thing only happened in movies. But my stomach sinks as I watch the red blood and bits of brain slide down the white wall.

I don't have time to breathe before a shot is fired at me, and I duck, narrowly missing the bullets. My cover's blown.

I wait for a break, but when I rise up, Luca is already firing two shots, taking down both of my shooters. He must have retrieved it from the floor. He turns the gun on Nico and pulls the trigger.

The loud click snaps through the air—the gun is out of bullets. Nico charges Luca, barreling into him like a football player. He pushes Luca into the wall behind him.

I've got one more man to find.

The final attacker retreated into the hallway when I shot the other guy in the shoulder, so I know which way he'll be coming from.

Luca raises his gun and brings it down hard on Nico's skull, and I swear I hear the sickening crack of bone. Luca strikes again and again, bringing Nico to the ground.

I crouch down, placing my gun on the counter. Sliding the spatula out of my belt, I suddenly feel a rush of air behind me and hear the thud of boots on the wooden floor.

There's a click behind me and the unmistakable cold press of a gun against the back of my head.

"Don't fucking move," the voice growls, low and gravelly, sending a cold shiver down my spine.

I close my eyes and release a sigh. *Fuck.*

I forgot about the hole in the ceiling from Luca.

My hand is near the second gun on my other thigh, and by some miracle, it's on the side of my dominant hand. The spatula is in my left hand, and I can feel the heat of the man as he takes a step closer. He's right behind me as Luca continues bashing Nico's face. His hands are coated in blood, and I know it's not his. It's his enemy's.

Gripping the spatula, I flex my fingers and prepare myself. I try to move all at once—small adjustments, not big movements. At the last second, I ram the metal handle of the spatula back, driving it hard into the crotch of the man holding me at gunpoint.

At the same time, I duck and pull my gun.

He fires a silenced shot, but it hits somewhere high on the wall behind me. I spin with my arm extended and level my gun at him. I pull the trigger.

The blast of my gun booms around the home like a cannon. The warmth of his blood splatters on me as his body thuds to the floor in front of me.

I turn to Luca at the same time he snaps his head to me. The terror on his face is quickly erased by relief when he sees I wasn't the one shot.

Luca gets off a lifeless Nico, and I try not to look at his face, but I catch a small glimpse. Let's just say I'll never look at ground beef the same way again.

"Are you okay?" Luca flings the brass knuckles away as I drop my gun, and we race toward each other across the room. I half jump into his arms as we collide, our mouths crashing together, tears free-falling down my face.

We're both covered in other people's blood, and bodies litter the floor like confetti after the ball drops in Times Square. It doesn't matter. We made it.

He pulls away from me, clasping the sides of my face with his hands. "You're okay? Are you hurt?"

I shake my head, catching my breath. "Enzo and Jax are—"

The sound of an explosion rattles us and shakes the house. Luca wraps his arms around me, turning me away as a black SUV plows into the home, splintering wood and shattering glass until it comes to an abrupt stop with its front half in Luca's living room.

Enzo and Jax explode out of the car with guns drawn.

"Enzo and Jax are here," I finish my sentence, breathless.

Forty-Three

"Y**ou're** fucking crazy, Len," Luca says, pulling me into him with an arm around my lower back.

Enzo and Jax look no better than us—covered in blood and out of breath. They step over bodies, coming toward us with the same fury and fire in their eyes.

"Fuck, you guys are okay?" Enzo scans both of us quickly, then gives Jax the same once-over. "They're okay." He releases a heavy exhale as he and Jax put their foreheads together, catching their breath. Enzo places his hands on each side of Jax's jaw, and they just breathe each other in.

Me, on the other hand? I am anything but okay.

It has to be the adrenaline. My body feels like it might explode with all the energy and sensations running through me. It's intoxicating. It's definitely lowering my inhibitions, demanding I feed it. I cross my arms, grabbing the hem of my shirt, and pull it over my head. With my arms low around Luca's waist, I pull him into me and capture his mouth.

"I need you to fuck me," I plead against his mouth, then kiss him again. He moves to my neck, and I look at Jax, then Enzo. "Please. I might die if I don't do something with all of this." Tears well in my eyes, and I can't explain why, but everything is dialed up to a thousand.

They seem to know what I need—or maybe they need it too—because Enzo comes behind me and unclasps my bra. His firm hands find my breasts, pinching my nipples and extracting a moan as I lean against him. Luca removes his shirt and unbuckles his pants. Jax kneels down and unlaces my shoes. I'm not sure who takes off my tights, but I'm naked in seconds.

Jax turns my head and captures my mouth. His warm tongue slides against mine, and it feels like I haven't tasted him in weeks. Enzo works on my neck, his hands kneading my breasts and pulling on my nipples. Luca kneels, taking one of my legs over his shoulder. I fist his hair, and Jax swallows my moan when Luca's mouth greedily sucks on my clit. His fingers slide into me, stroking me as my hips move along with him.

They strip off their clothes as they work my body. Luca brings me to an orgasm quickly.

"Delaney, we've waited so long for you, angel," Enzo murmurs against my skin, making me feel alive, like every nerve ending in my body is buzzing. "Let us make you feel good."

Luca stands and replaces Jax's mouth, wanting me to taste myself on his lips.

Luca grunts, and I feel Jax's soft hair against my thighs. He's sliding Luca into his mouth, his firm hand gripping Luca's cock.

"Fuck, Jax. Fuck," Luca growls, squeezing his eyes shut, fisting Jax's hair, and pumping into his mouth as Enzo turns my chin to him, kissing me deeply, wanting a taste of my arousal as well. His hands grip the globes of my ass, squeezing as he reaches around, circling my clit with his finger.

Jax pulls away, spitting on Luca's dick before standing up. I feel myself get wetter. Jax kisses Luca, circling his cock with his grip, sliding along his shaft.

"Go lay down," Jax tells him in a quiet tone.

He looks at Enzo and nods toward the couch. It's a wrap-around sectional, cream in color, with dramatic red splotches of blood, like someone threw a red can of paint at it periodically. Some of the bodies lie on top of each other. Others have fallen, landing between chairs and tables. Arms stick up awkwardly, held in place by the surrounding furniture.

Enzo picks me up, one arm under my knees and the other behind my back. I wrap an arm around his neck and kiss him as he carries me over the bodies and blood.

"I told you, the next time I fuck you, I'm taking this ass, angel," Enzo says as he puts me down on Luca's lap.

I straddle Luca's hips, fisting him as I lean down and kiss him, rubbing my wet pussy along his shaft before lining him up and working myself onto him.

Luca leaves his bloody handprints on my hips as he holds me, grinding me into him.

"Fuck, look at her," Jax says, practically panting, his hand sliding up and down his dick. He's taken off his shirt but has only lowered his pants enough to free his erection.

"Jax." I'm nearly whining as I lick my lips, staring at his cock.

"Goddamn, Peach. You want me to feed you my cock?" He pinches my chin, tilting my head up and taking my mouth in a rough kiss.

"Please." I break the kiss to beg, then kiss him again. "Fill me up. I want to feel all of you, everywhere."

"Christ, Lenny," Luca growls, sitting up and capturing my nipple with his mouth. "Your pussy is so tight."

He smacks my ass, grabbing my hip firmly. His teeth graze my nipple as he bites down gently, then sucks hard. He rocks his hips faster, his hand on my hip helping me grind my clit against him.

"Make her come again, Luca," Jax commands, his hand still sliding along his cock as Enzo steps closer behind him.

"Just a finger, angel," Enzo whispers, his voice low and teasing. "You look so fucking beautiful riding his big dick. Does it feel good, baby?"

Luca continues working my tits, thrusting and rocking me as Enzo slides his middle finger into my ass.

"Good, angel. God, you're fucking perfect. Now come for us." He kisses my neck, and a second later, another orgasm washes through me. Enzo adds another finger as pleasure holds me captive.

My cunt pulses around Luca, and he lets his head roll back, holding himself up with one arm. His free hand slides to Jax, gripping his cock while the sounds of my pleasure echo through the room.

"You're ready for me now, angel."

I glance behind me to see Enzo squeezing a lube packet onto his palm.

"Well, aren't you prepared," I say with a breathless laugh, though my voice is so rich with need that I barely recognize it.

"Come here, Jax," Luca says quietly.

I turn just in time to see Luca's tongue flick over Jax's cock before taking it into his mouth.

"Oh, fuck," I pant, my pussy clenching around Luca as he groans against Jax.

"Just like that." Jax watches Luca's mouth devour him. I only look away when Enzo presses his warm body against me.

"Lean forward," Enzo murmurs against my neck, his lips brushing my skin. Luca lies down beneath me, his hands gripping my hips and gently rocking me against him. I lean down to kiss him, arching my back to give Enzo access to my ass.

Jax kneels behind Luca's head, his hands rubbing down my back, his thumbs working into my tense muscles. All of them are focused on me—relaxing me, taking care of me, readying me so I can take Enzo's cock. If I've played my cards right, they'll fuck me within an inch of my life.

"Relax, baby," Luca whispers against my lips.

Enzo presses the head of his cock against my ass.

"Just kiss me," Luca murmurs. His hand guides my jaw back to his, and he kisses me through Enzo's slow, gentle slide into my ass.

Enzo moves carefully, pushing in until just the tip is inside. He pauses.

"You're doing so good, angel," he whispers, letting me acclimate to the stretch. He drizzles more lube on his cock, his movements inside me small and deliberate, ensuring he doesn't hurt me.

I brace myself against Luca's chest, leaning up slightly.

"More," I say, closing my eyes and savoring the sensation of being completely filled.

"Jax, more," I plead, opening my mouth, needing him there.

"I'll give you what you need, baby." Jax's husky voice cocoons me as he leans forward, sliding his cock into my mouth. I groan, tasting the salty tease of his arousal.

"That's a good girl, baby," Luca says, his hands firm on my hips as I begin to move. My cheeks hollow as I take Jax's cock deeper into my mouth.

"Fuck, you were made for us, Peach," Jax says, holding my chin sweetly. "Look at me. I want to watch you take my thick cock down your throat."

"My God, Jax," Luca pants. "Keep talking. She's squeezing me with everything you say."

I open my eyes, locking on Jax's. His gaze softens, and he smiles, his dark brown eyes warm.

"Beautiful," he whispers.

Enzo is fully inside me now, his hard cock adding to the fullness as Luca stretches my cunt. I've never felt so complete in my life.

He pulls back on my hair just enough to send a sharp tingle of pain down my spine—not enough to make me lose my hold on Jax's cock, but enough to hold me still. They're priming me, ready to take me how they want, ready to make me theirs entirely.

"We're going to fuck you until you can't walk," Enzo growls, his voice dark and commanding. "Then we'll carry you to bed."

He slides his cock nearly out of me, only to push back in, while Luca holds me up and pounds into me from below. I moan around Jax's cock, my body trembling from the sheer intensity of it all.

"Then, we're going to fuck you again," Enzo promises, his lips brushing against my ear.

"That's it, baby," Jax murmurs, his hips thrusting gently as he slides his cock deeper into my mouth. Their rhythm is perfect—one pulling out as another pushes in—leaving me no time to think, only to feel.

The burn is exquisite, a hurt that feels so good I want more.

I release Jax's cock with a pop, reaching for a hand to squeeze my nipples, desperate for more sensation.

Instead, my fingers brush against something cold and lifeless.

"Ew!" I shout, throwing the dead man's arm away. "Fucking bodies everywhere. Someone with a pulse better squeeze my tits until I—"

Luca takes the cue immediately, his hands gripping my breasts, pinching and twisting my nipples as he pounds into me from below. Enzo spits onto his fingers, then circles my clit, sending electric shocks through my body.

"Get your fucking mouth back on me," Jax commands, his cock pressing against my lips.

I obey, taking him back into my mouth as he thrusts deep, his pace quickening.

"That's it, baby. Suck this dick," Jax growls, his head falling back as his hands grip my head, holding me steady. "You were made to be our slut, weren't you?"

I can't answer—one, because my mouth is full, and two, because the most intense orgasm of my life is barreling toward me.

A sharp smack lands on my ass, making me yelp around Jax's cock.

"Answer, Delaney," Enzo demands, his grip on my hair tightening as he slams into my ass. "You belong to us, don't you? We own you. This pretty pussy—" he smacks my clit, making me whimper, my cunt clenching around both him and Luca—"this perfect ass. You're all ours, baby. Forever."

Their words unravel me completely.

"She fucking loves that," Luca growls, his thrusts becoming

more frantic. "You're going to come so hard on my cock, aren't you, Lenny?"

I mumble a yes, earning harder thrusts and a sharp pinch to my nipple.

"Come on, Peach," Jax says, his voice thick with desire. "Come with me. You're sucking my dick so good, I'm going to explode."

His hips jerk as he thrusts into my mouth, shorter and faster, his cock twitching against my tongue.

"Ah, baby. That's it." Jax's voice cracks as his orgasm overtakes him, and I feel him release.

The taste of him and the intensity of Luca and Enzo's thrusts send me spiraling. My body explodes with sensation, every nerve lit up as I scream through my climax. My cunt clenches hard around Luca, and Enzo's cock pulses deep inside me.

"Oh, goddamn it. Sit her up," Jax commands breathlessly.

Enzo pulls back on my hair, adjusting his hips to keep himself buried in my ass. Luca presents my breasts to Jax, who bathes them in his cum as I cry out, my orgasm still gripping me.

"Fuck," Jax breathes, his release dripping down my chest onto Luca. "So fucking perfect."

Jax's orgasm subsides but Luca and Enzo's are building, and I feel like mine is still pounding against me.

"Fuck me harder." I cry out as Enzo keeps hold of my hair.

Luca leans up, licking Jax's cum from my tits, sucking my nipples into his mouth with a whimper.

"Does his cum taste good on me, baby?" I hold the back of Luca's head against my breast as he keeps pounding into me from the bottom. Luca answers with another whimper and I squeeze my pussy, clinching my ass.

"Shit, Delaney." Enzo smacks my ass again. "You're so fucking bad, gripping my dick with this tight ass so you can make me come?" He pulls back more on my hair making me yelp it feels so fucking good. "Do it again because I want to punish you for how perfect you are." I clinch tight and moan when his hand cracks against the globe of my ass again.

Jax is kneeling beside Luca now lubing his finger. "You want some too Luc?" Jax seduces him as he runs his finger along Luca's ass. Opening his mouth and inviting Luca's tongue while he inserts his finger into Luca's wanting ass. "Fuck her hard, Luca. I want to feel you come with my fingers in your ass."

I clinch at his dirty mouth. I clinch because Luca pounds into me as he nips at my breasts. And I clinch again when Enzo's cock pulses inside me.

Smack.

Smack.

Smack.

"Such a bad slut." Enzo growls. "Now you're going to come for us again while we pump you full." He flicks my clit again and I cry out.

Luca's strong hands grip my hips and shows me no mercy. I feel him everywhere, so deep inside me and I cry out with each pound.

Enzo spanks me again, "Louder, baby. When we fuck you this good, I want all of Wisconsin to hear you." Another smack, then he's back to my clit rubbing and thrusting like his life depends on it.

It feels like a dozen orgasms crash through me at once and I actually do scream. Over and over, it seems to be the only way I can breathe through the intensity. Just when I think it's going to ebb again, Enzo pinches my clit, holding it as he and Luca fuck me senseless.

I don't know what is happening, but I feel like I can't control my body. The orgasm completely takes me over and it's like I'm demon possessed.

I need a fucking exorcism but god I never want this to end.

Finally, the peak begins to fade away and I open my eyes. Black spots dot my vision as I take in deep breaths before I look down at Luca.

He's not looking at me though. He's looking between us, where his cock disappears into my cunt.

"What?" I ask, looking down and I think I may have pissed myself. Luca looks at me with a cocked grin.

"Are you a squirter, Lenny?"

Forty-Four

Jax finds me a robe from Luca's closet. It swallows me whole, but it's so warm. Luca pulls a truck around to the front, and Jax carries me to the vehicle, so I don't step on shards of wood, glass, or blood—and probably some brain matter. Just thinking about it makes me shiver.

"You okay, Peach?"

I nod and smile. "I was just thinking how gross it would be if I stepped on some brain and it squished between my toes. Ugh!" I shiver again.

"Well, stop thinking about that." He laughs and sets me in the front seat of the truck. His warm hands rub my thighs, and I hold his face, needing to kiss him.

"I watched you on the video. I was so scared," I whisper, my voice cracking and my eyes watering.

"Hey, don't cry, baby." He kisses my cheek, catching my tear on his lips. "We would fight through the armies of hell to get to you." He wraps his big arms around me and holds me close.

I feel the truck tremble, followed by the sound of something heavy being loaded into the bed of the truck.

"Is that our new fingerless friend, Marco?" I murmur into Jax's chest, not wanting him to pull away.

He rumbles a soft laugh. I look up at him. "Sadly, our buddy caught a bullet with his skull and won't be joining us for the rest of the trip."

Ah.

Enzo steps around. "She good?" he asks Jax, his brow furrowed with concern.

"Yeah, I'm good," I say with a grin that I know comes across as a bit melancholy.

Jax leaves to get things from the back of the SUV, and Luca steps out of the wreckage from the recent "renovation."

"Hey, you didn't run over my computer!" He holds his laptop up in one hand, grinning like a kid in a candy store. "I can't believe you destroyed my house, though," he adds, standing by the truck, surveying the damage.

"Yeah, it doesn't feel good, does it?" I snap, suddenly remembering he blew up my house.

He throws his head back and barks a laugh. Setting the computer in my lap, he leans in and gives me a kiss.

"I didn't actually blow up your house, Lenny."

Oh. *Well, shit.* Those assholes let me believe my house was gone for five days. Payback is going to be a bitch for this.

We drive a few minutes down the property's main road to a lodge overlooking a small lake. I'm sitting in Jax's lap because... well, he wanted me to. The truck's headlights shine on the bodies littering the grass. I can see the murder barn in the distance.

"Jesus," I mutter, staring out the window. It looks like an old battlefield, bodies lying still where soldiers fell.

"I've already got someone on the way for cleanup, Peach," Jax says, rubbing my leg as he looks out the window with me.

Inside the lodge is a large open space with a living room and a giant couch. A long, rustic wooden dining table with two matching benches sits in the back corner, and the kitchen spans nearly the entire back length of the building. To the right is a pool table, where the boys set our bags.

"I'm going to get Lenny a shower," Luca says, taking my hand and leading me upstairs while Jax and Enzo finish unloading the truck.

In the shower, Luca holds me under the hot water, running his hands through my hair and helping wash away the blood and dirt of our battle.

"You came out there for me," he says, his deep blue eyes locking onto mine. Droplets of water hang from his tousled hair, and suds run down our bodies.

"Of course I did." I wrap my arms around him, standing on my tiptoes. "How could I let you fight alone?"

My eyes drop to his chest for a second as I recall the head exploding on the wall. I try to blink it away, but it's burned into my mind.

"It'll get easier," Luca says, rubbing my face gently. I think he knows the weight of the lives I took is beginning to press on me. "I'm here for you, baby."

He picks me up, and I wrap my legs around his waist, locking my ankles behind him. I swear to God, these men are never going to let me walk again. They seem to plan on carrying me... forever.

Turning off the water, he steps out of the shower and sets me on the counter to grab a towel from the warmer. Wrapping me in it, he hugs me to his chest, releasing a deep sigh.

"I'll be okay, I think," I tell him, sitting back to look at him. "I did it for you. They were going to hurt you."

I cup his face with my hands. "I would shoot them again if I had to." He leans down and kisses me. "I would burn this world to ash for you, Luca Bellini."

Luca smiles, and my entire world seems to calm.

"I'll never leave you again, Lenny." He rubs my arms, drying me and helping me stay warm. "I'll never leave your side. And I'll never hide you away during a fight again."

This time it's my turn to smile.

"From now on, every step is together," he says firmly.

I nod, and happy tears fall from my eyes as he hugs me tightly.

"I love you, Lenny," he whispers before kissing me again.

Two knocks against the doorframe make us turn. Enzo appears, a towel wrapped low around his waist.

I try not to stare, but the outline of his dick under the towel is impossible to ignore.

My gaze isn't the only one wandering—Luca's is too.

Enzo covers his chest with one hand and his junk with the other. "I am not a piece of meat," he balks.

"It's not our fault you look like a Greek god," Luca retorts.

"Jax is making us some food. Come help me move these beds together in the loft?"

I gasp. "Does my dream of being deliciously squished by all three of you while we sleep actually get to come true?"

Enzo gives me one of those rare smiles I try to memorize every time. But this one lingers. He saunters over, placing a hand at the small of my back.

"Every night, angel," he promises, pinching my chin gently

between two fingers and leaning in to kiss me. "Now that we have you, we're never letting you go."

Enzo and Luca slide two giant king-size beds together, securing them with zip ties to hold them in place. Meanwhile, I help Jax in the kitchen which consists of me snacking on mozzarella cheese while he slaps my butt each time he walks by.

There's a pizza oven here, and apparently, when money is no object and you order food for a one-night visit, all the kitchens get stocked with provisions. Jax works the pre-made pizza dough with practiced ease. In no time, the smell of melted cheese and garlicky sauce wafts through the lodge.

I take a swig of beer as Jax feeds me a bite of pizza.

Of course, a mouth-gasm activates instantly. It's so fucking good, and Jax knows it. His dimples are on full display as he watches me savor the food he cooked.

"Is it weird I want you to fuck me with this pizza?" I ask, tearing off a piece to feed him.

His eyes widen in surprise, mid-bite, just as Luca and Enzo join us.

Enzo pulls me into his lap at the table, his hands resting on my hips as I rub his shoulders.

"Are you sore?" he asks tenderly, his hands working magic on my thighs.

"A little," I admit, kissing him softly. "But it feels good. Like I've survived a gunfight and been well and properly fucked."

"Damn right," he says with a satisfied grin. "We'll keep you that way."

"So, Squirt," Jax teases, and I gasp audibly, my cheeks instantly heating.

"How. *Dare*. You." My face must look like a cherry tomato as I bury it in the crook of Enzo's neck. "It's so embarrassing."

"Hey, none of that," Luca says, grabbing my chin gently and turning me to face him. Jax and Enzo wear matching smug smiles, and Luca is trying—and failing—to hold his back. "You've really never squirted before? We were your first?"

I nod, still mortified.

"Oh, Lenny," he says, rubbing his thumb across my lip. "You shouldn't have told me that. We're going to make you flood our bed every time we fuck you now."

Jesus.

"God, that's fucking sexy," Enzo growls as Luca leans down to kiss me fast before abandoning me for his true love: the fresh pizza Jax is setting on the table.

"Peach, I'm telling you this right now," Jax says seriously, though the sucker stick hanging from his mouth kills the effect. "If you don't drown me the next time you sit on my face, I'm not going to talk to you for like... an hour."

"Ooh, don't threaten me with a good time." I wink at him.

Jax narrows his eyes at me playfully before sitting next to Luca, who shares a fresh slice of pizza with me. Luca uses his thumb to wipe some sauce from the corner of my mouth, then sucks it off.

"You sure you're okay, Lenny?" he asks, his voice softer now. "It was a heavy day... and an even heavier night."

I take a moment to think about it.

Luca and I working things out didn't feel heavy—it felt freeing. I felt lighter. Even after he told me about his mother, about how he killed her and everything else, it was a lot, but not heavy.

I take his hand, playing with his long fingers that I love so much.

"I killed strangers," I blurt out, and Luca flinches. I know he wishes I didn't have that experience weighing on my shoulders, but it's done now. "It should feel heavier, but it's not. Because it was for us."

"The first time is hard, baby," Luca says, his voice quieter now.

Jax places a hand on Luca's thigh, understanding the weight his mother's death still holds.

"No," I shake my head. "The weight of this is not the same. They were strangers. Nothing to me. Luca, you had a lifetime of memories with your mother that I don't have. I have one cup of hot chocolate…"

The memory surges through me, unlocking a chest full of forgotten moments. My father's voice echoes in my mind.

Il mio tesoro.

My treasure.

I freeze as the memory plays out, my eyes widening as tears form and spill down my cheeks.

"Lenny, what is it, baby?" Luca asks, panicked, cupping my face in his hands.

But I'm trapped in the memory, a prisoner to the flood of emotions.

"Is she having a panic attack?" Enzo kneels beside me, his gentle touch brushing my cheek. "Angel?"

His soft tone slowly pulls my gaze to him, and the room comes back into focus.

"I—" My throat feels dry as I try to speak. "I remember."

"What do you remember, Peach?" Jax is behind Luca now, kneeling on the bench and holding my hand.

"Everything."

Forty-Five

I t's not as odd, pulling up to my old childhood home, as I thought it would be. If you can even call this place a home. It's a goddamn fortress—let's not kid ourselves. I always remembered it as stark, cold, and empty. But it looks much different now, coming back after so many years away.

I didn't sleep much last night, and when dreams finally came to me, they were restless—full of lightning and a little girl staring at her reflection in a large window. I woke up first and snuck out of the massive bed, fashioned so we could all sleep together.

Enzo found me sitting on the wide wooden deck overlooking the lake behind the lodge. He's always been an early riser—a workaholic. But I suppose you have to be to run a multibillion-dollar empire.

He sat in the deck chair next to me, and I traded my cold chair for his warm lap. His massive frame swallowed me whole, and I felt like I could just nuzzle into his neck and disappear for the next twenty-four hours.

But the peace didn't last long. We needed to get ready for the reading of my father's will and still had an hour's drive to the Chicago estate.

Jax said a quick hello, then checked the grounds to ensure they were clean after last night's gunfight. Aside from the massive hole and damage inside Luca's home, you wouldn't be able to tell anything had happened. The house has been sealed off, and repairs will begin today.

Enzo brought his team to the lodge, equipped with a rack of clothes for me to pick from, a hair and makeup stylist, and fresh suits for themselves. Black on black on black seemed to be the color palette of choice, so I went with a fitted black gown. The draped front dipped low, hugging every curve perfectly. The long slit ran up to my upper thigh, and when I sat, crossing my legs, the dress fell open on either side of my knees, with the rest of the fabric pooling on the floor.

I touched up my deep-red nail polish, and Luca kissed my ankle as he helped me with my heels.

It was a ridiculous show of force as we pulled out of the long driveway from Luca's farmhouse to the main road. The timing was perfect. An entourage of black SUVs was already racing down the road. Our limo pulled out behind them, and an equal number of SUVs followed us.

Everything about today needed to be a statement, and it started with my arrival at the Caputo estate. We went over the plans again and again last night, and while I felt ready, at the same time... I didn't.

I grew up next to crime and mafia dealings my whole life and never knew it. My father was terrifying, and so was the company he kept. I was happy being separate from it.

Now, after running away for six years, I'm diving headfirst into a tank of bloodthirsty sharks. *Wonderful.*

I didn't remember the entrance from the road being so large, but there's no mistaking the Caputo "**C**" on the crest of the massive gates. The long driveway winds through a forest first, where the security gates are already open for us.

The trees clear, giving way to manicured lawns, and then I see it—the impressive home.

Tall cypress trees line the driveway and decorate the front of the opulent villa. The line of SUVs turns right, following the circular drive. The limo stops in the center, and the guards spring into action.

Some step out, taking positions on either side of the wide walkway leading up to the front door. Others remain by their vehicles, ever watchful. Several surround the limo, and one opens our door.

Enzo steps out first, adjusting his suit jacket. Luca and Jax exit from the other side while Enzo holds out his hand for me. I know he can feel the tremor in my fingers as he helps me from the car. He gives my hand an extra squeeze and a wink as I step in front of them, walking with my shoulders back and confidence in my stride.

The boys fall in step behind me, and while I want to look around, I know there must be no fewer than a dozen eyes on me as the long-lost Caputo heiress returns to claim her empire.

Luca had drones flying over the property all morning, so we watched from the limo as the heads of mafia families arrived. We practiced names as we watched the drone footage, then switched to the security feed in the house, watching them mingle.

Giovanni "Johnny Boy" Moretti was the first to arrive, and I chuckled, remembering my dance with Mr. Moretti and Eloise's confessions in the bathroom. He looked absolutely nothing like Mr. Moretti, so anyone with eyes could tell his first wife stepped out on him and had the milkman's baby.

Domenico "Dom" Ferrara, a strong enforcer of the Italians, and his men are often sent to collect debts from rival families. Raffaele "Ralphie" D'Angelo, a loan shark and extortionist, spent years working closely with my father. Now that my father's gone, D'Angelo is eager to position himself and his family at the top of Chicago's underworld.

Antonio "Tony" Vitale is Enzo's cousin. The Vincenzi and Vitale boys have been long-running partners, known for their involvement in high-end real estate and money laundering operations. If there's one family I know will be on my side today, it's theirs. And they're a force to be reckoned with.

I was especially excited to see Francesca "The Queen" Lazzarini arrive, and she did not disappoint. The first and only female boss, her icy demeanor and strategic brilliance were evident from a mile away. In black heels and a black pinstripe pantsuit jacket worn without a shirt, her buttoned blazer revealed just enough. Her ear-length black hair was styled in loose curls, with one side shaved. Her piercing green eyes scanned the property before she helped her wife out of their vehicle.

Lazzarini is a true story of rags to riches within the Italians, keeping her family under the radar while quietly expanding their influence. Now, she sits at the table with the other family heads—a formidable equal—and it's impressive.

Other families haven't survived the weeklong power struggle incited by my father's death. Some are recovering, licking their wounds and laying low. So, there's something to be said for those here today. These are the survivors.

After the Italians, the other mobs arrive, save the Sicilians who were wiped out in a mob war about four years before I was born. With the stature of the Caputo name, the heads of gangs attend in person. No representatives or dignitaries would be appropriate to meet the new leader of the Italians.

The Asian mobs and Irish arrive simultaneously. The Polish and Mexican mafias come next, with others filing in succession. The Russian Bratva arrives about five minutes before we do—definitely by design. They're setting themselves up as rivals or equals. Either way, they're someone to watch.

My heels click loudly against the concrete path as I pass the line of staff working full-time at the estate. I want to stop and say hello, maybe look for familiar faces, but there will be time for that later. These people work for the mafia—they know how these things go. All of them dip their heads in reverence as I pass, while I pretend this isn't weird as hell.

Two guards wait just inside and walk ahead of me. Enzo, Jax, and Luca follow behind, with more guards bringing up the rear. I keep my eyes forward while trying to take in the details.

Touches of our Italian heritage are everywhere—in the home's design and the art that hangs on the walls. It feels warmer now—not at all the drab, chilling place from my memories.

I had dreaded what it would feel like to be here again. I was certain I'd want to level this place and never step foot on these grounds again. But perhaps not.

The reading of the will is set in my father's wine cellar. It's vast—like an entirely separate estate underground. There's an elevator, but descending the wide marble staircase that curves into the cellar is much more dramatic.

And today is all about putting on a show.

Enzo takes my hand as we descend the stairs. I hold my dress with the other hand and take a deep breath as we head into the belly of the beast.

Forty-Six

As soon as the curve of the stairs reveals us, the family heads rise from their seats, their eyes fixed on me. They sit around the largest table I've ever seen. It must be twice the width and length of a standard table. Each family head sits in their designated space, with enough room on either side for another person or two.

I suppose it's better to spread them out rather than stack a bunch of killers on top of each other.

There's an open spot at the head of the table for me. Another seat next to it remains empty for Enzo, as head of the Vincenzi family. A few other empty chairs mark the families who are absent. On the other side of my seat is the executor of the will, who will oversee today's reading.

Giuseppe Thomas.

I can't stop fangirling over his name. Giuseppe.

I must have said it twenty times today, each time pinching my fingers together and saying, "Fuhgeddaboudit." Jax joined in, and I thought Enzo was going to burst a blood vessel on the way here.

"Giuseppe is going to be my new safe word," Jax announces with a gleam in his eye.

"I swear to God," Enzo huffs under his breath, "I will get out and walk the rest of the way."

"You'd be late then. You said twelve times the families can't arrive after I do," I remind him, echoing the rules he drilled into me last night.

"Hey," Luca rubs Enzo's knee, his eyes full of earnest understanding, "just fuhgeddaboudit." He cracks a smile on the last few syllables, and Jax and I burst out laughing.

"Not you too," Enzo groans, shaking his head.

Several minutes later, while Luca distracted Enzo with drone footage, I sneaked Enzo's phone away. Jax huddled close to me, holding down the button until the phone assistant popped up.

"Set a reminder in three days that Jax's new safe word is Giuseppe," he whispered into the phone. I quickly blacked out the screen and slipped it back before Enzo noticed.

As the man, the myth, the legend himself, Giuseppe, stands to greet me, I cast a quick, knowing look behind me. Jax and Luca suppress grins while Enzo rolls his eyes toward the ceiling, as if sending a prayer for patience.

"It's lovely to see you again, Ms. Caputo. Though I admit, the last time we met, you were just a girl and likely don't remember me," Giuseppe says, taking my hand with both of his.

He must be in his mid-seventies, with white hair and bushy black eyebrows. I imagine he's seen it all after working for the mafia for so long. "I knew Salvatore since he was a baby. I'm truly sorry for your loss."

"Thank you, Mr. Thomas," I reply politely. Hearing good things about my father isn't something I'm accustomed to.

"You are the spitting image of your father, but much prettier," he says warmly, his eyes gleaming.

"I would hope so," I tease back with a small smile.

"I have everything prepared as requested, Ms. Caputo. We can begin when you're ready." He nods and returns to his seat.

Enzo takes his place as one of the family heads. Jax and Luca position themselves behind my chair, with Luca pulling it out for me. A snicker from the table catches my attention, and I turn to see "Johnny Boy" Moretti sneering at me, shaking his head as if I'm carrying the zombie plague.

"Ah," I say, changing course and rounding the table toward him. "You must be 'Johnny Boy' Moretti." I extend my hand, and he can't refuse it in front of so many family heads. "I had the pleasure of meeting your father recently."

His eyes narrow, but he takes my hand. As he does, I yank him toward me, catching him off guard. He stumbles, nearly face-planting onto the marble floor as he grabs the table for support. His ear is now close enough for me to whisper.

"We both know there's not a drop of Moretti blood in your body," I say, my voice low and level. "I'd keep my head down if I were you, before a blood test proves you're just a low-level soldier pretending a limp dick is your daddy. M'kay?" I let go of his tie and watch him straighten himself, his face as red as a tomato. "Nice tie. Is that polyester?"

I walk back to my chair without waiting for a response.

"Thank you all for coming. Please, be seated." I take my seat, and Luca pushes my chair in. The guests follow suit, their companions and bodyguards lining the back walls.

Jax reaches around to the open wine bottle in front of me, pouring me a glass.

Being in my father's wine cellar, it's no surprise he had a

vast collection, including his favorite—a rich port wine. I was pleased to find bottles of my favorite wine stocked, so I requested some be opened for the guests.

Careful not to let my fingers tremble, I raise my glass. "To Salvatore Caputo."

The guests lift their glasses with solemn nods, some murmuring my father's name before taking a sip. I set my glass down, my deep-red lipstick staining the rim.

My new best friend Giuseppe begins the reading of the will. Gathering his papers, he steps to a podium. Clearing his throat, he begins to read the words that will change the rest of my life.

"This is the last will and testament of Salvatore Caputo," he announces, each word heavy with significance. "This document shall serve as the official transfer of power, effective immediately upon my client's death."

The tension in the room is palpable as his words echo.

Giuseppe clears his throat, turning the page as the weight of his words settles over the room. "I, Giuseppe Thomas, prepared this will with Mr. Caputo, drafted during a pivotal time in his life when he and Mrs. Caputo were expecting their first child—a daughter named Delaney Caputo. Salvatore, ever the protector and visionary, ensured this document would secure the succession of the Caputo name in the event of his passing."

His gaze flickers to me briefly before he continues, his voice steady. "Everything in this will was prepared with his greatest treasure in mind: the future of the Caputo family."

My chest tightens at his phrasing. *Il mio tesoro.* The words echo in my memory. To my father, the future of the Caputo family was his treasure—me.

"Salvatore Caputo, in his final wishes, bequeaths his entire estate and all assets, both personal and business-related, to his beloved wife, Stella Caputo. In the event of her passing, all estate responsibilities and assets are to transfer to his only child, Delaney Caputo. As his next of kin, Delaney will assume all responsibilities associated with the Caputo family, including its assets, operations, and the family business itself."

A murmur ripples through the room, but it quickly dies out. The gathered family heads exchange glances, their expressions ranging from wary to intrigued. I keep my face neutral, even as my heart races. This isn't just about inheriting a fortune; it's about stepping into a legacy of power, violence, and betrayal. The enormity of it presses down on me.

Giuseppe's voice cuts through the tension. "Is there anyone present who disputes the passing of Salvatore Caputo's assets or wishes to present a claim?"

Silence.

It's a silence that feels heavy, expectant, like the calm before a storm. My grip on the chair tightens, and I scan the faces around the table. No one speaks, but their eyes are on me—calculating, assessing. It's clear that my every move is being scrutinized.

Just as the moment stretches too long, the sounds of cars rushing the mansion sound outside. The guests within the cellar, their guards lining the walls, rustle in agitated nervousness.

I hold out a hand, "Please remain calm and seated. Everything is under control." I make a point to look at each family head as I speak.

There is no gunfire. Just another stretch of uncomfortable

silence before the sound of heels clicking against the marble floor echoes into the interior of the villa.

The rhythmic taps grow louder, echoing through the room. Heads turn, whispers break out, and my pulse quickens. I don't need to look to know who it is. I've been preparing for this moment.

An entourage of bodyguards walk ahead of their boss, lining the room and making a dramatic show of force that is to be an intimidation.

The steps stop just outside my line of sight, and I hear the metallic clink of jewelry. Slowly, deliberately, a manicured hand —long red nails, dripping with gold rings—rests on the table. The fingers curl as she steps into view, her eyes locked on mine. Her hazel gaze is sharp, predatory, and her smile is the kind that sends a chill down your spine.

The room holds its breath but being this is now *my* house; I break the silence. My voice is steady, carefully masking the undercurrent of tension and anger lacing my words.

"Hello, mother."

Forty-Seven

My mother's smile widens, relishing the chaos she's caused in the room. The heads of families who attended her funeral are reeling, trying to process the woman who's just walked in—alive, after twenty years of being presumed dead. It's clear she's enjoying this moment, watching them squirm. She looks at me, her gaze cold but pleased.

"Well, well, Delaney," she says, her voice silk-smooth, almost condescending. "What a lovely woman you've become."

I swallow down my temper, my heartbeat accelerating. This isn't the first time I've been face-to-face with her—not really. But it feels like the first time. I've spent years believing she was gone, buried under a sea of repressed memories. But now, after last night, the truth is as sharp as glass, and I'm not the little girl staring at her reflection anymore.

"No thanks to you," I respond, my voice steady but carrying the weight of everything I'll never be able to say.

She raises her wineglass, clearly expecting someone to serve her.

Just like the mystery hand I watched emerge from the shadows at Enzo's club in Butte. Those red talon nails and gold rings are what connected all the dots for me last night. I felt the weight of that woman's gaze staring at me from the dark booth, and it's just as heavy now.

"Serve yourself," I tell her, my voice sharp and decisive. "No one here will be doing your bidding."

For a moment, I see a flicker of something—maybe surprise, maybe offense—but she hides it quickly. She's used to getting what she wants, used to commanding the room, and it bothers her that I'm not playing along.

She stands, walking to the table behind her. Uncorking a bottle of port, she pours herself a generous glass with careful deliberation. The silence in the room stretches, everyone waiting as our family drama unfolds.

"Is this any way to treat your mother after twenty years missing at sea?" she asks, taking a sip, her tone dripping with faux sweetness.

"Missing?" I repeat, the disbelief clear in my voice. "That's an interesting way to put it for someone who faked her death for two decades."

She scoffs at my words, as if she's not used to people questioning her. With a flick of her wrist, she waves away the accusation like it's nothing. "Being the leader of a mafia family requires sacrifices you could never understand, Delaney."

I take a deep breath, my resolve hardening. "You're right," I reply, my voice cutting through the tension. "I don't understand. But I'm starting to."

The tension in the room grows thick, every set of eyes on me as Stella raises an eyebrow over the rim of her wineglass. She takes another slow sip, savoring the control she thinks she still holds.

"Giuseppe," she says, her voice smooth and dangerous, "since I am *still* Mrs. Caputo, despite your... widower's thoughts, it is my right to inherit my late-husband's estate, not my daughter's."

The air in the room shifts. Every eye turns to Giuseppe Thomas, waiting for confirmation. He looks to Stella, then to me, and nods slowly. "That is correct," he says, his voice even.

The room murmurs with speculation, the gossip rising as events no one could have predicted unfold like a stage play.

I raise my hand, cutting through the whispers. "Question, Mr. Thomas," I say, my voice strong. "I believe there is a clause in the will stating one cannot inherit the estate of someone they murdered. Is that correct?"

The tension in the room becomes a heavy fog. All eyes snap to me, and then quickly to Stella. She keeps her face neutral, the façade still in place, but the air is charged.

Gasps ripple through the gathered families.

Giuseppe's face doesn't waver. He nods again. "That is also correct," he confirms, his voice tinged with an unspoken understanding of the gravity of the situation.

My mother's lips curl into a cold smile, one that doesn't reach her eyes. She tilts her head slightly, as if amused by my boldness. Her laugh echoes in the room, hollow, sharp, and full of malice.

"My husband's death was ruled a heart attack," she says, her tone unbothered. "There was no evidence of foul play."

"Well, to be factually correct, there was evidence—lots of it. It was just... removed."

I stand, grabbing my wineglass and walking slowly toward her end of the table, my eyes never leaving hers. Several of her guards shift nervously which makes Jax and Enzo shift.

Stella holds her hand out to her guards, quieting them down.

"Funny how that works," I say, my voice calm but edged with something darker, as I take a sip.

Stella's face falters for only a second, but I catch it. Just a flicker of panic behind that polished mask.

"Next time you hire a hacker to erase video footage of you committing—a murder," I draw out the word deliberately, "ma-a-a-ybe make sure they actually, you know, delete it. Hackers like to keep insurance policies on their clients... especially the really shitty ones."

I pause for a moment, standing just behind Johnny Boy, watching her squirm ever so slightly before I cut my eyes to him. "Get the fuck up," I deadpan, and he all but teleports out of his chair to stand along the back wall. I lift myself onto the table, sitting with one leg crossed over the other as my dress cascades to either side. I rest my wrist over my knee, swirling my wineglass lazily.

"There's this thing hackers do that's really fun. It's called a 'dead man's chest.' Very old-school pirates, and I'm here for it."

The words hang in the air like a warning. Stella knows exactly what I'm talking about, and I can see the growing unease in her eyes.

"If that hacker were to ever be betrayed by said shitty client," I continue, "all their dirty little secrets would spill for everyone to see."

I smile at her sweetly, watching the tension mount within her. "Or if a better hacker beats them to death and then breaks open—everything they ever touched." She swallows hard, not sure if I'm bluffing.

"Oh, I get it. You think this is a bluff." I nod, lacing every word with sarcasm and disdain. "I can understand that. Well, show of hands, everyone." I hop off the table, looking to the guests. "Who wants to watch footage of my mother killing my father?"

I raise my hand, glancing around for others.

Francesca raises hers tentatively, looking around to see if anyone else joins her. They seem unsure whether I'm serious.

"Ah, Luca, see that. The Queen wants to see the footage, so... we've got to play it."

"This is getting good," Francesca whispers to the leader of the Russian Bratva, who looks at my mother's guards behind him with malice. Maybe we should have served popcorn instead of wine.

"Luca, play the clip," I say with a calmness that contrasts sharply with the heat running through my veins.

Jax snickers softly, and I narrow my eyes at him. That's exactly what he said to Luca the morning we reunited over breakfast—you know, when they played that clip of me faking an orgasm with... Malachi? No, wait. Marvin?

Luca leans over with a smirk. "Mark," he mouths, reminding me of the poor guy's name.

With that, he presses a button on a remote control in his hand. I keep my eyes trained on Stella, the monster whose womb I had the misfortune of being born from.

Above us, recessed television screens slowly descend from the ceiling, and the lights dim. The room falls into a hushed silence as the screens flicker to life, and everyone holds their breath as the black-and-white video footage starts to play.

Forty-Eight

The room is silent as the video plays, the footage crystal clear. It's my mother, walking through the front door of the Caputo estate. I watch her with a sense of detachment, almost as if I'm watching someone else.

"Pause here for me, babe?" I ask Luca, who halts the video on a close-up image of my mother's face.

"See her expression here? Like she's constantly smelling dog shit?" I point from the screen to my mother, wearing the same scowl then as she is now. "Yup, exactly like that. Same person."

I nod to Luca, and he lets the footage continue as she strolls into the house without hesitation.

I turn to the room. "So, what happened just before this was an EMP," I explain, pausing to glance at their wide-eyed faces. "An EMP is basically an electric bomb. It was set off, and it disabled the entire security system for about thirty seconds—just long enough for her hacker to take over the system without anyone knowing."

The screen splits, showing a side-by-side view of my mother entering the house and the footage from the security room. Everything looks normal. The security team is watching a looped playback, completely unaware that a killer is walking through the door.

Tension builds in the room. Subtle gasps and whispers ripple among the guests, while others remain silent, their attention glued to the screen.

My mother walks through the estate, heading toward my father's room. There is no hesitation, no remorse. She glances to the side, ensuring the coast is clear, then takes a deep breath and moves forward.

We watch closely as she reaches my father's door. She's wearing gloves—gloves that conceal any trace that a woman, presumed dead for two decades, was in the room the night her husband died.

The camera zooms in, and my breath catches as she reaches into her pocket and pulls out a syringe. With careful, practiced movements, she injects something into my father's foot, between his toes.

"Foot fetish," I whisper under my breath. A few chuckles ripple from the gathered guests. My continued jabs are chipping away at her composure, and I love it.

The room falls silent again as the footage continues. The scene unfolds with all the heavy weight of history. My mother sits on the bed next to my father, her tone calm, almost soothing. It's as if she's about to tell him a bedtime story, revealing everything he didn't know—everything hidden in the shadows.

My father looks at her, his face a mixture of disbelief and confusion. His gaze lingers on the woman before him—a woman who looks so much like his wife but is older, harder. He clutches his chest, trying to make sense of this impossible moment. His heart is betraying him.

"You're not... no," he whispers, his voice strained.

She doesn't rush to comfort him. Instead, she takes a slow, deliberate breath, letting the poison do its work. His body begins to spasm, his face contorting in pain as the venom spreads. He grits his teeth, fighting to stay conscious, but it's too much. His body jerks violently. His heart is failing, and the horror on his face mirrors the truth sinking in.

"I never wanted to marry you, Salvatore," she says, her voice low and detached. "I never wanted a child either. But I wasn't given a choice."

The room remains still, every guest listening intently. Even though I'm here, the chill I feel has nothing to do with the air conditioning.

"When my father lost the war, he handed everything the Romanos' built over to your father—me included. I became your reward for a job well done." Her eyes flicker with contempt. "You wanted a wife. You wanted a child. But I never wanted you. And I never wanted her."

She looks toward the camera, as if addressing me directly. Her gaze is cold, devoid of love or warmth. For the first time, I feel the full force of her disgust, but I smirk. I've waited years for this truth to come out.

"I hated you," she continues in the recording, her voice a deadly whisper. "I hated what you put inside me. I hated everything about this life."

My father's body spasms again, but his eyes remain locked on hers, his breaths ragged. He tries to speak, but the venom's grip holds him silent.

"You never figured it out, did you?" she asks, her tone almost amused. "All these years, and you really thought I was dead and never realized who your secret adversary was."

She pauses, letting the words sink in. "I faked my death.

'Lost at sea.' It's laughable, isn't it? Too ridiculous to be true. I was certain everyone would think you killed me, especially since I worked so hard to make it look like you were beating me. But instead, they declared me dead, and I had to adapt."

I shake my head, feeling a sick twist in my stomach. She's telling the truth, and somehow, I've always known it. But hearing it from her lips is something else entirely.

"I went after what you loved most," she says, her voice sharp, "your empire. Your treasure." She tilts her head, speaking of me now—the daughter she never wanted. "I rebuilt the Sicilian empire in secret, right under your nose, and I worked to kill the spawn you made me give birth to. Your precious little treasure."

My father's eyes are barely open now, his breaths shallow, his face ashen. "Soon, I'll have the Italians, stolen from you before your body will be cold in your grave."

He's heard enough. His body convulses one last time before going still.

The video ends, the final frame showing my mother's face frozen in a venomous smile. The silence that follows is thick—suffocating. Stella, realizing the game is up, tries to lunge at me in a rage, but instead, her body spasms violently. She collapses to the floor in a heap.

I don't flinch. I don't blink. I watch her contorted body with detached indifference. Several guards rush to her but none go near her, unsure what is happening to her.

"Oops," I murmur, a faint smirk tugging at my lips. "I forgot. We have another video to play."

The second video begins, showing Stella sneaking into the wine cellar weeks earlier, injecting poison into the bottles of my father's favorite port—the same wine she drank today.

The room watches the second video in horrified silence. Stella, cloaked in shadows, moves with deliberate precision, the small vial in her hand catching the dim light. The needle pierces the cork of each bottle, injecting its deadly contents with methodical ease.

"She planned everything," I say, addressing the room. My voice is steady, but there's an undercurrent of disgust as I explain the scene unfolding on-screen. "She poisoned these bottles, knowing my father's fondness for this particular port. What she didn't know was that he'd given it up months ago. High cholesterol. Doctor's orders."

Murmurs ripple through the guests. Several glance at their own glasses of wine, unease etched on their faces.

"But she couldn't be patient, could she?" I continue, turning my gaze back to Stella's spasming body. "When this plan didn't work, she returned with something stronger, something more direct."

The video shifts to show Stella a week earlier, sneaking through the same wine cellar where we now sit. The irony is almost poetic.

"And yet," I say, taking a deliberate sip of my wine, "her arrogance was her undoing. She never anticipated that her own poison would be her end."

Her body spasms revolt of the poison. Her body jerks violently, veins bulging and turning black as if something sinister is moving beneath her skin. Her skin takes on an unnatural, sickly purple hue, and I watch as the blood vessels in her eyes burst, turning them a deep, terrifying red. She foams at the mouth, her face twisted in agony.

"Enjoying your wine, Mother?" I ask, my tone sharp and unyielding.

The Bratva family leader stands, concerned they might have been poisoned too. The tension crackles in the air, and I hold up a hand, a smug calmness filling me as I reassure them.

"No worries," I say, my voice steady and smooth as I pick up her glass. "This wine was special. Only for my mother today."

Their faces twist into expressions of doubt and unease as the blood-curdling scene continues. Stella's body hemorrhages, blood thick and dark like tar, pouring from her mouth and eyes. I don't flinch. I watch as her agony drags on, and I feel nothing but cold detachment. The woman who haunted my every step, the woman who poisoned everything I loved, is dying before my eyes. For real this time.

The seconds feel like hours. I can hear the blood sloshing around, her body convulsing violently, but I don't feel anything.

And then—finally, after what feels like an eternity—her body falls still. She dies.

I stare at her, emotionless. The room is silent, save for the soft rustle of clothing as the others shift uneasily.

The doors around the cellar open. My father's guards and Enzo's file into the room. Each of them holding a gun to the head of Stella's guards, who raise their hands in resignation.

When we first arrived at the villa, the guards were instructed to enter the house through a rear exit and wait here. We didn't want a gunfight outside when my mother arrived.

Enough have died this week and I'm done with the bloodshed.

For now.

"Well, that was gross." I say, taking Enzo's hand and

hopping off the table. I had been watching my mother's death so intently, I hadn't even realized he walked over here.

"You okay, angel?" He whispers as we head back to my seat.

"Yeah." My heart skips a beat at his concern for me but he's not alone. Jax and Luca also carry looks of worry, communicating questions with their eyes. I give them a wink and take my seat again.

"Mr. Thomas, you brought my mother's will as requested?" I take another drink of wine. The fellow heads of families settle back to their seats. Some clearly frazzled, one downs his glass of wine and pours another. Poor Johnny Boy Moretti looks white as a sheet and hangs against the wall still.

He did pick a poor seat because now there is a corpse oozing black tar next to his chair and I can understand that would be a bit unsettling.

"I–I did, Ms. Caputo." Giuseppe exchanges one set of papers for another underneath. "Though I admit I was confused why you would want to see it. All the matters would be taken care of with your father's will."

"Well, I think we both know why now."

He opens the will, and the same formal, precise language fills the room as he begins to read. "I, Stella Romano Caputo, being of sound mind and body, do hereby bequeath all of my assets, properties, and any interests to my beloved husband, Salvatore Caputo, to be transferred upon my death. In the event of his passing, these assets and properties shall pass to my daughter, Delaney Caputo."

Francesca smirks, clearly catching on before the others. The ripple of realization spreads as the implications settle over the room.

I lean back in my chair, allowing the silence to work in my

favor. "So, to clarify," I say, my voice carrying, "since my mother faked her death, she couldn't have amended her will. And now that she's... indisputably deceased, I inherit not only my father's Italian empire but my mother's rebuilt Sicilian empire as well."

Giuseppe nods, a faint smile tugging at the corners of his lips. "That is correct, Ms. Caputo."

The weight of the moment presses down on the room. Two empires—one built by Salvatore Caputo, the other rebuilt in secret by Stella Romano—are now mine. The gathered families shift uneasily, each calculating what this means for their own power and alliances.

Our guards lower their weapons. The Sicilian muscle that have just landed under my jurisdiction now, look on in wide-eyed confusion.

Enzo stands, his cousin follows, raising their glasses in a toast. "To the new queen of Chicago," he says, his voice smooth and confident.

The other heads of families hesitate, their eyes darting to one another. But one by one, they rise, lifting their glasses, their movements deliberate, acknowledging my ascension.

"To Delaney Caputo," Francesca says, locking eyes with me. Her piercing gaze is a recognition, and a promise all at once. Of what, I'll have to wait and find out.

"To Delaney Caputo," the room echoes.

I raise my own glass, a cold smile on my lips. As the glasses clink and the weight of my new title settles over me, I know this is only the beginning. The world of power, betrayal, and bloodshed I've stepped into won't wait for me to find my footing.

But I'm ready. I've been preparing for this moment my entire life—even if I didn't know it.

Forty-Nine

Three Months Later

So, that's the story of how I accidentally took over the mafia.

I solved the mystery surrounding my mother's death, resolved my daddy issues, and amassed a fortune the likes of which I could never have imagined.

Jax, Luca, Enzo, and I jumped into action immediately. The mess my mother left behind was monumental—like trying to untangle a knot that just kept getting bigger.

Around thirty years ago, a family war broke out between the Romano's and the Caputo's when the head of the Sicilian's challenged my grandfather for control. The war was bloody and divided the city. After the Caputo's emerged victorious, retaining their hold over their territories, unification became their priority. My mother was betrothed to my father in hopes of ending the feud forever.

The Sicilian empire was distributed among Caputo allies, including Enzo's family, which acquired the members' club in Butte—still sporting the Romano family crest.

My mother, however, staged her death and rebuilt the

Sicilian mob from the ashes of the war, making it just as powerful as the Italians and they've remained completely out of sight, until the time was right.

She was supposed to be dead. The Sicilians, gone. No one ever had any notion to even consider either possibility the cause of all this trouble.

If she hadn't been a ruthless, murderous psychopathic cunt, it might have been impressive.

Now, combining both empires, the Italians are at the top of the criminal world, and I am their queen.

Something about that night at the lodge, eating pizza with my men, made everything come rushing back. Memories I had blocked out since I was six. Memories of my mother's cruelty and manipulations that shaped everything.

My mother wasn't the victim—I'd been wrong all along. My father wasn't the abusive one; she was. I saw the truth, the twisted games she played, the self-inflicted injuries she used to manipulate him.

"You made me do this. You always make me do this," I recalled my father saying.

That day was my sixth birthday. She had missed it again. My father made excuses for her, as he always did, convincing me that she really did love me—she was just busy. Lying to his treasure, justifying a mother who had never wanted her child.

That night, I heard my mother's voice and went to see if she had a birthday present for me. Their fight escalated, as it always did. She began hitting herself, slamming her body against the wall, trying to create a bruise. I stood there in the doorway, frozen, my little mind unable to process the bizarre scene.

She locked eyes with me in the reflection of the mirror and

smiled—a chilling, toothy grin, bloodied from her self-inflicted wounds. My father faced me, but he hadn't seen me yet. Her body blocked his view of me.

She arched her back, swung her arms, and threw herself down the flight of stairs. She didn't even try to stop herself. Tumbling and flipping, she landed at my feet.

Her arm was broken, the white bone sticking out of her skin. I looked up at my father, who stared back at me in horror, knowing what I had witnessed. "Happy Birthday." She said with a bloody mouth before she beat her head against the ground.

My father rushed me out of there, begged me to stay in my room.

An ambulance came for her. My father brought me out of my room, delivering me to the table with a cup of hot chocolate because I was shivering. The next morning, he woke me with a teddy bear. I clung to it a few weeks later when she disappeared.

After all these years, I finally understood why he shielded me. He was scared for me. We grew apart. The assaults, the hidden war always took him from me. My mother organizing hits or raids on important days like my birthday, made sure she tormented me too in all of this.

I grew to hate him. And he let me hate him.

He thought keeping me distant would protect me from the war's reach. In a way, he did what Jax, Enzo, and Luca tried to do—pushed me away, thinking it would keep me safe.

If only I could go back in time, I'd ask him to protect his treasure by keeping it close, never letting me go.

When we moved into the estate, I found journals my father had written to me. I spent hours in his closet, surrounded by his things, reading his thoughts, and mourning him, the relationship we never had. Some entries were advice on running the mafia, on being a good boss. Others poured out his regret —for the mother I had, for the father he wasn't.

I couldn't leave that closet; for weeks, I would end up in there at some point in the day, huddled on the floor with a journal or clutching a suit jacket and crying.

I knew we needed to clear his things out but I felt like I was getting to know him in there, surrounded by his scent and it panicked me thinking about losing it.

I had nothing else from him.

Enzo brought in specialists who tested the air and took samples. A week later, he handed me a custom candle that smelled just like my father's closet—a perfect blend of old cigars, expensive cologne, and leather. Now, I burn one every day in my home office.

Cleaning up the mafia empire wasn't easy. There were betrayals to uncover and "conversations" to be had—Jax and Enzo handled those. They were my guard dogs, protecting me from the mess my parents left behind.

Then I learned about my fifteen-year-old half-sister, Giulia "Gigi" Russo—the product of an affair between my mother and a Sicilian family leader who was spared at the end of the war.

My mother had his child and put her up for adoption, using her as leverage to get what she wanted from him. Threatened to ruin his marriage, destroy his family with an illegitimate child and proof of his betrayal.

Giulia had no clue where she came from, left on the doorstep in a basket only a day old. With Luca's help, I got her out of foster care, tied her to the Russo fortune, and secured her future. We'll teach her how to be a good boss and when she's of age, she'll take back the Sicilian's and we'll run the two families together.

Now, she's in therapy and attending a prestigious boarding school in the U.K.—one where mafia kids learn both survival and business. I said the place was just for heathens, but Jax and Enzo found humor in my objections.

"Don't worry," they laughed. "We all went there."

"My point exactly!"

Giulia and I talk almost daily. We're looking forward to spending the holidays together as a family. It's a fresh start for all of us. An unconventional one, but in this world, nothing is ever simple.

Six Months Later

Things are running much smoother now, with most of the family disputes settled. There's some tension brewing with the Irish that we're keeping an eye on, but otherwise, all is quiet in paradise.

I've fully adopted Gigi, and she's thriving. Not only is she acing her classes, but I hear she practically runs the school now. I guess the apple doesn't fall far from the tree and I'm very proud of her.

Running the mafia isn't just about the classic stuff—arranged marriages, cargo shipments of guns, and the whole "fuhgettaboutit" attitude. What surprised me most was the amount of humanitarian efforts, politics, and charity work involved.

Don't get me wrong, we still slice off fingers when people cross us—but there's more good in the mix than I ever imagined. Enzo and his cousins are buying up land to build factories, warehouses, affordable housing, and even nature reserves.

Francesca "The Queen" Lazzarini is making waves in politics. She's an expert at bribing and blackmailing, but she uses her power to sway lawmakers into supporting the people—lower taxes, neighborhood reforms, and better education in struggling areas.

The Lazzarini family didn't come from old money like the Caputo's or Vincenzi's, so Francesca knows what it's like to go hungry. Now she's making sure the kids in her old neighborhoods don't have to.

Jax, of course, is thriving in his own way—he's opened a five-star fine dining restaurant that's booked out for months. He even hired that guy—what's-his-name—who recently moved to Chicago and gave him a job as a dishwasher.

Even with his busier schedule, Jax still has plenty of time for games. Showing up at my office with a new toy. Watching me give a presentation while he controls a vibrator that is sucking on my clit. He loves to see how close he can get me to coming before I excuse myself for the restroom and basically tackle him for his cock or shove him to his knees and drown him.

Yes, he's still calling me Squirt from time to time.

Luca has taken Moanster23 to a whole new level. He's invented the highest quality earbuds I've ever used. When Jax blows him, Luca makes sure to Facetime me so I can hear every moan, every breath. It's Moanster23 in ultra-high-definition, and it's beyond euphoric.

We moved Caputo Enterprises into the same building as Vincenzi Consulting and now I can sneak to Enzo's office and hide under his desk with his cock in my mouth, anytime I want.

One of the reforms I've pushed through is a fight against domestic violence. Enzo and I work side-by-side and two businesses have never been more successful.

Today, I finished my announcement about our new rehabilitation facility and an office opening in Seattle.

The staff is buzzing with energy as I head to my private elevator. It's Enzo's birthday, and I've got something special planned for him .

I found a secret room in my father's downtown office where he had "conversations". I renovated the space into something much more suitable for–*us*.

Pressing the hidden button, the panel opens, and my stiletto heels click against the black marble tile. Removing the pin from my hair, I shake my head and let my long locks fall past my shoulders as Jax and Luca watch with hungry eyes. Both of them on their knees, hands patiently behind their backs.

Enzo is on his knees too, his lower legs strapped in and spread apart on a mounting stool. There is a bench to keep him cozy and hold his weight. Armrests to lock his arms and hands in place and a nice cushioned circular pillow for his head.

I walk in front of him, tickling him with a black leather riding crop. "Happy Birthday, baby." I whisper into his ear before I lick it. He can't answer me for the peach choke ball in his mouth but he moans for me.

We got him a new one after poor *Marc-oh-fuck-no* ended up choking on his other one... I think Jax shoved it down his throat, before they put a bullet in his head but he won't admit to it.

"You look so beautiful in your garter and stockings." I stand in front of him so he can see my heels but nothing else. I run my nails through his hair, and he moans again. "I'm going to fuck you so good today. Are you ready to see your present?"

He nods his head and groans a response against the gag.

I remove my white button-down shirt and my grey pencil skirt that matches Enzo's eyes. The lingerie I put on for him is largely a complex arrangement of straps in a rich deep red.

I crouch down, giving him a good view of what he doesn't get to touch. It looks almost painful for him to see me and he pulls against the bindings.

I stroke the riding crop over my peeked nipples, then rub down my pussy. Bringing it up to my mouth, he whines when I lick the taste of myself off it.

On the table next to me, I get the box with his present in it and open it.

"Please, can I have a taste first?" Luca asks so sweetly, that I have to say yes. I look at Enzo while Luca puts my leg over his shoulder and feasts on my cunt. Jax stands behind me, holding me up and fingering my ass while I grind my pleasure out on Luca's mouth.

"Can I clean him, Peach?" Jax is already licking his lips seeing how wet Luca's mouth is from my climax. "Please."

"You've been so good for me, waiting and asking." I bite his lip, pulling it back with me before I let it go. "Just a quick taste for my good boys." Jax is near starving and holds Luca's face with both hands. He licks along Luca's bottom lip before he invades Luca mouth with his tongue.

I run the riding crop along Enzo's jaw, gently stroking him with it. "Okay now, we need to get Enzo's actual present out now."

I keep my eyes on Enzo as Luca lifts the very long, very girthy silicone replica of his cock out of the box. It's so big and oddly heavy, a harness is necessary for me to strap it on.

I also will admit, I had to add weighted hip thrusts to my workout routine for a few weeks now and my ass has never looked better.

This strap-on is custom to the max, including a lovely feature that sucks on my clit as I thrust, and a curved g-spot stimulator that Jax puts in perfect position for me.

Enzo is nearly crying he's so happy.

Luca and Jax squirt lube in my waiting palms and I stroke the long shaft. "Are you ready for me to fuck you baby?" I ask Enzo and he can't shake his head yes fast enough.

With the riding crop, I tickle along Enzo's bare skin, running it gently down his back before slapping his ass with it. He jolts in surprise, then moans wanting more.

"Does my little brat want another spanking?" I reach between his legs and squeeze his balls. "Maybe one for each year?" His cock jumps and I kiss his firm ass cheek as I stroke him several time. "I think so."

Enzo took his spankings so well as I pumped my fist along his dick, commanding him not to come. Now that he's earned his reward, I tickle his ass around the butt plug he's been wearing to get ready for megalo-dong.

I remove the plug slowly and he protests the loss. "Aw, my greedy whore wants something to fill his tight asshole?" I tease his opening with the large head of dildo. "Ask me nicely and I'll fuck you like a good birthday boy."

I hear him moan please but the choke ball muffles it.

He gets another smack with the crop. This time on his balls and he arches his back.

"Oh, what a fucking slut you are. But I didn't hear you." I massage his balls, then move to his shaft for a stroke. "Ask your angel to stuff you full of her fat cock." I stroke him faster, twisting my hand and I know he's close to coming.

He groans and his breathes through his nose come in short, quick bursts. "No coming yet, baby. Ask for permission."

He whines and thrashes, moaning into the choke ball. "That's what I want to see from my whore, begging to have my cock." Drizzling his ass with lube, I line up and push into him slowly giving his praises with each tormenting inch.

Then I fuck my birthday boy like he deserves while I let Luca and Jax suck each other off. Removing the dildo and harness, along with the choke ball from Enzo, he pants heavily.

"Fuck angel." He gasps.

"You did so good baby." I lay down in front of him and spread my legs wide, stroking his cheek with the riding crop. I drag a replica of Jax's cock along my mouth, down my breasts and circle my clit with it. "Now I'm going to fuck myself until I squirt in your mouth, and you're going to take every drop, you fucking thirsty slut." I end it with a slap to his face before I turn the vibrator on.

And right there, I watch as Enzo falls in love with me, just a little bit more.

One Year Later

The guys are running around like chickens with their heads cut off this morning, and I've already threatened Enzo three times with the spatula.

Luca has no fewer than eight computer monitors going, looking like he's about to hack into the goddamn Matrix. Jax strolls in with a team of guards trailing behind him, heading straight for the kitchen to grab sandwiches.

"I've scouted that place twice this morning," Jax says, taking a big bite. "We should be good, Peach." He offers me some, and I grab his wrist, pulling him close to steal a bite. I swear, even his sandwiches taste better than mine.

"I'm connected to the entire grid. I could shut down all of Chicago from my phone if needed," Luca announces, barely glancing up from his screens.

"My loves, it's just a book signing," I mutter around my mouthful of food. "I think we'll be fine."

"Speaking of which, we've got a present for you." Luca grins mischievously, walking toward me with a box tucked behind his back.

He opens it, and nestled inside is a golden spatula. The handle reads, *My Stepbrother is My Stalker,* the title of Dela Montgomery's latest bestseller in her new interconnected mafia rivals series.

"Aw! My spatula looks so pretty!" I beam at it, and all three of them chuckle, rolling their eyes at my ridiculousness. "This one's not for spankings." I hold it up to the light. "It's going on the wall in my office."

"It's time to go, angel." Enzo kisses me on the head. "Everything will be okay."

"I know that. Do you guys know that, though? Because I'm not so sure you do."

As expected, the signing goes off without a hitch. Shockingly, none of the readers show up armed with Uzis, intent on shooting the place up.

When we get back to the house, Enzo scoops me up and

carries me to our bedroom—they've got a birthday surprise waiting for me. But I've got one of my own.

They tell me to wait outside the closed door until they're ready. When I'm finally allowed to open it, I'm met with the sight of all three of them, naked, hard, and grinning. Then they step aside to reveal our new, giant, custom bed.

I gasp, covering my mouth with my hands. "I love it."

The bed is sleek and modern. And it's huge—large enough so we can all sleep comfortably together.

They shower me with kisses and "happy birthdays" before I tell them I have a present too.

I grab a small box from the nightstand drawer where I hid it, and they step around me to see what's inside. When I remove the lid, they stare at the small T-shaped item sitting on the little pillow inside. Their confused faces make me giggle.

"Lenny," Luca gasps, figuring it out first. His mouth drops open as he looks at me in surprise. "She took her IUD out."

Enzo and Jax's eyes snap to mine, and slow smiles spread across their faces.

"You want us to put a baby in you, angel?" Enzo asks, stepping closer.

"Peach, you just triggered a deep-seated breeding kink that I hope you're ready for," Jax teases, his voice low and playful.

"I am." Their hands caress my body, removing my clothes. "We've talked about starting a family—"

Enzo interrupts me, nearly stealing my breath with a deep, hungry kiss. I moan against his mouth. "I want you to fill me so full of cum, it drips out of me for a week," I whisper against his lips.

"God damn, Lenny."

"At the same time," I pant when Luca bites my nipple. "I want all three of you to fuck me at the same time."

They hesitate, Jax's voice soft. "Are you sure, Peach?"

I whimper my answer as Jax's tongue traces my neck and claims my mouth. Enzo's finger flicks against my clit, sending jolts of heat through me.

We've done double penetration with Enzo and Jax. Then Luca and Jax fucked my pussy while Enzo took my ass. But I need this. All of them.

"More than anything," I manage to say.

"On your back, Lenny," Luca commands, his blue eyes dark with desire. His lips curve into a deadly smile as he adds, "Jax, get her nipple clamps."

"Oh," I moan, my body reacting instantly. Another one of Jax's toys: remote-control vibrating nipple clamps. Five words I never knew I needed in my life so much.

Enzo retrieves the lube while Jax rummages for the clamps. Luca's tongue slides up my slit in one long, slow lick, and I clutch his hair with both hands, arching into him. The position pushes my breasts together, and Enzo takes full advantage, lavishing each nipple with his mouth.

My hips roll, chasing the pleasure Luca is coaxing out of me. When Jax turns on the first clamp and presses it against my nipple, the vibrations send shockwaves through my body. He fastens it in place, and the sensations intensify.

The second clamp goes on, and when Jax activates them both, I shatter. My orgasm hits like a freight train, leaving me breathless and trembling.

Each of them leans down to kiss me—and each other. Their lips and hands are everywhere, exploring, teasing, and worshipping my body. I feel Luca's cock pressing against my entrance, his size filling me completely as he sinks into me. My moans fill the room as he sets a steady rhythm.

I will never fucking tire of this.

Jax hooks one of my legs over his arm while Enzo takes the other, spreading me wide. They align themselves with me, the anticipation almost unbearable.

"Let's give our queen a baby," Enzo growls, his voice rough and commanding. He pushes into me slowly, joining Luca, and I cry out at the overwhelming fullness. They move in perfect sync, stretching me in ways that send pleasure coursing through my veins.

"Fuck, Luca. I love you like this," Enzo murmurs, turning Luca's face to him for a kiss. Their mouths collide, tongues tangling as they lose themselves in the moment.

"Jax," I gasp, my body trembling with need. "I need you. Please."

He kneels between my legs, his hands gliding over my skin as he positions himself. "Anything for you, Peach," He eases into me and spits on my clit, rubbing his thumb in circles as they work to pump into me. The sensation is indescribable, and I'm lost in the intensity of their love and desire.

They move as one, their bodies pressing against mine, their touches driving me to the brink again and again. Their words are a mix of praise and filthy promises, each one making my heart race and my body ache for more.

When the three of them finally release, filling me with their warmth, the world seems to stop. I'm wrapped in their arms, their love surrounding me completely.

We lay in our bed together, fucking until the sun comes up and it was the best birthday of my life. They hold me and we share our dreams for our enterprises, our love, and for the future of our family: our very own treasure.

Our relationship may not make sense to everyone but it's really the only thing in my fucked up, crazy life that makes sense for me. I'm the crime queen of Chicago, a romance writer, a big sister, and a partner to the three most loving, caring men that have ever existed. Soon, I'll get to be a mother. I'll give my treasure the life, the parents that I never had.

We're a crime family, we make our own rules—and we'll burn down anyone who tries to stop us.

Epilogue

Two years later, and here I am, waiting in the back room, my nerves gnawing at me as the makeup artist puts the finishing touches on my face. The hairstylist is dousing me in hairspray like it's the secret to world peace, and I inhale half of it with every breath I take. Seriously, if I ever have to smell another can of this stuff again, I might just scream.

Behind me, Gigi stands, holding my veil, her eyes glistening with soft tears. I never could have imagined finding a sister, a best friend, out of all of this. But here we are, sharing this moment. It feels like some cosmic joke. The same angry cunt who gave us shitty childhoods, accidentally gave us one of the most precious gifts in the world: Each other.

Now Gigi has just turned eighteen and is helping me into the most important moment of my life.

"You ready?" she asks, her voice soft but full of emotion, her hazel eyes, just like mine, bright and brimming with tears.

I smile at her in the mirror. "As I'll ever be... for a second time," I answer, grabbing my bouquet of flowers.

My eyes catch the pale pink Delaney roses mixed into the arrangement.

When Luca told Enzo there was a flower with my name,

that was all it took. They've become a sort of obsession, and the creeping rose bushes have been planted all around our estate of offices.

But they are gorgeous, and I won't deny it, I love them.

Gigi walks ahead of me, her head held high as she's the first to make her way down the aisle as my bridesmaid. The doors close, and I steal a glance through the small window, catching sight of the triplets wobbling down the aisle to their waiting dads. The sight of them is enough to make my heart swell, their little hands reaching for their fathers, and I swear they've got all of us wrapped around their tiny fingers already.

Leo, with his chestnut brown hair and eyes. Isabella Rose, with her near-black hair and bright blue eyes. Antonio, with his dark brown hair and storm cloud grey eyes. They're everything to me. Everything I never knew I could have and more.

The bridal music begins as the doors open, and I walk down the aisle toward them. My three grooms stand there at the end, waiting, looking more handsome than I've ever seen them before. Each one of them holding one of the triplets, who point at me, smiling as if they can't wait for me to get to them.

The mafia families are in attendance—everyone seated, watching. But all I care about right now is walking toward the three men who mean everything to me, to become their wife. Theirs forever as they become husbands. To me. To each other and our family will finally be complete.

I'm about ten feet down the aisle when I hear the unmistakable sound of gunfire followed by screams.

Not again.

My shoulders drop as I roll my eyes, and I can't help but mutter, "You've got to be kidding me."

"Son of a bitch." Jax exclaims, his face turns a shade of red

I've never seen before. This is the second time we've been interrupted on our wedding day, and this time, I will not have it.

The doors swing open again, and before the attacker can make it more than one step inside, I reach into my bouquet of flowers and pull out my revolver hidden there. I aim straight at the would-be intruder's head. The room goes silent as I lock eyes with the threat.

"You picked the wrong wedding to crash, mother fucker," I say, my voice steady as I squeeze the trigger.

Acknowledgements

It was a Friday, late morning and my text message went a little like this:

> A why-choose

> I have to work out the story but... A contemporary

> One girl

> -Her step-brother

> -Her boss

> -Her ex fiancé who just got released from prison

> She doesn't know....they are all in the mafia....and they are all ex boyfriends

> •• - What are we thinking?

One thing lead to another, and before you know it, Gnome and I are discussing the intricacies of butt-plugs, peaches n' cream with hair pulling, just how many fingers is the right amount and... pegging.

You know, just another Friday.

This book goes out to you Gnomie.

Thank you for joining the emergency huddle about triple-penetration. That could have been a disaster.

This shit-show goes out to you.

That Time I Accidentally Became A Serial Killer

*For Poppy Hartwell, justice comes
with a touch of pink—and a trail of blood.*

I'm a prosecutor, not a
killer—or at least, I didn't use
to be. Now I'm armed with a
pink killing kit, a growing body
count, and two crushes I can't
choose between.

The worst part? I'm falling for
both of them.
Turns out, justice isn't just
blind—it's a whole lot messier
than I ever imagined.

*A Legallly Blonde meets
Dexter Mash-Up*

🔪 Stalker Romance

🔪 Love Triangle

🔪 Grumpy x Sunshine

🔪 Consensual Non-Consent (CNC)

*Coming Summer 2025
By: Rebekah Sinclair*

More Works By
Rebekah Sinclair

THE
FORGOTTEN GODDESS

A completed Series available on Kindle Unlimited

🛡 GREEK MYTHOLOGY 🛡

URBAN FANTASY

FATED MATES

STAR-CROSSED LOVERS

She is the goddess time forgot

He is the god that never
stopped looking for her

Rebekah Sinclair
Writes

To stay informed on my upcoming releases, book signing events, and more, visit my website and sign up for my newsletter.

www.rebekahsinclairwrites.com

If you'd like to chat with other readers, join the Rebekah Sinclair Writes discord!